T

Jean Stubbs is a frequent lecturer at writers' summer schools and seminars and in 1984 she was writer-in-residence for Avon. Her novels and short stories have been translated into eight languages and have been televised and adapted for radio.

She lives in Cornwall with her second husband.

Other books by Jean Stubbs

Jean Stubbs

The Northern Correspondent

Volume IV of Brief Chronicles 1831–1851

PAN BOOKS
in association with
MACMILLAN LONDON

First published in 1984 by Macmillan London Limited

This edition published 1993 by Pan Books Ltd
a division of Pan Macmillan Publishers Limited
Cavaye Place London SW10 9PG
and Basingstoke
in association with Macmillan London Limited

Associated companies throughout the world

ISBN 0 330 28705 2

9 8 7 6 5 4 3 2

A CIP catalogue record for this book is available from
the British Library

Phototypeset by Intype, London
Printed by Cox & Wyman Ltd, Reading, Berkshire

To first impressions and final proofs

Acknowledgements

My thanks as always to those who suggested, obtained, lent or gave research books: in particular, Ian Atlee and the staff of Helston Branch Library and Paul Bannister of the Library Van; Bob Gilbert of Gilbert's Print and Bookshop, Truro, Cornwall; Stella Thomas of the Press Gallery, House of Commons; my uncle, R. B. Darby, and Adrian Leaman, for scholarly beavering; my brother, J. G. Higham, for loan of a rare copy of *The History of Hyde* published in 1930 by the Clarendon Press, formerly owned by our family; and Mr R. H. Pratt Boorman, editor and proprietor of the *Kent Messenger* for fifty years, for generously giving time, books and advice. I have read and used the information from a great many sources to furnish the historical background to this novel, but I feel I should mention the debt I owe to David Ayerst for his *Guardian, Biography of a Newspaper*, and to R. J. Morris for his *Cholera 1832*. I am grateful to Frank Munday, general manager of *The Cornishman* in Penzance, for showing me round the newspaper premises on two occasions and answering all my questions. I thank both my editors, Tess Sacco and James Hale, for creative criticism and encouragement. And I thank my four grandchildren for being such good copy: Joanna Mathys continues to shine through the young Cicelys; Nicholas Mathys is all three Longe boys rolled into one, and the original creator of 'Little Voice'; Clare Brookes inspired Alice Vivian; very young Oliver Brookes makes an early appearance as Matthew Standish. Finally, of course, I am very glad of Felix – the man who has lived with me and the Howarths for so long that he thought of a far more subtle dedication than I did!

Contents

Part Three   New Editions

Part Four   By-Lines

Part Five   Postscript

'It may be desirable that some journals should be tools and instruments; and, if they refuse to obey the word of command, of course they do violate the contract . . . but we object to be judged by the rules applicable in such cases. We have not undertaken to obey, and we will not obey, any man or set of men whatever . . .'

Manchester Guardian 3 May, 1848
in answer to *Manchester Examiner,* 2 May, 1848

THE HOWARTH FAMILY TREE

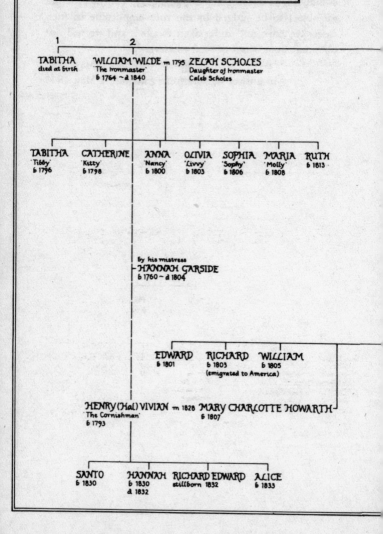

	1	2
	TABITHA died at birth	WILLIAM WILDE m 1795 ZELAH SCHOLES 'The Ironmaster' Daughter of Ironmaster b 1764 ~ d 1840 Caleb Scholes

TABITHA	CATHERINE	ANNA	OLIVIA	SOPHIA	MARIA	RUTH
'Tibby' b 1796	'Kitty' b 1798	'Nancy' b 1800	'Livvy' b 1803	'Sophy' b 1806	'Molly' b 1808	b 1813

By his mistress
- HANNAH GARSIDE
b 1760 ~ d 1804

EDWARD	RICHARD	WILLIAM
b 1801	b 1803	b 1805 (emigrated to America)

HENRY (Hal) VIVIAN m 1828 MARY CHARLOTTE HOWARTH
'The Cornishman'   b 1807
b 1793

SANTO	HANNAH	RICHARD EDWARD	ALICE
b 1830	b 1830 d 1832	stillborn 1832	b 1833

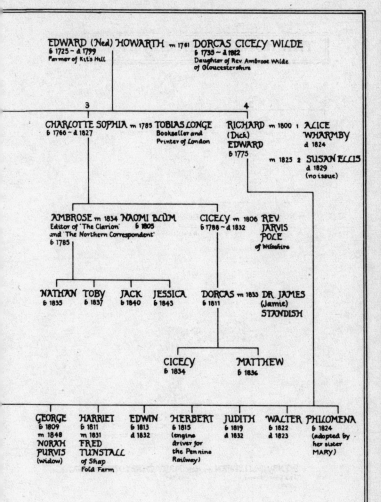

EDWARD (Ned) HOWARTH m 1761 DORCAS CICELY WILDE
b 1725 ~ d 1799   b 1735 ~ d 1812
Farmer of Kit's Hill   Daughter of Rev. Ambrose Wilde
                                         of Gloucestershire

3

CHARLOTTE SOPHIA m 1785 TOBIAS LONGE
b 1766 ~ d 1827   Bookseller and
                          Printer of London

4

RICHARD m 1800 1 ALICE
(Dick)   WHARMBY
EDWARD   d 1824
b 1775
        m 1825 2 SUSAN ELLIS
                 d 1829
                 (no issue)

AMBROSE m 1834 NAOMI BLÜM
Editor of 'The Clarion'   b 1805
and 'The Northern Correspondent'
b 1785

CICELY m 1806 REV.
b 1788 ~ d 1832   JARVIS
                   POLE
                   of Wiltshire

NATHAN   TOBY   JACK   JESSICA
b 1835   b 1837   b 1840   b 1843

DORCAS m 1833 DR. JAMES
b 1811   (Jamie)
                   STANDISH

CICELY   MATTHEW
b 1834   b 1836

GEORGE   HARRIET   EDWIN   HERBERT   JUDITH   WALTER   PHILOMENA
b 1809   b 1811   b 1813   b 1815   b 1819   b 1822   b 1824
m 1848   m 1831   d 1832   (engine   d 1832   d 1823   (adopted by
NORAH   FRED   driver for   her sister
PURVIS   TUNSTALL   the Pennine   MARY)
(widow)   of Shap   Railway)
          Fold Farm

Part One

Part One

Stop-Press News 1831–1833

Thunderstorm

chapter one

17 August, 1831

The August day turned so livid and sultry as to make folk wonder whether the Hour of Judgement was at hand. Air became taut silk which could suddenly rip, earth and sky bronze cymbals which could shortly clash. Women sensed oncoming headaches, men lost their tempers, children threw tantrums, and plans both humble and great went awry.

In the north-country town of Millbridge, Lancashire, Ambrose Longe, editor and owner of *The Clarion*, had chosen this particular Wednesday to move from his old home to the rooms over the printing shop. It should have been a simple matter. The paper had gone to press on Monday evening, leaving a modicum of leisure in its wake. Thornton House was no more than a few hundred yards away down the High Street, and his possessions were few. But first the lad with the handcart was late, then a chest of drawers got stuck on the turn of *The Clarion*'s stairs, and finally the woman whom he had hired to cook and scrub for him sent word that she was ill abed.

By six o'clock in the evening Ambrose decided that evil had been more than sufficient unto the day. So he sent out for a mutton pie from the bakehouse and a jug of beer from the Royal George, and set up camp for the night. In this fashion his uncle, the ironmaster, found him: an apron protecting his trousers, coat and waistcoat dangling from a peg, shirt sleeves rolled up, composing next week's leader on Parliamentary Reform.

Ambrose wrote as he had done from the age of six, with rapt dedication, rumpling his hair as he sought for an especially

3

neat phrase and twining one leg round the other in ecstasy as he found it. His thin brown face expressed a range of emotions. A glint in his light-brown eyes approved the fighting qualities of those who were shunting their Reform Bill through the Commons. His jaw lengthened as he feared obstruction from the Lords. His pursed lips reminded readers that nothing less than their say in the country's government was at stake. His grin marked the end of fourteen generations of feudal despotism in the Wyndendale valley. His short laugh promised victory, though his frown admitted that the battle was not yet won.

So deeply did he concentrate that his uncle was able to stand for several moments in the open doorway, observing and unobserved. A smile sat ready on his mouth but his bright black eyes missed nothing and disapproved of all they saw. In particular they despised this slim brown fellow intent upon his task, his careless pose, his shabby elegance. Above all they misliked the grin with which Ambrose tackled his inky revolution.

The ironmaster drummed a short tattoo on the doorpost with the silver head of his cane and cried heartily, 'Am I intruding?'

Not caring tuppence whether he did or not. Catching the fellow short and sharp. Fetching him down to earth.

Once more aware of reality, Ambrose found that it had not improved and some further demand was being made of him.

'By no means, sir,' he replied courteously, trapped, and pulled out a ladder-back chair and dusted it with the skirt of his apron.

William Howarth was used to better thrones, but sat down grandly. He had been the handsomest of men, was still handsome at sixty-seven, still held himself tall and splendidly. His hair grew white and thick, his countenance was ruddy, his smile wide and youthful owing to the teeth he bought and had fixed when his own failed him. He gave an impression of powerful benevolence, but Ambrose knew that power came first and ben-

4

evolence could go hang when business was in question. Then the narrow black eyes became pinpoints of insistence, and you looked to your own interests as best you could.

'I have an excellent proposition to put to you,' the ironmaster began in an engaging tone.

Then he wiped his forehead and the inside of his top hat with a peerless handkerchief, and muttered something about heavy weather.

Ambrose remained standing by the printing-press. He took a bite of pie and a swallow of beer, and waited.

'Which I think should please and certainly astonish you.'

Unmoved, the younger man stood at his ease, and did not answer.

'It concerns our bye-election, in part. You know, of course, that Lord Kersall is putting up his second son Humphrey as Tory candidate?'

Candidates were not only put up by the Kersalls, they were inevitably accepted, and any Kersall would do. But in these perilous days when Whigs were capturing Tory seats, and the second Reform Bill was being prepared for its second reading, the Tory party needed fighters, not leeches, in Parliament.

'Silly old fool! He must be in his dotage!' said the ironmaster contemptuously, though Lord Kersall was the same age as himself. 'None of that family knows anything about politics. All snobbery and inter-marriage, microscopes, gardens and balloons – and Ralph Kersall was a rotten balloonist, too. Can't let him get away with this nonsense any longer!'

'Have you ever thought of offering yourself as Tory candidate, sir?' Ambrose asked, straight-faced.

The ironmaster shook his cane roguishly at his nephew.

'Not *thought*, my boy. I've *done* it! And I don't think we need doubt the outcome. Well, why not? That tribe of stuffed puppets has had a stranglehold on this borough long enough.'

'I couldn't agree with you more, sir,' said Ambrose heartily. And he smiled.

The ironmaster missed the significance of that smile, saying under his breath, 'William Howarth M.P.'

'Yes,' he continued aloud, 'we could all do with a change. I'm not speaking of the Reform Bill, mind you.' Threatening. 'No, no. Too sweeping by far. But the aristocracy are out of touch with the people. I shall represent Wyndendale better than any Kersall ever did. So let us root these old-fashioned squires out of the House of Commons, say I, and replace 'em with men of business, men of sense.' He paused and wiped his forehead again. 'Your ordinary workman don't want to think for himself. He wants his master to think for him, and to tell him what to do. I know this valley, and I know what's best for it.'

'I daresay the Kersalls thought that, too, sir!' said Ambrose with fine sarcasm.

The ironmaster's colour rose in a way which would have alarmed his personal physician.

'What do you mean by that impudence, sir? The Kersalls think that God invested them with some divine right to rule. I know that a man has to be a good servant, and to learn how to make his way in the world, before he can become a good master. And that's what I am, and intend to be – a good, straightforward, honest Master!'

Though Ambrose still smiled he was oppressed by more than the heat. His beer had gone flat. His pie tasted sour. Still, he spoke with courtesy and detachment.

'Your intentions sound excellent, sir, but I don't quite see how I can serve you.'

The ironmaster's expression belied his tone, which was amiable.

'Oh, I know we have had our political disagreements in the past, Ambrose, but it is a narrow mind that never changes its opinions. I flatter myself that mine has always been open. And then, I thought a great deal of your mother. I loved and respected Charlotte. I should like to think that her son and I did not quarrel. For her sake.'

His nephew's brown skin lost its warmth. His eyes flickered.

'Are you asking me to refrain from exposing your more unpleasant business deals in my newspaper, sir?' he asked coolly.

'More than that,' said the ironmaster curtly, keeping his notorious temper under control. 'Much more than that. I want your unqualified support. Wait a minute!' Silencing Ambrose with a peremptory gesture. 'Hear me out before you answer!'

There was a pause, and he spoke again in another tone.

'I happen to know that you're short of capital.'

'I am short of cash, sir,' Ambrose replied lightly. 'Capital is a luxury to which I have never aspired.'

'I should advise you to save your wit for a more suitable occasion. Your present position scarcely gives reason for humour.'

The ironmaster slid one hand inside the breast of his coat as if to soothe a savage heart, and drew out a sheet of paper on which was written the brief, sad tale of Ambrose's financial situation. He hooked on his spectacles, held the document out at arms' length, and began to read its contents aloud with great deliberation.

'As far as general printing goes, your rival *The Wyndendale Post* still gets the best orders in the valley. Old habits die hard, as you have no doubt discovered, and established society pays better than any of your liberal-minded Johnnies. The rent on this place is not much, but then you have such limited space that you cannot expand even if you could afford to. Your mother, Charlotte, left you an income which prevents you from starving but will do little else, and is tied up so that you cannot realise the capital – I daresay Nick Hurst advised her on that point, and very wise too. You was always a spendthrift, Ambrose! So that leaves *The Clarion* to make you rich.'

He cleared his throat and recited the facts with relish.

'You have at present one old Koenig and Bauer steam-driven press which prints a thousand sheets an hour. You publish the paper, classed as Independent, price sevenpence a copy, once a week. Your circulation is around a thousand, which is quite good for a local journal. Still, you will not make your fortune that way!' His voice thickened. 'And you also waste time and make no profit from printing that damned radical rag *The Recorder,* which dodges stamp duty by selling a straw for tuppence and giving the paper away with the straw! That sort of nonsense will have to stop.'

'One moment, sir,' said Ambrose lightly, though somewhat pinched of countenance. 'We appear not to understand each other. Neither *The Clarion* nor *The Recorder* will give you any support whatsoever. If you are looking for a newspaper to sing to your tune then try Arnold Thwaites of *The Wyndendale Post.* They say that his coat has two linings, one for Kersall and the other for Howarth. I am sure he won't mind turning it again!'

But the ironmaster could not now be deterred.

'Fine words, sir, fine words. Listen to my proposition. I am prepared to buy you a new Napier double-cylinder printing-press which will produce over two thousand sheets an hour. I will pay for a reporter's wages, so that you don't have to double up for both jobs. You can publish twice a week. Once on Tuesdays, as at present, and again on Saturdays, which means that you can report the Thursday debate in Parliament. All my business houses, here and overseas, will be alerted to send you foreign news – your foreign coverage is paltry! I can engage agents in Liverpool, Bolton, Preston, Blackburn, Clitheroe, Wigan – anywhere you name – to sell copies of *The Clarion* outside this valley. Furthermore I can bring you any amount of advertising revenue. All you need to do, my boy, is to expand and flourish!' And in the same breath he added, 'By Jove, this room is too damned hot and close for my liking!'

Ambrose jerked up the lower half of the window, and stood moodily by it, looking out onto the deadly languor of the market square. An odour both rank and sickly assailed their nostrils.

'Fo! What a stink!' cried William. 'Why won't the council do something about those cess-pools? Now, there's an issue on which you and I agree, my boy. Sanitation! That one-time partner of yours, the cartoonist fellow, what's-is-name Topp. Johnny Topp . . .'

'Tripp, sir, if you please,' said Ambrose through his teeth. 'His name was Jeremy Tripp.'

'Aye, aye. Poor talented fellow!' cried the ironmaster, who had detested him. 'Well, he might not have died of typhoid fever if Millbridge council had paid more attention to the drains. I warned them about those wooden pipes thirty years since. Gave them a fair estimate to provide iron pipes in their stead. We must take it up again. Fight for improvement. Stand together. What do you say?'

'Our opinion on that issue may be the same, but our interests differ, even so, sir,' Ambrose replied drily, 'since your company stands to profit by the sale of the drain-pipes, and my objection is purely on grounds of public health.'

'Well, I can't sit here bandying words all day,' said the ironmaster testily. 'Are you willing to bury the hatchet for Charlotte's sake, or not?'

Ambrose threw the rest of his pie through the open window into the street, where it was gobbled by a passing cur.

'I must tell you, sir, that when the next election comes, I shall actively encourage Wyndendale to choose a man with a social conscience – a title which hardly applies either to you or any Kersall.'

The decision was harder to make than he would have believed possible. He saw the newspaper of his dreams float out of that window into the lurid evening light. But he spoke on sturdily.

'My mother and father were radicals and risked their lives for their beliefs. I have been in Millbridge jail half a dozen times for printing and distributing *The Recorder*. And *The Clarion* is rightly called an Independent newspaper, since that means

9

it is at liberty to throw stones or shower praises on the decisions made by any party whatsoever. You and I are not the same political animals, sir.'

'Gently, gently!' soothed the ironmaster. 'I am not holding your past against you. Yes, you have suffered for your beliefs, mistaken though they were – and poor, brave Charlotte suffered most. Whereas the sensible thing to do in life is to look about you, weigh matters up, use your head instead of your heart, and get your own way in the end. Just look at *my* past record.

'I began life as the son of a yeoman farmer on Garth Fells – your grandfather Ned Howarth. A better fellow never breathed, God rest his honest bones, but I've worked my way up to become one of the richest and most powerful men in this valley. I haven't reached my present position without knowing all the ropes and how to pull them. I'm not against social improvement – like the sanitation we were talking about – and I run a model ironworks down at Snape. Nobody can point a finger at me there. And I can promise you this, lad. When I am elected you can be sure they'll take notice of me in Parliament. And if you back me, Lancashire will take just as much notice of *The Clarion*!'

Ambrose said bitterly, 'Oh, I don't doubt you will make all your wishes and opinions known, sir – *and* put them to profitable use.'

'I thought you would see my point of view,' said the ironmaster, satisfied. 'And another thing, my boy. We must look about us for bigger premises. Give *The Clarion* a new name. Make a fresh start altogether. Find you proper lodgings and a decent landlady to look after you. None of this gimcrack rubbish.'

He lifted a very fine old silver watch from his waistcoat pocket, and consulted the time.

'Too late to go home for dinner,' he observed. 'Nor do I fancy riding down the valley with this storm threatening. There will be the very deuce of a cloudburst, by and by. No, I shall

10

send a message to Zelah and put up at the Royal George for the night. Ah! I have an excellent notion. Let us dine there together and discuss details.'

Ambrose spoke composedly, but a muscle twitched in his brown cheek.

'Sir, I cannot compromise either myself or my newspaper – unimportant though we may seem to you – on a matter of principle.'

The ironmaster was amazed, incredulous.

'Stuff and nonsense! What have principles to do with business? It's all money, whichever way you look at it. The newspaper will benefit. You will benefit. I shall benefit. Where is your difficulty?'

Ambrose made a gesture of amusement and despair.

'The difficulty, sir, is that you do not see the difficulty.'

The ironmaster's face became as thunderous as the evening sky.

'Never mind your coffee-house parlance, sir. Yes or no? I am a plain man. Give me a plain answer.'

'Then – plainly – no, sir.'

'Are you telling me that you prefer to live from hand to mouth in this piggery, rather than work for the future I envisage?'

'Your vision of my future newspaper could not sound more to my liking, sir, but its cost in personal terms would be too heavy.'

The ironmaster rose with surprising speed and agility for such a big man. He towered over Ambrose Longe. He gripped his cane to his side lest he be tempted to use it on his nephew's head and shoulders.

'You arrogant fool!' he shouted. 'What do you think will become of you, eh? No home, no wife, no friends, no property. Living alone and scratching a living from one day to the next. Producing a couple of paltry rags which barely make ends meet. Still in the same position that you were in when you came here fifteen years ago, and nothing better to look forward to. Well, I have done my duty by you. Do not trouble to beg of *me* when the time comes.'

Ambrose walked past him, not without an inward tremor, and made a gesture of holding the front door open, though it already stood as wide as it could go, and the air and sky grew fouler yet.

'You will find the offices of *The Wyndendale Post* almost directly opposite, sir,' he said with deliberate insolence. 'I am sure Arnold Thwaites would need no persuasion to ditch his present patron – providing you made it worth his while.'

Then William stopped short, as if seeing his opponent for the first time, and put the truth into words.

'I am not blind to quality,' he answered slowly. '*The Post* has none, and its editor is a toady and a hack. I want a newspaper of authority and style which will be the envy of the provinces. *The Clarion* could have been made so! And I need an editor who can stamp his individual mark upon it, and yet be a loyal friend to me and the party I shall represent. I want, in short, exactly what you want – a first-rate provincial newspaper – for I believe you to be honest enough to recognise *The Clarion*'s shortcomings. And you may prate of principles until you are blue in the face, sir, but what your paper needs is capital investment. Without it you must stagnate.'

He had made up his mind as to the next move. He set his top hat firmly upon his head. He even smiled at his nephew, though the smile was not a kind one.

'I shall put my money to better use elsewhere. I shall found my own paper. I shall install my own editor. I shall get what I want.'

He mounted his great black horse. He turned its head towards the Royal George. He sat looking down at Ambrose Longe.

'And when that happens, my lad, I promise you that my newspaper will cut *The Clarion*'s throat. Which will leave you no option but to cut your own. And good riddance to the pair of you!'

The heavens were now so enraged that two young women, drawing up in a carriage a few hundred yards further down the High Street, stopped at the very house which Ambrose had left that morning and made haste to reach its shelter.

Had the ironmaster seen them, he would in a moment have turned his horse's head about and engaged them in conversation. For the vivacious young woman with copper-coloured hair was his favourite niece, Mary Vivian; and her companion, Naomi Blüm, tall and dark and stately, was the daughter of a Jewish merchant with whom he had dealt in the past. Mary wanted to sell a house, and Naomi wanted to buy one. William Howarth had been the means of bringing both ladies together.

Though their acquaintance was only hours old, they had liked each other immediately, and would have declared a friendship were business not so pressing. Now little Mary Vivian hurried her visitor up the steps, talking all the way.

'What a pity that we muddled the dates between us. For had you come next month, as I intended, the house would have been ready for viewing. As it is, my cousin Ambrose only moved this morning, and of course I have not had time to inspect it, let alone engage a cleaning woman. But since you have come so far, and it is a charming property, perhaps you would excuse a little dust and disorder?' Over her shoulder she cried imperiously, 'Alfred, take the carriage and horses round to the yard at the Royal George and shelter there. They will not mind.'

Her coachman was not so sure, but sighed and touched his hat and did as he was told.

Artlessly, Mary sought to impress her prospective buyer.

'As you can guess, knowing my Uncle William, he has done so much business with the George over the years that they are only too delighted to oblige us at any time.'

She concentrated on turning the front-door key.

'Let us hope that the storm soon blows over,' she said, in some difficulty. 'Not that we shan't be very comfortable resting here for an hour or so. Still, I hate thunder and lightning. The one gives me a headache and the other makes me jump so. Drat this key! And then, I don't like the idea of leaving the children at home. My housekeeper, Polly, is wonderful with them, but she is getting old, and I fear they tire her. There! The lock needs a drop of oil – not that Ambrose would notice anything like that!'

Then she smiled most delightfully, opened the door with a flourish, and cried, 'Welcome to Thornton House, Miss Bloom!'

Only the ominous weather outside could make the place seem welcome. Dust and disorder were not the only faults. It had been long and grievously neglected.

'Of course, two bachelors working odd hours are no inducement to good housekeeping,' Mary explained. Adding to herself, 'That wretched servant-girl must have been bone-idle!'

Her stream of chatter, springing from enthusiasm, was quickly doused. Her companion was by nature quiet and contemplative. In silence they trailed through silent rooms which still bore the faint stale scent of dried rose-petals, and saw webs float from leaf to plaster leaf across the moulded ceilings, and heard mice scuttle in the empty larder. Mould spotted the piles of linen, laid away in tall cupboards. The long clock in the hall had stopped. In the bedroom where poor Jem Tripp had died that Spring, the furniture was carelessly shrouded in old sheets, the curtains drawn close, the air stuffy. So that Mary almost felt the presence of his coffin, saw again upon his waxen face the look of mild astonishment, and closed the door gladly on his ghost.

'Ah, you should have seen the house as it used to be!' Mary cried, in a passion of self-reproach for the long kind years it had given her.

But Naomi Blüm, taking an inner view, gave one of her rare smiles and asked, 'Whose room was this?'

14

A palpable presence was here also. Grave and serene, triumphing over the masked looking glass, the stripped four-poster bed, the faded square upon the carpet where the sun had shone on many an afternoon.

Mary's forehead became smooth, her smile returned.

'It belonged to Aunt Charlotte. She lived in Thornton House with Great-Aunt Wilde for a time when she was a young girl. When her husband died she returned here as mistress. Then there was a political scandal, and she went abroad for some years, but came back again in her old age and made a home for Ambrose and Jeremy and me. There is her desk under the window. She wrote in her journal every day, and taught me to do the same. The desk is something of hers we would wish to keep.'

This reminded her of another omission.

She cried, 'Oh, what a muddle I have made of it all! There should have been a proper inventory of furniture, and everything cleaned and polished before you arrived. Uncle William said you had lived in the best hotels in every capital of Europe. What must you think of us?'

Naomi replied soothingly, 'Mrs Vivian, I think very well of you.'

She stood by the long window, looking down at the darkening High Street, smiling still. The smile illumined her.

She said, 'Mr Howarth is right. I have had every luxury and every excitement that city life could offer. But now I am looking for a home, Mrs Vivian, not an hotel. I wish to belong somewhere, not always to be the passing stranger. This house has known much living. And I like your Millbridge. Very old, very handsome.'

She answered Mary's silent question with another smile, 'Yes, Mrs Vivian, I should like to buy your house and the furniture you don't want for yourself. For I feel I have come home.'

Mary stood quite still and silent, marvelling at the double favour which Naomi Blüm had conferred on her. Hal Vivian's debts could now be paid, without secret recourse on Mary's part to the ironmaster, and this exotic stranger could become a friend.

'Oh, that would be . . . Oh, goodness, I was so afraid . . .'

Impulsively she held out both gloved hands, which were warmly clasped, but was immediately distracted by what she saw outside.

'Oh, look at that! Oh look!' cried Mary.

The air had become a thick black vapour. The heavens opened, lit and hurtled spears upon them. Almost simultaneously, low and threatening at first, then loud and confident, came the growl and crack of thunder.

'Oh, let us close the shutters, pray!' cried Mary. 'We shall be struck dead else!'

But Naomi was too awed and Mary too frightened to move. So they stayed where they were, their hands now clasped for mutual comfort, watching. And the storm, finally let loose, filled Thornton House with fury and outraged its rooms with light.

In the Town Hall a special council meeting was still in progress. Had old Hamish Standish, the director of Millbridge Hospital, still been alive the argument would have been decided long since. But his successor and nephew, Dr Jamie Standish, was too young to master the councillors and too obstinate to let go of them. So while one storm broke over their heads, another threatened to engulf them as they sat around the table. The chairman hastened to intervene.

'I think I may say, on everyone's behalf,' he began soothingly, 'that we are most grateful to Dr Standish for the vigilance, enterprise and public spirit he has shown this afternoon.'

For he wanted to go home to his tea.

'Hear, hear!' they murmured in relief.

'And I believe I speak for all of us when I say we shall sleep sounder at night knowing that the health of Millbridge and this valley is in such capable hands.'

They endorsed this statement with great enthusiasm.

'All Dr Standish's remarks and suggestions have been carefully noted, and I can promise him they will be just as carefully considered. I regret that so many of our members are absent, but this is a holiday period. Meanwhile, I thank Dr Standish for giving us so much of his valuable time, and perhaps we can discuss the matter at a later date.'

They clapped and nodded at the young doctor as if he had been knighted, and began to rise from their seats and collect their papers. But the gangling red-headed fellow brought his fist down upon the table with a thump that rivalled the thunderclaps outside, and shouted in a strong Scottish accent.

'Will you sit down? I have not yet done!'

'Oh dear,' said the chairman to himself.

He had been afraid of this. Like uncle, like nephew, he thought, and sat again. The others followed suit.

Jamie spoke with quiet emphasis, for his time and patience were not so important as the issue at stake and he must win his point.

'Gentlemen, this is not a matter you can put off, nor even put to one side. We are not speaking about a seasonal attack of measles, or a local epidemic of scarlet fever, bad though they be. We are discussing a deadly disease of pandemic proportions, for which there is no known cure. We are confronting *cholera*, gentlemen!'

They were listening impatiently, frowning, staring at their hands.

'I feel I have not made myself understood, and I grant you that my own limited knowledge of the disease is acquired from professional journals such as *The Lancet*. But I am not alone in believing that this country faces one of the most serious health crises in her history. For the first time, Asiatic cholera has entered Europe and is moving westwards along the routes of trade and war. Only last September it devastated Moscow. Soon it will reach the Baltic ports, a few days' sailing time away.

17

Less than a week after boarding ship, gentlemen, it could be on our shores. It is too late to prevent an epidemic when the first victim drops dead in Millbridge High Street.'

In the little silence that followed he asked permission for his colleague, Mr Bailey, to speak to them. Who had been sitting on a hard chair outside the door waiting for just such an emergency.

So very shortly a wiry, yellow-faced, pock-marked fellow was ushered in and introduced as the chief surgeon at Millbridge Hospital; but more importantly as an ex-army surgeon who had served in India, when the regiment to which he was attached suffered severely from cholera.

The members of the Board stared suspiciously at him, as though the fellow carried plague in his pocket, but Jamie Standish addressed him cordially, for he respected this unassuming man.

'Mr Bailey, these gentlemen find facts an unconvincing argument. Would you be so kind as to tell us what to expect if the cholera catches us unprepared?'

The surgeon was as modest as his status, but eloquent. He fixed his eyes upon the opposite wall, wet his lips, and recited his piece like a child called upon to give hideous entertainment.

'Sirs, it is like this. A man is out of sorts. Nothing much. A touch of summer diarrhoea, a feeling of heat at the pit of the stomach. You prescribe a dose of calomel or rhubarb and magnesia. Suddenly he begins to vomit and purge so violently that he cannot hold medicine down. He is seized with the most agonising muscular cramps. You cannot help him, try though you might. And so it goes on until the poor wretch is passing the linings of his own damaged bowels, and too weak to scream. He shakes with cold, he sweats with fever. Even in his final collapse he is wracked by excruciating spasms. If he is fortunate he will die in a few hours. If he is not, he may suffer thus for three or four days, while all around him his comrades are dying in a like manner. And when death comes they call it mercy.'

18

He looked at them directly, and said, 'If you had seen even one case of cholera, gentlemen, you would do everything within your power to keep such an evil at bay.'

They were subdued, studying his pock-marked face. Then one councillor, who had no time for such gloomy flights of fancy, made a practical objection.

'Aye, it's all very well to scare us with tales, but what about the cost? Dr Standish, here, has been talking of lime-washing poor folks's cottages and tenements, and hospitals and workhouses and prisons and such-like, from roof to floor, and purifying every drain and privy in Millbridge and the valley!'

This reminder brought forth a host of grievances.

'Aye, and giving idle folk warm clothes, and feeding them up for nothing, to help them fight this sickness better!' added another.

'Why, we should be put to no end of expense,' grumbled a third, 'and the poor cost us enough already, Lord knows!'

Which revived all their former prejudices.

'You say the cholera starts in poor quarters and poor folk suffer most?' cried an alderman. 'Then I say it is a poor man's disease. And if we keep them apart from the rest of us, as the sick were kept in times of plague, then we have naught to fear!'

'Sir,' said the surgeon very clearly, 'cholera, like death itself, knows no distinctions between rich and poor. Healthy folk stand a better chance of resisting the disease, but in my regiment the officers died along with their men.'

This was not the answer they wanted.

'Surely we should leave such decisions to those who are best qualified to deal with them?' the chairman suggested. 'The Privy Council in London has set up a Central Board of Health to deal with this very problem, and so far they have seen no need to issue a national directive.'

'Too damned busy sipping port!' said Jamie Standish savagely.

The alderman's tone was cautionary, reproachful.

'Seven illustrious medical men of the highest integrity, working without payment for the public good, Dr Standish!'

'Seven rich and idle drones, sir, who don't care a fig for it!'

'Gentlemen, gentlemen!' chided the chairman.

'Besides,' said another councillor comfortably, 'surely cholera can be held at bay like the yellow fever was. We have the benefit of being an island. If an infected ship comes into port it can be quarantined. That's how we've dealt with it in the past.'

But this brought forth a protest from the businessmen present.

'Why, you talk of quarantine as though that were nothing! Ships and goods and men standing idle for above a month! Let us hope we do not come to that pass. Quarantine will cost more than lime-washing!'

'I believe we can reach a compromise,' said the chairman loudly, as though light had suddenly shone upon him.

He felt that he had been harassed quite enough for one afternoon. And by now the thunder had reached such a pitch that they were almost shouting at each other in order to be heard.

'Both Dr Standish and Mr – er – his colleague have convinced us of the gravity of the situation. For which we thank them. But there seems to be a general agreement that we should wait for instructions from a higher authority before we act upon their suggestions. Which, of course, in the event of cholera, we should certainly do.'

Defeated, Jamie Standish reached for his hat.

'Yes,' said the chairman, relieved, 'I think that should meet the case. Meanwhile, we all have homes to go to – and are doubtless anxious about the safety and well-being of our loved ones . . .'

Doctor and surgeon lingered in the empty council chamber, marvelling at the power and fury of the elements.

'We had best gird our loins for the fray,' said Jamie grimly, 'which may be on us sooner than we think.'

'If it is not already in our midst, as yet unrecognised.'

'That's a terrible thought, Mr Bailey!'

The wiry surgeon had faced worse thoughts. Nor did he flinch from the cannonade of thunder, the swords of lightning.

'With regard to cholera, Dr Standish,' he said, surveying the war without. 'Whose side did you favour in the recent medical debate? Do you believe it to be borne upon the air as a poisonous vapour? Are you a miasmatist?'

'No, I am not – for what my opinion is worth!' Jamie replied modestly. 'I favour the theory of contagion. I think it more likely that cholera is bred in dirt, and we pass it from one to another.'

'I have, as yet, reached no fixed conclusion,' said Mr Bailey soberly, 'but if the miasmatists are right – this wild storm might well bear cholera upon its wings.'

Naomi Blüm

chapter two

Over the rectory tea-table in Millbridge that September afternoon, all talk was of a foreign Jewess who was shortly coming to live in the Old Town, for such a thing had never been known before.

'Of course, one expects to find such people in Trade or in the big cities like Manchester,' said Mrs Warburton, smoothing the skirt of her second-best grey silk, 'but not to meet them socially. And I believe I speak for all respectable and right-minded folk.'

The rector's wife, Cicely Pole, was divided as usual between what she felt and what was required of her. She compromised.

'Surely, we are all equal in the sight of God?' she suggested.

And would have liked to remind them that the Jews were, however inexplicably, God's chosen people.

Mrs Warburton disposed of her at once, in a tone both firm and jocular. For one should not forget that Cicely Pole, however respectable, was sister to Ambrose Longe and daughter of the late revolutionary Charlotte, and blood will out.

'I think we must draw the line at heathens!' Mrs Warburton said.

Mentally, the rector's wife counted the cakes and biscuits and divided them by six, wondering whether she should order more. She had noticed that controversy sharpened the appetite.

Plied with hot tea and gossip, conversation flowed. Cap ribbons wagged beneath plump chins. Cashmere shawls slithered from buxom shoulders. Faces became flushed and intent. Only Mrs Wheeler, the bank manager's wife, was inclined to listen rather than talk.

'Well, I must say, Cicely, I was horrified to hear that Thornton House was being sold at all,' Mrs Beardsall began, 'since it has been in your family for four generations!'

'. . . and was your childhood home,' added Mrs Hurst. 'Why ever did dear Charlotte leave it to Mary Vivian, who was only a niece, after all. Surely you or Mr Ambrose should have inherited?'

'The Will was fair and just,' said Cicely, who would have liked to give her mind either to the tea or the conversation, but was not being allowed to do so. 'When my mother adopted Mary she felt she must provide for her as for a daughter. Ambrose and I approved the decision.'

'Dear Cicely. So understanding always,' murmured Miss Glossop. 'Such a forgiving nature. Did Mr Ambrose not mind Mary turning him out of Thornton House?'

'Again, that was a matter of mutual agreement and arrangement,' said Cicely firmly, closing that avenue of attack. 'A large family house is not suitable for a bachelor.'

'*I* heard, though of course I do not know how true it is, that poor Mr Vivian was in serious financial difficulties,' said Mrs Hurst, 'and that is why Mary needed to sell.'

'You will excuse me a moment?' Cicely said, as though she had not caught the remark. 'I have something to see to in the kitchen . . .'

Behind her back the conversation leaped into ferocious life.

'*I* am surprised that the Vivians did not borrow from the ironmaster. After all, Mary is his niece and Mr Vivian his natural son. Pray don't nudge and shush me, Evelyn, everyone knows *that*!'

'*I* heard that the ironmaster would be only too pleased to help, but Mr Vivian prefers to remain independent of him. Not so Miss Mary, who is very thick with her uncle, and tucks many a secret banknote into her purse! Well, she was never one to throw away an opportunity. Look how well she has done for herself! To start life as the daughter of poor Dick Howarth in that windy farm on Garth Fells, and to end up as mistress of the

23

Old Hall and owner of Thornton House takes a great deal of cunning, my dears!'

'But why did she sell to a *Jewess?*'

'Because,' said Mrs Hurst, 'she wanted a high price quickly. And the Jewess – being a foreigner and not knowing any better! – paid what she asked without argument, and bought all the furniture, too. For she seems to have nothing of her own. Mr Hurst declares that her troubles have only just begun, for Thornton House is in a shocking state and will cost more to put to rights than it did to buy. Sure enough, it is swarming with workmen already!'

'Who is this person? Has anyone met her?' Mrs Warburton asked.

'She is called *Miss Naomi Bloom,*' Mrs Wheeler offered. 'The surname is not, of course, spelled as we pronounce it. But I thought it rather a pretty name.'

It did not appeal to the other ladies.

'What age might she be?' asked Miss Glossop.

Here Mrs Beardsall broke in.

'Oh, she is not in her first youth! My husband saw her when she came to Millbridge to consult the painters and carpenters, and apparently she stayed overnight at the Royal George with her maid!'

This caused a small commotion. The Jewess had been made manifest.

'Oh, what is she like?'

'How was she dressed?'

'How did she speak?'

'He did not speak with her, naturally. Not being acquainted. She was dining alone – which seems rather *outré*. Would you not have thought she would stay at the Old Hall with Mary Vivian? Anyway, Mr Beardsall said that she was uncommonly dark, heavy-featured, and shockingly over-dressed. False curls and bare shoulders, and the most trumped-up jewellery he had ever seen!'

'Poor thing. She will be quite a wallflower!' cried Miss Glossop, who had first-hand experience of such a state.

The bank manager's wife waited for them all to finish before she delivered the *coup de grâce*. She spoke in a die-away voice as though she regretted a subject so vulgar as wealth.

'*I* heard – Mr Wheeler happened to say – that Miss Bloom had been highly educated both here and abroad and spoke several languages fluently. And I believe that she has refused many offers of marriage so far – one of them being from a German baron. Nor is she quite the stranger we imagine, for her late father was a business connection of our ironmaster. It was Mr Howarth who advised the lady to look at Thornton House and suggested that she might find Millbridge a salubrious place to live in.'

This unexpected revelation caused instant silence.

'Yes,' Mrs Wheeler continued, in the same cool, pale voice, 'Miss Bloom could have lived anywhere she chose – London, Paris, Berlin – but apparently she took quite a fancy to the property and the place. Oh, I know that Thornton House has been neglected, but it is by no means as bad as Mr Hurst says. Miss Bloom is simply sparing no expense in restoring it to her satisfaction. Oh, certainly she bought *some* of the furniture, but only the best pieces. She has never had a settled home, you see. Always travelling! And, far from being *trumped-up*, Mrs Beardsall, her jewels are worth a fortune in themselves. You see, her late father was an expert in the buying and selling of precious stones. But then, Mr Beardsall would naturally think they were paste, wouldn't he?'

Here she flung up her hands and gave an arch little laugh.

'Oh yes, my dears, Miss Bloom can afford to indulge her every whim! When her father died she inherited a most substantial fortune.'

Another short silence followed.

'Oh, money, money, money!' cried Mrs Hurst, fanning

herself vigorously. 'What difference does money make?'

She wondered whether it was tens or hundreds of thousands.

'Would you say she was *very* rich?' whispered Miss Glossop.

The bank manager's wife shut her eyes and fluttered her fingers, as if to answer that this was the poorest of descriptions.

'All I can tell you, my dears, is that Mr Wheeler is most grateful to Mr Howarth for introducing him to Miss Bloom. In fact, Mr Wheeler says that Millbridge is most fortunate to have such a distinguished personage in its midst!'

They realised at once that Miss Blüm must have lodged a mighty sum in Mr Wheeler's bank, and thought it incredibly sly that all this information had not been confided earlier. Cicely Pole, returning to the fray, found the ladies unusually quiet. She had refreshed herself by consulting her husband Jarvis, who was hiding in his study writing Sunday's sermon, which would fall upon deaf ears.

'I have just discussed the subject of our conversation with Mr Pole,' said Cicely resolutely, 'and I must tell you that both he and I are of one mind upon this matter. As soon as Miss Bloom moves into Thornton House we shall be leaving our cards, welcoming her to our social circle, even though she cannot join our religious communaity.'

Their response amazed her.

'Dear Cicely!' cried Miss Glossop, patting her hand. 'You are a true Christian. Did you say the poor lady was alone in the world?' Looking round at the relieved and expectant company. 'Ah! I have trod that thorny path myself!' And seemed likely to continue to do so. 'I, too, shall follow your charitable example and call upon her!'

'We must *all* call upon her!' cried Mrs Hurst generously.

'You know how narrow in their views our good townsfolk can be,' added Mrs Beardsall. 'It is up to us to set a good example.'

'Cicely,' said Mrs Warburton curiously, 'did Mary not tell you that this person . . . that Miss Bloom was very rich?'

Then Cicely Pole understood the reason for their change of attitude, and regretted it.

'I see very little of Mary these days, living out at Brigge as she does, and busy with her children. So we have not discussed the matter,' she replied, somewhat wearily. 'Does money make such a difference?'

'No, of course not!' cried Mrs Hurst, who knew what was due to a rector's wife. 'It is what we are that matters, not what we have.'

The others concurred automatically.

'And as Mr Pole said last Sunday, we must love our neighbours as ourselves!' added Mrs Beardsall.

To show she had not been asleep at the time.

'And if some of us did not extend the hand of friendship,' murmured Miss Glossop, now on safe ground, 'Miss Bloom might find herself ignored by society.'

Then Cicely Pole spoke drily and composedly, as her late mother would have done.

'Oh, not since she is so *rich*, surely?'

On one point at least their charity was unfounded, and Cicely uninformed. They were not taking pity on a heathen. Naomi Blüm had been received into the Church of England at birth, and so would attend Sunday morning services in St Mark's church with the rest of them. And the elegance of her dress, the magnificence of her jewels, would capture and hold the attention of his flock as the Reverend Jarvis could never hope to do.

Her grandfather, Daniel Blüm, had been born in a German ghetto at a time when a highly intelligent boy could hope to escape the consequences of being born a Jew. Life behind the pale was poor and narrow, rigidly orthodox. Outside lay a broad fair Christian world of freedom and opportunity. By means of good patrons, good luck and hard work, Daniel became a distinguished member of the intelligentsia, who accepted him in spite of his origins. Only the cleverest Jews gained entrance to these charmed circles, and once there they made the most of this new freedom. By the time Daniel Blūm's sons came to manhood the Jewish salons of Berlin were the brightest stars in Germany's social firmament.

These sons were raised as Jews in a Christian society, an exhilarating and uneasy position which made them unsure of their identity. The burden of his religion lay most heavily upon the second son, Nathan. He was a dark and secretive young man, forever seeking to escape himself and his origins. He could have been a scholar like his father, but money gave him a greater sense of security. He became a dealer in precious stones. He travelled widely. He lost touch with his family deliberately. He was drawn first to Holland and then to England, whose attitude towards Jews was more emancipated. Here, he prospered exceedingly and was highly respected.

For the first time in his life he found sufficient confidence to think of someone beside himself, and in this state of contentment fell in love with Jessica Samuels, the daughter of a London merchant. He was then nearly forty, a powerful, complex and sophisticated man, whilst Jessica was an innocent eighteen, bred solely to be the queen of a Jewish hearth. They married in the summer of 1804.

Within months the dream had faded. Nathan was not by nature a family man, and the Samuels insisted upon family closeness. Moreover, they were strictly orthodox. The nervous brilliance of German Jewish salons, their fine food unhampered by Kosher restrictions, their wide and ever-changing spectrum of ideas, were delights unknown to and unwanted by the Samuels. They clung to the Judaic rules. To him, his marriage proved to be another kind of trap, and Nathan made his final escape. It was ruthless and brilliant, and so obvious a solution to all his inner difficulties that he wondered why he had not thought of it before. He became a Christian.

He was quite prepared to be generous with his young wife if she should decide to leave him, but despite her inner turmoil the girl remained loyal to her husband, and the Samuels cast them both forth in ritual fashion.

Jessica had sacrificed her family and her religion for him but she refused to share his Christian state. A deeply devout Jewess, she remained in limbo to the end of her days, observing the festivals alone. In the autumn of 1805 Naomi was born, a child of a divided house. Thereafter, no other infant survived and a few years later Jessica gave up trying to atone for her sins.

When the war with France was just over, Nathan Blüm felt able to visit his family again, taking his nine-year-old daughter with him. The Blüms were not orthodox Jews, and some of their Jewish friends had been converted to Christianity, so they received Nathan without reproach. To the motherless Naomi they extended such a welcome, and the child reciprocated with such warmth, that he left her in their care for a few months.

Naomi's need to live fully, to love and be loved, had so far remained unsatisfied. She hardly knew her father and her mother's affection had been constricting, but in the vast galaxy of the German Blüms she shone bright. Nathan returned and saw his daughter for the first time. He had not realised what a quick and vivid little girl she was. In the sombre mirrors of her eyes he saw an intelligence and self-awareness which Jessica had lacked. Secretly he claimed her for his own but knew that only his family could give her a stable childhood. So for the next eight years Naomi lived in Berlin until her father could take her over.

She was an eager pupil in this worldly education and, whatever his faults as husband and father, Nathan was an excellent teacher. He made a companion of her. In his strange possessive way he loved her. Whilst she, given permission as it were to love him, loved without reservation.

He never said that he did not want her to marry, but he spoke bitterly about the narrowness and mediocrity of the married state. He regretted the waste of intellect in a woman, of adventure in a man. He described procreation as the subjection of the woman to a gross indignity, and childbirth as a passport to ugliness, agony and death. His singular views made a strong impression on the girl's mind. In delivering himself of them Nathan seemed to become a dark priest condemning the sins of the world.

Naomi was also made subtly aware of his deep displeasure when she became interested in anyone of either sex. The painful outcome of one early attachment dissuaded her from trying again. She must have no friend but him. Gradually, she shaped herself to his requirements. They travelled much abroad. He even taught her something of his business. Few people were so close. But the price of the relationship was high, and she could not escape it.

She was twenty-five years old when her father suffered a massive heart attack and died before a physician could be summoned. Naomi knelt beside his body, thoughts and feelings in conflict.

'Thank God he knew I was with him!'

'I can finish this business in Amsterdam for him.'

'He would hate a great family funeral. I think he would have liked to be buried here quietly. I can go to Berlin afterwards and tell the Blūms myself. Yes, that would be best.'

'I must ask Mr Feinberg about investments.'

'My wanderings are over. I can find my own place in the world.'

But her recurrent thought would have struck a central chord in Nathan, however cruelly.

'Free! I am free!'

Newspapermen

chapter three

The ironmaster wasted no time at all. The day after his ulti-
matum to Ambrose Longe he cast a wide net and within the
month came up with a couple of very interesting catches.

The Millbridge Advertiser, instituted in 1792, was exactly what
its name implied. It had known only one owner and editor –
Dickie Thoroughgood – and only one home, which was his
home, 38 Cornmarket. Newspaper and man alike were popular,
reliable and unpretentious. In their fortieth year of partnership
they seemed likely to go on for ever. Then early one evening
Dickie Thoroughgood was found slumped at his desk, face awry,
staring at the pen which he could not grasp.

His physician ordered him to bed and refused to say how
long he might stay there. He forbade him to have anything
to do with his newspaper for the present and to be prepared to
delegate most of its work in future. But Dickie's love for *The
Advertiser* had been a jealous one and no one but he was capable
of taking charge. The paper lingered, like her master, on the
verge of extinction.

While he lay helpless over his shop, and *The Advertiser*
came out late and lacking – with the aid of old journeymen and
raw apprentices – the ironmaster approached Mrs Thoroughgood benevolently behind her husband's back.

Between them they reached the decision Dickie could not
make on his own. A sum of one thousand pounds, in the shape
of five hundred pounds down and five annual instalments, was
just that much more than the newspaper could have fetched in
the open market. It would have been stupid to refuse. So Dickie
accepted, and died a week later.

Then rumour had it that a certain reporter, on a Yorkshire newspaper of Tory persuasion, deserved better opportunities than he could ever hope to get. Whereupon the ironmaster's private secretary made discreet enquiries, reduced the reporter to three pages of personal and professional information and served him up with the ironmaster's breakfast.

William Howarth smiled and said, 'So Jack is better than his masters? He sounds a likely candidate. Tell him that if he is interested in editing *The Advertiser*, and we suit each other, I will offer him double his present salary.'

Sam Pickering was typical of many a poor and clever man who has been at the mercy of those less able than himself – he bore life a grudge. But he also possessed a shrewd head and all the energy accumulated in years of frustrated ambition, which made him a formidable prospect.

A bachelor of eight-and-thirty, he was not ill looking, though somewhat stooped and cadaverous. There was a threadbare quality about his cuffs and elbows, a melancholy droop to his long moustache, but his eyes were sharp and green and missed nothing.

For a long time he had felt that recognition of his talents was overdue, yet William Howarth's offer took him by surprise. He was by nature suspicious of grand gestures, and decided to keep his counsel until he had met the ironmaster and satisfied himself that the man was genuine. And since he did not intend to jeopardise his present job, he arranged his appointment so that no one would know what he was about.

The following Sunday being his day off, and he known as a keen botanist, Sam Pickering set out to walk the thirteen miles which lay between him and Kingswood Hall. The October morning was crisp and fine. He preferred his own company to that of anyone else. And some sort of adventure was afoot, whatever the outcome. He arrived on the ironmaster's doorstep in high spirits, which he hid behind a sober mask, believing them to be bad for business.

His caution and the ironmaster's impassiveness were well matched. They lunched casually and alone in the ironmaster's study, dispensed with compliments and empty assurances, and dealt in plain facts. By the end of the meal Sam Pickering had accepted the job on terms which suited them both. The ironmaster crossed his legs, drank coffee and spoke in a conversational tone.

'With regard to other local newspapers,' he began, 'only a couple need concern you. One is *The Wyndendale Post*, long-established in the valley, which Lord Kersall and his circle use for their own ends. The other, *The Clarion*, calls itself independent but has radical proclivities. It is run by my nephew.'

He read a question on Sam Pickering's face and answered, 'That is of no importance. He and I are not close.'

Some instinct made him refrain from saying just how far apart they were. He contented himself by observing that even relatives must take care of themselves, that business was business, and honest competition the order of the day.

'I am not asking you to join in the squabbling and backbiting that goes on between *The Clarion* and *The Post*. I want this newspaper of ours to stand head and shoulders above the fray. It must have quality. It must be the best, Mr Pickering.'

Sam fingered his moustache carefully.

'The best in Millbridge?'

'The best in this valley. For now.'

'What about later on, then?'

The ironmaster looked at him meaningfully.

'That depends how good you are at your job, Mr Pickering. My money will always be good.'

'*I'm* good,' said Sam quietly. 'Given half a chance I can be even better.'

The ironmaster smiled on him.

'Then we can both look forward to a great newspaper.'

'But I'd be less than straight if I didn't tell you there was an element of luck in it, Mr Howarth. A newspaper has to find its way and take its own chances, just like a man does. And while

I can promise you that *The Advertiser* will never get less than one hundred per cent from me, I can't promise aught else, and that's the truth.'

'Good enough!' cried William heartily, and settled down to details. 'Now we need a new name which will express our intention of becoming widely known. I like the idea of using *Lancashire* in the title, and then a fine ringing noun to follow. How do you fancy being a *Herald*, Mr Pickering?'

Joking. Serious.

'*The Lancashire Herald?*' said Sam, pulling his whiskers thoughtfully. 'There's only one objection that I can see. Don't you think that *Herald* sounds a bit like *Clarion?*'

'Do you think so?' William replied blandly. 'Oh, but the name of the county gives it far more weight, don't you think?'

'Aye, it's a grand name, for sure. And it's *your* newspaper, Mr Howarth. You're entitled to call it what you like.'

'I should like *you* to be satisfied with it, too,' said William graciously. 'Of course, we must use the old name along with the new one for a while, because I want to keep *The Advertiser's* business. But that side of the paper will be a secondary concern. Dickie Thoroughgood's journeymen should be able to look after it. So we shall be known as *The Lancashire Herald and Advertiser* for a twelvemonth or so, and then we can emerge in our true colours.'

The ironmaster poured out a measure of brandy, observing that it would warm Sam for the road.

'Now, Mr Pickering, everything is ready at thirty-eight Cornmarket, including the living quarters. We can engage a servant to look after you. All you need do now is to name the hour that you arrive by coach, and someone will meet you. So how soon can you take up the post?'

'Well, I should give reasonable notice to the Keighley *Chronicle*, Mr Howarth. Suppose we say a week tomorrow?'

'Why give them a week?' asked the ironmaster, astonished. 'They have treated you shabbily for upwards of fourteen years.

34

I will employ you as from today. Tell them to go to the devil, and come straight back. If it is a question of money I will advance you whatever you need. In any case, take this to cover your expenses.'

Seldom had a sovereign been accepted so reluctantly.

'Thank you, Mr Howarth, but if it's all the same to you I'll work my week out on the *Chronicle*.'

'Why, man? For heaven's sake. You owe them nothing.'

'I owe myself something,' said Sam Pickering judiciously. 'I've got the reputation of being trustworthy, Mr Howarth. I shouldn't like to mar it for the sake of a week's notice.'

The matter was settled.

'Well, I'd best be off if it's all the same to you,' said Sam. 'The light wanes early this time of the year.' He added awkwardly, 'It's been a champion day, Mr Howarth, and I thank you for it.'

That same month the cholera reached Hamburg, only thirty-six hours' steaming-time away, giving rise to an urgent question in the House of Commons. At British ports all incoming ships were quarantined for fourteen days, and the Central Board of Health produced its first cholera circular, in a shrill command for national vigilance.

Only a few days later the Wyndendale Board of Health was formed. The list of its members read like a roll of honour, being composed of all the town's magistrates, the four most important men in the district – including Lord Kersall and the ironmaster – three physicians, Mr Bailey the surgeon, and leading representatives of Church, Chapel and Quaker meeting house.

Led by Dr Jamie Standish they went to work immediately. A small fortune was spent on chloride of lime and its application. They composed a brief and simple printed notice, giving details of cholera symptoms and whom to contact, and issued a copy to every family in the valley. Charity committees were set up, organised by wives of the Board, to receive and distribute gifts of food and clothing.

Before the second circular was published on November 14th, the Wyndendale Board had taken possession of an old disused poorhouse on the outskirts of Millbridge and were rapidly throwing up two temporary buildings near it, to form a complete cholera unit: hospital, isolation house and convalescent ward. With a little difficulty, owing to his lack of medical status, Mr Bailey was put in charge of this. And with even more difficulty, the town council were persuaded to pay for it out of the public rates.

The ironmaster, who was known to be a staunch admirer of the new London Peelers, himself organised a voluntary police force to guard the unit. Up at Millbridge Hospital, Mr Bailey interviewed poor men who would be paid to take the risk of fetching, carrying and burying cholera victims; and poor women who would be prepared to nurse the sick and to care for those who recovered. Wyndendale was ready. So it was highly infuriating to find someone out of step with the crisis, and Jamie Standish stalked into *The Clarion*'s printing-shop one late November morning brandishing the latest edition, and shouting over the noise of the old Koenig printing-press.

'Have you gone quite mad, Mr Longe?'

He pointed with theatrical emphasis to a headline which said:

NO CHOLERA! JUST ANOTHER TORY PLOT!

He rapped the leading article which informed its readers that the usual intestinal disorders, due to poor sanitation, were being used as a means to divert public attention from the Reform Bill.

Ambrose transferred printing ink from his hands to his apron, ready but wary. He had been annoying people for fifteen years and was prepared for any reaction from hard words to hard blows.

Cheerfully, he shouted back, 'Not mad, Dr Standish. Just tired of being hoodwinked by a panic-stricken opposition!'

'What is this nonsense about plots?' cried Jamie, shaking the newspaper at him furiously. 'You cannot be serious! And how can I make myself heard over this damnable racket?'

Ambrose motioned him to come outside into the passage, and closed the door. They were old acquaintances, connected through Ambrose's mother and Jamie's uncle, and through Mary Vivian whom Jamie had once hoped to marry. It was not a friendship but they respected each other, even liked each other in a cautious fashion.

'Your attitude, sir, is nothing less than irresponsible!' said Jamie, now quiet and emphatic. 'The new Board of Health in London is composed of men noted for their medical ability and experience, and this second circular is based on a five-month study of cholera in European conditions. Surely a reputable newspaper like *The Clarion* cannot discount such a document? *The Post* and the new *Advertiser* have printed it upon their front pages in full!'

Despite his concern and anger he described Ambrose's latest rival as delicately as he could, though even in so short a time people were forgetting Dickie's homely paper and referring to its sophisticated replacement as *The Herald*: a good resounding name which tripped off the tongue much as *The Clarion* had done in its early days.

'Damn the other papers,' said Ambrose deliberately. '*The Clarion* thinks for itself. Oh yes, the government sent me copies of both documents to print, as they always do. It is the only bonus provincial newspapers can expect! I printed the first circular and I trounced it for reading like a leper's charter – all that talk of shutting cholera victims up in their houses, and daubing SICK upon the door, as though we lived in the days of the Great Plague, and threatening to use troops and police cordons to enforce such measures. To me that smacks of civil war. You did not, I notice, object to that.'

'You were criticising the tone, not the truth, of the document.'

'Well, I grant you that this second circular is cooler in tone, but I cannot help noticing how the epidemic flares up afresh whenever the Whigs present their Reform Bill! I am not alone in my opinion, I do assure you. The radical press is quite convinced that this is a political plot. And I shall continue to urge my readers to ignore the hysteria, and to question this sudden interest in their health and welfare! You can have me put in prison for it if you wish. I am not unacquainted with the inside of Millbridge Jail! – and there, Dr Standish, I rest my case.'

'You're dafter than I thought, man!' said Jamie more kindly, realising that Ambrose was wholly sincere. 'Have you not heard rumours from the North?'

'I am suspicious of rumours,' said Ambrose, smiling slightly.

'Then I'll tell you the truth, and I can quote you names, dates and places. But this is only for your private ear. No printing, mind! The authorities are hoping to contain the disease, and they don't want to cause a panic. The news came to my chief surgeon, Mr Bailey, in a letter from an old friend up in County Durham.

'Three weeks ago a keelman by the name of William Sproat was taken desperately ill. His own surgeon could do nothing for him and advised a second consultation. Dr Clanny, a leading physician thereabouts, was called in and professed himself to be suspicious but uncertain. Then they asked Mr Kell, who is the person known to Mr Bailey, to take a look at the patient. Mr Kell is surgeon to the reserve units of the eighty-second regiment, now stationed at Sunderland barracks, and has served in Mauritius. He had no doubts at all. He diagnosed Asiatic cholera.

'The keelman died on the twenty-sixth of October – the first *confirmed* case in the country, but not necessarily the first *case*. Cholera has probably been with us for some time – thriving on the ignorance of doctors who have not the experience to recognise it, and the fears of those who know and dare not name it.'

He struck *The Clarion* with the back of his hand.

'*That* is why I cannot let you use your influence in this manner, Mr Longe. You must think in terms of saving lives, not votes. Cholera has nothing to do with Tory politics. It is an evil of nature beyond human control with which we must deal as best we can.'

After a little silence Ambrose said, 'I thank you for telling me, sir. I am sorrier than I can say for my part in this – though it was the result of honest conviction . . .'

He had suffered a body blow. The truth revealed a narrowness of view, a lack of political judgement in him, which worried him deeply. Sam Pickering and *The Herald* had shown more wisdom and infinitely more common-sense. He discounted Arnold Thwaites on *The Post*, who had probably also believed the cholera to be a Tory plot and gleefully covered up for his masters.

'I shall retract my allegations,' said Ambrose stiffly, 'but without betraying your confidence, of course. Perhaps you would be kind enough to tell me how *The Clarion* can make amends.'

Now Jamie turned away, a little sorry but much more relieved, saying, 'You could reprint and distribute our own cholera circular, if you would, Mr Longe. I believe that order was given to *The Post* last time, but I doubt they made sure all the poor folk had a copy! I understand that you have your own lines of communication, which reach all those in most need of help!'

He said this with a twinkle, that Ambrose might know he referred to *The Recorder*, and had quite forgiven him.

Two Friends

chapter four

Once she was established in Millbridge, Naomi Blüm proved to be a curious mixture of the sociable and the solitary. She seemed eager to be accepted, as was only proper, and when Mrs Warburton informed her that Tuesday used to be Calling Day at Thornton House before Charlotte Longe became 'odd', Naomi reinstated that afternoon ceremony of tea-cups and talk. But she proved socially difficult in ways they would never have imagined, and her only friend seemed to be that sly cat, Mary Vivian.

It was not Naomi's wealth they minded. They expected her clothes to be more fashionable, her possessions newer and costlier, her food richer, her wine older, her servants softer-spoken and softer-footed than their own. It was her intellect to which they objected. Her purse of conversation lacked the common currency of small talk, while abounding in the silver of perception and wit, the gold of integrity. In short, they found her heavy-going. Sometimes even her wealth was not sufficient to excuse her.

The Warburton family were noted for their musical soirées. Indeed these evenings could be said, like Atlas, to support the cultural world of Millbridge, and were regularly reported in the society columns of the local press. Only a philistine such as Ambrose Longe would have described their rendering of Haydn's Trio in F Major as 'the battle of three blind mice'. But then, he could not afford to pay a reporter and had to act as his own music critic, so very likely he knew nothing about it. The reporter from *The Post* always wrote lovely notices. The old *Advertiser* had never come, of course, but the new *Herald* did and was courteous if non-committal. Consequently they stopped sending invitations to *The Clarion*, which everyone said served it right.

There were obviously fine folk in the valley who did not move in the same circle as the Warburtons and therefore made do by hiring musicians or attending concerts in Manchester. This was tacitly understood. But genteel members of the middle class felt privileged to spend an evening at 'The Elms': yawning behind their hands and fans, dozing off lightly, being nudged if they snored or their feathered head-dresses nodded forward and tickled the person in front, and finally waking up in time to clap and say quite truthfully that they had never heard anything like it.

So Mrs Warburton, as a leading light of Millbridge society, was among the first to leave her calling card at Thornton House. And when she heard that Naomi had stayed with relatives in Germany who held regular musical assemblies and that as a child she had seen and heard the late Ludwig van Beethoven perform his own work, the lady was overjoyed. At last, she thought but did not say, someone capable of appreciating us. Her invitation cards, issued judiciously but widely in the New Year of 1832, read 'To meet Miss Naomi Blûm, and enjoy a little music.'

On that January evening Mrs Warburton stood proudly in her entrance hall and received her guest like royalty. And very regal Naomi looked in her Chinese green silk gown with sleeves *à la Medici*, and the cuffs of dark green velvet. Her blue-black hair was dressed in full curls high on her head and encircled with a *chaperon* of artificial roses. The other ladies present were also very dressed and curled, but they had to share the services of Miss Barlow the seamstress and Mr Babbage the hairdresser, whereas Naomi's gown had been bought in Paris and she was fortunate in her personal maid.

So far so good. Millbridge was delighting in the double spectacle of Miss Blûm and the gifted Warburtons together, and a great many compliments were exchanged by those present, but the most delicate flattery of all was paid by the Warburtons to Naomi. In deference to her foreign origins they had devoted the evening to the work of German and Viennese composers.

The music critic for *The Post* once wrote in his fervour, 'I even delight in the tuning-up! Such vivacity and dedication! Such a promise of the cultural feast to come!' To which Ambrose Longe unkindly responded by saying that he could endure the tuning-up if only they would decide upon the same note.

This evening the Warburtons scraped and twanged with more than their usual energy, paused for a few hushed and portentous moments, and then pitched into Bach without mercy.

A faint line appeared between Naomi Blūm's black brows, which deepened as the concert progressed. Innocent of her reaction, they sawed away conscientiously, pausing only to turn over the wrong pages and to smile and nod at one another in a haze of self-congratulation.

Having executed Bach, and acknowledged the applause, they made way for the hostess herself, who refused to be intimidated by the Moonlight Sonata, and made a number of gallant runs at it before the piece submitted. As Ambrose Longe once said on a similar occasion, 'There are sometimes advantages in being stone-deaf. Let us hope that Beethoven can only hear in *heaven*!'

Breathing and bowing deeply, the triumphant pianist tried to catch Naomi's eye, but her guest looked steadfastly elsewhere.

Finally Haydn was put between the shafts and taken out for a family drive. They set off together at a quick trot, but he ditched the Warburtons in the second movement, leaving them to stagger home one by one behind him.

There was another pause until the audience realised that the performance had ended and then everyone except Naomi clapped very hard and shouted, 'Bravo! Bravo!' raising their eyebrows in silent acclaim, shaking their heads in wonder and crying, 'Never heard them on such form before!'

Naomi had no wish to hurt anyone's feelings. She struck her gloved palms lightly together in token payment. Her smile was a mere stretch of the lips. She became aware of her frown and erased it. She hoped they would not ask her what she thought, but of course they did.

'And we require you to be horridly truthful, Miss Bloom!' cried Mrs Warburton, shaking her forefinger archly at her guest of honour. 'We know you have heard a great deal of good music in your travels, and our poor efforts will seem nothing beside that. So do scold us. We are always willing to learn.'

Her guests glanced at one another in smiling disbelief. Such modesty, they were thinking.

Naomi replied carefully, 'A most commendable effort.'

Mrs Warburton's smile began to ice over.

'Of course, we are not *professionals*!' she said, with tremendous emphasis on the word.

Naomi unfortunately seized upon this truth as an explanation.

'No, no, I quite understand,' she said graciously. 'I was not judging you as professionals.'

Mrs Warburton could hardly believe her ears.

'I fear I made one or two mistakes in the sonata,' she offered, and her smile was a false ghost of itself.

Naomi hesitated.

'You *know* I did!' cried Mrs Warburton.

She laughed lightly. She struck Naomi's hand playfully, but not quite so lightly, with her fan. She dared her to agree. Behind her, a semi-circle of curious faces, ready to look hostile in a moment, waited for an answer.

Embarrassed, a little afraid, Naomi endeavoured to reassure her.

'Well, that is no matter. Even good musicians make mistakes.'

There was a short silence.

'Even *good* musicians,' Mrs Warburton said thoughtfully. 'Thank you, Miss Bloom.'

Ambrose stopped the printing-press.

'She said *what*?' he cried, delighted.

Mary giggled, drew herself up to imitate Naomi, and repeated the comment which was that moment enlivening the tea-tables of Millbridge.

'She'll *never* be asked there again!' said Mary, in mock horror.

'Fortunate Miss Bloom!'

'*You* have been rude about them, too. Often.'

'Ah! But I meant to be rude, and they expect it of me. Miss Bloom told the simple truth and that's much more devastating.'

'But poor Naomi minds very much, and blames herself dreadfully.'

'The lady obviously lacks a proper opinion of her talents. I must ask her to write my music column for me.'

He spoke idly, but Mary cried, 'Oh, why not? I sometimes feel that she finds life a little dull. And she knows so much about music.'

'Then she is over-qualified for the post. Her readers know so little. I should not dream of subjecting her to further ordeals.'

'Oh, don't be a tease, Ambrose. She won't expect to be paid.'

'I *couldn't* pay her, my dear girl. Well, well, I must get on. What have you done with your three brats?'

'I left them at Thornton House while I came to tell you the latest gossip. Naomi loves having them.'

'How very peculiar of her,' said Ambrose unkindly.

'And, Ambrose, it's Naomi's Calling Day today, and the only ladies to come were Warburton Enemies. It makes life very difficult.'

'I should have thought it made life a great deal easier. If she can now make an enemy of the Enemies she will be free of everybody. As I am – and you are.'

'I am very popular with everybody!' Mary cried indignantly.

'Trot away, pisey cat!' said Ambrose, and started up the printing press to indicate that he had done with gossip for that day.

'Oh, you!' said Mary rudely, sticking out her tongue.

She ran down the steps into the market square, and was lost in a crowd of Tuesday shoppers.

The April evening had come in so quickly that the lamplighter made his rounds an hour earlier than usual. Now the gas lamps shone like angels down the wet, dark High Street, each wearing a misty halo.

The York Mail rattled into Millbridge, punctual to the minute, and as it passed Thornton House the long clock in the hall chimed nine strokes of approval. This reminder of time passing caused the lady of the house first to judge the degree of steam rising from a silver spirit-kettle, secondly to inspect the contents of a silver muffin-dish keeping nice and hot on the hearth, thirdly to lift the corner of one lace curtain and peer out, and finally to sit down again. She had repeated this routine two or three times, for her guest should have been here long since.

It was interesting to observe that though Naomi Blüm had kept most of Charlotte Longe's furniture, and the lay-out of the parlour was pretty much the same, the room had a distinctly foreign air.

Perhaps the carpet was too new, lush as a golden meadow beneath her bronze kid shoes. Perhaps the freshly upholstered chairs were too grand in their yellow velvet coats. Perhaps the degree of polish was too high, the gas light a little too bright, the fire too hot, the general effect too luxurious. Whatever the reason, the place was entirely different, a fact of which its present owner remained delightfully unaware. For she believed she had re-created a typical English, Christian, middle-class parlour, and politeness had so far forbidden anyone to rob her of this illusion.

45

The sound of hooves and wheels brought Naomi out of her chair. The noise of the lion's head door-knocker fetched her parlour-maid rapidly down the hall. In another moment Mary Vivian burst in out of the rain, carrying a bundled child, and full of explanations even before she had been divested of her wet coat and bonnet.

'Oh, Naomi! Such a time as I have had getting here! Hal was home late, and I had waited dinner above an hour, and we had scarcely finished when someone came about the tunnel, so he went back again.'

Mary set the child down on the hall floor, where he stood wide-eyed, dripping quietly.

'Then I ran round to the stables to tell Alfred we were ready for the carriage, and he was drunk again, Naomi! Dead drunk. So I harnessed the pony and trap myself – oh, do you think Joseph could take them over to the Royal George . . .?'

'My dear, of course. But you should not have driven out alone at this time of night!'

'Oh, I wasn't going to be robbed of my evening, no matter what!'

The soft-footed manservant appeared, wearing a mackintosh, and within moments was heard driving up the High Street.

Mary knelt down, half-laughing, half-crying, and began to unwind the wet woollen scarf which bandaged her son from head to foot.

'And then this naughty boy had a nightmare and would not be left alone, and I was afraid the two girls would wake up as well : . .'

'Bring him into the parlour,' Naomi cried. 'He will be cold out here. Oh, Santo Vivian! What bad thing did you dream about?'

Mary was not possessive about her offspring, and allowed Naomi to carry the boy into the hot, bright room, to remove his outer clothes and to give them to the parlour-maid to dry. The reason for this personal attention was soon plain to see. The disposal of his tasselled cap meant that Naomi could stroke his black curls and kiss his scarlet cheeks, the lack of gloves allowed her to rub warmth into his small hands, and when she had unbuttoned his little overcoat she hugged him very hard.

Young Santo Vivian was a sturdy fellow, not long past his second birthday. Folk said how like his father he was, but the way he held himself and looked boldly round was William Howarth all over, and secretly rejoiced the ironmaster's heart.

At first Santo stared at his hostess with solemn grey eyes, but gradually her blandishments made him smile, and the hug brought forth a shout of laughter. Whereupon Naomi laughed too, sitting back on her heels, loving him.

Tenderly the two ladies embraced, standing back to admire each other's dresses before settling down by the fire; and at last Naomi could infuse the tea, order warm milk for her unexpected guest and cut a buttered muffin into strips.

'I see you still take all three Millbridge papers!' Mary cried irrepressibly, spying them on a side-table. 'Have you not made up your mind whether you are for or against *The Clarion*, then?'

'Must I be either?' Naomi asked reasonably, tucking a linen napkin round Santo's neck.

'Yes, indeed! I like people to be positive in their opinions. My country, right or wrong, say I!'

Naomi held the cup of milk to Santo's lips and answered teasingly but firmly.

'Then *you* are wrong, say I!'

Mary was quiet for a moment, but soon plucked up spirit and began again.

'Well, let us agree to disagree on that score. What do you think of our three respected papers?'

Naomi answered with devastating frankness.

'*The Herald* is a shrewd teacher. *The Clarion* is a promising pupil. And *The Post* is best for lighting the parlour fire!'

'Goodness!' cried Mary, impressed. 'We shall never get you married if say things like that. No one cares for a clever

47

woman. There are exceptions, of course,' she added quickly, fearful of hurting her friend. 'Aunt Cha was very clever and didn't care what anybody thought, but that was as she grew old.'

Naomi drew the child on to her lap and wiped the butter from his chubby fingers with a fine cambric handkerchief, which brought forth an affectionate admonishment from Mary.

'You should have babies of your own to spoil, Miss!'

'Ah, if one could have them without the husband!' Naomi replied.

'Husbands are very nice creatures. At least, mine is.'

Naomi shrugged, unconvinced.

'And what about love?' Mary continued. 'How do you manage without that, I wonder? I have been in love with something or somebody all my life. It is an absolute necessity for me.'

'Oh, love!' cried Naomi scornfully. 'Love is a usurer who first persuades you that his loan is a gift, and then demands a high rate of interest for it!'

'There you go again, Naomi! What a cynic you are, to be sure! You must have been crossed in love. Were you?' Without waiting for a reply she ran on, 'I was, frequently. Lord, what a goose I made of myself! It is much better to be married and sensible, I assure you.'

Naomi smiled to herself and rocked the handsome boy in her lap while Mary retailed gossip from one end of Wyndendale to the other. Santo's eyelids drooped with heat and sleep. Naomi touched one side of his flushed face to make sure they were not sitting too near the fire, and a great contentment crept over her. She could have stayed like that for ever, but Mary would not let her.

'What do you mean by calling *The Clarion* a promising pupil?' she asked suddenly. 'Ambrose is a very good journalist. Even those who don't like him must admire him.'

'What do I mean?' Looking drowsily into the flames. 'I mean – he is a clever fellow, your cousin Ambrose, but he is capable of so much more than this comedy he plays. He is like

Mr Punch, who will hit anybody with his stick. Like a little boy who knocks at a door and runs away. Oh, he is brave and amusing, one cannot help liking him – and yet one cannot take him seriously, either.'

'But why not?' Mary protested. 'He is serious in his beliefs and he has suffered for them, too.'

Loyalty was one of her strong suits, but a deeper grievance was besetting her.

She went on, almost querulously, 'I adore Uncle William, and he is always very kind and generous to me, but it was not at all nice of him to set up a paper in direct opposition to *The Clarion*. And why do you call *The Herald* a shrewd teacher, as though Mr Pickering knew more than Ambrose?'

Her tone made Naomi look up, but she answered Mary calmly.

'*The Herald* is politically better balanced, and in particular fields – such as foreign and financial news – it is better informed.'

Mary's colour was high. She showed every sign of the temper which people of her complexion were supposed to possess.

'It is easy for *you* to talk!' she cried impetuously. 'You and Uncle William are rich and can do as you please. Ambrose is poor and must manage as best as he can. And I think he does very well, and if I could help him I would do so. The only thing he lacks is opportunity.'

'Gently, gently, my friend,' said Naomi. 'Surely we are not going to quarrel over a difference of opinion?'

She descried the meaning beneath Mary's words and anger.

'Are *you* worried about money again?' she asked, wondering what had happened to the proceeds from the sale of Thornton House.

'Oh, no matter!' Mary said miserably, deflated. 'Look how late it is already! There is never enough time for anything these days. We must go. And poor little Santo is fast asleep.'

'You cannot drive him back by yourself through the dark and wet,' Naomi cried. 'Why not stay here with me tonight?'

'No, love,' said Mary, composing herself. 'I must go home. Polly was very worried when we went out. She won't sleep until we get back. And Philly or Hannah might wake up and find me gone. So let me have the poor little fellow . . .'

She held out her arms. Naomi gave up the child reluctantly, rang the bell, and ordered the maid to bring their coats.

'Will you not tell me what troubles you?' she asked, for she wanted so much to help.

'No, I think not,' said Mary stoically. 'Aunt Cha always said, "Don't talk about troubles. Deal with them." She disliked grumblers.'

'I wish I had known her,' said Naomi simply.

She coaxed Santo's arms into his sleeves.

'I thank you for your company,' she said, smiling at her friend. 'You leave two empty spaces behind you.'

Mary spoke more briskly than she felt.

'You really should get married, you know, Naomi. It would leave you no space at all!' She added, with a touch of humour, 'We must find you a husband like Hal. That would suit you very well indeed. You would have lots of babies, and hardly ever see him!'

She could keep up her spirits no longer. Two single tears formed, trembled and slid down her cheeks. The parlour-maid, without a hint from her mistress, tactfully disappeared.

Mary said in gasps, 'Oh, cuddle Santo for me! If he sees me crying it makes him cry too! I shall be myself again in a minute.'

She kept wiping away the tears very firmly and just as firmly they welled up, until at last she sobbed the story out.

'I'm expecting another baby in November – and let's hope it won't be twins this time, though Santo and Hannah are sweet. And Hal is in trouble with his tunnel. It's taking longer than he

50

estimated and they are working at night by torchlight to cut the costs, which has its dangers and difficulties. So he has no time to listen to me. And Polly leans on me, instead of the other way about. And, though I love the Old Hall dearly, there is always something that needs doing to it, and paying for. And it is no use consulting Hal, for he knows nothing about houses and is always busy. And Uncle William helps out when he can, but Hal would go mad if he knew – all because Uncle William didn't marry his mother nearly forty years ago. But at least I have *you*,' crying hard, 'and what I would do without you, I don't know.'

Santo roared in sympathy and mother and child sobbed together, while Naomi endeavoured to comfort them both. After a while Mary drew a deep breath, blew her nose and said resolutely, 'There. That's better. I'll go home now. Do be quiet, Santo, or I might be tempted to leave you behind and have one less to cope with!'

Naomi said firmly and compassionately, 'No, I shall not let you go. It would be rash and foolish to risk yourself and the child twice in one night!' It was her only hint of reproach for Mary's impulsive behaviour. 'Let us send a message to the Royal George and one of the ostlers will take it to Brigge. We shall say that you were feeling faint, and I am keeping you here. That they are not to worry, for you are quite safe with me, and will be home in the morning.'

She was at her best and most beautiful, caring for them, offering rest and shelter. Now she took them both back into the parlour and ordered a hot cordial for Mary.

'Ah, how well you shall sleep tonight, and in the morning – not one moment earlier than nine o'clock! – you shall sit up in bed and drink hot chocolate, with no one to worry you. I will take care of Santo. Then we shall breakfast together, and talk things over and make many plans, and all your troubles will fly away. How does that sound to you, my Mary?'

It sounded so wonderful that her Mary wept without restraint, and so was helped to bed in a borrowed nightgown,

51

relieved and beloved. The old spell of Thornton House was still working. It soothed her body, rested her mind, and brought peace to her soul. Under that quiet roof she slept as soundly as her son in his makeshift cot.

Naomi sat before her looking glass, punishing her curtain of black hair with a silver brush, and her face grew dark and stern. Money could patch the holes in a marital fabric, but not renew it. A child was growing in Mary's womb, and three small creatures already dragged at her hands and skirts. An ardent lover had turned into an absent husband. Her house of dreams must be cleaned and repaired, over and over again. The clocks were ticking time and beauty away.

Then Naomi walked her bedroom floor, shaking her head over Mary's woes which were the woes of women, and Nathan Blüm spoke through his daughter.

'So *this* is marriage? For *this* they wish me to give up my freedom?'

A Gift from a Stranger

chapter five

July, 1832

Despite a third cholera circular in December, the passing of a Cholera Bill in February which enforced regulations, and an official day of fasting and prayer in March, Wyndendale had almost forgotten the threat of an epidemic. By the summer a sense of anti-climax prevailed. Cholera existed, certainly. The monthly lists of confirmed cases proved that, but the numbers had grown perceptibly fewer of late. Was it not, after all, the real thing? Might it not be, as some newspapers suggested, a milder English version of the disease?

Whereas, eight months ago, the valley had admired Dr Standish's promptness in dealing with such a challenge, people now thought he had over-reacted. His unused cholera enclosure seemed to be a monument to apprehension. Birds nested, tramps slept, children played, in the damp deserted buildings. The rates had soared beyond even the council's expectations, and charity was dispensed sourly.

The three major newspapers, reflecting the interests of their readers, were much more concerned with the diseases of the body politic and the harsh medicine of Parliamentary Reform. So far the Reform Bill had fetched down two governments, been twice rejected by the House of Lords, and caused riots throughout the country. The great Duke of Wellington, formerly a national hero, had lost power and face by opposing it. Finally King William had been forced to create several new Whig peers to ensure that the Bill would be passed, and at last it became law on June 7th, 1832. The ironmaster, ably supported by his *Herald*, began to pave the road to the next election with gold, while Ambrose and *The Clarion* prepared to battle against them with the frail weapons of audacity and a sense of injustice.

A few people noticed that the June figures for cholera had substantially increased, but the authorities had cried wolf once too often for them to be perturbed.

At six o'clock one Saturday evening in mid-July, the Carlisle Flyer rumbled through the archway of the Royal George and into the yard, delivering its passengers for a half hour of food and rest. From the back of the coach, where he had clung unobserved for the latter part of the journey, jumped an Irish navvy by the name of Sweetheart Reilly. At once the guard gave a shout, and the driver raised his whip. But the navvy lifted a hobnailed boot significantly and gestured towards the shovel in his kit, smiling all the while. So they glared for a moment longer, to show him that they were not to be trifled with, then scrambled down peaceably from the box and made their way into the hostelry.

'Is there a sup of beer to be had in this place, me darling lads?' Reilly demanded of the ostlers, who were hurrying tired horses away and running out with a fresh team.

'Not for the likes of you!' said the head stable-man, who had been watching the incident. 'Get out afore I have you throwed out!'

The Irishman's broken nose and quick little eyes bespoke a fighter of courage and repute, but his bearded face was bland, and he spoke with the honeyed tongue which had earned him his nickname.

'Then, could you be telling a poor stranger that has been tramping the roads for a week or more where to sup?'

The stable-man spoke disdainfully.

'They're not over particular at the Red Lion. You'll find it in Shooter's Lane, at the back of market square.'

'God bless you!' said Reilly fervently. 'I suppose a grand gentleman like yourself wouldn't be having the price of a night's lodging on him, would he?'

54

'Be off with you!' Spoken with derision.

'Only as a loan,' said Reilly persuasively. 'I'd be paying you back and buying you a drink into the bargain in no time at all. I've a fine job waiting for me.'

The stable-man did not even reply.

'Then could you be telling me where they're building the grand tunnel?'

'Ah! You're one of them blackguards, are you?' said the man significantly. 'Yes, I can tell you. You've got a long walk ahead of you. It's nigh on ten miles down the valley, outside a town called Garth. So you'd best be legging it!'

Reilly touched his battered hat, which had once been white. Next to fighting folk, he liked irritating them.

'Could you be lending me a horse?' he asked, straightfaced.

The stable-man said, 'Are you going or do I call Bert?'

'I'll not be troubling you further, sor,' said Reilly, grinning.

He set off at a smart pace, but had only taken a dozen steps when he turned round and came back again, full of apologies.

'Perhaps you could be telling me where Mr Henry Vivian lives?'

'No, I couldn't.'

'Then God blast *you*!' cried Reilly, out of patience with him. Adding reverently, 'God pardon *me*!'

'Bert!' shouted the stable-man. 'There's a funny customer here as needs sorting out!'

The Irishman lingered to see the size of the Royal George's bouncer, all the while making a great show of filling his clay pipe and lighting it. He judged the man's strength, temper and experience at a glance. His expression changed from interest to appreciation, but the luxury of an encounter must be postponed. Meanwhile, Bert stood arms akimbo, waiting for orders.

'There'll be no need to disturb the gentleman,' said Reilly, grinning. 'I shouldn't like to spoil his looks. Any further, that is.' And as Bert clenched both mottled fists and began to advance on him, he cried, 'A very good evening to *you*, sor!' engagingly, 'and God bless all here!'

He swaggered off, whistling, but once out in the market square his whistle faded. A ten-mile tramp at night, with a dry throat, an empty belly and empty pockets, was no joke. Still, there were ways and means. You could stand over a small man at the bar and ask him to buy you a drink. You could steal a hot sausage and a chunk of bread from other people's plates, sup tankards which had just been put down, appropriate change which had not yet been picked up, or work your way round the room begging. When they all got tired of being bullied or coaxed, you could punch your way out, refreshed.

The good citizens of Millbridge were partaking of light suppers when they heard the stentorian voice of cheer coming down the High Street, in a medley of songs and curses. The navvy had celebrated his evening at other people's expense. His pockets jingled with small change. His kit lurched drunkenly on his back. Someone had punched his right eye and then punched his dirty white hat over it. His face was swollen and his velveteen coat and moleskin trousers spattered with blood and beer. Still he continued to call down the blessings of God upon all present. If ever a man was happy and gracious in his cups that man was Sweetheart Reilly.

He paused for a moment to relieve himself in the gutter and then looked round for further entertainment. The town seemed uncommonly dull. He peered into the darkness of a shop front, for they were all shops at this end of the street. Then he noticed a stately terrace of Queen Anne houses, across whose windows the curtains had not as yet been drawn, whose interiors spoke of leisure and grace. He started to run up the steps of each house and bang the brass door knockers, bawling greetings to the occupants and demanding entrance.

Wisely, folk ignored his noise and pleas. The navvy could cause chaos, and it would take more than one constable to restrain him, even if any could be found at nine o'clock at night.

So he gave up trying to provoke them, and began to make his way out of the town, hoping to beg a lift. Those he asked either rattled past as though they had not heard or fetched him a cut with the whip and told him to be off. Miles of unknown territory lay before him. At regular intervals the sky blushed rose from the cupola fires at the ironworks in Belbrook and Snape.

A whistle sounded somewhere to his left. On her final trip of the day, the valley's famous steam-engine, 'Pioneer', was setting out from Millbridge station. He could hear her chuntering behind him in the distance, gathering speed.

Reilly stumbled towards the track as fast as he could, waving his hat, shouting to the driver and stoker to stop and let him aboard. They neither saw nor heard him, and the train roared by at a good twenty miles an hour or more, throwing a shower of sparks into the air, the coals in her belly glowing red and gold.

He stood craning his neck, watching the little train diminish, listening to the mournful sound of her whistle. Then he sank down and laid his arms along the cold smooth metal of the rails, and bemoaned his friendless and penniless condition. All that he had lost, all that he had never possessed, haunted him. As the spurious warmth of alcohol faded, he began to weep. For men like him had dug that land and laid that track, with their strength and sweat and sometimes with their lives, and it was not for them, never for them.

Then as self-pity gave way to common sense, his boisterous spirits rose again. He remembered that his present situation was nothing out of the ordinary. He had always been short of money except for a few hours on payday. His friends were picked up literally by the wayside and left there when the job was done. His home was the road. So he wiped his face, rammed his greasy hat on his greasy head again and strode on, sobered.

In Lower Flawnes, the poorest part of Flawnes Green, a wretched creature of the night asked Reilly for custom, and he spent a few urgent minutes with her up against the wall of an alley. Then, hearing that she had a room nearby, he took advantage of her kind hospitality and enjoyed her favours at his greater convenience. Moreover, she gave him clear directions to Garth, which cost him all his small change and his blanket in payment. She was older and harder and shrewder than she had looked in the shadows but Sweetheart was always generous with the ladies.

On his way out of Lower Flawnes he was fortunate enough to hail a simple fellow in a cart, who lived at a farm not half a mile from Hal Vivian and was willing to give the navvy a ride. It was well past midnight by the time they turned off the main road and came to the village. The moon was shining like a silver penny, and through the trees at the other side of the river Reilly could see the ghostly chimneys of the Old Hall.

Unperturbed by its grandeur or the hour, Reilly hammered upon the imposing front door with knocker and fists, bawling, 'God save you, Mr Vivian, and God bless your lovely lady, and the pretty children that say their prayers at her knee!'

The manor house seemed to have been struck dark and dumb with his impudence, but in a few moments a casement window opened above the navvy's head, and the person they called the Cornishman leaned out.

'Who the devil are you?' he asked.

There was humour in his voice, and kindness. Sweetheart warmed to him at once and spoke in his most mellifluous tones.

'A poor navvy, your honour. Hoping to find work at your famous tunnel. That, owing to a generous nature and an open hand, finds himself temp-o-rarily short of silver and a night's lodging.'

'What idiot told you where I lived?'

The voice was still humorous, but Reilly sensed that his privacy was strictly guarded and he did not welcome intruders.

'Now, who should need to tell me, your honour?' he

answered. 'When all the world knows where such a famous gentleman lives!'

A vivacious little lady appeared beside the Cornishman, curious to see the navvy and to find out what the commotion was about.

Reilly had already doffed his crushed and filthy hat. Now he held it reverently to his breast and bowed low to Mary.

'God help me!' he heard the Cornishman say. 'Even at this hour in the morning! No, I don't know him from Adam! Hey, you there, have you worked for me before? Who's your contractor? What's your name?'

'I haven't had the honour of working for your honour before, and I don't belong to no contractor in particular. I tramp from place to place, sor. But I've worked on railways before. I was on that devil of a line across Chat Moss – the Manchester to Liverpool railway – and have a paper to prove it. And me name is Seamus Reilly, but on account of me kind heart and loving ways the lads call me *Sweetheart*!'

A shout of laughter from the Cornishman, and an answering giggle from the lady told Reilly that he would lie snug that night.

'Are you hungry?' cried the Cornishman heartily.

'Thirsty, your honour!' Grinning.

'Aye, they're always thirsty,' said the Cornishman to himself. 'Well, we're all abed, Reilly, but I'll come down and draw you a pint of ale. You can sleep in the stable tonight. They'll give you bread and cheese from the kitchen in the morning, and I'll find you half-a-crown to help you on your way.'

'God bless you, sor!' cried Reilly, from his heart.

He worshipped the man. At that moment he could have died for him. So he spent the few remaining hours of darkness snoring happily in the straw of the Old Hall's stables, and set off again in the cool of the summer morning, with a full stomach.

At Thornley Mill, being overcome by a call of nature, he

dropped his breeches and excreted in the bushes near the stream.

His half-crown was spent in a tavern at Whinfold, on the edge of Swarth Moor, where he found good company in the mine workers coming off their night shift. They toasted each other royally and quaffed each other's tankards, and Reilly managed to drink rather more than he had paid for before he staggered out of the door.

At Childwell he drew himself a bucket of water from the well and had a good spluttering wash before letting it rattle down again into its cool cavern.

Then he crossed the wooden bridge to view the railway line at Upperton Cutting, where so many poor navvies had been broken or buried when they blasted it out with gunpowder, four years back. 'Pioneer' thundered past him on its first journey of the day, as he stood on the side of the deep ravine. He waved his hat and shouted an obscene and friendly greeting, and the driver waved back. Three small girls, playing in the front garden of their house in Medlar, had thrown their ball over the hedge into the road. And Reilly, who was fond of children – though he had consistently deserted his own – tossed it back to them, enjoyed a few minutes of conversation, and gave them an orange apiece from his bundle before a servant chased him off.

He saw the chimneys of Kingswood Hall on the skyline, but decided against the long climb, and so tramped over the iron bridge to Coldcote, which he thought was a poor sort of place, neither town nor village. He did not bother to stop there.

Garth, on the other hand, was a typical product of the railway age: all sheds and works and smoke and noise and a hillside mounted with drab houses. He took the wrong turning by the church, climbed up and up into the thin, clear air of the fells, realised he was lost and opened the gate into a cobbled farmyard.

A lanky girl of twelve came to the back door and stared at him. Her vacant look and vacant smile told their own tale.

Ninepence in the shillin', poor soul! thought Reilly.

'Could you be telling me where the tunnel is, me darling?' he asked and looked hopefully beyond her into the hot kitchen, where he could see and hear and smell their Sunday dinner roasting on a spit over the fire.

The comely young woman who was basting this joint caught sight of his wild appearance and immediately shouted, 'Judith! Shut that door and come back in!'

The girl slammed the door in his face.

He waited. He knocked again.

In another minute or so it opened and he looked into the mouth of an old brass blunderbuss, held by a weather-beaten farmer. Close behind him came the lanky girl, holding on to the tail of his coat. In the background the bonny young woman was shouting for Fred.

Hypnotised by the blunderbuss, the navvy repeated his request humbly, holding his arms wide to show that he carried no weapons and came in peace.

Still suspicious, the man gave him instructions. Now he was joined by a younger fellow with a newer gun, who seemed to be his son-in-law. The simple girl laughed and clapped her hands.

Reilly asked, in his sweetest tones, if there was a drop to drink or a bite to eat in this good Christian household on God's Holy Day?

They would not let him in, but they gave him a mug of home-brewed ale and a bit of fat pork on his crust of bread. Both men stood guard over him as he ate, and the womenfolk watched him as though he were some strange beast which had escaped from a menagerie.

Reilly thanked them kindly but his feelings were hurt. He wanted to show them that he was a human being like themselves.

The lanky girl stared at him with vacant eyes, smiling her vacant smile. He set down his empty mug, wiped his mouth and ferreted round in his bundle.

61

'I thought so!' said Reilly, delighted. 'I thought I had one of them oranges left!'

And he gave Judith Howarth the last thing he possessed.

The navvies had built a shanty town round the crude hole which would one day be the Wyndendale Tunnel. They had been paid the night before, and were enjoying their brief holiday. Beer flowed. Beef roasted. Wives and mistresses were being used as women should be, children cuffed as they ought to be, and babies put in the brat cage and pulled up close to the ceiling to keep them out of the way.

'Now God bless all here!' cried Reilly from a full heart.

'Blast me eyes, if it ain't old Sweetheart come begging again!' roared one bull of a navvy named Teapot Flanagan.

'Ye're out o' luck, Sweetheart!' bawled Fisty Dooley, who was considered to be a great wit. 'There's jobs a-plenty here. No need to give ye the tramping bob this time. Ye can stand us all a drink on payday instead!'

Others recognised him and came forward to shake his hands and thump his back in a friendly fashion. Tons of earth, miles of iron rails, years of wandering from job to job in exile had bonded both strangers and friends into a brotherhood. Penniless and blanketless though he was, they brought him in and made him welcome because he was one of them.

All afternoon they sat drinking and talking. First, Sweetheart gave them news of the outside world. Then they outlined the task on which they were engaged.

They reckoned that the tunnel would take at least three years to build, and it posed particular problems. Working like moles in the dank earth, the men were wringing wet in half an hour and could not get dry again, which laid them open to all sorts of minor ailments. The fumes from the gunpowder got on their chests and made them cough, and there had been two or three roof falls in the tunnel, with some bad casualties. Still, taken all in all, it could be worse. The pay was good, the contractor was honest, and Mr Vivian was a gentleman. So drink up, lads, there's more in the barrel!

Towards evening, Reilly withdrew into himself. It was one of the best Sundays he had ever spent, but he had grown weary of it. His beer had lost its flavour, his tobacco its taste. His head felt woolly. He couldn't hear as well as usual. Flanagan had to ask him twice what in the name of Jesus was the matter with him. It was nothing, he said, he just felt out of sorts, tired-like after the journey. Someone gave him a blanket and he dossed down on the dirt floor.

In the middle of the night he had a fit of diarrhoea so quick and so violent that he soiled himself. He managed to get outside, where he vomited and lay on the ground for a while, shaken by the fierceness of the double attack. But before he could summon the energy to go back into the hut the sickness and griping returned, and though he emptied the contents of his stomach and bowels time and time again, it was never enough. He strained to bring forth, to fetch up, anything in response to a demand that would not be satisfied. The sound of his retching and purging became so inhuman that he woke the occupants of his hut, and Flanagan and Dooley came out to help him.

He cried that the pit of his belly was afire but the rest of him ice-cold. As he shivered and groaned for relief he was suddenly and cruelly contorted by muscular spasms, and fairly screamed with pain.

'Best fetch the surgeon,' said Teapot Flanagan, afraid.

'That bugger wouldn't come out at this time o' night. Not if we was *all* on our last legs!' said Fisty Dooley.

'But poor old Sweetheart's puking his guts up!'

'Well then, we'll fetch him inside and get the women to look after him, while we find a 'pothecary!'

They roared round Garth at two o'clock in the morning, rattling shop doors and throwing stones at shutters to rouse their occupants, but their reputation had gone ahead of them, and nobody stirred.

Reilly was worse when they got back. The women had

made him a rough bed on the dirt floor, and were keeping him as clean and warm as they could. His bowels and belly seemed to be settling down, though occasionally a watery motion would escape, but now he was tormented by convulsions during which he screeched and jerked without control. In moments of respite he fell back whimpering, staring pitifully at the circle of spectators with little sunken eyes. A used puppet.

Gradually the cramps eased, but then he began to shiver and to wail that he was freezing to death. They laid more blankets on him and heated two bricks and wrapped them in flannel, setting one by his feet and one upon his breast. The skin on his hands was wrinkled like that of an old washerwoman. His voice, when he could gather strength to speak, was hoarse and faint as though it came from a great distance. Then he fell into a still, white coma.

All night they watched by him, but as dawn broke they saw the sweat of death shine on his livid flesh, and knew he was leaving them as surely as if they stood on shore and watched the tide draw him out.

Demented, Teapot and Fisty descended again upon Garth, found an apothecary just taking down the shutters of his shop, and fetched him back unceremoniously by the scruff of the neck. The little life that was left in Reilly issued forth in one long mournful sigh as the man turned him over.

The inquest, though immediate and unofficial, was long-winded, owing to the amount of evidence everyone insisted on giving.

'It's difficult to tell what he died of,' said the apothecary cautiously. 'It sounds as if you'd all eaten and drunk enough to kill yourselves twice over! I'm surprised there aren't any more of you throwing up after a party like that!'

Incensed, they described Reilly's sufferings in vivid detail.

'Sounds like food-poisoning,' said the apothecary.

'Then why wasn't the rest of us taken like it?' demanded Fisty.

'Well, you say he only got here yesterday. He could have

eaten something on the way here that you knew nothing about.'

'What about them cramps?' asked Teapot, in awed recollection. 'I never seen nothing like them cramps before!'

'Well, you don't die easy with food poisoning. He'd be bound to hop about a bit.'

Then a fearful thing happened. As if to illustrate the truth of their descriptions, Reilly stuck first one and then the other leg in the air. His limbs vibrated, his toes twiddled – as Fisty said – like he was playing a heavenly harp. And all the while his sunken eyes stayed tight shut and he grinned into his beard as if he was having the very devil of a joke on them.

'Holy Mary, Mother of God!' cried Flanagan, kneeling and crossing himself. 'Don't play them sort o' games wid us, Sweetheart!'

'Jesus, Mary and Joseph save us!' echoed Fisty.

Some navvies fell to their knees alongside him, praying for succour. The rest stampeded from the hut, yelling blasphemies. For the dying man had been horrific to watch, but the dead one chilled them to the marrow of their bones.

The apothecary had never seen this grisly comedy before, but he was not superstitious and he assumed he had made a mistake. He persuaded Flanagan and Dooley to hold their comrade down while he examined him afresh, but found neither pulse nor breath.

'Nerves!' said the apothecary, very practical. 'You've seen a chicken run with its head off, haven't you? Well, that's nerves, too!'

He knew better than to ask for a fee and departed unobtrusively while the behaviour of the corpse was being discussed.

Reilly would not lie still. For upwards of an hour, the body went through a hideous mime of its former agonies, and at one time even snapped open its eyes. So that the navvies, who had presumed they were afraid of nothing and nobody, were quite unable to stomach Sweetheart's antics; and though at last he lay cold and tranquil, no one would enter the hut until the undertaker came to carry him away.

A Lady Financier

chapter six

The sun poured down on Wyndendale and everyone rejoiced.
Mary Vivian was at that happy stage of pregnancy where early
ills are over and the child is not yet a burden. She blossomed
in loose flowered gowns, her quick step slowed to a saunter, her
quick temper softened. Mud in and around the tunnel had
dried as the good weather continued, making working conditions easier. The navvies only swore out of habit, and Hal
Vivian came home early for dinner.

William Howarth, M.P., divided his attention between Parliament, the constituency, the ironworks and *The Herald*. With
his self-earned fortune, his image as a man of the people, and his
hard common sense, he appealed to a wide range of voters.
Parliament being in recess, he was presiding over Kingswood
Hall, relishing a domestic triumph. His youngest daughter Ruth
had made an excellent match and was to be married in August.
William planned to give her the finest wedding of them all.

Even the family black sheep, Ambrose Longe, whistled
that hot summer afternoon as he wrote a leader guaranteed to
make the ironmaster sit up and take notice, if not to beg outright
for mercy. His other uncle, Dick Howarth the farmer, had
dropped in to pass the time of day on his way home from the
Monday market and told Ambrose in all innocence that there
was an outbreak of summer diarrhoea among the navvies in
Garth. One of them had actually died of it the previous week,
and the apothecary had said he was not surprised. He said Garth
had grown too big for its boots, and the Wyndendale Railway
Board should have provided a better water supply and a new
draining system when they took the village over eight years since.

As soon as Dick had gone, Ambrose sent his apprentice and journeyman home for their teas, with instructions to return in an hour, by which time he should have written a new editorial. They would then typeset it, substitute it for the old one, re-arrange the inside pages, and be ready for the old Koenig printing-press to roll out that week's edition of *The Clarion*. Now he sat on the high stool at the high desk and tried out a possible headline for his latest broadside. His concentration was so deep, her step so light, that he did not become aware of his visitor until the air in the musty shop smelled of essence of violets, and a feminine shadow curved across the threshold. Ambrose read both signs as an infuriating distraction.

Without turning round, he said curtly, 'Go away, Mary. I'm busy.'

The answering chuckle was deep and soft, the voice a gentle contralto. The shadow straightened and became too tall for Mary.

'It is not your cousin, Mr Longe, but her friend.'

'I beg your pardon, Miss Bloom!' he cried, and slid down from the stool in some confusion.

'It is I who should beg yours, Mr Longe,' said Naomi sincerely, 'for I see I have interrupted a flow of thought. I should have knocked and waited – but the front door was wide open, as though you expected your callers to walk in.'

'Yes. Well. Not exactly. It is a necessary form of ventilation in this place, at this time of year.'

'But you should have a notice on the door, asking people not to come in unless it is absolutely necessary.'

'That wouldn't stop Mary, I can tell you!'

'Ah, you always joke!'

'And how may I be of service to you?' Ambrose asked, as politely as he could, wondering how soon he could return to work.

'Perhaps we may be of service to each other, Mr Longe. I have come upon a matter of business.'

He hesitated. He sighed. Business, with Millbridge ladies, was either an account of their latest social event or the offer of a poem for publication under a pseudonym such as *Ariadne*. He glanced wistfully at his unwritten leader and reluctantly at the ladder-back chair in which visitors sat and wasted his time. Naomi bowed her head.

'I understand. You would rather I went away?'

'No, no!' he cried, and cursed the conventions that forbade him to answer in the affirmative. 'I must ask you to excuse my apparent abstraction. It is just that we go to press this evening, and I have some work to do at the last minute which I did not expect. Pray do sit down, Miss Bloom.'

He spoke courteously, but with an undertone of firmness which she could not mistake. She smiled with the utmost good humour, and remained standing.

'I can state my business in a few moments, Mr Longe. I merely wished to invite you . . .'

There it is! he thought. Another damned soirée.

'. . . to call upon me at your convenience, to discuss the possibility of my investing money in *The Clarion*.'

'Well, I'm damned!' said Ambrose.

He sat down in the chair himself, quite winded.

Naomi smiled serenely upon him. There was a gleam of amusement, of satisfaction, in her lustrous eyes.

'You are surprised?' she asked, raising her eyebrows. 'You do not think your newspaper warrants such an interest?'

He put his head in his hands and his elbows on his knees, trying to collect himself.

'You will excuse me, Miss Bloom. I hadn't thought about it at all. And it . . . really . . . is . . . a bit of a. . . . swinger!'

His memory warned him. He wiped both hands over his face to erase the dream. He looked up sharply. He asked his question deliberately.

'On what terms, Miss Bloom?'

She replied easily, still amused, 'That would surely be the subject of our discussion?'

'Yes,' said Ambrose. 'Yes, of course.'

'When shall we arrange? I regret to say, but I am ignorant of newspaper work. As you print today shall you be free tomorrow?'

'That would be perfectly . . .'

But he owed three months' rent, and there was not so much as the price of a pie in the house, and he could no more write the leader now than fly.

He jumped up, crying, 'Miss Bloom, why don't you sit down here and tell me what you had in mind?'

Her gleam of amusement faded. Her gaze seemed to penetrate the empty larder, the empty cash box, and his empty hopes. She rustled forward to the proffered chair, and settled herself in it as gravely as though it were Chippendale, resting both gloved hands on the head of her parasol.

'Excuse me a moment!' said Ambrose hastily.

On a sheet of paper he scrawled 'BACK IN AN HOUR', and pinned it on the front door, which he then shut in spite of the heat.

'You see, Mr Longe,' said Naomi, very friendly, very noticing, 'what a good idea that is?'

He perched on the office stool opposite to her. The first moments of euphoria were fading. From his experience of life he knew there had to be a snag somewhere, and the greater the offering the larger the snag. It occurred to him that she might be looking for a husband. Not that he was much of a catch, but women of her age could be desperate. Not that she looked desperate, either. She looked uncommonly cool.

'Before we begin, Mr Longe,' said Naomi, as though he had asked the question outright, 'I should like to make my motive clear. I give you a brief account of my circumstances.

'I was an only child, and my mother died when I was very young, leaving me in my father's care. He was a successful businessman, who gave me the sort of education he would give a son. He did not care for domesticity and never re-married. For the last eight years of his life I was both companion and confidante and acted as his private secretary. There was good and bad in this for me. I saw and knew a great deal more of the world than do most women. But it also meant that I had no permanent home and no friends of my own age.

'When my father died his business friends were very kind with help and advice. Among them was your uncle, Mr William Howarth the ironmaster, who introduced me to our dear Mary. I am happy to live at Thornton House, and to make many pleasant acquaintances, but always the other field is more green, Mr Longe! I speak frankly. My heart is grateful for what I have, but I miss,' and she fluttered her fingers to express the word, 'the *frisson* of the business world.

'It is of no use to grumble. Therefore, I thought, why not do business on my own account? Why not invest in a good and interesting proposition? Something on my doorstep that I can watch! Our dear Mary so often says that she would help you if she could. Well, she cannot, but – if I feel the risk is worth taking – perhaps I can.'

Ambrose sat quite nonplussed.

'You think I exaggerate my business knowledge?' Naomi asked. 'I shall show you letters and papers which will act as my credentials. My father was a good financier. I learned from him.'

Ambrose recovered his sense of humour.

'I wish I could say the same, Miss Bloom. *My* father had simply no idea of finance at all, and neither have I!'

'Ah! You joke of serious matters?'

'No joke,' said Ambrose seriously. 'I'm down on my luck, Miss Bloom. If you saw the books – if there were any books . . .'

'You keep no accounts?' she asked, horrified.

He shook his head. Her horror soothed rather than annoyed him. He began to see that she was very serious indeed, and about business.

'So how shall you convince me that my money will be well spent?'

She was handsome, but then so were many women. She

talked to him as one person to another, without lure or guile, and that could be said of very few women. He liked her, and liked her idea even better. He wished he knew the right words or actions, but could not find them.

'I don't know,' said Ambrose, smiling helplessly.

She lifted her eyes to heaven, that it might witness this lack of business acumen.

'So what can you offer as collateral, Mr Longe?'

He gestured round the hot, cramped shop, then touched his breast with one thin, brown hand.

'I work hard,' he said. 'The newspaper is my life.'

Naomi pondered his reply. Her expression was unreadable.

'Your shop is too small,' she observed.

'I have frequently regretted its lack of space, myself. Forgive me, Miss Bloom, but might *I* ask *you* a question?'

She inclined her head graciously.

'I presume, excuse my own frankness, that you have a thousand or two lying around doing nothing very much?'

'You can presume I have sufficient capital, but I assure you that it is not lying around. It works hard for its living, Mr Longe!'

'Lord above!' said Ambrose, half to himself. 'A lady financier!'

Naomi smiled. The title pleased her.

'To return to our onions,' Ambrose continued, beginning to enjoy himself. 'Do I understand you to mean that you have looked into the business side of newspapers in general, and believe you can make money out of *The Clarion* in particular?'

She inclined her head again, but put up one finger to stay him.

'Your newspaper would be a viable proposition only if it was conducted on a much larger and a more business-like scale, Mr Longe.'

'That's what my uncle, the ironmaster, thought.'

'He was right. Your uncle, the ironmaster.'

'He didn't – you haven't . . .?'

'I am on social terms with Mr Howarth, only. Your name has never been mentioned. I have told you that I wish to conduct my own business, Mr Longe.'

'Quite so,' said Ambrose quickly.

She was formidable, this lady, with her strong features and her sombre eyes. He found himself trying to take care of her interests, though heaven knew he could not even take care of his own.

'Miss Bloom, it would require a considerable outlay on your part with no guarantee that you would ever get the capital back, let alone make a profit!'

'Mr Longe,' she replied, a little impatiently, 'that is *my* problem. Yours is to convince me that I am making a sound investment.'

He sat for fully a minute, thinking. Then he shrugged, got down from the stool, stuck both hands in his pockets and walked as far round the room as the Koenig press would let him.

'I fear I cannot do any such thing, Miss Bloom,' said Ambrose finally. 'I have no idea how to market myself. I never had. All I can tell you is that if I was given the same opportunities as Sam Pickering I'd do at least as well as he does! How *is* he doing, by the by?'

'Very well. I looked into the finances of *The Herald* also.'

'I thought perhaps you might have done,' said Ambrose, grinning. 'Did you think *The Clarion* could compete with *The Herald* in the open field? For that's what it would amount to!'

She nodded.

'Bless my soul,' said Ambrose, and leaned on the old Koenig. He felt extraordinarily moved. 'A knightly combat!' he remarked quietly.

'That is what you and *The Clarion* need, Mr Longe. A fair contest and a worthy opponent. With *The Post* you may amuse yourself. With *The Herald* you will not play games!'

He looked at her absently.

He said, 'If I had a newspaper with the weight and authority of *The Herald*, Sam Pickering and I would finish *The Post* off!'

Naomi shrugged. It was a wonderful shrug. If Arnold Thwaites had seen it he would have shut up shop the same day. Yet another idea was now disturbing Ambrose.

'You haven't any secret ambitions to be a lady journalist or anything of that sort, have you?' he asked in trepidation. 'You're not thinking of taking the paper over and changing its policy? Or advising me, pressurising me, altering and confounding me generally? Or of employing relatives and friends who are unable to find work elsewhere? No? Because if I can't run my own newspaper the whole idea is strictly out of the question.'

She shook her head emphatically.

'Mr Longe, I have no wish to curtail your freedom or the freedom of *The Clarion* in any way. It remains your newspaper. But I shall offer practical help in order to increase its circulation and to broaden its scope. I have access to foreign and financial news sources. I believe I could bring in more advertising. I can help you in many ways. My business connections are quite as good as those of your uncle, the ironmaster. You do not object, I take it, to that sort of assistance?'

'I see no reason why I should,' he answered cautiously.

'But there *is* some work I should like to do for *The Clarion*.'

'And what is that, Miss Bloom?' he asked, once more afraid that this magic carpet was about to be whisked from under his feet.

She said, almost shyly, 'I should like to keep the books.'

He burst out laughing with relief and delight.

'I am quite serious, Mr Longe,' said Naomi sternly. 'Providing you have no objection, of course. If you have, then we must employ a book-keeper.'

'Not the least objection in life, I do assure you. The books couldn't be in better hands.'

'And of course we must put this matter on a proper business footing and discuss all the details, so that we both know exactly where we stand,' She produced a small notebook and pencil from her reticule. 'What is the name of your solicitor, please?'

Ambrose was floored at once.

'I suppose . . . no, old Nick Hurst is dead now, poor devil. He used to deal with my mother's affairs. Well, someone else in the firm would do, wouldn't they? Ah, but his partners took over when he died! What would the name of the firm be now? At any rate, I know they're still down at the bottom of the High Street.'

She gave him another minute to reflect, and sighed impatiently, saying, 'Never mind, Mr Longe. I shall find you a good solicitor.' Then she cried, 'This is ridiculous! I buy, I sell. I ask questions, I answer them. I demand evidence, I provide it. What kind of business is this, I ask you?'

'Oh, I leave that to you to decide,' said Ambrose grinning.

She glanced quickly at him, and smiled too.

'I think you are not aware that you give me a great deal of power by allowing me to handle the financial side,' she remarked. 'Do you know that? To keep a company's books is to know the company – and sometimes to know it better than it knows itself.'

'Not this company,' said Ambrose, grinning. 'You'll learn a great deal more about a newspaper by coming in on press day. And if you don't leave now, Miss Bloom, *The Clarion* will be a day late!'

She gave a triumphant little laugh, and closed the notebook.

'Sometime you must invite me to press day. Meanwhile, Mr Longe, perhaps you will call on me soon? Shall we say Friday evening at six o'clock? My solicitor will be there in an informal way, to make everything plain to you. Then, when you are quite satisfied, we can enter a legal business partnership.'

'Oh, anything you do will be all right by me,' said Ambrose.

She said, warning him against himself, 'That is not a business-like remark, Mr Longe. It is well that I am honest.'

He bowed and kissed her hand. He hardly noticed that she had left. The scent of violets remained.

He felt incredibly free. The shop seemed larger and lighter and cooler than before. Anything was now possible. He was young again, and the world gaped like an oyster. As he bent forward to swallow it whole he saw a great pearl lying at its heart, and the name of the pearl swam into his mind, so that he ran out of the shop like a boy, banging the door behind him, and calling after her.

'Miss Bloom! Miss Bloom!'

She was sauntering gracefully down the length of the hot, bright market square. Now and then the brim of her Leghorn straw bonnet inclined to a passing acquaintance.

'Miss Blo-o-o-m!'

She turned, astonished. The fringe of her parasol was all a-tremble. She began to walk gracefully back, puzzled, but he could not wait for her to reach him. He started to run towards her, oblivious of public stares and comments.

Ah, how he wished that his mother was alive to share the moment. How many years ago had he promised that one day he would revive the name of her own news-sheet? Thirty? He was only a boy then, but he remembered his vow and Charlotte's answering look most vividly.

Naomi was near enough for him to see the amusement on her face, but he did not care. He halted before her, breathless and exalted.

'Miss Bloom . . . forgive me . . . but why not have . . . a new name . . . for the new paper?'

'Mr Longe. It is *your* paper!' Guessing that he had thought of something momentous. 'What name would you suggest?'

'Mr Longe! Mr Longe!' bawled the journeyman from the doorstep of *The Clarion*. 'T'door-latch is snecked. Have you got t'key?'

'Oh, Lord!' cried Ambrose and turned to run back.

Naomi caught him delicately and tightly by one sleeve. She was smiling openly.

'The name, Mr Longe. The wonderful name, if you please.'

'I'll be with you in a minute, Mick!' Ambrose shouted back. Then, 'Oh, Miss Bloom, better than *The Clarion*, better than *The Lancashire Herald*, best of all. All that I've ever wanted!'

'Oh, la!' she cried, laughing at him outright.

He watched her expression to see how she registered the title.

'*The Northern Correspondent*?'

'*The Northern Correspondent*!' she repeated, trying the syllables on her tongue. 'I like that. I like that very much. Yes, yes. That is a good name. A name of great importance.'

Then he laughed too, out of sheer joy, and saluted her triumphantly, and began to run back to the shop – slapping his pockets, trying to find the key he had left hung up inside the office.

Grim Harvest

chapter seven

On Tuesday morning, *The Clarion* duly reported an outbreak of severe summer diarrhoea among the navvies in Garth and lambasted the Wyndendale Railway Company for failing to provide proper living and working conditions.

This was not the first time that Ambrose Longe had taken gossip for truth and made a political issue out of it, and Sam Pickering never let him get away with anything. So *The Herald* sent their reporter down to Garth to check the story. The man came back with a rumour which Sam dared not print until it became official fact, but he set up a hasty 'Postscript' as the paper went to press on Tuesday night, to the effect that Mr Bailey, chief surgeon of Millbridge Hospital and an authority on Asiatic diseases, had been called to Garth for consultation. That same evening the Board of Health was summoned to hear a full report from Mr Bailey. At first light on Wednesday morning the cholera unit was opened, to be cleaned and made ready for the first victims.

Life relishes little ironies. It was given to Arnold Thwaites, rightly described as the best chair-polisher in local journalism, to scoop this historic news. On Thursday morning *The Post* headline screamed – CHOLERA STRIKES WYNDENDALE.

By Friday reports of other cases were coming in from all over the valley. On Saturday the weekend edition of *The Herald*, and a special edition of *The Clarion*, pushed national and international news to the back page and gave inside coverage to a full report of the epidemic, reprinting the substance of the cholera circulars so that people should know what to do if they fell sick.

The ironmaster marshalled his voluntary police force with the minimum of fuss to mount guard over the enclosure. At Kingswood Hall, Ruth's grand wedding was postponed, and her five married sisters and their families warned to stay away. Zelah, the ironmaster's Quaker wife, and Anna his Quaker daughter, expert in nursing the sick, prepared and set aside two rooms in the great house as convalescent wards. For, as Zelah Howarth pointed out, the official unit might well be glad of outside help as the contagion spread.

Harold Bailey had snatched a few hours' sleep at the cholera hospital, and now stood opposite his director in the small bare room which served him as an office and general living quarters. They were careful to keep a certain distance from each other and had not shaken hands. Dr Standish did not touch any article of furniture or take refreshment of any sort during this short visit. His identity had been carefully established by guards at the gate before he was allowed to enter, and he held a handkerchief to his nose and mouth as he crossed the drab compound. This he stuffed into his pocket, and on reaching the office, he set down that morning's *Herald* without comment. He had marked the paragraph which gave the national cholera figures for July, and the little surgeon whistled as he read them.

'Will it get worse than this, do you think, Mr Bailey?'

'I should think it more than likely, sir.'

Harold Bailey was concerned with a matter which seemed of greater moment. An old campaigner, he had drawn a rough diagram of the valley and circled the outbreaks with a red crayon. He was studying the tactics of the enemy.

'Take a look at this map, Dr Standish,' he said, with a little grin of triumph. 'I think you will be interested!'

He spoke rapidly, with enthusiasm, despite the fact that his eyelids were reddened and he had obviously slept in his clothes.

'I have always thought I might catch sight of King Cholera's footprints if I got up early enough,' he said cheerfully, 'but

India is such a vast continent that you cannot hope to track him there. No, it is this small valley of ours that has made the glimpse possible. Mark you, this survey only represents our first batch of patients. Already out of date by several hundred, I fear, but still relevant.

'Starting with Millbridge, we had cases scattered casually across this poor district near Market Place. No apparent pattern to them at all – except that they were working men. But the landlord of a local tavern, the Red Lion in Shooter's Lane, was one of the first to die. I think that some or all of them could have been his customers!

'Now look at the poor quarter of Flawnes Green. Sporadic cases again. And again, mostly working men. But we have another clue here. A prostitute from Lower Flawnes was found dead of cholera in her cellar. It seems reasonable to assume that she was early infected. Could not these other cases have been infected clients?

'Further down the valley we have mill-workers from Thornley, coal-miners from Swarth Moor, and a handful of cases from Childwell. Again, poor people from poor districts. I hear well-fed councillors crying, "A poor man's disease!" Not a bit of it! King Cholera don't mind expensive provender!

'He crosses the river into Medlar and tries more respectable folk. Three little girls from the same family. And – mark how and where he moves! – he is travelling either along or within sight of the railway line. The only stop he seems to miss is Coldcote. At Garth he comes to an end – and to the beginning of our epidemic.

'Now far be it from me to judge my fellow men, but navvies are crude and filthy folk. Their habits and conditions encourage our royal foe. Once among *them* he can expect choice pickings, so an outbreak at the tunnel is understandable. But why not begin in the town of Garth where he can butter his bread even thicker? Why wander up into the hills, and put a cold finger on a child at an outlying farm?

'I believe I can show you the answer!

'In the early hours of Monday the seventeenth of July, at Garth, a navvy called Reilly was taken ill. Not unexpectedly, if you consider the circumstances. The navvies had been paid on Saturday night and spent the whole of Sunday – and most of nine weeks' wages – drinking. Upset stomachs and bowels would be common enough after such an orgy. So Reilly's friends nursed him until he was obviously at his last gasp and then fetched in a local apothecary, who diagnosed food-poisoning. The fellow was buried, and no one thought any more about it.

'When I went down there eight days later, at their surgeon's request, two of the cases were convulsed. As you know, Dr Standish, cholera convulsions are an awesome spectacle. Once observed there is no mistaking them. I was about to inform the surgeon of my conclusions when one hulking fellow, lounging in the doorway, remarked that his mates were "going the same way as Reilly". Intrigued by this comment, I asked a number of pertinent questions.

'Apparently, Reilly had arrived there only the day before his death, making his way by foot and coach from Glasgow – where the epidemic is exceedingly bad. Everything they could tell me pointed to his symptoms being those of virulent cholera.

'I have set down my evidence for you to see. *Now* look at the map, Dr Standish! Reilly reaches Millbridge and drinks at the Red Lion. He has to get to the far end of the valley which is unknown to him. What would be the most sensible thing to do in such a situation? To follow the railway line to Garth! All these victims are contacts on the way. He takes a prostitute. He drinks with working men. He begs from those who are better off.

'It is as though King Cholera himself jumped down from that coach in Millbridge and strode Wyndendale from end to end.'

The two men were silent for a few moments. Then the dry little surgeon spoke again, meditatively.

'Every day this picture changes. The original trail is almost

80

obliterated, but I have been keeping a short account of each case. One line, no more. Name, address, age and sex of patient. Admission date. Length and severity of illness. Outcome.

'Dr Standish, I have a favour to ask of you. If I had a number of lined sheets with these headings printed upon them, they could be used by any reasonably intelligent member of my staff. For I shall not always be able to keep the entire inventory and might indeed become a line of information myself!'

He spoke with deliberate lightness, but Jamie answered earnestly.

'Nay, God forbid, Mr Bailey! We have more need of you than of anyone. Aye, you shall have your printed headings within the day, if you will give me details. *The Clarion* would be glad of a little custom. How many shall you need?'

'With thirty lines or so to the page? Let us say a hundred. And if we order a gross then that covers all eventualities.'

'You envisage three thousand cases or more?' cried Jamie aghast.

'It is a rough estimate, based on the national averages so far. It could be better or worse than that, but many of these will recover, particularly towards the end. His grip slackens at the last – though in the beginning he is murderous and greedy and does not like to let go. Then afterwards, if I am spared, I can add the notes I made in India to the information I have gathered here, and together we shall see what we can make of the disease.'

'We should perhaps allow a few young physicians and surgeons to share this knowledge, Mr Bailey? In the event of *both* our deaths.'

'May God preserve us *both*, sir! Yes, I agree.'

Jamie was too young and untried to be termed a great man, and yet there was greatness in him, and great humility also. For he could have allowed either fear or pride to rule him, but was striving instead to fetch order out of chaos, and to listen to and learn from a man inferior in medical and social status.

'Well, Mr Bailey, we are in the same case as those unfortunate navvies at the moment. We stand, as it were, at the entrance of a long tunnel which as yet has no light at the end of it. But with God's help we shall come through. And when that blessèd day dawns, I trust we shall be allowed to keep this present hospital as a fever hospital. Cholera is not our only, not yet our worst, enemy!'

Jamie hooked his hands behind his back and strode over to the window. Even the August sun could not brighten that grey compound, in the centre of which an iron basket of fire was burning. One of the expurgators, a creature either too simple to know what dangers he ran, or too poor to care about them, was wheeling a barrow from the grey main building, piled high with ragged clothes.

'Typhus, scarlet fever, measles and smallpox rage amongst us,' said Jamie to himself. 'We make no preparation for them. We scramble our resources together to meet the need of the moment, and afterwards we make haste to forget. There should be special provision against such disasters. It is not enough to treat them. We should learn from them, study them in order to fight them better. No man would try to live for the rest of his days upon a handful of guineas earned in his youth, but most doctors expect the knowledge gained as a student to last them a lifetime!'

The expurgator lifted a pitchfork and began to feed a heap of clothes to the flames. Black smoke coiled slowly on the heavy air.

'We need a fever hospital, Mr Bailey, which is also a teaching hospital, offering facilities for research . . .'

The little surgeon said, 'I could not agree more, Dr Standish. But you know that such a decision does not rest with me.'

'Nor with me, unfortunately. Though I shall do my utmost to bring it about.'

The guards opened the high wooden gates to allow the cholera van through. The horses galloped in, ears pricked, eyes starting, coats lathered with haste. The van rattled and swayed. As the gates closed behind it, a hail of stones spattered against them. The driver reined in the horses and sat stolidly in his seat, seeming to study the tip of his whip. Two more expurgators hurried out, cloths tied over their faces, rough gloves protecting their hands and arms. They began to unload patients from the vans with more speed than ceremony, stacking them on the ground in rows until the stretcher-bearers should arrive. Some were too far gone to notice, but others wailed and screamed for succour and were answered from beyond the walls with angry cries.

'You appear to have more work ahead of you, Mr Bailey,' said Jamie grimly, 'and I must get back to my own!'

In the far corner of the enclosure two grave-diggers stood back from the finished trench, and while the living waited, the sheeted dead were carried past them and laid in the earth side by side.

The man was trundling his barrow away to collect more rags. He glanced neither to his left nor right. For sixpence a day and a full belly, his eyes, his ears and his compassion had been stopped.

A dark spell lay over Wyndendale. Dr Standish's official report to the Home Office confirmed that the valley was in the grip of cholera, and consequently in quarantine. Coaches stopped there only long enough to deliver and collect mail, and to change horses. Most of their passengers chose to stay mewed up inside, and those who joined the coach at Millbridge sat like lepers outside. All communications were clearly marked as coming from a stricken place, so that their recipients could take what precautions they fancied.

The whole country was in trouble, that nightmare summer, as the monthly tolls doubled and trebled, and the holding of local fairs and wakes was forbidden. Now, in addition to the cholera figures, the newspapers were printing more and more obituary notices. It was expected that the poor should suffer, but it seemed strange and horribly improper to find the great and important suffering also.

Cholera mounted marble steps as easily as wooden stairs. Its calling card lay on silver salvers as well as on earthenware plates. Its evil spirit could sparkle in champagne or wink from the bottom of a beer tankard. In the open market stalls it blessed all produce, lingering a little longer in some than in others. It laid wait in baskets of soiled laundry, in blankets, in stable straw. It rose again from the clothes of the dead. It seeped from water closets.

Down in Garth all work on the tunnel had ceased. The remaining navvies struck camp and tramped out of Wyndendale to escape further affliction, and carried the affliction with them.

Like another king, cholera best loved the poor and was always with them. They drank to keep the thought of it away. But it sat by their sides in the cellars and tenements, kept them company at work, watched their revels, brooded over them as they slept. Nowhere was too deep, too filthy, too dangerous to daunt it: following miners down the ladder roads of Swarth Moor, unravelling the spinster's thread, helping the shuttle to wear a weaver's life away. It reeked in middens and sties. Flies were its messengers. Water its chief carrier. The pedlar displayed it, tradesmen bought and sold it, cattlemen drove it, vagrants wandered with it. Cholera was the streetsinger's song, the prostitute's love, the prisoner's freedom, and undisputed it reigned.

Zelah Howarth had been right. As the August slaughter mounted, the isolation unit could not deal with every stage of the sickness at once. All schools in the valley had been closed. Now they were opened and used as receiving stations. The official ambulances were supplemented by a fleet of carts, upon which the name of CHOLERA VAN was roughly printed. Houses such as Kingswood Hall, whose women were willing to ease the nursing load, were placed beneath the same restrictions as the official unit. Social life almost ceased. Even in church each worshipper was wary of his neighbour.

Only devotion prevailed against the terror. Love might and must yield in flesh, but never in spirit. The mother rocked her tortured child and was afraid of nothing but to be separated from it. Husband nursed wife in secret and in secret gave a kiss to the lips that would infect him. Whole families locked and bolted themselves inside their homes and defended the privilege of dying together. Fearless among the sick moved such Christians as Zelah and Anna Howarth, out of humanity. And those who could not help themselves, and were carried forcibly away to hospital, had the bitter satisfaction of seeing their abductors showered with abuse and stones.

At first Jamie Standish had hoped to run his little army of helpers from a distance, so that he could fulfil his obligations as a private physician and as director of Millbridge Hospital. But when the pestilence moved into the genteel precincts of the Old Town and passed through the marble portals of Kersall Park, Jamie rolled up his shirtsleeves and fought the enemy at close quarters. He could make no distinction between one patient and another and avoided the eyes of old friends, noble clients and important acquaintances, as he issued the instructions which would turn them into social outcasts. Money could buy certain comforts and privileges, but it could not protect its owners against the ignominy of the disease.

Every newspaper in the valley placed its facilities at the young doctor's disposal. All rivalry was laid aside in favour of the common cause. News was shared and exchanged freely. Local cholera figures were published weekly and posted on noticeboards in each district. Mr Bailey's file grew thick.

'What a capricious rogue he is!' the surgeon said to himself, standing back from the cadaver on the mortuary table. 'Why take some members of a family and leave others? Why should one expurgator last a month and another die in the first week? Why do I still go unharmed, though I face him a hundred times a day?'

The hubbub attending the arrival of the cholera van was noisier and more forceful than usual. He laid down his scalpel and looked through the window. The guards were struggling to let the van in and keep the people out. For a few moments the result could have gone either way. Then, like a cork from a bottle, both van and mob burst into the compound. The guards fired their rifles into the air, and shouted for assistance. The invaders scattered in all directions, without particular purpose, yelling and brandishing homely weapons. A shabby fellow, who appeared to be a ringleader, knocked the driver from his seat. Some snatched spades from the grave-diggers and began to unbury the dead. Others dragged the sick from the van and staggered towards the open gates with their stricken burdens.

A face flattening itself suddenly against Mr Bailey's window, became an open mouth of horror, crying, 'He's burking a body, lads! Come over here!'

The little surgeon was out of the door in an instant, striding towards the shabby ringleader. Two guards ran to his side, fixing their bayonets, and threatened those who came near.

'You!' roared Harold Bailey, pointing to the man. 'As you value your life, and the lives of all poor souls here, tell me what in the name of God you think you are doing.'

The fellow walked slowly but defiantly towards him.

'We know what you're up to,' he shouted, so that his cohorts could hear him. 'You won't find no rich folk in this place. They're all poor folks as canna speak up for theirselves. There's nowt wrong wi' them as a dose o' rhubarb won't cure, but you're murdering them and selling their bodies to be burked. It's a right Bastille, this place, and we've come to set 'em free. You won't stop us, because there's more of us than there is of you!'

'Tell your friends,' replied the surgeon, very clearly, 'that if they stay here peaceably, and in good order, I'll take you to inspect the hospital for yourself. You can go anywhere, and see anything you want to. You can ask any questions and I will answer them honestly. Does that seem fair to you?'

The fellow hesitated, then nodded. The mob stood,

hushed and waiting. The soldiers were watchful, holding their rifles ready. Harold Bailey escorted the ringleader across the compound at a brisk pace, and opened the door of the main ward.

'What's your name?' he asked curtly.

'Jeremiah Vetch.'

'Then welcome to the nethermost depths of hell, Jeremiah Vetch!'

A vile stench assailed their nostrils. The surgeon paid no attention to it, but Vetch's eyes watered and his stomach heaved.

'Walk in, man. Walk in.'

Vetch swayed on the threshold, assaulted by the sights and sounds of terminal cholera. He was staring down a long room full of the living dead, most of whom were of necessity left to their own devices. Mops and pails appeared to be most in use. Half a dozen poor women were cleaning up the worst messes. Two medical assistants were working their way steadily down each side of the ward, gauging the condition of over a hundred patients. The number of beds was not sufficient, and victims were crowded head to foot, and tossing on straw mattresses laid on the floor. The only peaceful occupants of this hospital bedlam were the cases in coma, lying white and shrunk and still under their soiled blankets.

Jeremiah Vetch's expression changed from disbelief to terror.

'Is there anyone here whom you think should be released?' asked the surgeon sternly. 'You may take them with you, if you wish.'

Vetch shook his head and tried to push past Harold Bailey to reach the open air, but the wiry surgeon held him fast and shook him.

'Would *you* like to cure any of them with a dose of rhubarb?'

Vetch thrust him away, and vomited on the ground.

'Oh, you will do better than that later on,' said Mr Bailey

grimly. 'You should study the experts in that ward, my friend. They will show you how to fetch up what is no longer there!'

The man wiped his mouth on his sleeve, shaking.

'Shall I show you the mortuary?'

The man shook his head.

'Then leave us to do what we can for them, and take those idiots away with you! *Now!*' said the surgeon, very low and fierce.

Jeremiah Vetch turned obediently and walked across the compound, and kept on walking. His fellows watched him approach and pass them. One man cried, 'What's up, Jem?' Vetch shook his head. He could not speak. Reading his face, they fell in behind him, silently. Silently, the guards saw them all out, and closed and barred the gates.

The grave-diggers picked up their spades and smoothed the long mound which had been disturbed. Two stretcher-bearers came quietly from a side-building, and began to carry away the sick. A fresh load of coffins was delivered and stacked up against the walls of the laundry. The iron fire-basket received its tribute.

Mr Bailey returned to the mortuary and picked up his scalpel. The eyes of the corpse seemed to be stretched to their utmost width, and stared from the hills of his cheekbones like green brilliants.

The number of cases reported for the month of September was half that of August. October saw fewer still, and a greater percentage of victims was recovering. In St Mark's church, Millbridge, on the first Sunday in November, the Reverend Jarvis Pole held a special service of supplication for both the living and the dead. He spoke eloquently and movingly, not at the congregation but with them, having his own great loss to bear. His eldest daughter, Dorcas, now took her mother's place in the family pew.

'Let us sing in His praise,' said Jarvis Pole, steadfast.

But as they lifted their voices more hopefully and heartily

than at any time in the past terrible months, nineteen-year-old Dorcas was seized with stomach pains and sank to her knees moaning. Those present hovered between prudence and charity, but the Reverend Jarvis dropped his hymn book in his haste to reach his daughter's side and carried her from the church, still moaning pitifully, and most pitifully followed by his other children.

Six weeks earlier he could have hunted all day in vain for medical assistance, but it so happened that Jamie Standish was riding between his two hospitals and met the little procession at the head of Rectory Lane, and so came home with them.

A maid and Dorcas's old nurse, Sarah Pratt, undressed the girl and put her to bed. There, in their presence, Dr Jamie most carefully examined her. But he could reach no conclusion other than the hideous one to which they had already come. Cholera.

Yet she has youth on her side, and the epidemic is declining, he thought. It is bad, but not hopeless. And since we have nothing to lose by it, we might as well try the saline treatment.

Aloud, he said, 'No, I shall neither bleed nor purge her, for I am of the opinion, particularly in the light of recent experience, that such violent methods weaken the organism still further. I believe we might save her if we act quickly. I shall be back within the hour with Mr Bailey and one of his assistants. Meanwhile you must keep her warm. Wrap her in hot blankets, build a good fire, put hot bricks to her feet and warming pans to her sides, and give her as much hot negus as she can take. If she complains of pain, apply a linseed poultice to the affected part.'

Then he was off, full of apprehension and excitement. For the saline method, first published in *The Lancet* the previous December, and tried two months later by Dr Thomas Latter of Leith, had struck him as being eminently sensible. Several lives had been saved by it, provided they caught the disease in its earliest stage. Yet other victims had failed to respond, and in the end its trials proved inconclusive. Finally the Edinburgh Board had rejected the treatment outright, and so he and Bailey had never attempted it.

Now he rode for the cholera hospital like a madman. Within the hour, as he had promised, the three of them were back. With them in the hospital van was a Read's Patent High Quality Syringe, a bottle of saline solution, a wicker frame, a copper tube, a pint of pure alcohol and a thermometer.

Dorcas Pole had lapsed into a restless doze and already her eyes seemed too deep in their dark sockets for comfort. At the foot of the bed her father knelt and prayed. By her side sat the middle-aged woman who had seen her into the world and might well see her out of it.

'Mr Pole,' said Jamie kindly, 'it would be best if you left us with Miss Dorcas and Mrs Pratt, and interceded with the Almighty downstairs. Each to his post, sir. I can assure you that we shall do everything within our power to help her.'

For good or ill, they were about to make medical history in Wyndendale, but that he did not say.

Jarvis Pole bowed his head, took out a lean purse, and murmured something about no expense being spared.

'Sir,' said Jamie, as kindly as before, 'I am not concerned for my fee but for your daughter's life. Put your purse away, sir. We can discuss such matters later.'

Harold Bailey automatically dipped his silver-tubed syringe into the alcohol, explaining with a little laugh of apology that this was an old habit of his in India, where water could be particularly foul.

Jamie turned his attention to the young medical assistant, and proceeded to instruct him in the heating of the saline solution, which must be kept at a steady 112 degrees Fahrenheit.

'Above all else, we must maintain the patient's bodily heat!'

They placed the wicker frame over her legs to create a

miniature cave, and piled blankets upon it. The assistant filled a spirit lamp with alcohol, lit it, set it at the end of the bed, and connected the copper tube so that a current of hot air passed continually into the little cave beyond.

'Keep your eye on that, too,' Jamie ordered the lad, 'and check the temperature inside the frame from time to time. It should be held at 140 degrees Fahrenheit.' Then he turned to the surgeon, saying, 'We may well be several hours before she is over the worst, and until then this treatment will keep all three of us employed! We shall have to rely entirely upon our judgement every step of the way, since we have neither the time nor the equipment to estimate accurately how much fluid and salts she is losing, or has lost already. But I believe that if we inject the solution now, and then each time she vomits or purges, we should be able to maintain a reasonable balance.'

Sarah Pratt spoke up, basins and towels to hand.

'How do you want *me* to manage, sir? I must clean her, and that means disturbing your arrangements, no matter how careful I am.'

'We'll lift off the wicker cage when that is necessary. You must be as quick as you can, and we must start all over again. The method requires patience above all else.'

'I think I can see why the Edinburgh Board discounted it!' said the surgeon, only half-joking. 'When a single patient demands the skill and energy of three medical men for an undetermined length of time, using sixpenn'orth of alcohol an hour, that is a treatment only to be ordered for the rich!'

'Hang the cost,' said Jamie briefly. Then, asking a great favour, 'Can you spare a few hours from the hospital?'

The surgeon nodded, though he would have liked to sleep.

The girl gave a shriek and a gasp. Mrs Pratt held a basin in front of her, and wiped her face and forehead with a wet flannel when she had done. Then there was a violent attack of diarrhoea. They removed the frame, and withdrew. A maid came

91

in to help, and as soon as she came out with her bundle of soiled clothes and her pail of dirty water, they were back again, setting everything up.

This must have happened a dozen times or more, and each time they went through the same process. To combat the pain and soothe the patient they gave Dorcas small doses of opium. They administered the homely remedy of rhubarb and magnesia. They injected the saline solution. An apprentice to these sorcerers, the lad hovered between attending to the temperature of the blanket cave and the temperature of the solution and filled up the spirit lamp when the flame faltered.

Each time this routine occurred, Jamie checked his watch. As late morning became late afternoon, he noted that she was suffering less and lasting longer between bouts. Their ministrations were taking effect. Whereas the girl should now have been in convulsions, she was dozing, albeit restlessly. The two doctors dared to hope. Evening came and the purging and vomiting had almost ceased. Towards midnight she lay clean and comfortable at last, and being no longer plagued fell fast asleep in her warm nest.

Now Harold Bailey and his assistant took themselves back to the cholera hospital, but Jamie Standish stayed, dozing in an armchair on one side of his patient's bed while Sarah Pratt dozed on the other. From time to time he got up to replenish the spirit lamp, or take the temperature of Dorcas's little cave, to feel her pulse and put a hand upon her forehead, smiling slightly as he listened to the state of her body and heard the right sounds.

November's national figures for cholera were not a quarter as great as those of October. By the end of December only three hundred cases were reported in the British Isles, and none of these was from Wyndendale.

The spring of 1833 seemed to be the most beautiful the valley could remember, but that had little to do with the weather.

Those who had survived the cholera discovered life to be a most precious gift, and began to renew themselves. There would be an abundant crop of marriages and babies that year. A kinder harvest to reap.

In the grey light of a late March afternoon, Jamie Standish rode up Rectory Lane, showing every symptom of the most infectious and contagious disease known to man. His pallor, his dry mouth, his palpitating heart and rapid pulse and shallow breath, a certain queasiness of stomach, and a continual movement of the lips as though he were repeating some magical phrase over and over again, bore witness to the gravity of his complaint.

Yet he had hopes of both palliative and cure: clutching, in one cold hand, a basket of primroses for the dark and lovely Dorcas Pole.

Part Two

In Circulation 1833–1834

The Opening Round

chapter eight

January, 1833

In Lower Millbridge, on the left-hand corner of the crossroads, you would find *The Lancashire Herald* at No. 38 Cornmarket. On the right-hand corner stood another building which might have been its twin. These three storeys of grimy brick, with a damp cellar and two spidery garrets, faced on to a different road and so were called No. 21 Middleton Street. At the height of the cholera epidemic Naomi Blūm cast a favourable eye upon this property, which was cheap enough, the owner being on the verge of bankruptcy and glad to sell. Still, she liked to bargain, and in the late summer of 1832 she obtained the premises and freehold very reasonably indeed.

Cleaners scrubbed and fumigated the house throughout. Carpenters and painters transformed a neglected dwelling into an efficient set of offices. The place swarmed with workmen, and Naomi inspected their progress daily. Even in the midst of uncertainty and death her nerve remained steady, her business sense unblunted. She ordered a new Napier double-cylinder printing press.

'But we may never live long enough to open, Miss Bloom!' cried Ambrose, aghast at such industry.

'We act as though we shall, Mr Longe!' Naomi replied.

Her expression was a curious compound of derision and pity.

'How sheltered all you English are,' she observed, 'on your safe little island. So the cholera may strike? Well, it may not! My father's race are born to trouble. They wake at dawn, knowing that they may not see night fall. Every joy casts a long shadow. Death can be the kindest friend, and life the worst enemy. Still, they endure. Let durance be your watchword, Mr Longe!'

Ashamed, amazed, he endured. Death passed close by, took his sister Cicely, nieces and nephews, friends and neighbours, but spared him. An unbeliever, Ambrose nevertheless attended the Service of Thanksgiving at St Mark's on the first Sunday in the New Year, and sang as heartily and gratefully as any member of the congregation. Then, like the rest of Wyndendale, he prepared to start life anew.

On the second Tuesday in January, the final edition of *The Clarion* asked its readers to stay faithful, and promised them a better newspaper than ever before in *The Northern Correspondent*. The following day Ambrose helped to load his few possessions on to a cart, locked up the old shop for the last time, and rode with the carter to Middleton Street.

Swinging signs were long since out of fashion, but Ambrose and Naomi eschewed even brass plates in this progressive age. No. 21, being a corner building, had the advantage of two sides on which to advertise the newspaper. So just below the roof sixteen rows of brick were painted white, and upon them in huge black letters ran the legend THE NORTHERN CORRESPONDENT

They would never have dared to commit such a vulgarity in the Old Town, but here it was new, brash and highly effective.

Sam Pickering stood at his office window on the first floor front, watching the removal and giving his moustache a meditative tug now and again. His light green eyes were thoughtful but a little smile hovered on his lips. If the Longe fellow wanted a battle royal he should have it, and with this sort of backing they were now well matched. But what the devil was going on between him and Naomi Blüm? He was, like Sam himself, a sworn bachelor. She, apparently, liked to keep the reins in her own hands, providing the cash but making sure that it was spent well. Nor could anyone think they were in love. Not a bit of it! Very friendly, very brisk, never a word or a look wasted. Yet, in the end, they were man and woman still.

Aye, there she came, not far behind her protégé, in the private carriage she kept at the Royal George. Robed and furred against the January cold. That coat and muff had cost a pretty penny! How much was she worth? No one knew for sure. Hidden depths! She must have sunk two or three thousand into the venture already, and would need to act as banker and backer while *The Correspondent* found its feet and its readers. If it ever did! So she had money to spare. But she lived surprisingly modestly for a rich woman, her lifestyle being comfortable rather than extravagant.

He had hinted as much to the ironmaster, who replied by putting one finger to the side of his nose and saying, 'Portable property, Sam! Jews don't change their natures by wearing Christian coats. Miss Bloom comes of a race which has survived constant persecution. She is always ready to travel light, and carry her fortune in her pocket!'

Sam supposed she was handsome in her way. A fine figure of a woman. But her features were too strongly marked, her character too independent for his taste. He fancied the small, fair sort himself, with bright blue glances, winsome manners and harmless prattle. Not that he could afford such a luxury. The most innocent women tended to breed and to clamour for attention, and he couldn't be tied up like that. No, he was married to *The Herald*, which meant he could fight with both hands free and his mind on the job, not be for ever pulling his punches and looking over one shoulder.

Snow had fallen that morning, but only a thin covering still lay on roofs and tarpaulins and in drifts along the gutter. The rest had been trodden to grey slush. It was cold, though. He could see their breath smoking as they talked and looked up, admiring the name which ran round the top of the building. Aye, they'd got some brass to think up a cheeky idea like that.

99

But then, they were starting behind the line. *The Herald* was already fifteen months ahead of them. Still, a right good idea! He expected the ironmaster would come foaming round to best them. Probably have *The Lancashire Herald* embossed in gold on the roof-slates of No. 38, or else in tiles down one corner! And *he* was none too pleased about Ambrose Longe's change of fortune. It was a good thing that the old war-horse had been elected Tory M.P. for Wyndendale. Kept him quiet for most of the time. Kept him down in London, too.

A breath of freedom filled Sam's lungs at the thought. He pushed up a sash window and leaned out, hands planted squarely on the sill.

Crying, 'Good morning, Miss Bloom! Good morning, Mr Longe!'

Naomi turned gracefully, smiled and inclined her head. Ambrose grinned and bowed very low. What a puppy the fellow was! High time he grew up. Well, *The Correspondent* would test his mettle all right.

'I see we're going to be neighbours,' Sam remarked sarcastically, nodding at the legend as though he had only just caught sight of it.

'Why, so we are!' Ambrose replied in mock astonishment. 'I didn't notice *your* sign!'

'Oh, la!' Naomi murmured to herself, eyebrows raised.

Sam twirled one end of his moustache, unperturbed.

'What have you done with that cubby-hole full of iron-mongery in Market Place, Mr Longe?' he asked drily. 'Sold it for scrap?'

'Too many pickings there for a scrap merchant,' Ambrose replied, very cool. 'I advised him to come down to you instead.'

'Gentlemen!' said Naomi pointedly, sternly. 'I leave you to your business. Good day, Mr Pickering. Good day, Mr Longe!'

Slightly chastened, they watched her carriage return up the High Street. Sam was the first to break the silence.

'It's just after half-past eleven,' he remarked, consulting his pocket watch. 'If you're going to get that lot sorted this afternoon you'd best eat a good dinner first. Something as'll stick to your ribs. How about joining me at Pendleton's Chophouse?'

The world once more belonged to men.

'Just give me five minutes to pay the carter and lock up!' Ambrose replied cheerfully. 'And I'm with you.'

Situated in Croft Street, off Cornmarket, Pendleton's was one of those businesses which is a product of time and place. It had begun life as a modest pie-shop. Peggie Pendleton cooked, Harry served and young Walter hawked the streets with a tray on his head. Over the years, business and the family increased. Harry bought the shop next door, enlarged the kitchen and extended the premises to take wooden tables and benches so that customers could eat there.

The shop now sold a variety of cold savoury delicacies to be taken away in paper bags. A side-window service was instituted in the kitchen, whereby poorer people could bring their plates and basins and be served directly from oven or cauldron. Finally, old Harry bought the shop on the other side, obtained a licence to sell beer, wines and spirits, and instituted a bar and a chophouse.

The little world of Millbridge was changing so rapidly that it was not a matter of swimming ahead so much as keeping abreast of a strong current. Pendleton's coasted along with the 1830s. They were open before the factory whistles blew at six o'clock in the morning. They did not close until the last reveller had fallen in the gutter long past midnight. Though obliged through pressure of work and numbers to employ outside help, they were still a family business. Old Walter Pendleton, who had once carried a tray on his head, now carried it in his hands – and as chief waiter he ruled the staff, customers and customs of the chop-house. Daughters and nieces baked the mountains of hot and cold food. Sons and nephews acted as waiters, grandsons as errand-boys.

Pendleton's catered for a wide circle of clients. Working

men drank in the tap room while their wives fetched covered basins from the side-window. Business men dined and supped in the chop-house while their servants made purchases from the shop. Bachelors gratefully patronised all four establishments.

The two editors hung their hats and coats on a couple of pegs by the door, and rubbed their hands in anticipation. After the grey cold of a January morning the heat was a blessing. Being near the new gasworks, Pendleton's had been among the first to install this modern form of lighting, and on that dull midday every lamp was ablaze. A mighty fire roared up the chimney-back at the far end of the room. Savoury smells, floating through the serving hatch from the kitchen, made their mouths water and their nostrils twitch.

'If you get here before noon,' said Sam Pickering, 'you can choose your seat. Come half an hour later and you'll either wait by the door or find somewhere else to have your dinner!'

The chop-house gave itself no airs, being a long, low room with a blackened ceiling and a flagged floor. Wooden tables and high-backed settles against the walls provided little hutches in which customers could eat, drink and talk with reasonable privacy. The Royal George in the Old Town might court its clientèle with comely serving-maids offering handwritten menus, but Pendleton's only employed waiters, who reeled off the day's dishes as though they were joined together, and shouted their orders through the hatch.

The kitchen was most famous for its steak and kidney pies and puddings, but also did tasty stews of tripe and onions, succulent pig's trotters, liverish black puddings and glutinous cow-heels. Only one vegetable was served with any dish, this being mashed potato, but you could have as much as you pleased. For dessert there was a standard choice of suet roly-poly with jam or treacle, rice pudding or apple pie, all served with cream from the Croft Street dairy.

Sam led the way to a table at the far corner of the room.

'Quickest service here, and the coolest place,' he explained. 'You can run a temperature sitting atop of that blaze with one o' Pendleton's puddings inside you! And you can't hear yourself talk if you're too near the hatch!'

'I can imagine,' said Ambrose, fascinated. 'I didn't even know this place existed.'

'No. Well. You've been up at the posh end of Millbridge, and that part of town is a dead duck as far as progress goes. I don't know what reason you had for coming here but you chose the right address. We may be a bit rough round the edges but we're alive and kicking. Oh yes. The Old Town's all right for genteel folk with private incomes, but there's no fresh blood there, and the social circles are as tight as a pig's backside. Down here there are new people, new ideas, constant change. In short, my lad, the staple nourishment of journalism!'

A small, bald waiter stood before them, wearing old-fashioned knee breeches and buckled shoes. His shirt-sleeves were rolled above the elbow. A clean, white apron was tied where his waist should have been.

'Good morning, Walter!' said Sam, very affable. 'This gentleman is Mr Longe, the editor of *The Northern Correspondent*.'

Walter nodded and pursed his lips judiciously.

'We'll have a bottle of claret to start with,' Sam continued, very easy and pleasant, 'and what do you recommend today?'

'Well, as the gentleman hasn't been here before, Mr Pickering, I think he should try our steak and kidney pudding. They're just being lifted out!'

'Right you are, Walter. Two steak and kidney puddings it is!'

The bottle of claret and a couple of thick glasses appeared almost immediately. The noise, the heat and the activity of the chop-house were increasing with every minute. In the same easy and pleasant manner, Sam poured the wine and lifted his glass.

'Here's to *The Northern Correspondent*!' he said. 'Long life and health to her!'

'That's uncommonly generous of you,' Ambrose replied, touched.

'It's all right,' said Sam drily. 'I'm looking forward to a good punch-up. I could hardly get going on *The Clarion*, now could I?'

'You did your best,' said Ambrose, equally dry. 'Here's to *The Lancashire Herald* and long may we both battle!'

They clinked glasses and drank deeply.

'Why did you refer to my newspaper as *she*?' Ambrose asked.

'The original paper was edited by a lady, wasn't it?'

'Yes, by my mother. But as it was short-lived, and closed down forty years ago, I'm surprised you ever heard of it.'

'I was the youngest of thirteen children,' said Sam, 'and my father was a weaver who taught himself to read and write. He always had some book open by the shuttle, so's he could learn as he worked. He was a great radical, was Father. He belonged to one of those working-men's groups – there were dozens of them and they never seemed to do much but talk! Anyhow, he and seven other weavers used to club together, a farthing apiece, to buy their weekly copy of *The Northern Correspondent*. And Father chose to read it last because that meant he could keep it. How long did the paper run, by the way?'

'Just over two years.'

'Well, it had come and gone by the time I was born, but Father knew the editorials by heart. He used to quote bits to us. I was reared on *The Northern Correspondent*, in a manner of speaking.'

'Well . . . I'm . . . damned!'

'Small world, isn't it?' said Sam, watching him. 'Here's the steak and kidney pudding! Don't let it get cold.'

There was little likelihood of that. The plates were sizzling.

'So that's why I always think of *The Correspondent* as a lady,' Sam continued, speaking between mouthfuls. 'Y.L.C. were the initials your mother used, if I recollect aright.'

'You do indeed,' said Ambrose, disarmed.

Sam wiped his mouth.

'And now that the present newspaper is owned by another lady,' he added, so casually that Ambrose was taken by surprise, 'it seems to earn the female gender twice over. Whereas *The Herald* is a *he*. No doubt about that, either!'

Ambrose laid down his knife and fork. His bonhomie vanished along with his appetite.

'Miss Bloom does *not* own my newspaper,' he said coldly. 'She has merely invested money in it, and will eventually be repaid.'

Sam's face was expressionless, but his green eyes betrayed a twinkle and his appetite was unimpaired.

'No need to get on your high horse about it,' he remarked. 'I don't own *The Herald* and I never will. I don't want to, neither. Let somebody else worry about the money side. Miss Bloom is a lady investor, then, though there's nothing "mere" about the investment, from what I've heard! Still, what's the difference? I tell you, Mr Longe, if *The Herald* was on the rocks I'd take a shove from the devil to get it off again!'

He popped a large forkful of meat and suet crust into a cavernous mouth, chewing reflectively.

Ambrose resumed eating, but slowly and without zest. He endeavoured to match his companion's easy flow of conversation.

'So you were brought up a radical?' he observed. 'When did you become a Tory?'

'When I got my first job on a Tory paper! Besides, radicals are forever sticking their necks out, wanting to run before they can walk. Can't wait for things to take their natural course. Always push, push, push. Oh, times are changing. We all know that. But they won't change overnight, nor next year neither. It's no good knocking your head against the door because it won't open when you want it to!'

Again he paused. Again launched another broadside.

'But then, you're not what I'd call a full-blooded radical, are you? I've seen you turn against *them*, before now, if their ideas weren't quite to your liking. Aye, *The Clarion* was a popular little paper, no doubt about it. Folk enjoyed seeing the local bigwigs slip on your banana skins. It'll be interesting to see what you make of *The Correspondent*. None of my business, mind, but if you're aiming at a wide market you need a strong line and a firm policy. They want more than a joker and a fence-sitter out there.' Then genially, 'Are you thinking of keeping *The Recorder* on?'

'I hadn't really thought about it at all,' said Ambrose coldly, declining to be drawn on that question.

'Well, no problem there. I daresay there's plenty of likely young radicals about who wouldn't mind taking it over, provided you printed it for 'em for nothing!' Sam remarked casually.

He sopped up his gravy with a bit of bread. His tone altered, became hospitable, persuasive.

'Now, how about a slice of apple pie to finish, Mr Longe? Could you manage that? Walter! Apple pie for two, and a ladle of cream on each of 'em!'

He lifted the bottle to the light and squinted at the level.

'Shall we see this bottle off, then, Mr Longe? No, no! Put that brass back into your pocket! I'm doing the treating. Today is by way of being a special occasion. The opening round, as you might say.'

A Shrewd Assessment

chapter nine

'He was pleasant. He was frank. He was sensible,' said Ambrose, in the parlour of Thornton House. 'Then having called the tune, he paid the piper.'

He had reported every remark except the one relating to herself.

'In short, he bested me!'

He leaned on the mantelshelf and stared moodily into the fire.

Naomi had put aside the letter she was writing, and listened carefully. Now she rang the bell for tea.

'You were on his territory, at his invitation,' she replied. 'When he is on your territory, you shall best him. But he is a formidable man. If I must choose who shall be my enemy – your uncle the ironmaster or Mr Pickering – I hesitate, yes. But Mr Pickering I do not choose.'

Whenever she was particularly disturbed or concerned, her phrases betrayed a foreign influence which made Ambrose smile.

'Well, I haven't any choice at all, my dear Miss Bloom,' he answered lightly. 'They are both my enemies! At least, Sam Pickering plays an open game.'

'No, no, he does not,' she answered vehemently. 'He is deep, this Mr Pickering. Very deep. And he has no vanity, like your uncle. That is a great strength. It means that he must be convinced, that he cannot be persuaded.'

She mused, leaning back in her armchair, hands clasped in her lap. Though she had been expecting no one to call, she wore an evening gown and a full complement of jewels. Which also made him smile.

'If I were in your place,' said Naomi, at length, 'I should wonder what reason he has for talking to you, because he would only tell you what he wished you to know.'

'In other circumstances we could have been friends,' said Ambrose, brooding. 'I have always disliked my uncle and everything he stood for, but somehow I cannot dislike Sam Pickering.'

She was up in arms at once, gesticulating.

'Like? Dislike? What does that matter? Friendship is based on mutuality and trust. How can you be friends? Love your enemy if you must, but know him for what he is – your enemy!'

The maid's knock at the door silenced her. She transferred her attention to the spirit-kettle, eyebrows drawn darkly together.

'Well then, what was my enemy's purpose today?' said Ambrose peaceably, accepting tea. 'Naive as it may seem to you, I thought he was being sociable. However, I appear to be ill informed on the subject of enemies, Miss Bloom. Pray do hold forth!'

She was quiet again, reflective.

'Of course, he would wish to find out what kind of man you were,' she began. 'Until this morning you were only a newspaper and your uncle's prejudice. And then, you are bound to meet. After all, your offices are on opposite sides of the road.'

'Did you arrange that especially?' he asked, grinning.

She ignored the remark.

'You say that he made you feel of no importance? Well, that would suit the purpose of a small-minded man, but for Mr Pickering it is not reason enough. How does a buyer act when he wants something?' The expressive gestures of hands and shoulders were again in evidence. 'Does he say, "That is a most beautiful jewel, and I must have it at any cost?" No. He purses his lips. He frowns. He shrugs.' All mimed. 'Then he points out a flaw – it does not matter how small – because the flaw makes it appear cheap! Remember that a flaw must be present, or there is nothing to bargain about. Remember, also, that the jewel is worth a great deal, or he would not be bargaining at all.

So, Mr Longe. Find your jewel, identify your flaw, and there is his reason.'

Ambrose set down his tea untasted. His face looked thin. His linen was as immaculate as ever, but showing signs of wear. His brown frock-coat and trousers, though elegant and well brushed, were in the fashion of a previous decade.

'Deuce take it! I never had to think twice about the machinations of Arnold Thwaites!' he remarked, only half-humorously.

'Why should you think of him even once?' she cried, taking his words literally, 'Mr Pickering would not be afraid of *him*!' She leaned forward, coaxing his appetite with a plate of delicacies. 'Will you not eat a few little cakes? They are so very little!'

'But so very rich,' Ambrose replied, smiling. For he knew her ploys to distract him. 'Thank you. Yes. *Afraid*, did you say?'

'But of course afraid!' Her tone was scornful. 'Did he trouble to acquaint himself with the editor of *The Clarion*? No! "This is the editor of *The Northern Correspondent*!" he said to the waiter. And yet both editors are the same man. He fears what you could make of *The Correspondent*. Remember who employs him. What will happen to him if your newspaper does better than *The Herald*? That thought has certainly occurred to him, and troubles him deeply.'

The lines on Ambrose's forehead had not entirely vanished.

'He hit me hard, you know, saying I was not a full-blooded radical. Suggesting I had no firm policy.'

'He meant to hurt you. And did he speak the truth?'

'I suppose he did. It depends what value you place on an open mind. Sam Pickering believes in being a Party man, which has a simpler and more popular appeal. I say what I believe to be right, whether it's got a Party label on it or not. Sam Pickering will support Tory policy and William Howarth M.P. even if he thinks they're both wrong! And that's about the size of it.'

'This *Recorder* he mentioned. What of this?'

'Well, it is a newspaper for working people, simply written and produced for their benefit. No frills and straight politics. To be honest it is somewhat old-fashioned. Sad to think that the truth – as one always believes it to be! – must conform to fashion like anything else. Sam Pickering was quite right when he said it could be taken over by any young radical, provided I printed it free! In fact, it probably needs newer blood than mine in its veins!'

She did not answer at once, sipping tea and watching him. She was obscurely grateful to Sam Pickering. The subject of *The Recorder* had been one on which she felt she could not question him. Politically, she did not care one way or the other. Business-wise, she was anxious that *The Correspondent* should have the best of his time and ability, and be in no way hampered by a secondary concern.

'On the other hand,' Ambrose continued, 'he is right in thinking *The Clarion* was lightweight, and that *The Correspondent* must be handled with authority and conviction.'

She set the problem before him as enticingly as though it were a plate of rich little cakes.

'I have no objection if you make *The Correspondent* a radical newspaper. I tell you, I invest money for a return. I do not mind the nature of the investment.'

He felt as uncomfortably full as though he had eaten every crumb.

'But that would narrow the field of *The Correspondent* as I perceive it.'

'Indeed?' Eyebrows raised.

'Oh, yes. I see it on far broader lines. I see it as a newspaper which is able to be independent of all parties, reporting news from every side without fear or favour. I see it as a newspaper which will be widely respected because it does not court popular prejudice and because it can be relied upon to give a fair hearing to anyone.'

He paused a moment, remembering, and said frankly, 'It

110

hit me, though, that Sam Pickering's father used to read the original *Correspondent*. He was the sort of reader my mother wrote for – the self-educated working man. And then, my parents showed such courage. Their paper was written, printed and distributed at the risk of being imprisoned or transported for life. It makes my present notion of the newspaper seem like a cowardly compromise.'

'How very clever of Mr Pickering!' Naomi answered quietly.

They were both silent then: he thinking hard, she observing him. He drank up his cold tea, rose, and returned his cup to the tray, thinking aloud.

'All my life I have revered and loved my mother above all other people – had you known her you would not wonder at that confession. Yet I fear that I take after my father, who was a likeable fellow but somewhat of a failure at close quarters!'

He faced her, saying, 'Consequently, I cannot hold myself in high esteem, and in the very moment that I seem most sure of success I am most deeply afraid of failure. It was a great deal safer, my dear Miss Bloom, to starve with *The Clarion* than to risk running *The Correspondent*. There is my flaw, and no doubt Sam Pickering perceived it. For he is one of those dogged fellows who never doubts himself.'

Naomi's smile lit her face, but still she did not speak.

'However, that is old history,' he said more cheerfully. 'Whether I succeed or not, I have a vision of what *The Northern Correspondent* could be, and I shall endeavour to realise it. Pray remember, my dear Miss Bloom, that I warned you I was a shaky investment!'

'Mr Pickering and I have a belief in common,' she answered calmly. 'We envisage a newspaper that will outrival *The Herald*.'

For a moment his face reflected his emotions of relief and humility. The next moment these were masked by dry amusement.

'And I will hand over *The Recorder* to someone else!'

Her expression changed.

'For how much?' asked Naomi, interested.

'My dear Miss Bloom, no one would give me a penny for it. It is a financial and legal liability. It is not even supposed to be printed. I have lain in Millbridge jail before now, because . . .'

She lifted one hand like a prophet of old.

'Enough!' she said, once more disappointed in him.

He threw back his head and laughed as he had not laughed for a long time. She sat very upright, very handsome, frowning with incomprehension. His humour was alien to her.

'Oh, do forgive me,' Ambrose gasped, wiping his eyes, 'but I find your attitude absolutely priceless, Miss Bloom.'

'I wonder why?' she answered, genuinely puzzled.

'Well, never mind. Pray don't be offended. You do me so much good. I am so much obliged to you in so many ways.'

He kissed the hand that had admonished him.

'Thank you,' Ambrose said sincerely. 'God bless you.'

She was touched and pleased. She withdrew her hand, but smiled.

'What an utter ass I am,' Ambrose continued, striding about the parlour, shaking his head at his own stupidity. 'Here you are, investing a small fortune in me and my newspaper, and all I can do is to fetch my fears and woes to you – and eat too many cakes! I should be reassuring you that all is well and nothing can fail!'

Naomi murmured to herself, '*He* should reassure *me*?'

He stopped in front of her.

'I am deeply and humbly aware of your generosity, your wisdom and your forbearance, madam.'

'Such compliments!'

'I shall endeavour at all times to do justice to your confidence in us – in me and my newspaper.'

'Fine speeches!'

'And even without the vast sum I could have procured from the sale of *The Recorder* . . .'

'I knew it!'

'. . . I say with confidence that your money shall eventually be returned to you, with interest!'

'Do you know how much interest?' Gazing intently upon him.

'Doubtless it is written into the contract. What matter whether it be ten, twenty or even one hundred per cent?'

'You hear him?' Hands raised to heaven.

'And until that blessèd day, madam, when you will be free to help other struggling provincial editors, let us enjoy the prospect of the battle before us!'

'Before *you*, Mr Longe. I play no part, remember, in the running of the newspaper.'

But he could not let her get away with such a hypocrisy.

'My dear Miss Bloom, what have you been doing this very evening but reviving its editor's faith in himself, resolving the paper's problems and helping to decide its future policy? Let us have no more of this feminine pretence. I am well versed in the ways of strong-minded women. My family has produced many a matriarch.'

'I am not a matriarch!'

'Not yet, madam, but you have all the makings of one. No doubt some enterprising king of industry will carry you off – but not yet, pray God, not yet. *The Correspondent* deserves a run for your money.'

'Mr Longe!' she cried, in warning. 'You go too far.'

She stood up. She switched the stiff silk skirt of her gown into position. She pulled the bell-rope.

'Deuce take it, Miss Bloom, I was only joking,' said Ambrose, abashed. 'Though joking in earnest, for all that.'

'I shall not marry,' cried Naomi passionately. 'I shall never marry. Marriage is not for me.'

He shrugged, nonplussed at such a serious rejoinder to his fun.

'I thought that women always wanted to marry, no matter what.'

'Then you see before you one who does not, no matter what.'

The parlour-maid removed the tea-things and fetched his overcoat.

In the hall he held out his hand. Naomi's frown disappeared. She came forward and clasped the hand frankly and firmly, like a man.

'Shall I tell you why I remain single, Mr Longe?'

'By all means, Miss Bloom.'

'Because I choose *not* to marry, *not* to change a way of life which pleases me, *not* to merge myself in another person, *not* to risk losing life itself in the bearing of more life. Most women have no choice. A woman of independent means and mind is more fortunate. I choose liberty, Mr Longe.'

Amazed, Ambrose asked, 'But what of love, Miss Bloom?'

'Love costs too much.'

He nodded. She had expressed his lifetime's philosophy in a few words. He was dumb with admiration. Holding his top hat under one arm, he spoke again, as one who consults an oracle.

'Why does everyone else not know that, Miss Bloom?'

She answered darkly, 'Because they do not *think*, Mr Longe. They worship a graven image of love, and expect it to solve all their problems. Whereas it merely causes greater ones. And then, having made life impossible for its victims, it leaves them!'

They were his own beliefs again, succinct and clear.

'Good Lord,' said Ambrose. 'What an astonishing woman you are!'

'Besides,' said Naomi, 'why should I give my property to a man? Why should I let a man use my money?'

He burst out laughing again.

'I do not think money is such an amusing matter!' she chided him.

She saw that his great-coat had worn thin, and regretted the fact. She spoke in a different tone.

'We should raise your salary, Mr Longe. I do not mean to keep you poor while my money is repaid.'

'We'll keep me exactly as I am, Miss Bloom,' he replied grimly. 'Remember you do not own me and my newspaper. You are an investor.'

Surprisingly, her face softened.

'Was Mr Pickering able to make you doubt *me* as well as yourself?' she asked, smiling. 'Ah! he is very clever, that one. Very subtle. You should watch him carefully. Goodnight, Mr Longe.'

One of Those Golden Days

chapter ten

The time when Ambrose Longe acted as general dogsbody of *The Clarion* was over. This Monday morning he sat at his desk in 21 Middleton Street, presiding over a meeting with his three most important members of staff: Frank Ormerod, head printer, from the Manchester *Exchange Herald*; Bob Bullock, overseer, formerly a compositor on the Manchester *Observer*; Charlie Ainsworth, reporter, trained on the Manchester *Chronicle*.

These men had been chosen not only for their ability, but for the experience gained on three major and entirely different provincial newspapers. Each man had improved his salary and his status by coming to *The Correspondent*, and was as keen as Ambrose to make a success of this venture. Two of them had brought wives and children. One had brought his bride. And all had uprooted themselves to move more than sixty miles from the place in which they had been born and bred.

Copies of every newspaper in the valley were spread before them, from the eighty-year-old *Wyndendale Post* to the two-year-old *Garth Advertiser*, and including the final edition of *The Clarion*.

'With regard to layout,' Ambrose was saying, 'I want *The Northern Correspondent* to catch attention without clamouring for it. It should give the impression of being reliable and dignified, but never dull or pompous. We must interest readers outside the valley, without losing sight of the fact that we are primarily a local paper. We aim to appeal to, and cater for, intelligent and enquiring people in every walk of life – self-educated artisans, as well as professional and business men. Bearing this in mind, I welcome your suggestions and comments.'

Frank Ormerod, the head printer, spoke first: a burly,

florid fellow who looked older than his forty-two years.

'I daresay I'm prejudiced, Mr Longe, but I don't think you can beat *The Exchange Herald* for good looks. It's half the size of the usual paper and twice as thick. Instead of having five or six narrow columns on each page you've got three broad ones. I don't like a crowded appearance to the print, myself. I wouldn't like it as a reader, let alone a printer. I think it tends to put folk off. Gives them mental indigestion. This way, there's just as much word space. And being smaller, it's easier to hold.'

'Thank you, Mr Ormerod,' said Ambrose. 'Would you like to fold this blank news-sheet into four, to show us how the paper would look compared to these others? Good. Now, who would like to speak next?'

'I'm not against the size,' said Bob Bullock, the overseer, 'but the smaller a paper is the more striking the masthead should be. You've got to shout *The Northern Correspondent* at them! *The Observer* has an eye on its masthead, as you know. I see you had a trumpet for *The Clarion*. Now I think the title should stand out – blackletter or condensed roman – with some such illustration either to one side or in the middle. *Correspondent* suggests a pen. What about a pen in an inkstand?'

Ambrose took the dummy newspaper from Frank Ormerod, sketched three broad columns on the front page, printed the title in thick dark roman letters across the top, drew a dummy stamp in the top righthand corner, and a jaunty quill between NORTHERN and CORRESPONDENT.

'Mr Ainsworth?' he enquired, of his reporter.

'Well, that layout is different to the rest of the Wyndendale papers. No doubt about it!' said young Charlie Ainsworth. 'But it would be a deal livelier with a few woodcut blocks between the advertisements on the front page, and leaded columns.'

Ambrose nodded. He held the dummy *Correspondent* and considered it at length, head on one side.

Then he said, 'I like this.'

They accepted the statement in silence. He was the editor.

He moved to other matters.

'Now, the Liverpool–Leeds mail coaches go through Millbridge, so we shall get the Liverpool and the Irish papers direct. But the strength of a really good paper lies in its Parliamentary news. In Manchester you have the advantage of an overnight express mail service from London, which means that London news arrives the following morning. I have made arrangements whereby an agent meets the express mail coach in Manchester and sends a full selection of London morning and evening papers on to us via the York Flyer. We shall thus be able to publish Thursday night's Parliamentary debate in our Saturday morning issue. Which brings us in line with *The Herald*!'

He reflected on this with some satisfaction, for *The Herald* had advertised itself 'first and best' with London and Parliamentary news from the beginning.

'The usual ministerial documents and Manchester newspapers will arrive with them. So by Friday teatime we should have all the latest intelligence. It will be our policy to acknowledge the sources of our information and to give credit to them. Political news will be reported in an unbiased and unprejudiced manner.' He paused and added with a smile, 'Even Mr Cobbett's *Political Register* will be accorded a consideration he would not extend to any other paper!'

They chuckled a little at that.

'Foreign news!' Ambrose announced, and they all sat forward. 'We shall continue to use the foreign news quoted in the London press, but we now have our own sources as well. Miss Bloom, our chief investor, has family and business connections in most of the European capitals. Of course, these mails will be subject to the same delays and hazards as any other news from abroad, but they have the advantage of being personal and reliable – and *The Herald* cannot poach them!'

They liked that.

Young Charlie Ainsworth said, 'It's ridiculous, the way that the authorities deal – or *don't* deal, I should say! – with

118

foreign mail. The Channel crossing is a lot easier and faster than it used to be, now we've got steamships. If I was in power I'd set up a public mail service between Dover and Calais that worked seven days a week. Right now, if the foreign news arrives at the weekend, you don't get it for two or three days because there's no delivery on Saturdays and Sundays – not unless you pay for a private express mail.'

'Which we shall do,' said Ambrose.

'No expense spared, like?' Bob Bullock asked.

'Within reason, no.'

Bullock pursed his lips and nodded. Frank Ormerod smoothed his chin and looked thoughtfully at the freshly painted ceiling. Charlie Ainsworth examined his shirt cuffs, which were a credit to his young wife's laundering.

'I like your notion of a steampacket mail service,' Ambrose said to him. 'I think that could well be one of *The Correspondent*'s personal campaigns. Which brings me to another important point. Though we give fair hearing to all parties we are not simply a mouthpiece. We have concerns of our own. *The Correspondent* wants a better daily life for the majority. We shall take up cudgels for shorter working hours and better working conditions. We shall expose the inhumanities behind the Poor Law. We shall back social reform.'

'Mr Longe,' said Frank Ormerod judiciously, 'might I make a point? Businessmen are an important part of our readership, and you're making special provision for them – advertisements and Stock Exchange reports and so on. But they're employers, Mr Longe, not workmen. They won't like too much reform.'

'They blooming well need it, though!' Bob Bullock growled.

'*The Correspondent* will assume that its business readers are *good* employers,' Ambrose replied, smiling, 'anxious for the welfare, and therefore the increased productivity, of their workers.' But for a moment his confidence faltered. 'By George!'

he added. 'It's going to be damned difficult to strike the right balance!'

Frank Ormerod and Bob Bullock nodded, but Charlie Ainsworth was too young to feel more than general jubilation.

'I had planned to keep the same format as *The Clarion*,' Ambrose went on, 'so that our present readers would know where to find everything. But as we are adopting Mr Ormerod's suggestion of an eight-page newspaper we shall have to split it into smaller sections. For instance, the back page, formerly page four, is now pages seven and eight. I propose we put bankruptcies, editorial letters and sporting features on page eight and leave the social chatter to page seven. Incidentally, the social columns have, in the past, caused me more problems and grief than the rest of the newspaper put together . . .!'

The three men smiled conspiratorially at him and each other.

'. . . so I am delegating this task. Since society is the province of the ladies, I propose to put our page seven into the hands of two very competent and lively members of the female sex. I refer to our chief investor, Miss Bloom, and my cousin, Mrs Henry Vivian. They will be fully responsible for attending and reporting on all the usual events, selecting literary items, and making this page as interesting as possible to the wives of our readers.'

The three men looked very doubtful indeed. Ambrose understood and proceeded in a brisker tone.

'This is an experiment, and until they have proved themselves to be professionally reliable their post will be a temporary one. I have impressed upon them the necessity of their copy arriving on time and being legibly written. They know that my word upon it is final and that they will have no part or say in the rest of the newspaper. They can claim reasonable expenses but they will not be paid a salary.'

This made all the difference. Frank Ormerod spoke good-naturedly.

'Well, to be sure, the ladies have a nice eye for detail and a neat way of expressing themselves. Their pens lack power, of course. But then – power isn't their province. Which is right and proper.'

'I knew one lady who wielded a powerful pen,' Ambrose replied pleasantly, 'and I wonder whether it is opportunity rather than ability which the ladies lack. We shall see. Still, I digress. So, Miss Bloom and Mrs Vivian are page seven, and will entertain our readers' wives. We have no dearth of voluntary reporters to entertain their husbands, either! Mr Ainsworth, when his more serious duties permit him, can take his pick of boxing matches, racing meetings, eating and walking contests, field sports and the like. But in his absence we can rely upon the services of a number of amateur enthusiasts.

'Last, but not least in importance, a half column will be kept free on the back page for late news – the *"Postscript"*.'

He came to the end of his notes, and said, 'I think that maps out the course and sets the character of *The Northern Correspondent*.'

They contemplated its image with considerable satisfaction.

'Our first copy goes to press on Friday night,' said Ambrose, 'so we have four clear days in which to create a damned good impression on the reading public. Meanwhile, the printing presses must earn their keep and the rest of the staff be kept busy. We already have a number of printing jobs to hand. You and I can discuss that part of the business this afternoon, Mr Ormerod. Outside work will provide our main source of income until the newspaper is established.'

He consulted his pocket-watch.

'I should like to mark this occasion by inviting you to be my guests for dinner today. It is now fifteen minutes short of noon. We should be in good time to find seats at Pendleton's Chop-house.'

The four newspapermen set off in double file down the narrow pavement. They formed an interesting quartet. Ambrose, slim and dandified, walked with the burly, rosy Frank Ormerod. Behind them came Bob Bullock and Charlie Ainsworth: the one truculent, the other talkative. All four of them were experiencing the euphoria of a newly-formed team which promises to work well.

The heat of Pendleton's enveloped them. The sharp eyes and encyclopedic memory of old Walter came to Ambrose's assistance.

'And good morning to *you*, sir,' said the head waiter, bustling forward to help him take off his coat. 'Mr Longe of *The Northern Correspondent*, isn't it? I thought so. Good to see you again so soon, sir. Now, where would you like to sit?'

As editor of *The Clarion*, Ambrose would instantly and impudently have chosen Sam Pickering's favourite corner. Today he felt that such tricks, though delightful and enjoyable in themselves, were not quite in keeping with his present status as editor of *The Correspondent*. He shifted the responsibility on to Walter's shoulders.

'Where would you suggest?' he replied tactfully.

Walter's eyelids acknowledged this piece of diplomacy with a blink of approval.

'Well, sir, a gentleman in your position likes to see and be seen, as you might say. Supposing you was to take a table on the far wall? You've got a good view of the door from there. You're out of the draught, near enough to the fire and not too near the hatch.'

Within a minute, four top hats and four greatcoats hung side by side on the wooden pegs, and four pairs of cold hands rubbed themselves together in anticipation.

'Should I fetch you something to drink while you order, sir?'

'Yes, if you please, Walter. I shall drink wine, but these gentlemen may have what they wish.'

'Beer for me, Mr Longe,' said Bob Bullock immediately.

'I'd like to join you with a glass of wine, Mr Longe,' said

Charlie Ainsworth, playing the man of the world.

'I'll have tea if you make it this early, ' said Frank Ormerod to the waiter, 'and water if you don't.'

'Tea, sir? Certainly, sir. Milk and sugar? Very good. A bottle of claret for you, Mr Longe? A pint of home-brewed for this gentleman? Coming immediately, sir.'

'I'm a teetotaller,' said Frank Ormerod, in explanation.

The other three looked slightly dashed.

'Nay, I shan't preach!' he said, smiling. 'A man's opinions and beliefs are his own business, but I never touch wine nor spirits.'

'I haven't given much thought to teetotalism,' Ambrose confessed, 'though it has become a very popular issue.'

'It's been going a while,' said Frank Ormerod, 'but it was the cholera that really persuaded folk. Heavy drinkers went down like ninepins with the cholera. I've not had much time to look about me, as yet, but I've been told there's a big teetotallers' society in Flawnes Green.'

'Ah well, there will be. Flawnes Green has been a Methodist stronghold for donkey's years,' Ambrose replied.

'I'm a Methodist, too,' said Frank Ormerod.

'I'm an atheist,' said Bob Bullock, defying anyone to tackle him.

'I'm a Catholic,' said Charlie self-consciously.

Unobtrusively, Walter set down a bottle of claret, two thick glasses, a tankard of foaming beer and a mug of thick sweet tea.

'Then I consider that *The Correspondent* is fortunate to have such a wide range of beliefs among its staff,' said Ambrose gracefully. 'I can almost match you in my own family. My maternal great-grandfather was an Anglican clergyman. My father was an atheist. And we have a fair sprinkling of Low Church and Quakers.'

A gust of cold air caused them to look up. Sam Pickering, caught off guard for once, had left the door open.

The two editors looked at one another for a long moment.

Then Sam shut the door, flipped his hat on to a peg and began to shrug off his overcoat with tremendous nonchalance.

'Good morning, Mr Pickering,' Ambrose called, pleasantly.

'Good morning, Mr Longe,' Sam called back, equally pleasant.

Preening the ends of his moustache, he strolled over to be introduced. His green eyes were pale and expressionless as he registered the strength of the opposition.

'All Manchester newspapermen, I see,' he commented. 'You've swum out of your way a bit, haven't you? Manchester's a big pond! Oh, Millbridge will be, given time. But it's a puddle as yet.'

The three men intimated, modestly, that Ambrose had made it worth their while to come so far. Ambrose smiled. Sam Pickering, however unwillingly, was impressed.

'First copy of *The Correspondent* comes out on Saturday, I believe?' said Sam. 'I shall look forward to reading it.'

'I'll send you a copy, Mr Pickering,' Ambrose replied.

'Thank you, Mr Longe. I'll send back a copy of *The Herald*.'

'Your usual corner, Mr Pickering?' Walter asked, appearing at the right moment. 'This way, sir. Any guests today, sir?'

'Two unexpected guests, as it happens, Walter,' said Sam, loud enough for them to hear. 'Our Member of Parliament and his personal secretary will be joining me in a few minutes.'

Oh, that's a point to Sam! thought Ambrose. But it did not diminish the feeling that all was well with his world.

The expression on old Walter's face was quite indescribable. This was the first time that Pendleton's had entertained a man of national note. He hastened to the kitchen to apprise them of the honour. In another moment the wooden tables were being given an extra polish, the fire made up quite unnecessarily, and Walter had gone down to the cellar himself to find a special bottle or two of wine, prior to bowing low before William Howarth M.P.

124

Sure enough, at twenty minutes past twelve, when the chop-house was thick with smoke and noisy with feet and voices, a white-headed giant paused tremendously on the threshold, deigned to enter, and was followed by an unctuous shadow.

For a couple of seconds, as the ironmaster met his nephew's bland, brown gaze, his brow furrowed and his mouth thinned. Then he recalled the value of good public relations and strode up, holding out his hand. The palm was soft, the nails manicured, but the grip was that of a blacksmith.

'How are you, my boy?' cried William, in a voice that caught the attention of everyone within earshot.

Ambrose responded with equal cordiality. In the background Walter waited, ready to escort the great man to the end of the room.

'Good to see you!' said William heartily.

His false teeth smiled splendidly on all. Even those who did not recognise him stopped with their forks in mid-air, aware that they were in the presence of an august personage.

The ironmaster nodded amiably at Ambrose's henchmen, to indicate that he wished them well but did not want to be introduced. Then, in the bustling wake of Walter, he walked majestically to Sam Pickering's corner table.

Due to the ironmaster's importance, *The Correspondent*'s order for four slices of jam roly-poly was slightly delayed, and accompanied by Walter's apologies.

'But I see that Mr Howarth is no stranger to *you*, Mr Longe,' he remarked with some deference.

'He is my uncle,' Ambrose replied, light and brief as became one who was so well connected.

An unexpected and unlikely foundation-stone had been laid for his reputation at Pendleton's.

The occupants of *The Herald*'s table were still eating when *The Correspondent*'s men prepared to leave. Once more, Walter came forward to help Ambrose with his coat, and this time stood on tiptoe to speak a confidential word in his ear.

'I just thought I'd mention, Mr Longe, that Pendleton's make one or two exceptions among their better customers – though that's not generally known, mind you, and when we're full up, we're full up. But if you send me word that you're coming in, any time before eleven o'clock of the same morning, I'll see that your table is kept, sir!'

It was one of those golden days, rare but precious in any man's life, when everything conspires to please him. A box of fine cigars was waiting for him on his desk when he returned, delivered by special messenger. An accompanying note, written in an elegant cursive script, read: *To the Editor of* The Northern Correspondent, *on his first working day.* It was signed, *Naomi Blüm.*

How long had it been since he smoked a cigar? He thought back and reckoned that the last one had been given to him by the ironmaster one Christmas Eve, seven years ago. He could never remember buying, or being given, an entire boxful. Obscurely gratified, he put them into an empty drawer of the desk and locked it.

Then, as he was penning a note of thanks, the two o'clock Leeds Mail rattled up from the turnpike road and stopped at the crossroads. Here an office-boy from each newspaper waited, on opposite pavements, pulling terrible faces at each other and shying the occasional stone. And when the lad scampered up the stairs he held letters from four of *The Correspondent*'s agents, each increasing the order for Saturday's edition. So Ambrose added the good news to his thanks.

The early dusk descended. Gas lamps were lit in streets and offices. Mail came in by the Manchester coach at five o'clock. Charlie Ainsworth delivered his first local report. Ambrose read and marked the London and provincial papers, sorting out material for his articles into separate piles, sketching out ideas for the inside pages. A rough outline of the first *Correspondent* was emerging.

At half-past five iron hooves and iron wheels proclaimed

that the kings of industry were driving home to dine in comfort. At six o'clock the factory whistles blew, and the cobbles rang to the tune of a few thousand clog-irons as their workers hurried back to cold poverty. The printing-presses completed their labours. The staff bade Ambrose and each other good night. Ambrose worked on.

This was his best and most peaceful time of day: the hour of assessment, correlation and creation. The office clock ticked on the wall, unheeded. Darkness fell. Lower Millbridge prepared to enjoy the delights of evening. And before the first thought of food or drink could cross his busy mind, there came a small boy from the Royal George delivering a tray of hot dishes under metal lids, covered with a clean white cloth.

'All ordered and paid for, Mr Longe,' said the lad, looking hopeful, and was dazzled by the three-penny bit which Ambrose bestowed upon him. 'I can collect the tray when the Preston coach goes out, at nine o'clock, if convenient.'

Another note was tucked between the Davenport fowl and the orange trifle. He broke the seal. Her three sentences conveyed three different messages from three sides of her character.

First, the woman.

I know you will work too late today and forget to eat.

Second, the friend.

Pray do not regard this as a form of intrusion, but as a sincere concern for your well-being.

Third, the financier.

If the promise of future sales is fulfilled, I will consider a further loan – and at seven per cent instead of seven-and-one-eighth per cent. Yrs. Naomi Blüm.

Across Ambrose's face flitted alarm, appreciation and finally amusement. He read the note again. This time he chuckled and shook his head. Then he poured himself a glass of chilled white wine and proceeded to do full justice to the Royal George's supper.

The day was not yet over, nor did he want it to depart. In

a new and delightful ritual he unlocked the cigar drawer, selected a fine specimen, shook and listened to it, smelled it, cut it, lit it and finally smoked it at his leisure.

At nine o'clock the lad came for his tray. At ten Ambrose buttoned up his mulberry great-coat, cocked his beaver hat at a fashionable angle and sallied forth, swinging his cane.

'Good evening, Mr Longe,' said a familiar voice.

He had descended from his own bachelor apartment on the top floor of his own office probably for the same reason as Ambrose: a breath of fresh air and a look round the town, after a long day's work.

'Good evening, Mr Pickering.'

They were both at a loss for a moment.

Then Ambrose said, 'If you're not going anywhere in particular, would you like to come to the Ship for a drink?'

He was aware that Naomi would have disapproved of this move and privately resolved not to tell her. Privately, he also wondered why he must resort to subterfuge.

'I don't mind if I do,' said Sam laconically.

They walked side by side, and Ambrose sought some topic of conversation which did not pertain to newspapers.

'Strange to think that this was part of a Roman road which connected Lancashire and Yorkshire once,' he said, striking the cobbles of Middleton Street lightly with his cane. 'What astonishing fellows they were! Building and marching their way across the Pennines in the mist and wet. Millbridge didn't exist then, except as a corn mill and a packhorse bridge. The town evolved a thousand years later. A thousand years!' He swung his cane up at the stars, as if to call them to witness. 'Later on the local farmers called this road Ship Street, because they drove their sheep along it to market. And here is an example of how the past stays with us, but in a slightly misunderstood form . . .'

He pointed to the swinging sign above the Ship tavern, which depicted a galleon in full sail.

'Fond of history, are you?' Sam asked, as they crossed the

128

threshold and entered a low room full of light and noise.

'Yes, when I am in a philosophical frame of mind. It puts time and ourselves into perspective,' said Ambrose.

The green eyes regarded him impassively.

'I study botany,' said Sam. 'I get that from my father. He'd walk miles to find a particular flower.'

'Ah, you have the advantage of me there. I am no countryman, either by birth or inclination. I was born in London, just off Fleet Street, and lived there until I was seven. I went back again as a young man, to be trained on *The Morning Post.* I like the mainstream of life.' He ordered a bottle of claret, saying, 'My treat, this time. Shall we sit over here out of the general fray?'

'I'm not a domestic man, myself,' said Sam. 'This is *my* sort of parlour.' Nodding round at the crowded tavern. 'I saw enough of cottage poverty when I was a lad not to inflict it on anybody else.'

'So the fair sex have no hold on you at all?'

'I don't mind a pair of arms in Flawnes Gardens,' said Sam, with a twinkle of humour. 'What about you?'

'I come into the same category,' Ambrose admitted.

'So do a lot of married men, and all,' Sam remarked. 'Which makes me wonder why they bother to saddle themselves with a wife and children in the first place.'

They finished their wine and took to the night again.

'When I was a lad,' said Ambrose, 'Lower Town was mostly fields.'

Now, offices and tenement houses shouldered the ancient corn market, once a centre of rural commerce. The High Street, so broad and fine in the Old Town, narrowed and darkened into a busy thoroughfare. Taverns proliferated. Mill chimneys mushroomed. To their left, the new railway line ran into the new station. To the right loomed the new gasworks. Millbridge Hospital stood on the hill above.

For an hour they explored side-streets, looked into shop windows, talking of everything but newspapers, until at last they came to a halt. Here, round the foot of the whole town, curled the great grey River Wynden – crowded by warehouses, jammed with barges, floating with a variety of refuse and the occasional drowned cat. On its opposite bank the turnpike road connected Millbridge with the outside world.

'Progress!' said Sam, in his dryest tone, surveying their miniature metropolis, 'I suppose we know what we're doing!'

'Oh, I doubt that exceedingly,' Ambrose answered. 'With rare exceptions, people are either opportunists or sheep. One lot grab what they can from life, the rest do as they are told. Neither group ever stops to consider the consequences.'

Sam smiled unwillingly and said, 'That's a good line, Mr Longe.'

'*My* line, Mr Pickering,' Ambrose replied, smiling back.

They parted at the crossroads, lifting top hats, expressing thanks for each other's company.

It was almost midnight. Ambrose stood back in Middleton Street to savour the full beauty of the offices of *The Northern Correspondent* by moonlight.

'And *that*, Sam Pickering,' said Ambrose to himself, 'is our first score settled!'

He was tired, but still he lingered, under pretence of finding his keys. Then the clock in the black church tower of St Stephen's struck twelve, to indicate that this dog had had his day.

Ambrose unlocked and opened his own front door.

At the Vivians'

chapter eleven

August, 1833

You could not wish for a more delightful house than the Old
Hall at Brigge, nor a more delightful couple than Mr and Mrs
Henry Vivian. Had an artist been painting that family group as
they sat on their front lawn, he could have named his picture
Idyll.

Pregnancy always suited Mary. She ripened and bloomed.
Her blue and white sprigged muslin gown complimented rather
than concealed her state. Her copper side-curls were caught up
with matching blue ribbons. Shaded by a parasol tied to the
back of her chair, she was engaged in writing her contribution
to *The Correspondent,* but from time to time she glanced up at
her husband and children, partly to make sure that all was well
and partly to share their enjoyment.

Hal Vivian, chief engineer and architect of the Wyndendale railway, had spent much of that summer Sunday afternoon
trying out another kind of railway. In his brief hours of leisure
this gifted man had made a scale model of his steam-engine
Pioneer and had ordered an ironworker at Snape to fashion ten
feet of metal track to the same specifications. Supported by a
series of wooden bricks, which could be removed or raised to
form different heights, the track sloped sufficiently to allow the
engine to trundle downwards in a highly realistic manner. The
Cornishman's alleged purpose was to show his children how to
play with this new toy, but as the afternoon waned they began
to realise that all railways were their father's province. They
stood by his side, watching him experiment.

Philomena, a solemn child of nine, had Mary's fine-boned

131

face but her hair was as black as that of the Cornishman. Strangers took her to be their daughter, though in reality she was Mary's adopted sister. She fell victim to every minor ailment, clung to her childhood, and needed much affection and coddling; whereas three-year-old Santo was a vigorous and sociable little fellow who longed to grow up. At this moment Philomena was contenting herself with wistful observation. But Santo clutched his hands so that they should not be tempted to touch the track and stamped his feet softly from time to time like an impatient little pony.

Two maids now came from the house, bearing trays, and Mary put her pen and paper away and called her family to the table. Hal Vivian strode over to sit in a wicker chair at his wife's side and accept a cup of tea, but the children soon ran back, gulping milk and nibbling bread and butter, to enjoy the railway undisturbed.

The Cornishman was brooding about something, looking uncommonly like his father the ironmaster. Mary's smile vanished. She loved him to excess and could be excessively hurt in consequence. He loved her too, but lived far more in a world of visions than in the world about him. They never quarrelled nowadays. There was nothing new to quarrel about. He went his way, and Mary occupied herself in trying to interest and please him.

'Is something troubling you?' she asked, wondering which thorn in his crown was pricking him at the moment.

'No, no,' he answered quickly, for he must respect her condition. Then, as the condition came uppermost in his mind, he said with some apprehension, 'Do you think it might be twins again?'

'Pray heaven not!' Her mock horror was not all mockery. 'No, no. For I'm not half as big as I was with Santo and Hannah. Goodness me, I was as big as a house with them. As big as the Old Hall itself!'

The Cornishman smiled. Her extravagance amused him.

Her chatter usually provided a cover beneath which he could think of something else, but her next remark brought him back to attention.

'I should so like another daughter,' said Mary quietly.

Cholera had taken its toll of their household, and a head-stone in Brigge churchyard marked the worst passage in their lives so far.

> Here lies Hannah Charlotte Alice,
> Daughter of Henry and Mary Vivian,
> Died 15 August, 1832, Aged 2 years, 7 months.
> Also her infant brother, Richard Edward,
> Stillborn, 17 August, 1832.
> 'The Lord Giveth, the Lord Taketh Away.
> Blessed be the Name of the Lord'
> Also Polly Slack, Servant and Friend,
> Died 20 August, 1832. Aged 70 years.
> 'Thy Will be Done.'

For a few moments sorrow joined them.

'How Naomi wept!' said Mary. 'I was past tears by that time. I could feel nothing. First, poor little Hannah, then my baby, and at last my dear old Polly who had nursed us all so faithfully.'

Hal Vivian put his hand over hers, saying, 'No more sad thoughts, love. The rest of us were spared, thank God. Drink your tea.'

She wiped her eyes with a little handkerchief, sipped and said, 'Oh, it is cold. Let us have a fresh cup.'

'Have you thought of names for the infant?' he asked, concerned to distract her.

She glanced at him shyly, sadly, because they had discussed this already, and she suspected that he never listened.

'A daughter would be *Alice*, of course, after my mother. And a son – well, I could not bear to call him Richard or Edward . . .'

133

Her lower lip trembled.

'My dear love, there is no need. There is many a Richard and an Edward among your father's family. Neither name will die out among the Howarths, at least!'

'You would not consider – since Uncle William is always so good to us . . .?'

'No, I would not. Besides, "William Vivian" is an awful mouthful. And there is another reason, with which I don't want to trouble you.'

But she knew she had to hear it. She begged him to tell her.

'The tunnel will not be finished. He has postponed the project indefinitely. Apparently he is finding politics a costly business. He himself has no money to spare, and so far he has not been able to interest other investors.' He added reluctantly, 'And I have not enough to carry the venture through, even if I dared spend more.'

'Lord, no. We have spent enough already!' Mary cried, aghast. 'The tunnel is worse than this house for wanting money spent upon it!'

She heard a lack of sympathy in her tone, and softened it.

'Still, I should have thought Uncle William would want to finish it, after all the work you have done already.'

He was silent for so long that she feared she had offended him. Then she realised, with a familiar pang, that he was not disturbed by her reaction but by his own thoughts.

'Mary, I have something to tell you. To ask you. To discuss with you. We need not be hasty in our conclusions, but I have been thinking of the future. There will not be enough work for me here now.'

'Do you want us to go abroad?' she asked, afraid.

'No, no, but I must do something. I have to earn a living. I have ideas to realise, plans to fulfil. I must work.'

'Has Uncle William offered nothing to keep you here?'

'What reason has he for keeping me in Wyndendale when

he lives in London for most of the year? He has offered me introductions down there, certainly.'

Her spirits rose a little.

'Are we to move to London, Hal?'

'No, I do not choose to be at his beck and call, either there or here. I shall go back to Manchester. I shall resume my old position in the firm of Vivian & Son, instead of being a sleeping partner.'

'You want us all to live in Manchester?' she asked miserably.

'I want to decide what is best for us all. We need not live in Manchester itself. There are charming properties only a few miles outside Manchester, in the countryside. When I was a boy we lived in Ardwick Green, and you could not have had a prettier prospect.'

He studied her downcast face and tried an alternative proposal.

'Or I can live above the office in Manchester during the week, and come home at the weekend, while you and the children stay here. I know you love this house, and value your family and friends.'

'Papa!' called Philomena. 'Papa! It's all Santo's fault!'

The engine, sent off with a strong push down a steeper incline, had tumbled over. Its wheels threshed in the grass.

Santo shouted, 'Papa! Papa! It wasn't my fault!'

'Oh, yes, it was!' said Philomena indignantly. 'Who put the bricks up too high, and didn't listen when I told him to be careful?'

Santo clutched his head in anguish as he bent to inspect the engine, then shouted with relief, 'His chimney's not bent, Papa! He's just spinning his wheels a little bit, as if he's cross.'

'No harm done!' cried the Cornishman cheerfully, jumping up.

He was reprieved. He kissed Mary's hand in contrition.

'Think it over, my love, and do what you think best,' he

said. Then to the children, 'All right, I'm coming.'

She was glad not to have to answer him straightway, for her response would have been unwise and bitter. To cover and soothe her feelings, she set the portable writing case on her knees and began to scribble and erase industriously. At first she crossed out more than she wrote, then her face and forehead relaxed, her interest was recaptured, and a calmer spirit ruled her.

Her husband, whose glances had been frequent and guilty, now settled down to the toy railway in earnest. This time, as though made aware that he did not consider others sufficiently, he allowed his children to take part. Certainly he was soon off in a realm beyond them, explaining about impetus and momentum, but they were happy to let him talk so long as they could play.

The tea things were carried away. Mary finished her article for Tuesday's *Correspondent*, laid down her pen and sat musing. She had come to the end of her tether with regard to Hal's moods and absences. She must find another way of conducting her marriage.

Think a problem through by writing it down, Aunt Charlotte would have said. Grandma Dorcas Howarth, faced with the uneasy choice of being a genteel spinster or the wife of a hill farmer, had written down the reasons for and against both states, counting the cost with cool veracity. Ambrose possessed that document now, locked away with Charlotte's papers. She would ask him to let her read it again. For the moment she must give Hal his liberty and give herself time to think.

The Cornishman now dared to rise to his feet, brush the grass from the knees of his trousers and approach his wife with a hopeful smile. Mary held out her hand in truce and he kissed it tenderly. She answered his unspoken question.

'I think it best if I stay here with the children for the time being, and you come home to us at the weekends, Hal.'

He sat down with such a sigh of relief that she knew this was what he wanted.

'*I* think that is the best solution, love.'

He was anxious that she should not think his attitude cold.

'Only for the time being, as you say!' he added. 'When the baby is older, and you are thoroughly recovered, you may decide to join me. We should get a good price for the Old Hall, and you can choose what you like in Cheshire. The climate there may suit you better. It is a milder county than Lancashire in every way.'

She knew that the selling of one house, the finding and buying of another, would be her responsibility. She knew that, bereft of friends and family, she would find life in a strange place even more lonely than it was at present.

'Let us give ourselves a year of grace in which to make up our minds,' she offered.

A slight breeze made her shiver. As he reached solicitously for her shawl, his attention was drawn to the writing case.

'Do you find this fellow a help?' he asked, gratified, for he had designed and made it many years ago for his own use when travelling.

'Indeed I do. I can carry it with me and write wherever I happen to be, and that is a great advantage.'

'Then you shall keep it for your own use, Mary.'

Her face was joyful.

'But how will *you* manage, love?'

'Oh, I shall make myself another. I shall have plenty of time,' he added thoughtlessly, 'when I am on my own in Manchester.' He saw her joy vanish and hastened to say, 'Is Ambrose pleased with your articles? You seem to spend a deal of time and trouble over them.'

Wearily she replied, 'I believe so. At least, Naomi and I are still employed, and he does not complain.'

'You, too, will have more time when I am gone,' said the Cornishman humbly. 'You spend your life on me and the children and leave nothing for yourself.'

She turned her face away, pretending to collect her papers

137

together. She willed her tears not to fall, and they did not, though her throat hurt.

'I know I am not the best of husbands,' Hal Vivian continued, still humbly, 'but I believe you knew my faults when you married me.'

'Oh, our trouble is an old one,' she answered, keeping her voice controlled. 'You want too little of me, and I want too much of you. And whereas your life has hardly changed at all, mine has changed altogether, and I cannot always find my way in it.'

He looked dark and lost, unable to help her.

She said more cheerfully, 'But that is a common problem in marriage. I shall come to terms with it, somehow.' She took the responsibility away from him. 'What fun it will be to look forward to each weekend! We shall have so much news!'

The need for tears had gone. Her natural good spirits rose again. She smiled upon him triumphantly, as though the idea had been hers and was good. Hal Vivian put his arm around her shoulders, drew her to him very lovingly, and kissed her upon the lips.

The indomitable engine ran down its rails for the thousandth time, heeled over on to the grass and stopped. Santo, red and belligerent, stamped with frustration. Philomena jumped up, white and fretful, and ran to Mary.

She whimpered, 'My legs ache, Mamma. They ache and ache!'

'The children are tired, love,' said Mary gently. 'Shall we take them inside?'

They made a delightful picture together: Mary and Philomena walking hand in hand, Santo riding on Hal's shoulders, against a background of the Old Hall, one evening in late summer at the Vivians'.

Page Seven

chapter twelve

The Northern Correspondent did not soar to fame and fortune in the first twelve months of its life, but it did slot into place as though a place had been waiting for it. Smaller and stouter than the usual newspaper, its distinctive masthead and spacious columns persuaded the casual reader to give it a try. Moreover, the times were with it. The flat rate duty on advertisements had been reduced from three-and-sixpence to one-and-sixpence in 1833, which meant a perceptible leap in the number of advertisers, and its front page now looked lively enough even to please Charlie Ainsworth.

Politically speaking, the Whigs shared with Ambrose a distinct taste for social reform. In one year they had emancipated slaves in the British Empire, passed a Factory Act and an Education Act and were now thinking of amending the Poor Law. Mind you, *The Correspondent* reserved the right to argue even as it approved. So it must point out that the slave-owners had been compensated to the tune of twenty million pounds; that the education grant in contrast was only twenty thousand pounds, and had been divided between two national societies whose system of teaching left much to be desired; and asked why Althorp's Factory Act did not apply to silk and lace mills as well as other textile businesses. But then, it was never satisfied.

The ironmaster's high-minded image of his *Herald* had vanished from the moment its rival came into being. It was all very well for Sam Pickering to cuff the ears of an impudent *Clarion*, but on a serious *Correspondent* he must wage total war. Without more ado William ordered his editor into the fray, and from this change of policy came Sam's sardonic nickname for his rival, *The Northern Weathercock*, to be capped by Ambrose's contemptuous sobriquet, *The Lancashire Flunkey*. Their sales went up in the valley as people scented battle. The two editors belaboured each other, but they were still far too nice for the ironmaster's liking. Brought up on purring matches, he wanted blood to flow, to hear the kicks and watch the throttling, to know that in the end one contestant would lie on the ground without strength to get up again.

So far the fight was clean and *The Correspondent* was doing well. Starting with *The Clarion*'s faithful thousand and moving out ever wider into the Lancashire world, its circulation had trebled, and its sales and reputation improved from week to week.

Perhaps Ambrose's happiest notion had been the employment of female reporters, particularly as they were unpaid, for between them Naomi and Mary took the burden of Page Seven completely off his shoulders. They organised and divided the work, wrote sprightly and legible copy which he seldom had to edit, put forward new ideas and undertook all social obligations.

Unobtrusively, Naomi was laying the foundations of a future music society in Millbridge and encouraging an interest in theatre, with a view to building a municipal cultural centre. Mary had introduced four new items to the Saturday edition. 'Household Hints' and 'My Favourite Recipe' were both supplied by readers, but she wrote 'Fashions of Today' and 'Health and Beauty for Ladies'.

From the moment these features were established, Saturday sales increased perceptibly and soon outdistanced those of *The Herald*, though that paper's mid-week edition sold far better than *The Correspondent*. This caused Ambrose some mild speculation. At sevenpence a copy only the prosperous bought newspapers lightly. Were *Herald* husbands indulgent enough to buy a Saturday *Correspondent* for their wives as well as a *Herald* for themselves, or did they give up one in favour of the other? He could not tell, but he certainly set down this success to the feminine appeal of Page Seven.

Despite his championship of women, he had experienced twinges of fear – knowing Mary, not knowing Naomi – that they might fail to keep a deadline or fill their columns, and consequently have a fit of hysterics in his office or be found in a swoon on the parlour carpet at home. Nothing of the sort had ever occurred. When they could not manage some assignment they found someone else who could.

His own niece, Dorcas Pole, now become Dorcas Standish, had been scurrying round for Mary since last September as that intrepid lady grew great with child. And late one Friday afternoon, while they awaited news of Thursday's debate in Parliament and wondered what had happened to the fashion column of Page Seven, young Dorcas stepped down at Cornmarket from the very mail-coach which brought the London papers, smiling in triumph. She had caught an early stage-coach to Manchester that morning, taking a maid-servant with her as chaperone, to view the latest collection of winter furs at Kendal, Milne and Barker in Deansgate. Since there was an hour or so to spare afterwards she walked round Manchester's shopping centre, filling a notebook with sketches and suggestions for family Christmas gifts. Then, as the coach jounced and rattled its way back home, she had composed her article and transcribed the result in a jerky but readable hand ready for press.

Dorcas admitted that the trip had been Mary's inspiration, but her air of modest self-importance told Ambrose that she was quite prepared to be praised for her own efforts. So he congratulated her, smiling to himself, and being in a hurry to put the paper to bed quite forgot to mention expenses.

The girl was too shy to ask, but Naomi was not. On the following day she presented Ambrose with a bill which he would have refused to accept from anyone else, and wrote out an official receipt which he shortly mislaid. Even so, he did insist that future expeditions should first be agreed with him, since this one had been unusually costly. Naomi's reply was firm.

'In the first six months of this year Mr Ainsworth has claimed thirty pounds seventeen and eightpence in travelling expenses. I should not have thought that one pound twelve and fourpence was excessive for one special occasion. Besides, Dorcas has furnished us with sufficient material for the Christmas Feature as well as the winter fashions.'

'I cannot afford to finance feminine whims,' Ambrose replied, equally firmly. 'Page Seven must first agree the necessity of such journeys with me – or I shall have Mary dashing off to report the London and Paris fashions and expecting *The Correspondent* to foot the bill!'

'You pay us nothing and grudge us expenses!' she cried, incensed. 'Admit that your entire female staff costs less than one reporter!'

But he would not let her have the last word.

'With regard to coach fares, ladies cost twice as much,' he observed mischievously, knowing this would annoy her. 'Whatever Charlie Ainsworth's expenses may be, he doesn't need a chaperone!'

Naomi had swept the sovereign and five half-crowns into her purse, placed twopence change smartly upon the desk and clipped her reticule shut. For the moment she had no answer, but would doubtless find one and keep it for a later occasion.

On that early January evening in 1834, Frank Ormerod gave the door a perfunctory knock and walked in, carrying a mocked-up *Correspondent* which he placed before Ambrose.

'It's looking good,' said Ambrose briefly, appreciatively.

'We're just being held up by the Manchester coach – and Page Seven again!' said Frank, slightly reproachful. 'The ladies have taken to keeping us waiting the last few weeks – as ladies tend to do.'

'Ah well, half of Page Seven has been lying in,' Ambrose replied, grinning. 'As ladies also do!'

142

Frank pursed his lips. He approved the childbed but not the journalism. His expression suggested that he had been right to doubt this eccentric appointment.

'Page Seven will soon be back on its four feet again, Frank,' said Ambrose easily. 'What are we having from Pendleton's tonight?'

For on Monday and Friday evenings at half-past nine o'clock two waiters trotted up to Middleton Street with hampers of hot food and the Ship Tavern sent over a firkin of home-brewed ale. Then everyone on *The Correspondent*, from editor to errand boys, sat down in the lower printing office and ate a hearty supper.

'Meat and potato pie, Mr Longe,' said Frank. He cocked his head listening. 'There's the mail!' Then in a moment or two, 'And this sounds like Page Seven!'

A quick light step sounded on the uncarpeted stairs. An unusually submissive knock heralded Naomi and her copy. She entered in a flurry of fur and velvet, bringing with her a cloud of cold air and a scent of violets. Her countenance was troubled.

'Late again, Page Seven!' cried Ambrose sternly, keeping a straight face. 'You have held up the entire newspaper. Frank here is at his wits' end. We really can't go on like this, you know.'

Naomi's conscience was stronger than her sense of humour. She took his mockery with perfect seriousness.

'I am *so* sorry. I cannot tell you *how* sorry. Mr Ormerod, to you I apologise a thousand times.'

'Once is enough,' said Ambrose briskly. 'All right, Frank, I'll let you have this as soon as possible.'

Frank gave him a short nod, and Naomi a deeper one, and shut the door behind him.

In his usual amiable tone Ambrose said, 'Naomi, for heaven's sake sit down and stop fussing. There's plenty of time. We haven't sorted out the parliamentary news yet!'

The office boy, out of breath and considerably powdered by *Herald* snowballs, slapped the newspapers down on Ambrose's desk and received an editorial stare of disapproval.

'Thank you, Jimmy. I hope Mr Pickering's lad looks worse than you do. Remember that the honour of *The Correspondent* is at stake!'

A wink accompanied the rebuke. The lad grinned shame-facedly and ducked out apologetically, but was heard to whistle on the stairs.

'Now, Page Seven,' said Ambrose, skimming through the copy, 'what do you mean by this disgraceful behaviour, eh? Have you been gadding about at the newspaper's expense?'

His gratitude and admiration for her were undiminished, but he no longer stood in awe of Naomi. Sometimes he wished she would take life more lightly. Her wit was neat and quick, her play of humour gentle. Her smile was lovely but rare, her conversation animated but never frivolous. Her attitude towards everything, from music to investments, was one of dedication and concern. Yet, as a friend, he found no worse fault in her. He could rest in her company and rely upon her wisdom and commonsense, whether she be in a worldly or womanly mood. He could tease her without mercy or compunction, and she did not mind a bit. Most of the time she did not realise that he spoke in fun, which was even better. He loved baiting her.

Now she answered, in her own defence, 'No, no, I do assure you. I have not been out of the valley for weeks. It was a coincidence that I arrived at the same time as the Manchester mail-coach.'

'I'm relieved to hear it,' said Ambrose gravely. 'I thought,' with an enquiring glance at her ensemble, 'that you had not only been reporting on winter furs but buying them as well!'

'Oh no, no!'

She was horrified at the suggestion. Her gloved hands fluttered in deprecation of the pelisse she wore, to indicate that it was old and unworthy.

'This I bought in London a long time ago, but of course you do not notice such things.'

144

As though he had never seen her before, Naomi came sharply into focus. She wore her mantle with the dignity of a high priestess. When she stood it flowed from her. When she sat it moved into graceful folds. Few women could have worn that shade of purple, fewer still possessed such amethysts. Her velvet bonnet, lined with lavender silk and trimmed with grey ostrich feathers, was in the latest fashion, but the face within was millennia old. Ambrose had seen its likeness depicted countless times on Eastern vases and tombs and tiles. He recognised the long and noble nose, the sombre eyes lined with black lashes, the strong curve of the eyebrows, the tender and heavy mouth. Strange to see such a face tied up in lavender ribbons and set off by three white silk roses.

He failed to notice that haste had made her complexion gleam and that lack of time had prevented her from repairing the damage with a *papier poudre*. The mole on her left cheekbone might be considered a blemish by some, but not by Ambrose. He thought her hands shapely rather than large. He would not have sacrificed an inch of her height, though only of medium height himself. The threat of too much flesh at a later date, if she did not take care, was of no concern to him.

She was his creation of this moment, and henceforth he would see her thus. And, as the years blurred her image, he could lay this picture over it and so renew her.

He became aware of two lustrous eyes staring back at him in captivated horror.

He said at random, pointing to the silk roses inside her bonnet, 'Those flowers are not real!'

Naomi moistened her lips and swallowed, unable to respond to such an absurd statement. Ambrose returned to the text of her copy and was unable to read it.

'How is Mary?' he asked, as casually as he could.

Naomi studied the tails on her ermine muff.

'Oh, she is taking longer to recover from this confinement than from the others. She is allowed to get up in the afternoons

145

now, but she tires easily. That is why I am late. I went over to the Old Hall to collect her copy, and found she needed me. I have been there for most of the day.'

Her voice strengthened during this recital. She was finding safety in the commonplace, after a perilous moment.

Ambrose said inwardly to himself, This cannot and must not be.

To her he replied, 'And how is young Charlotte?'

Naomi was momentarily bewildered.

'Isn't that the new infant's name?' he asked, embarrassed.

She gave a little laugh of amusement.

'No, no. Her name is *Alice*!'

'I can never remember all their confounded names,' Ambrose muttered. 'What with the Howarths, the Poles, the Vivians – and no doubt the Standishes in due course! – there are too many children in the family already!'

She passed over this remark, regaining confidence as he lost it.

'Alice Vivian is both healthy and hearty. A fine infant. And she seems, as far as one can judge, to have inherited Mary's bright hair.'

'Good God! What an affliction!'

'She is a very pretty baby,' said Naomi, now quite composed. 'Ah! I forgot! – I shall forget my head next!'

He dared to look at her again.

'But never your bonnet!' he countered swiftly.

She laughed. He smiled.

'I am forgetting to tell you that Mary and Hal wish us to be Alice's godparents. Mary says that you must not refuse her.'

Ambrose put down the sheets of paper which would become Page Seven in a few hours' time. He could not concentrate on them while she was there. He got up and strolled to the window, hands in pockets, and saw only her image superimposed on the bustle of Middleton Street.

'It is typical of Mary to pay lip-service to a title and ignore its meaning,' he began sarcastically.

The tone sounded wrong, false.

He said simply, 'To tell you the truth, I am not fit to be anybody's godparent. I am not even a convinced Christian. How can *I* be expected to take on a child's spiritual welfare?'

'But that is not why you have been chosen,' she answered. 'Mary knows what you are *not*. She wishes you to take a special interest in her child because of what you *are*. Because of what you can give.'

'And what am I? And what can I give that is of the slightest value?' he remarked bitterly.

He was not prone to ask such questions as this, rather to assume that there was no God, the world was a bad joke, and one must make the best of it. But he had just suffered a profound emotional upheaval.

She heard the trouble and fear in his voice.

'Do you not know yourself?' Naomi asked in surprise.

'I know I have not an atom of reverence in my nature!'

Naomi said, 'You know how to enjoy life. That is a great gift. Teach Alice how to delight in life also.'

He was moved and amazed. To make much of little, to transform nothing into something, had always come so naturally to him that he could not regard it as admirable. Immensely comforted, he returned to his chair.

He said, as airily as he could, 'Oh, that's my father in me. That's old Toby! My mother used to say that he could make a banquet out of a pie from the cookshop and a bottle of indifferent claret. But that's more of a knack than a virtue. I don't suppose it will help Alice Vivian to lay up treasure in heaven or on earth.'

Then he fell into the contemplative pools of her eyes, and floundered there.

Naomi rose gracefully, picking up her muff.

'You wish to get on with your work,' she told him. 'I will go.'

He hurried to open the door. He bowed deeply, reverently.

She inclined the brim of her bonnet in his direction. The roses shivered.

'Alice will be baptised very shortly. Shall I tell Mary that we both accept?'

He shrugged, endeavouring to be an old self which he feared had gone for ever.

'Oh, if it pleases her. Yes. Of course. But you can tell her from me that I think the whole thing is quite ridiculous!'

'Ridiculous, perhaps, but very necessary. Good evening, Ambrose.'

He now found himself unable to pronounce her name, so he caught up her hand and kissed it humbly.

He watched her descend the stairs.

Only when she was no more than a whiff of perfume did he return to his desk.

'It *is* ridiculous!' he assured himself. 'Damned ridiculous. Come to think of it, everything is ridiculous!'

He caught sight of the papers on his desk. He glanced at the clock on the wall.

'But very necessary!' he added.

He began to read Page Seven.

Flesh and Blood

chapter thirteen

On Mondays and Fridays *The Correspondent*'s presses were busy with her own concerns until the early hours of the following morning. During the three remaining weekdays they worked steadily on other people's printing until six or seven o'clock at night, and left the evening to Ambrose to spend as he pleased. So it became known that if you wanted a private word with Mr Longe, whether it be a small grievance of watered milk or a larger one of social injustice, you could best hold his attention when the presses were silent. In fact, if he wanted any privacy at all except in his sleep, Ambrose soon realised that he must find it away from No. 21 Middleton Street.

Over the past year, according to his mood, he had divided his free time between Mary, Naomi, and a certain lady in Flawnes Gardens, but in his present state of disturbance he could do none of these things. Delicacy forbade him to approach Naomi, Mary's eyes and intuition were far too sharp, and the thought of Mrs Evans made him feel uneasy. He was, therefore, liable to be troubled, and a series of double knocks at ten o'clock one gusty February night hardly surprised him. He would have liked to ignore the summons, but a sense of duty fetched him downstairs, candlestick in hand.

'Who is it?' he called, pausing at the front door.

The stranger apparently bent down and applied his mouth to the keyhole, answering in such a hurried and embarrassed fashion that Ambrose could not catch the name.

'Who did you say?' he enquired. 'Cuzzins?'

The man again applied himself to the keyhole and enhanced his original statement, but no more intelligibly.

'Would you mind speaking a little more slowly?' Ambrose asked.

His visitor sighed like the wind, but replied syllable by syllable, patiently and hollowly through the keyhole.

'It's your cousin George. Dick Howarth's lad. From Kit's Hill.'

'Oh, George, of course!' said Ambrose, trying to remember which one of Dick's seven sons he could be. 'George, to be sure. Hold on, George, while I unbolt the door. You must forgive me for being so uncommonly cautious, but I have to take care who I let in at this time of night, in this part of town.'

The voice, deep and laconic, said, 'Aye, I know.'

He had stood back while the bolts were shot. Now he came shyly into the hall, pulling off his cap. Ambrose reckoned him to be in his twenties, but like many a working man he looked older than his years. Though the night was raw he wore nothing more protective than a brown fustian jacket and a muffler. His hands and face were scarlet with cold, and he wiped an incipient drop from the end of his nose. He was short for a Howarth, but his thatch of wheaten hair and straight blue gaze were pure Howarth, and he held himself as tall as he could.

So far as Ambrose knew they had never met before, but he shook the proffered hand, said he was looking well, and invited him to come upstairs into the warm.

They mounted two flights in silence. Ambrose's slippers flapped in homely fashion on the uncarpeted stairs, but George's boots creaked and echoed; and his breath came short and heavy with unease, like that of a man who has run a long way.

'Here we are!' cried Ambrose heartily. 'Come, draw up that other chair for yourself and I'll mull some ale. Should you like that?'

Again the laconic answer came, 'Aye, I would.'

Then George sat down and pushed his cap into his pocket and held out his hands to the blaze.

Not a tremendous conversationalist, Ambrose thought. If this is a family visit it's going to be a heavy one!

He thrust a poker into the heart of the fire and poured out two tankards of the Ship's best ale.

'And to what do I owe this unexpected pleasure?' he asked, with automatic courtesy.

George considered the question. His reply, when it came, was truthful rather than polished.

'Nay, it canna be any pleasure to you. We don't even know each other in a manner of speaking. I only saw you two or three times when I were a little lad. And I haven't come to talk of pleasure, neither. I've come on a matter of business.'

'I see,' said Ambrose, amused by his honesty. 'Well, now you mention it, George, you're perfectly correct. I don't know you from Adam. Which son are you?'

'I were the fourth lad. The one as went for a drummer-boy the year my Mam died. I come back when my time were up. I wouldna have stayed longer, not if they'd hung every hair of my head with a golden sovereign. I come back three year since, and it were then as they told me she were dead.'

He paused and brushed his sleeve across his eyes. It was a very simple gesture, and without shame.

'But there warn't no place for me at Kit's Hill. Our Hatty's taken over! She might be Fred Tunstall's wife but he's not her master. Nor's our Dad. And our Mary's got that grand! I hung about her place for a while, but in the end I dursen't knock. So I cleared off and looked up our Dickon and our Willum and our Edwin, and they got me a job at the colliery on Swarth Moor. I haven't been back since.'

'I see,' said Ambrose, who did not.

The ale hissed round the hot poker.

'Drink up!' said Ambrose.

George drank loudly and appreciatively, drawing breath between each sup and staring into the flames. He grew grave with reflection.

'What might you call them coals, Cousin Ambrose?' he asked quietly, pointing to the fire in the grate.

'That's Wigan coal. The best I can buy,' said Ambrose easily.

The blue eyes looked at him steadily above the scarlet cheeks.

'That's flesh and blood,' said George Howarth.

Ambrose sat down, silenced.

'This newspaper of yourn,' George continued, his tongue loosened at last. 'It's not what you'd call a working man's paper, is it?'

'No. But it speaks for the working man.'

'Aye. I thought that'd be the case. But it's bought and read by t'others, isn't it? The masters? Them as might do summat for working men if they liked?'

'Yes, and I hope that *The Correspondent* will eventually have some influence over them.'

'That's what I hope, and all!' said George with a touch of humour, but he found life too hard to take lightly.

He set down his pewter tankard and drew a sheaf of soiled and crumpled papers from the breast of his jacket.

'I haven't had what you'd call an eddication, but it's the truth as I've set down there. You've had an eddication, haven't you?'

'Yes,' said Ambrose, taking the papers with reluctance.

'Then make summat of that,' said George. 'I've wrote down what I know to be truth, and what I feel. The words don't allus come right but you'll get the meaning. I don't mind if you turn it upsides down and insides out, so long as you make sense of it and print it. I want folks to know what's going on. I want them to feel whenever they see coals in the grate as them coals is flesh and blood. That's what I come to tell you.'

He drained the last of his ale and stood up. He pulled his cap from his pocket and settled it dead straight on his head. His appearance was both earnest and comical.

'I'd best be off,' said George. 'Thankee for making me welcome.'

Ambrose's conscience was stricken. His welcome had been

courtesy of the emptiest kind. He put a restraining hand on George's sleeve.

'Won't you stop a bit longer and tell me more about this?' he asked, indicating the sheets of paper. 'Why, we haven't finished the ale, and you've told me nothing about yourself. I don't know where you live or whether you're married. Sit down, man, for heaven's sake!'

George hesitated, and again his honesty made nonsense of good manners.

'Nay, I'm no talker, cousin. And I've done what I come for. You've hearkened to me and I canna ask more nor that. I know as you and our Aunt Charlotte have spoken up many a time for the likes of us, but you're not one of us. I walk on t'other side of the street, as you might say. We're as different as chalk and cheese, thee and me.'

'Very well,' Ambrose replied, with equal frankness. 'We have nothing in common. But we share the same grandfather, and we care what happens to our fellowmen. Won't that do for a start?'

George's eyes became bluer, his face a deeper shade of red. He moved from one foot to the other, pondering. Then he snatched off his cap, stuffed it back in his pocket, and sat down again, breathing hard. Ambrose mulled more ale and endeavoured to mine some information out of this taciturn relative.

'I'm a bachelor, myself. Are you married, George?'

'Nay, I've got more to do than get wed.'

'Ah. I live alone here. Do you live with your brothers?'

'Nay. Our Edwin died of the cholera, and our Dickon and Willum emigrated two year since. To Americky.'

Ambrose maintained a few seconds' silence for the news of Edwin.

'A great many people are emigrating nowadays. Didn't you want to go with them?'

'Who, me? Nay, I'm not running away from owt. I've got summat to do here!' He paused then and added reluctantly,

153

nodding his head towards the papers on Ambrose's desk, 'Every word of that's the truth, but I dursen't put my name to it, else I'd lose my job.'

'I understand that. You needn't worry. I shan't mention names.'

George seemed unwilling or unable to part with more words at the moment, so Ambrose tried again.

'What is it that you feel you must do, George?'

The man looked up, and said simply, 'Tell folks. I must tell folks how it is. For they canna know, or they'd do different by us.'

'Would you mind if I read your article now?' Ambrose asked. 'I should have a better idea what you're talking about.'

George shrank a little at the thought of such public exposure, but nodded. He watched apprehensively as Ambrose began to decipher his cramped writing, and after a minute or so he burst out defensively.

'I can but print my letters!'

'I prefer printing,' Ambrose replied. 'Some people's handwriting is so difficult to read.'

His face changed. He settled back in his chair, leaving his ale untouched, and read on to the end in complete absorption. When he looked at his cousin again it was with amazement and respect.

'I shall publish this as it stands,' he said.

'What?' cried George indignantly. 'Put me to shame? The masters won't take no notice of a working man's words! If you do it proper they'll read it proper.'

'They'll read it as it is,' Ambrose replied just as fiercely. 'I'm not serving it up on a china plate. I'm going to shove it down their throats and hope it sticks!'

George leaped out of his seat, jerked his cap from his pocket and struck it against his thigh with frustration.

'Dang me!' he swore under his breath. 'And I thought as I could trust him!'

154

'Man, man, you have a gift of expression which I wish to God was mine. I'm a good journalist by any standards. Now and then I can be very good. But I haven't your power of expression. To polish this article in the way you mean would be to spoil it and weaken its case. I publish it as it is, or not at all. Take your choice.'

George simmered for a couple of minutes. Then he glanced sideways. He made up his mind.

'You're not having me on, are you, cousin?' he asked shyly.

'No, I'm not. I'll tell you something else. I'd be prepared to help you with your schooling, and later to employ you on the paper. It would take time and hard work, but you'd make a splendid journalist. That's my opinion. There's my offer. The rest is up to you.'

The meaning of the words had penetrated at last. George breathed harder. His eyes fairly bolted with pleasure. Evidently praise did not usually come his way. He fairly twirled his cap between his hands in an effort to contain himself. When he did speak he did not look in Ambrose's direction but straight ahead.

'You've knocked me all of a heap, cousin,' he admitted. 'Nobody called me owt but a clown afore. I'm right grateful to you. I'd be glad of the schooling. I feel, many a time, like a workman wi' poor tools. If the tools was good I could say more. Thankee.'

Then he managed to turn and look his benefactor face to face.

'But I shan't work on no newspaper,' he said emphatically. 'I'm not here for that. I could get led astray. I'm here to speak out as a working man, for working men.'

Ambrose was impressed and annoyed at the same time.

'Don't belittle other men's gods, George!' he said, light but firm. 'There's no finer weapon, to my mind, than a great newspaper. *The Correspondent* has a long road to travel before she becomes what I want her to be, but she'll get there in the end.'

George was watching his lips as well as his expression, unused to all this verbal play.

'Well,' he said finally, 'no offence meant, and none given, I hope, cousin. Only, I'm a working man and that's *my* road. Eh! Look at t'time. I must be off. I'm on t'six o'clock shift at Prospect!'

'Half a minute, George. Give me your address.'

The man printed it laboriously at the bottom of the sheet, adjusted his cap and muffler and followed Ambrose down the stairs. At the front door they shook hands: Ambrose warmly, George solemnly.

'It's a dirty night, I'm afraid,' said Ambrose, of the raw wind, the driving rain.

Time and place being creations of the mind, George replied, 'Nay, I shan't notice owt. I'st be tramping in good heart. Nor wind nor rain can mither me now. It's the best night o' my life, cousin.'

Ugly Days
chapter fourteen

The Northern Correspondent   *10 February, 1834*

A Prospect of Hell

A sound education is a vital tool with which we can fashion and improve the lot of mankind, and we shall not be satisfied until every citizen in this country can regard it as a birthright. Nevertheless, the most rudimentary learning can serve the ends of humanity, truth and justice. The following article has been written by a collier, and is printed exactly as it was received by us, without alteration or amendment. It is an essay from Hell itself.

The lot of our colliers on Swarth Moor is so harsh that they are brutal even to each other. Cruellest of all is the plight of their women and children. Little creatures of six work thirteen hours a day in the dark. Their mothers, even in an advanced state of pregnancy, crawl along tunnels dragging a heavy wagon behind them by means of a chain fastened round their waists. And all of them toil underground in conditions of total degradation, for the few shillings each week which keep them badly fed and badly sheltered.

Have they committed some abominable crime to be treated in this fashion? No! They are suffering because they had the misfortune to be born poor and powerless! We have recently emancipated negro slaves in our colonies abroad, but here at home a vast army of industrial workers are slaving their short and wretched lives away in conditions as harsh as any negro suffered.

What is the reason for this state of affairs? It is that a few rich and powerful men, standing high in public esteem, are making profits at the expense of an underprivileged majority. It is horrifying to think that we daily warm ourselves on the misery of our fellows. But if, knowing what we do, we continue to ignore their plight, we shall be as guilty of inhumanity as those who abuse them.

In view of the evidence given here, we demand that the local authorities investigate the collieries of Swarth Moor. Furthermore, we urge the government to set up a Royal Commission to examine working conditions in all collieries, for our own cannot be the only running sore in the country.

Then followed, George's *Flesh and Blood.*

The ironmaster flung *The Northern Correspondent* down upon Sam Pickering's desk and stamped round the office in a rage. His mood, veering from the defiant to the defensive, was laced with venom.

'That miner, whoever he is, is a liar, bribed by my nephew to damage me. Find him and sack him! For God's sake why did none of my own people tell me this? Do folk think I have the time to amble round Swarth Moor, inspecting my investments? Great Heaven, how will this sound in Parliament? Everybody knows that some of these are *my* collieries! Ah! I'll have that nephew of mine hanged yet!'

Then he wheeled upon his silent editor, crying, 'Well, what are you going to do about it, Sam? Sit there with a smile on your face while this radical rag smears me?'

Sam Pickering's light green gaze remained cool. He pulled his moustache thoughtfully, watching his master.

'We'd best investigate the matter for ourselves first,' he remarked. 'We can say nothing until we've got the facts right.'

'Facts? Facts? This Longe fellow is out to ruin my political reputation! It is obvious that I am one of the men he mentions. He even makes a pun on the name of one of my mines! I call that libel!'

158

'He hasn't mentioned *your* name, and how do we prove that "Prospect" was a pun, Mr Howarth? He seems to be more careful than he used to be! What's more, if it's the truth then it isn't libellous. But, either road, it does you no good, as you say.'

'Snape is a model ironworks! I am among the foremost masters in the country for workmen's benefits and improvements.'

'It isn't Snape he's talking about.'

'My collieries on Swarth Moor are merely an investment.'

'If you make money out of them, Mr Howarth, you're liable to be thought responsible for the way they're run.'

'Which, I daresay, is no worse than the way others are run.'

Sam's moustache was receiving an unusual amount of exercise.

'If the other collieries are run like this,' he remarked, 'there's bound to be a national investigation sooner or later.'

'Stop telling me what I already know, for God's sake, Sam.'

'I'm thinking what I can do, you see, Mr Howarth. It's no good me saying black's white when I'm liable to be proved wrong! That makes the pair of us look guilty, and there's the reputation of *The Herald* to consider, and all.'

This silenced William.

Then Sam said, 'How about giving me a statement for *The Herald*, Mr Howarth? Something on the lines of being shocked and appalled to realise what's going on, and you're ordering an immediate enquiry. We'll remind them what you've done for the district of Wroughton – workmen's cottages at low rents, medical benefits, cricket club, brass band, public park, and all. Then we'll run a series of articles on the improvements you're making at Swarth Moor – which you'll have to do, Mr Howarth, to get the story to stick. I can't see any other way.'

'And what about my damned committee and my damned shareholders? I don't *own* Swarth Moor, Sam. I'm simply a major investor.'

'Aye, but you can be – persuasive,' said Sam, smiling.

The ironmaster took a briefer, quieter turn about the

office, and fetched himself up short at the window, hands clasped behind his back. *The Northern Correspondent* advertised its presence blatantly. He gazed upon its whitened bricks with furious eyes.

'He couldn't do it without her money behind him,' he remarked.

Ambrose had set forces into motion which were to prove beyond his control. He had expected the coal magnates of Swarth Moor to defend their position. Instead, they attacked.

The ironmaster, too, was having his problems, for he found his committee far less sensitive to public opinion than he was himself. Due to the diligence of *The Correspondent*, and the new Factory Act, a number of members were being investigated already. Arnold Harbottle, one of the richest men in Wyndendale, had three cotton mills under government scrutiny and was the first to speak.

'It's time we put a stop to this social reform nonsense. If the Whigs and radicals have their way we'll *all* be poor. As it is, *some* of us has something!

'There's two good reasons why we can't afford to alter the present colliery system. Number One is plain arithmetic. Shorter hours, higher wages, or the loss of cheap and unpaid labour – which is women and children – means less profit. Less profit means lower dividends to the shareholders. Lower dividends means they'll take their money elsewhere. If we're not careful we'st be out of business altogether.

'Number Two is common sense. You can't deal with a factory worker or a collier the same way as you deal with other folks. They're not human beings like us, they're animals. They've got no morals. Their women are all whores, and their whelps are thieves. As for the men – why, I never knew such foul and filthy beasts. And all that prate about inhumanity! If you want to see proper inhumanity you turn a working man into an overseer and see how he treats his own kind!

'It beats me how anybody can print such bloody rubbish after what happened with the Luddites in 1812. It was villains like these colliers as set fire to my father's mill, and burned his house down and murdered him. And I'll tell you this, if we give our workers an inch less stick, or an inch more kindness, they'll do it again.

'Now, Will, let's talk straight. It isn't the first time we've had trouble from *The Correspondent*, and it won't be the last. Ambrose Longe is related to you. Why don't you stop his mouth?'

He flung himself back in his chair, acknowledging the applause with a grave nod. He had spoken in the mood of the meeting.

'So far my nephew has failed to respond either to friendly or hostile overtures on my part,' replied the ironmaster coldly.

'Maybe you wasn't hostile enough!' remarked another member, and raised a laugh which was ugly rather than amused.

'Well, blood is thicker than water,' said Arnold Harbottle, smiling. 'We can't expect Will to try as hard as *we* might.'

A curious sound, as of bees swarming, warned the iron-master that the meeting was not on his side.

'While agreeing in general with Arnold's statements, I think it advisable,' cried the ironmaster, over the hum of comment, 'to prepare for investigation on a local and possible even a governmental level. I suggest we inspect working conditions at Swarth Moor and then convene another meeting to discuss what needs to be done.'

'Why?' asked Arnold Harbottle pugnaciously. 'I don't give a bugger what the conditions are like!' He pointed one forefinger directly at the ironmaster. 'I'm not going to spend time and money for the sake of whitewashing *your* reputation!'

This was open war indeed. William Howarth, undisputed lion of every industrial committee in the valley for twenty years, now heard the roar of a younger lion.

161

'Then what exactly do *you* suggest we do?' he asked, biting off every word.

'Hire the bully boys,' said Arnold briefly, 'and shut everybody up. That miner, for one. Ambrose Longe, for another. And anybody else connected with *The Correspondent* who could be persuaded.'

'You realise, I suppose, that public opinion would be strongly against that sort of behaviour?' William demanded.

'I've said – I think you didn't hear me, Will – I don't give a farthing dip for public opinion. *I'm* not a Member of Parliament! I mind my own business. Let everybody else mind theirs. That's my motto. Why don't we put it to the vote?'

The response was instant.

'I will have nothing to do with this,' said William decisively.

'You don't have to,' said Arnold, counting the forest of raised hands. 'I've told you. We'll get somebody else to do the dirty work.'

'So long as we can't be charged with aught illegal!' interjected a more cautious member, wavering.

'We shan't be within sniffing distance of the law,' Arnold replied. 'I know a chap who takes care that even *he's* not found out, never mind us! If any of his lads get caught they take the blame, and he looks after their families until they get out of jail again. It'll cost us plenty of brass but it's worth the expense.'

They began with what they considered to be the least powerful link in the chain. Less than a week later, George Howarth was fetched up from the four-foot seam and left for dead on the floor of the boiler-house. By tacit consent everyone ignored him, but when he did not return from his shift at teatime his landlady sensed that something was wrong. George had few friends, but she was one of them. In strictest confidence he had reported his meeting with Ambrose Longe, and had later shown her – in pride and trepidation – its result. So she waited for two hours

162

in mounting suspense, and then sent her eldest boy to the offices of *The Northern Correspondent* with an urgent message.

The ambivalence of the ironmaster's nature was here most clearly delineated. His decision to take no part in the affair had been mainly a question of prudence. He had no objection to Ambrose and his accomplices being punished, but he intended to remain blameless. Indeed, he had already decided that he would condemn any acts of aggression in the columns of *The Herald*, thus giving himself and his newspaper a reputation for fair play.

Another side of his nature unwittingly assisted his nephew. For a long time he had been in favour of policing streets to keep them safe. When the London Peelers came into being in 1829 he had renewed his efforts, and Millbridge had recently become one of the first provincial communities to have its own small police force. Consequently, Ambrose Longe arrived at the ironmaster's mine that evening with a couple of the ironmaster's peacekeepers at his side.

It is strange how the many are held in check by the few. The three men could so easily have been thrown down a disused shaft, and nobody would have been any the wiser. By himself Ambrose might very well have suffered that fate, but the sight of his two constables, top-hatted and smartly dressed, holding leather truncheons at the ready, caused minds to change and tongues to wag.

George's body was suddenly discovered, wrapped tenderly in a couple of old sacks and brought out on an improvised stretcher. Six miners were produced to give evidence of a roof-fall in the four-foot seam, from which they had rescued their comrade at the risk of their own lives. While they were giving false evidence Ambrose took down their words in shorthand, and the constables made notes. A hospital wagon was sent for, and George was jolted the six long miles to Millbridge Hospital, mercifully unconscious for most of the way.

He came to for a moment or so when they arrived, recognised his mentor and tried to speak. Ambrose bent over to listen.

'I were feared – when you called it – *Prospect of Hell* – as the masters'd guess – where I worked . . .'

Ambrose's face changed. He had been too clever for George's good.

He knelt and spoke softly into the bruised ear, 'May God forgive me, George. I meant it to point to my uncle.'

'Well – it pointed – the way to me – but dunnot fret thysen – that lot'd have found – a needle in a bloody 'aystack,' George whispered. Making a final effort, he added, 'Take care of thysen – they said as I was – only the first – and they mean it – cousin.'

The information was given factually and without reproach, and George managed a nod before he foundered again.

Ambrose drew back ashamed and afraid. In truth, he had neither expected nor encountered such a savage reaction before. The weapons of newspapermen are words. So far even the most pugnacious readers had contented themselves with knocking his hat off or pushing it down over his eyes. Only once had he been struck with an umbrella. It seemed that those gentlemanly days and ways were done. Mutely, he sat by the humble hero and waited for Jamie Standish's verdict.

'This man's injuries are unlikely to be the result of a roof-fall – that would damage a particular portion of the body, and they are too multiple and diverse. Also, he bears the marks of different weapons. I would say he has taken a professional beating, administered by fists and boots, a chain, and blunt instruments.'

'Would you be prepared to testify to that in court?'

'I would. In fact, when I have prepared a detailed report I can send you a copy.'

'Did they intend to kill him?'

'He would have died if he had been left without succour long enough, certainly. But I think not. I believe they meant to incapacitate him and break his spirit. He will bear some of these marks for life.'

'Poor George!' said Ambrose to himself. Then to Jamie,

'Do the best you can for him. No expense spared. Send the bill to me.'

In view of George's warning, he ordered and waited for a hackney-coach to take him safely home. Nothing and no one stirred in the early hours of that Friday morning in Middleton Street. Ambrose entered the offices of *The Correspondent* unhindered and unscathed, double-bolted the front door and took refuge in his eyrie at the top of the house. There he spent the rest of the night writing a new leader, and had a nap at daybreak.

Shaved and breakfasted, he considered the situation from every possible angle. He was not only shocked but puzzled by the physical violence. The ironmaster's tactics, though they could be dirty, were usually more subtle. Well, *The Correspondent* had set her course for good or ill. There was no turning back.

'... but we shall not be intimidated!' Ambrose told his assembled staff. 'Our Saturday edition will publish full details of the affair, giving the identity of the miner involved, and urging an official enquiry into the supposed accident at Prospect Mine. By this evening we shall be able to include a detailed medical report from Dr Standish, and his professional opinion as to the true cause of George Howarth's injuries. Finally, we shall ask our readers why this man should be beaten almost to death, and what his attackers could hope to gain from it.

'Now, while our enemies pursue their present policy, none of us can consider himself safe. Even *The Correspondent* herself is at risk. Machines could be broken, the offices damaged or set on fire. We must find ways to protect ourselves. There are two obvious ones. No one must enter this building without his business and identity being checked – and no one must leave the building, except in the company of others. I shall presently be conferring with Mr Bullock, Mr Ormerod and Mr Ainsworth about this. In the meantime, if you have any good ideas of your own – speak up!'

The silence that followed was most eloquent. Then the

least important member of staff did speak up, and poignantly.

'Who's going t'help me punce that lad on t'*Herald*, Mr Longe? He's bigger nor me, though I *can* run faster!'

Laughter relieved them all. They patted Jimmy's head and slapped his back, and pretended to square up to him in sporting fashion.

'I wasn't referring to *The Herald*, you blithering young idiot!' Ambrose cried, though he could not help smiling. 'And if I catch you saying so I'll box your ears properly!'

Arnold Harbottle may not have been concerned with public opinion, but others were or had to be. The ironmaster, through the columns of his newspaper, professed himself amazed and horrified by the reports of bad working conditions at Swarth Moor, reminded everyone of the earthly heaven he had created at Snape, and promised to enquire into the matter personally.

The assault on George Howarth he regarded in quite a different light. Though George was William Howarth's nephew the relationship was never mentioned, and *The Herald* dodged the tell-tale surname by referring to him as 'a collier'. At first Sam Pickering hinted that the injuries were probably sustained during a drunken brawl. Then, as evidence to the contrary mounted, he chose to ignore the embarrassing implications of George's affair in favour of a general campaign against hooliganism, with special mention of the ironmaster's part in establishing a local police force.

The Correspondent proved that George was attacked, but was unable to find the attackers. No case could be made in court, nor could they on such slight evidence accuse the Swarth Moor magnates of conspiracy. This left them open to harassment. So Ambrose affected to join *The Herald* in campaigning for safe streets and, under cover of his own leading article, told his enemies that *The Correspondent* was on guard, and that the police were keeping an eye upon its premises at night.

For a couple of weeks an uneasy stalemate prevailed. Then

the long silence between Ambrose and Naomi was broken by her calling on him at the office. Since that fateful Friday afternoon she had taken care that Mary should deliver Page Seven, so for a moment he was torn between confusion and joy. Her first sentence dispelled both sensations.

'Ambrose, I think someone is trying to frighten me!'

They had succeeded. Her face was sallow and heavy, her eyes deep-sunk as though she had not slept.

'Sit down and tell me,' Ambrose said, and felt cold.

As she talked, head bent, she peeled off her gloves, finger by finger, and then smoothed them on again.

'I feel I am being watched, followed. Mostly after dark. Once I saw a face at the window. Sometimes I think there are figures in the shadows. Of course, we have Joseph in the house. The doors and shutters are bolted at night. No one has actually tried to break in. But I know you are all in danger, because of what you wrote about George Howarth in *The Correspondent*, and from what Mr Pickering says in *The Herald*. These are ugly days. And I am afraid, Ambrose, in case these people are going to punish me for lending you money. I have this feeling – and I cannot help it – that something terrible will happen. Do I sound foolish? Am I imagining things?'

He knew the answer, but not what he should say to her.

'Of course, the George Howarth affair was bound to upset you,' Ambrose began, diplomatically, 'and when we know such things are possible we tend to think the worst. But Millbridge has always had its share of rogues and footpads – you may well have glimpsed one of them. Certainly, you should continue to take all the usual precautions – and if you go out in the evening use your carriage and arm your manservant. The new station-house is not far from you, at the end of the High Street. I can ask one of the constables to keep a regular watch on Thornton House for a while, if you wish – just until this general unpleasantness has blown over. Otherwise I should advise you to enjoy sound nights and peaceful days, and forget about it.'

Naomi stared anxiously at him, trying to read his expression, but Ambrose was a master of concealment. After a moment or two she sighed, smiled and sat back in her chair.

'Of course, you are right. My nerves are shaken. I am sorry to have troubled you, but I had no one else to turn to.'

'Had you not?' Ambrose enquired, astonished at his unexpected eminence in her life.

'Why, no. Who should I ask? My poor Mary? She also lives alone – at least for most of the time. Your uncle? He is cool towards me these days – and with some cause, I must agree! My acquaintances in the High Street? The old ladies over the tea-tables? My servants?'

Then she became aware that her tone was high, that she was perhaps expecting too much of him.

'You are always busy and I must go,' said Naomi, rising. 'Ah! Once more I forget. I came to bring you our copy.'

He took Page Seven and set it down on his desk without a glance.

'Like me,' he said, 'you appear to have everything you want. But what we call our solitude is often loneliness, and then the much we have seems very little.'

'What little?' she cried, firing up in defence of her solitude. 'I need nothing. I need no one.'

'Well, you needed me – or at least,' correcting himself hastily as he read her expression, 'my advice.'

'We are good business friends,' said Naomi, very firmly indeed, 'and now I leave you to your work!'

She did not wait for him to open the door. With amusement and chagrin he watched it close behind her. He walked over to the window, hands in pockets, to glimpse her sweeping out into Middleton Street. He saw her stop and look questioningly at a shabby fellow lounging on the street corner, shake her head as if to chide her fears, seat herself gracefully in the carriage, and order Joseph to drive away.

Ambrose scrutinised the fellow too, but no one could have

said whether he meant any harm by being there. After a while the man detached himself from the wall and walked off whistling, in the opposite direction from that of Naomi's carriage.

Help! Murder! Thieves!

chapter fifteen

A sound as of quiet footsteps on the stairs. The wind grumbling in the chimney. The shutters talking back. The creak of a door bolt, straining against its bonds. All these are nothing to those who sleep fearlessly, but when violence has been done and promised to be done, then sleepers tend to start awake and people the void with fears.

So Ambrose told himself at four o'clock of a cold March morning, but what impelled him to walk up Millbridge High Street alone and unarmed, at an hour when any sane man stayed safe abed at home, was difficult to imagine. Did the cherished melancholy of all lovers draw him to watch and sigh beneath his lady's window? By no means. Ambrose had not the slightest idea in which room Naomi slept. The whole affair seemed non-sensical, and yet as urgent as stop-press news.

He was, in fact, driven by something which is generally regarded as a woman's prerogative: intuition. Charged by this strange feeling which causes a mother to rise unsummoned in the night, knowing that something is amiss with her children, he dressed and came out into Middleton Street.

The moon was high and acted as a lantern for him. The air was cold and gusts of wind hunted up papers and straw in the gutter. His boots sounded hollowly on the cobbles. No one was about. There were no coaches. The Scarborough Diligence had departed at midnight. The Carlisle Flyer would not arrive until a half after six. He hurried on, obsessed by the idea of arriving in the nick of time.

The Old Town lay in a silver hush. The stately steps of Thornton House came into view, donkey-stoned to a creamy white, unsullied and at peace. He walked more slowly now, keeping close to the area railings, somewhat shame-faced. A sense of proportion, a sense of humour, and above all a sense of the ridiculous, returned. Even supposing that Naomi and her property were attacked by a gang of robbers, who was he to confront them? Had he ever been a boxer, a swordsman or a fine shot with a pistol? Not a bit of it. The first blow would fell him. A sword would be more of a hazard to him than to his opponent. He did not even possess a pistol.

He found the condition of love wholly exasperating.

Still he marched doggedly on, and presently heard the lonely sound of hooves and wheels behind him in the distance, whereupon he stepped prudently into a doorway and waited.

The carriage bowled rapidly up the High Street. He recognised Naomi's manservant, Joseph, on the box, glimpsed the lady inside, and wondered what on earth they were doing out at this hour of morning.

The carriage stopped. The manservant jumped down, pistol in hand, and looked carefully all about him. Nothing. No one. A dog trotted by. An empty bottle rolled drunkenly in the wind.

Joseph was off guard only for the moments in which he opened the carriage door. Naomi's hand was on his arm, her foot touched the pavement. And in those moments four men were running soundlessly out of the shadows at the other side of the street.

They moved with incredible speed, and yet to Ambrose it seemed that the event unfolded like the petals of a flower, silently and with graceful deliberation. A hand floated over Joseph's mouth, another detached the pistol from his fingers. Two men pinioned Naomi's arms and rendered her as voiceless and helpless as her servant. The last man held and soothed the horses.

Ambrose's pulse quickened. His heartbeats hammered in his head, throbbed through his body. He paused on the edge of the scene for what seemed a long while but was only seconds. Then, without thought or plan or hope, he charged into the noiseless tableau.

His boots pounded on the narrow pavement. His voice rang again and again in the silent street. He threw himself heedlessly into their midst, crying, 'Help! Murder! Thieves!'

Everything became much too sudden, close, and indistinct.

'So this is what battle is like!' he thought.

He hit out wildly at one of the men holding Naomi. The other kicked him savagely in the jaw and he fell backwards. Undaunted, he scrambled up again, shaking his head to clear it. His intervention had broken the spell. Naomi was struggling fiercely. The fellow who was holding Joseph hit the servant with his own pistol and joined the fray, leaving the manservant lying unconscious on the pavement.

Remembering his school-days, Ambrose ducked his head well down and ran full tilt at the man's belly, temporarily winding him. Now one of Naomi's captors slapped her hard on both cheeks and, as she hung dazed with shock, left his comrade to hold her.

Ambrose was aware of fists punching his head and chest, of boots kicking him in the kidneys and groin. Down he went for a longer count, and this time he could only struggle up on to all fours. So he crawled the few paces towards Naomi's captor, wrapped both arms round his legs, and held on obstinately, croaking, 'Help!' until they hit him over the head. Naomi sank her teeth into the hand that gagged her, and screamed the instant it was snatched away. The horses began to whinny and plunge. Unnoticed, the manservant stirred and stared.

Windows were thrown up and shutters unbolted. Faces in nightcaps bobbed over the sills. Three aged spinsters flung up withered arms and shrieked, 'Rape!' A retired army major discharged the entire contents of his musket into the air without sighting a single target. And two top-hatted policemen pelted up the High Street, flourishing their truncheons and shouting, 'Stop, thief!'

Now Naomi strove to hold rather than to escape her captor, while his fellows ran away. Guessing her intent, Joseph crawled forward and fetched him down by the legs just as he freed himself.

Ambrose, recovering consciousness for a moment, wound his arms round a lamp-post, and whispered, 'This is one of them, constable!'

'You were so brave!' Naomi said, weeping, trembling, kneeling by him on the hall tiles. 'And so foolish! It was very brave and foolish of you, Ambrose, and you might have been killed.'

He sat up and felt his jaw.

'I think he knocked a tooth out,' he said.

Naomi held a cold compress to Ambrose's forehead, which felt extremely pleasant. To his amazement a great deal of time had evidently passed. Here was Jamie Standish with his nightshirt tucked into his trousers, no cravat, and an overcoat covering the rest of his deficiencies. There was Joseph, sitting on a hall chair with his face buried in his hands and a bandage round his head. Outside, the sky turned a lighter shade of plum, the world was beginning to stir.

'Yes, you've lost a tooth in the lower jaw at the side, Ambrose,' Jamie said, grinning, 'and you're going to ache all over for a while yet. But nothing seems to be broken. You'll fight another day!'

'Oh, good,' said Ambrose and tried to get to his feet.

'You must not!' said Naomi. 'He must not, Dr Standish!'

'Oh, yes, I must,' said Ambrose firmly. 'I have an important appointment to keep. Help me up, Jamie.'

Naomi wrung her hands, crying, 'No, no. Do not let him.'

'Naomi, do hush! Would someone be kind enough to order me a very quiet horse from the Royal George?' Ambrose asked.

'No!' said Jamie Standish, supporting him. 'You're not fit to ride, and your appointments must wait – but I've no objection to your being driven home, and going straight to bed.'

'Very well,' said Ambrose, resolved to humour them all rather than be diverted from his purpose. 'Order me a hackney-coach!'

The manservant stood up resolutely, if rather unsteadily. He looked very white and sick, but pulled himself together and endeavoured to dust and straighten his livery.

'I can drive you home, sir.'

Naomi cried, turning from one man to the other, 'But you are not well, Joseph! You are not well, Ambrose!'

'I'm quite fit to drive, madam,' said the manservant. 'I shall take care.'

'And if you start arguing about it, I shall *walk* back, Naomi!' warned Ambrose.

She saw that his mind was made up. She gave a resigned shrug.

'Then you must both drink tea before you go!' she said, having her own way in this at least.

'There was something puzzling me, Naomi,' Ambrose went on. He passed one hand across his forehead, but could not recall the question. 'Ah, well, it will come back.'

'The police tell me you took a crack on the head with a pistol before they could reach you,' said Jamie, watching him, 'so we shall have to keep an eye on you for the next twenty-four hours or so. If you feel a wee bit dizzy, or find yourself dozing off when you least expect to, send for your regular physician. Who is your doctor?'

'I don't think I have one,' Ambrose replied vaguely. 'I am never ill, you see.' He endeavoured to be helpful. 'Your Uncle Hamish used to be our family doctor . . .'

Naomi made a sound of exasperation.

'Aye, well. Send for me, then!' said Jamie, amused.

Ambrose nodded. He was conserving energy for what must be done.

'And, as your physician, I must insist that you delegate your work today, and that you go to bed immediately. Is that understood?'

Ambrose nodded again.

'He will not do what you say, Dr Standish!' Naomi cried, suspicious of this unwonted obedience. 'Does he think I forget that *The Correspondent* is printed this evening?' She plucked her copy from where it lay by her muff on the hall table. 'Here! Here is your Page Seven!' Thrusting it into Ambrose's fumbling hands. 'I tell you, Dr Standish, he will go home and work all day and all night, and disobey all your orders. I know him!'

'Well, if he's daft, he's daft,' Jamie replied philosophically, 'and I must be away to my breakfast.'

'On my honour, I promise you that I will go to bed immediately I get home,' said Ambrose, telling part of the truth. 'Now, are you satisfied, Naomi?'

She was not, but there was nothing she could do about it.

Ambrose begged leave to wash. Dollie, the parlour-maid, escorted him to one of the guest rooms and fetched up a copper jug of hot water and clean towels. The looking glass showed him a face that was either white or bruised, and a head with a plaster on it. Dollie brushed his suit, but it had been elderly in the first place and was now past revival. With shaking hands he re-tied his cravat so that the blood-stains hardly showed. He borrowed a comb.

Somewhat refreshed, he drank tea in the parlour, avoiding Naomi's reproachful eyes. Then he and Joseph walked out to the carriage together, making light of the fact that the boot-boy had to help one of them on to the box and the other into his seat. Joseph raised his whip in salute, and Ambrose waved goodbye cheerfully, though the action hurt. He waited until Thornton House was out of sight. He lowered the window, put out his head very carefully and called to the manservant.

'Kingswood Hall, if you please, Joseph!'

*

The ironmaster needed very little sleep and had been an early riser from childhood. His wife Zelah, accustomed to the management of a vast household and a large family, still left her bed at six o'clock each morning even though all her children were grown and gone. So husband and wife were breakfasting when Ambrose was announced.

'Show Mr Longe into the library and say I shall be with him presently,' said William, waving Zelah back into her seat.

For she would be ordering another place to be laid, and making the fellow welcome, if he were not careful!

'Shall he not join us, love?' Zelah asked.

'No, no. It is a matter of business, and will not take long. He has come a little too soon, that is all.'

She smiled assent, but did not believe him.

'You shall see the damned idiot before he goes, if you wish,' said William magnanimously.

Yet when he entered the library such a sorry gallant met the ironmaster's eyes that he did growl, 'Should you like some coffee?'

He was answered, 'If it is not too much trouble, sir. I might fail else. And would you be so kind as to offer Miss Bloom's coachman similar hospitality in your kitchen? He is in like shape.'

'Sit down, sir!' said William curtly, ringing the bell. And, as Ambrose lowered himself with infinite care, 'Have you both been in some sort of scuffle, then?'

'Did you not arrange it, sir?' Sarcastically.

The ironmaster replied, very short and sharp.

'My views on public violence have been made quite clear in *The Herald*. But perhaps you read no newspaper other than your own?'

'Oh, I know your public views, sir, but what you say and what you mean so often differ.'

William surveyed his nephew gloomily.

'Well, speak up. What have you come for?'

Drumming his fingers on the arm of his chair.

'Naomi Bloom was attacked by four ruffians in Millbridge High Street in the early hours of this morning. Fortunately, I happened to be there at the time and was able to summon help.'

The ironmaster's exclamation of horror did not stop him. He spoke on sturdily, though his head jingled at every consonant.

'There are several points to be cleared up as yet, but the number of these villains, the speed and skill with which they acted, and their presence in the street at that hour, indicates a deliberate and premeditated assault on her.'

The ironmaster held up his hand.

'Was Naomi hurt?'

'Not hurt. Shocked and frightened, yes, but not hurt.'

'I am relieved to hear it. Pray continue!'

'Whether they planned to abduct her, rob her, or simply to terrify her, we don't know. The police are holding one of them, but he is a hardened rogue and I doubt he will tell them anything.'

William nodded slowly, as though he were answering himself.

Ambrose said bitterly, 'You know, of course, that this is all of a piece with that cowardly attack on George Howarth? You realise that when they knew *The Correspondent* was ready for them they had to look for a victim elsewhere?'

William did not answer, did not look at him, drumming away with his fingers, but softly now.

'I have known you to be a ruthless man these many years, sir,' said Ambrose, shaking, 'but I always gave you credit for being a gentleman. I had not thought you capable of ordering a poor miner to be beat almost to death because he told the truth. Still less of seeking to harm a lady whose only fault is that of helping me.'

The ironmaster's fingers stopped in mid-tattoo. He crim-

177

soned. He paled. He drew his dignity like a great cloak about him.

'What, sir? You name *me* as being the cause of these disasters? You consider *me* to have no more morals than the lowest criminal on the streets? Why, what would Zelah say if I stooped to such acts as these? How should I face my father and my mother in heaven with this upon my conscience? Oh, what a wrong you do me!'

Ambrose opened his mouth and shut it again. He could not but believe him, and yet could not believe him entirely.

'Well then, I am sorry. But even if you are not directly culpable, I dare swear you knew something of this,' he said.

The ironmaster looked down, considering his position quietly.

'Let us say that I have suspicions as to where the blame can be laid. But I have no intention of confiding my business to you, sir.'

'I did not expect you to do so!'

'Some events get beyond one's control. I care not a fig for your opinion,' the ironmaster said very fiercely, looking up, 'and I shall not shed tears over Dick's hamfisted fool of a son, either!' Then he looked down again, and added, 'But no woman of any class or kind need ever fear me.'

'Then tell them to call off their dogs, for I will not have her subjected to this sort of ugliness!' cried Ambrose.

'It is different in business, of course,' said William, thinking aloud. 'She adopts the role of the man in that capacity. She must take her chances with me, there.'

'I would back her against the world, in any quarter, any day!' cried Ambrose with the utmost conviction.

The ironmaster looked up again, surprised.

'I intend to marry Naomi Bloom!' said Ambrose.

He heard this decision with tremendous astonishment, and inwardly bowed before it.

'To marry her? Why should she have *you*? She is worth ten of *you*!' said William Howarth contemptuously.

'I know,' said Ambrose with humility. 'Most women are worth ten of most men, but that is a peculiar misfortune on their part, and I cannot think it an accident of fate – rather a design.'

'Well,' growled the ironmaster, who was not worth his wife's shoestrings, 'you may have a point there.' And he considered it before putting his next question. 'Will she accept you, do you think?'

'She will have no choice, in the end.'

'God help her!' said the ironmaster. 'What a waste! She could have played consort to a king.'

'There were no kings available,' said Ambrose. 'Only one fool.'

William Howarth dismissed the situation as hopeless. He returned to their original subject of discussion.

'What I say now I say only to you. The situation slipped out of my control. Temporarily, that is. I hold a great many horses in check – now and again one will bolt! But I have not got to my present position without knowing how to rein them all in. Neither Naomi nor anyone else will be troubled further. You have my word upon it.'

'Thank you,' Ambrose said. 'I shall respect your confidence.'

Curiosity overcame him. He leaned forward.

'Did you see the conditions at Swarth Moor for yourself?'

'Of course.'

The look Ambrose gave him was eloquent. The ironmaster shrugged.

'They were bad. Very bad. As are industrial conditions everywhere – except in show-places like Snape.'

'Well? Is that all you can say? Is that all you care?'

'I can speak as charitably as you please, and feel as deeply, but it won't alter the fact that a great deal of money is involved in modern industry and those who make it are not going to relinquish it.'

'Good God!' cried Ambrose in disgust.

'I'll tell you this much more. I shall see to it that *my* collieries are cleaned up sufficiently to pass inspection. But I doubt they will be inspected for a long while. Our local council won't be in any hurry to investigate, and you'll wait a good few years for a Royal Commission. And don't expect anyone else on my committee to lift a finger until they are threatened with a court of justice!'

'How can you live with such a philosophy?' said Ambrose in sheer disbelief.

'Very comfortably,' said the ironmaster. 'You see, I accept life for what it is. You imagine you know what's best for everybody. That's nonsense. Of course things change, but they change at their own pace and time. Anyway, I can't spend all morning on you, so I'll be brief! I reiterate that I have complete faith in myself and my politics, and in Sam Pickering and *The Herald*, and we shall continue to fight you with all the strength of our convictions. But there will be no more ugly days – such as these last have been. So tell Naomi that there is nothing to fear. I have everything in hand.'

But you are old, thought Ambrose, and the time of your greatness is passing.

Still, he did not say this. Waiting for leave to go.

'Funny thing! Your father and I got on well together,' said William, remembering. 'Of course, I only met him once and we were both young then. I don't know how the friendship would have worn if we'd been under one another's noses all the time! Yes, I travelled down to London on one of the first Royal Mail coaches to find out how Charlotte was keeping. We hadn't seen hide or hair of them since they eloped the previous year, and my mother worried about her being so far away.' He shook his head, smiling. 'I stayed with them at that pig's muddle of a place off Fleet Street. And – bless my soul! – *you* were born, just a few days before I went back. The damned doctor was in a drunken stupor, and Toby and I ran in different directions to find a midwife. Poor Charlotte! Poor Toby! Well, well!' He frowned.

'Of course, Toby's politics were anathema to me, even then. You take after him in that way. And you're the dead spit of him to look at.' His expression softened. 'But now and again you remind me of Charlotte. And I loved Charlotte.' He held out his hand. 'So goodbye to you, Ambrose. You've faced up to me at last, instead of sniggering behind my back with that Johnny Topp fellow. I don't intend to get any closer to you. I wish you well, and I wish you well away!'

He considered another possibility.

'I daresay – if Naomi will have you, that is! – that Zelah will insist on entertaining you both. Pity! Still, we must make the best of it. By the by, Zelah would like to see you before you go. Yes, she was always fond of you. But then, she is an astonishing woman, and could find good points in the devil himself.'

In spite of this statement they shook hands firmly.

'Goodbye, sir. I'm . . . goodbye and God bless,' said Ambrose in confusion.

The shade of Charlotte approved of them, was amused by them.

The ironmaster pulled the bell-rope, clasped his hands behind his back, and watched his nephew limp gingerly from the room.

'Good God!' Ambrose whispered to himself, as Joseph turned the carriage round and headed towards Millbridge. 'I've got to propose to Naomi! How on earth shall I do that?'

A Tree Full of Stars and Birds

chapter sixteen

Excitement and tension had kept Ambrose on his feet so far,
but in the carriage he felt suddenly drained of energy, and
arrived at Middleton Street in a poor state. On consulting with
Joseph as to the wisdom of telling Naomi a part-truth, he found,
as he had suspected, a mutual masculine sympathy. The message
was worded carefully.

> *My dear Naomi, I have just received Information from a Reliable
> Source that there will be no more Attacks on* The Correspondent
> *nor on Anyone connected with it. You will be quite Safe, hence-
> forth. I do apologise for sending Joseph back so Late, but I had
> this Business to transact, and thought it Best he should Wait to
> bring you the good news.*
>
> *You will be delighted to hear that I am Fit for Nothing
> and shall spend today in bed! One of my staff will stay here at
> Night until I am safely on the Mend. I shall send you a daily
> Bulletin of my Health, so please don't Worry!*
>
> *I shall be Better by the weekend and we have something to
> Celebrate, so may I take you out to Dinner at the Royal George
> on Saturday evening? I can call for you at seven o'clock, if that
> is convenient. Yr friend, Ambrose.*

Then he let the world take care of itself while Frank Ormerod
and Bob Bullock took over his work.

News is not spread by newspapers alone. Throughout the
day the tale was embroidered, as it passed from one gossip to

the other. In the end folk were saying that the editor of *The Northern Correspondent* lay at death's door, having been attacked by twenty desperate villains in Millbridge High Street while preserving the honour of Miss Naomi Blüm. Still, this did no harm to the reputation of either him or the paper.

A letter of sympathy and dry good wishes, written by Sam Pickering and accompanied by a bottle of claret, arrived from *The Herald*. From the Ship tavern came a bottle of port. At lunchtime two lads arrived with trays: one a goodwill tripe-and-onions and apple pie from Pendleton's, the other a roast fowl with bread sauce and a tansy pudding ordered by Naomi from the Royal George.

In the afternoon the ironmaster's personal physician called, and almost bumped into Jamie Standish who had dropped by on his own account. Each of them pronounced Ambrose to be in no immediate danger of extinction but advised him to stay abed. Throughout the day his staff kept one eye on him and the other on the Tuesday edition, and dozens of people left messages of goodwill and even little gifts of eggs and cream and home-made cakes. He had not known he was so popular.

At six o'clock a full-scale dinner was sent from the Royal George, with a brief note.

'My Friend, I should like very much to see you on Saturday, and I accept your Invitation with much Pleasure. Yrs, Naomi.'

Ambrose was relieved, delighted and perturbed. He asked if Charlie Ainsworth would be kind enough to step upstairs for a few minutes. Though now poorer – and richer – for the birth of his first infant, the young man was still something of a dandy, and Ambrose needed a sartorial adviser. He explained as casually as he could that he was taking Miss Blüm out to dinner at the George, and wanted to make a good impression for the sake of the newspaper. He did his best to indicate that this was cold-blooded business, but by now every member of his staff was nourishing most pleasurable suspicions.

'So if you'd be good enough to glance over that

cupboardful of clothes, Charlie,' Ambrose said nonchalantly, 'and give me your opinion as to what I should wear, I'd be uncommonly obliged!'

The reporter's face brightened. He had expected to be sent down a coal mine at the risk of life and limb, not treated as a confidant. He rubbed his hands and opened the cupboard smartly, which was unwise since it lacked one hinge and the other was rusty.

'I meant to warn you,' said Ambrose, as Charlie staggered back holding the door, 'but you were a bit too quick for me. Are you hurt?'

'Not me, Mr Longe,' said Charlie, 'but I think I'd best lean it against this wall. There! No harm done. Now, what have we here?'

Diplomacy and natural good manners forbade him to be honest. He fetched out old coats and examined them judiciously. He went through Ambrose's collection of mended and unmended shirts. He inspected boots whose polish barely concealed their defects. He lost hope over the cravats. He approached the problem obliquely.

'I can tell you've been quite a dresser in your day, Mr Longe – and you've still got the figure for it, too.'

'As bad as that, eh?' said Ambrose, trying to sound unconcerned.

'Oh, they're good enough for everyday,' Charlie hastened to add, 'but if you're taking such a fashionable lady as Miss Bloom to such a fashionable place as the Royal George . . . well – none of it will do, Mr Longe, and that's a fact!'

Ambrose stared at him helplessly.

'But even if I could afford a whole lot of new clothes – which I can't, Charlie – how on earth would I get them before Saturday night?'

'I tell you what, Mr Longe,' said Charlie confidentially, 'we're much of a size, you and me. I'll lend you my wedding outfit!'

'Your wedding outfit?' Suspiciously. 'What's that like?'

184

'Oh, not one of your formal rigs, Mr Longe. I couldn't run to that. But it's a right bobby-dazzler. Black silk topper. Tobacco brown tail-coat with black velvet collar. White double-breasted waistcoat with mother-of-pearl buttons. Fawn strapped trousers cut in the peg-top style. White stock.' He measured the sole of one of Ambrose's scuffed boots against his own, adding, 'and we're even in luck with the footwear!'

Dollie the parlour-maid said demurely, 'Mr Longe, madam!' and did not smile until she had closed the door behind her.

Naomi also looked splendid, but then she usually did, and Ambrose had seen that Chinese green gown on other occasions, whereas the impression he created was downright spectacular.

'Oh, but how changed you are!' cried Naomi, throwing up her hands in admiration.

Quixotically, he felt piqued. Why should his borrowed finery make such a difference?

Naomi descried the shadow on his face and hastened to dispel it.

'Ah, but I have always said you were the most elegant man in Millbridge. How well they suit you, these beautiful new clothes! Why did you not warn me, Ambrose? I would have matched you, new for new! Oh, turn around. This is the first time I have seen them!'

He reflected that it was likely to be the last, and basked in her praises while he could.

He said airily, 'Oh, I really had to cut a dash when I was taking such a fine lady out to dinner—'

In her old relaxed fashion, friend to friend, she had caught his sleeve and turned him about. He tipped his hat over his eyes, spread his arms and pirouetted. She laughed aloud and clapped her hands, and he caught them in his own, laughing with her.

She stopped, afraid and shy at once. She moved away from him.

'Why! Look at the time!' she cried, pointing to the clock

185

on the mantelpiece, and examined her image in the looking-glass.

Ambrose, mirrored behind her, echoed her change of mood.

'By Jove! We must be setting off!'

Outside, the evening was cold but dry. The parlour-maid enveloped her mistress in furs. Joseph appeared, trimming a lantern, to escort them all three hundred yards of the way to the Royal George. Ambrose offered Naomi his arm, and she accepted it gracefully. Together they strolled up the High Street and across the market Square: a most distinguished couple.

The evening was a paradox. Though Ambrose intended it to be a private occasion, their entrance caused a public sensation.

Heads turned, conversations were suspended, waiters smiled and bowed. Old Benjamin Tyler, the landlord, hurried to welcome them. Then one gentleman, warming himself by the fire, strode forward to bow to Naomi, to shake Ambrose by the hand, speaking loud enough to be heard by everyone in the room.

'Your servant, ma'am. Good evening, Mr Longe. Anthony Clerk, at your service. My name will mean nothing to you, sir, but I am one of your many admiring readers. May I congratulate you on the courageous stance of *The Northern Correspondent* with regard to certain local evils, and on your own gallantry in defending this lady last Monday against a crowd of ruffians? I trust, ma'am, that you have recovered from such a shocking fright – and that you, sir, are feeling pretty much yourself again? I shall not trouble you further, Mr Longe. I simply wanted to shake you by the hand!'

Naomi smiled and inclined her head. Ambrose murmured a polite response. Pleased, confused, they began to make their way to the George's private parlour, but Mr Clerk's statement had dissolved the usual diffidence of collected strangers. To their astonishment, everyone in the room stood up and applauded, and those nearest to them stretched out their hands to be shaken likewise. Astonished, they acknowledged as many as they could, and heard the door of the parlour close behind them with a profound sense of relief.

'I did not know you were so famous, Mr Longe!' cried Naomi, smiling, laughing.

'It is not fame, Miss Bloom, merely notoriety!' he replied.

The foreign habit of an aperitif had become fashionable of late, and they sipped little glasses of aquavit. For several minutes they were able to make fun of their reception, to consider the menu and consult the waiter and choose their food and wine with care. Then silence and shyness stole upon them. The joy of celebration was shadowed by thoughts of a more serious nature.

They both began to speak of some triviality at once. They stopped. They excused themselves.

'Pray do continue,' said Ambrose courteously.

'It was nothing,' Naomi said, which was no more than the truth.

They were rescued by the entrance of two waiters, who came in at that moment trundling a trolley full of good things.

Reprieved, they discussed the soup, brown and creamy, flavoured with Madeira, and consumed it fairly rapidly in order to talk of the oysters which followed. They drank Chablis in a manner suggestive of desperation rather than delight. Between courses they used the parlour as a topic, praising the comfort bestowed by red velvet curtains, a turkey carpet, and a generous fire.

A dish of veal cutlets found them more relaxed. Roast beef and potatoes with a rich, dark claret persuaded them to joke again. An apricot tart made with bottled fruit caused them to speculate on the future of canned foods which were both a novelty and a luxury. Naomi said that at that moment her larder held a tin of genuine truffled hare paté from the Périgord, but she was half-afraid to try it. Ambrose promised to act as guinea-pig when it was opened.

They toyed with the savoury. They ate a morsel of Stilton, for appearance's sake. In a warm and leisurely mood, they drank coffee.

At last Naomi was able to say quite naturally, 'And how are you? And how is your poor head?'

Ambrose struck his forehead theatrically and replied, 'Almost as good as new!' Then, as if the blow had revived his memory, 'By the by, Naomi, I was puzzled to understand why on earth you were out last Monday at such an hour of the morning?'

'And I meant to ask you – how did you come to be there also?'

Their former camaraderie had been re-established.

'You answer first!' cried Ambrose.

'As you wish!' she replied and proceeded to act out her tale.

'On Sunday afternoons, when Hal has gone back to Manchester, I go to see Mary. I help her to put the children to bed, and then we have our supper together and talk, and work on the fair copy of Page Seven, and then I come home at ten o'clock. It is very nice for both of us. But this Sunday one thing upon another happened.'

She lifted her eyes as if to ask help of heaven.

'Poor Mary had not seen Hal that weekend, because he is down in the south of England. Philomena was ill with the croup and Mary had sat up with her all night. Her article was still in notes. Ach!'

Naomi pressed both hands to her brow.

'So! So at length everything is done, and I tell Mary to take a little sleep and I will stay with Philomena, just for an hour or two. But Mary is exhausted and sleeps like a child, and I do not want to wake her. It is very, very late. She wishes me to stay the rest of the night – which would have been sensible. But by that time, you know, I did want to come home!'

'Oh, I do understand!' Ambrose said solemnly, amused.

'And, after all, I thought myself quite safe. Joseph was with me, and he had a pistol.'

'Much good it did him!' said Ambrose drily. 'So Philomena has fallen sick again? That child is a cross which Mary will bear to the end of her days. Ah, well! How is Santo? How is our god-daughter?'

'They are both hearty!' she replied, smiling. 'Mary is keeping them away from the sickroom, in charge of a nursemaid, so that they do not catch the croup. Alice is a very lively baby, and Santo grows taller and handsomer every day!'

'They are the product of young and healthy parents,' Ambrose remarked, 'whereas Philomena was the last of a long litter.'

Then he fell silent, as certain thoughts occurred to him, but Naomi chattered on.

'The haughty young Santo – who said all girls were silly, and quarrels with Philomena at every trick and turn – simply worships Alice. It is quite charming to see them together!'

She saw that he was no longer interested and changed the topic.

'And now, sir, how did *you* happen to be in the High Street at such an hour, last Monday?'

There was no help for it. Ambrose looked directly at her.

'I woke up in the early hours of the morning, feeling that you were in danger and that you needed me.'

She did not answer him. She looked down at her wine glass and slowly twirled the stem. Her lips moved slightly, as though in prayer. Ambrose could not tell whether it was a plea for help or words of thanksgiving.

'You did need me,' he added firmly.

Still she neither answered nor looked at him.

'I was afraid that the only need was mine,' he went on humbly, sincerely, 'but in the last month or so I have begun to think and hope that our needs are the same. There are two main obstacles in the way. The first is me, for I am a poor bargain in the marriage market. The second, Naomi, is your suspicious nature!'

He had hoped to draw her fire, but she smiled a little, frowned a little, gave a little shrug.

'Are you not going to assist me at all?' Ambrose asked ruefully. 'You must know what I am trying to say. I don't ask for an answer outright, but could you not give me some indication of how you feel?'

She hesitated. Then said, eyebrows raised, eyes resolutely on the wine glass, 'I am considering your two obstacles!'

'Consider away!' he cried, relieved. 'I am not asking you to commit yourself one way or the other without due thought.'

Now she regarded him gravely.

'Why are you a poor marriage bargain? Tell me that.'

'Oh, that's easy,' Ambrose said, almost cheerfully. 'I earn only enough money to keep myself, and have no prospect of becoming rich. I have no home or property of my own. I am devoted to a profession which keeps unsociable and inconvenient hours – Mary was always grumbling about cold or burned dinners! And I am considerably older than you.'

The last remark interested her most.

'Indeed? How much older?'

'It would be indelicate to be exact in my arithmetic,' he answered, smiling. 'Let us say that I was a student at Cambridge when you were born.'

'So?' she mused. 'I did not realise that. You look and seem young for your age and I have always *felt* much older!'

'Well, so you are, in one way.'

She consulted her wine glass again.

After a moment or two she said, 'All those other things about you, I knew anyway – and they are not of great account.'

Hope blazed in him, but the result was too important be jeopardised by haste. He let her take her time.

'As for my suspicious nature. I have good cause to be

suspicious of men and marriage – but not of your intentions.'

Again she looked at him, so that he should understand the import of her words.

'I do not suspect you, for instance, of being a fortune-hunter, or you would have found a rich wife long ago!'

'You're very kind,' said Ambrose, flattered.

'I do not suspect you of looking for a home – although I think you need one! – or you would have found that also. Your strange hours do not frighten me, either. My father left all domestic arrangements to me. True, we lived in hotels. We had plenty of money. But he expected his clothes to be brushed, his shirts to be clean, his bills to be paid, his suite of rooms booked, his meals ordered, his business appointments made, his sec-retarial work done. I speak five languages. I tell you, I needed every word in every one of them!'

'What an astonishing woman you are!' he cried, proud of her.

Naomi gestured his compliment away.

'So it is not those things which I suspect. No, I am sus-picious of what you and I would become if we were married.' She paused and asked him, 'Do you remember talking of the cost of love?'

'I was only being clever,' said Ambrose fearfully.

The waiter had swept the cloth clean and fetched a decanter of port and a bowl of walnuts.

'Will you not join me?' Ambrose asked, pouring out two glasses.

She sipped her port composedly and set it down again.

She said, 'My father told me that a marriage contract was the most binding legal document he knew. Other partnerships can be changed or dissolved. Not so, this one. If you are fortu-nate, well and good. If you are not then you face every difficulty which life can heap upon you, and there is no way out. There are no escape clauses.'

Somewhat dashed, Ambrose replied, 'I take your point.

But on the other hand we know each other pretty well by this time. We have been good friends and partners for two years, and our mettle has been tested more than once.'

Her cool approach incensed him. He spoke more sharply, more passionately now, than he had done.

'You believed in me and the future of *The Northern Correspondent* though we were in a sense unproven! You found premises and bought machinery at the height of the cholera epidemic when most people would have held back and waited! When I suggested that we might not live to publish the paper, you replied, "We act as though we shall!" You put forward a philosophy that life should be lived courageously, risks taken, misfortune – and even death – accepted. "Let durance be your watchword!" you said. Do you remember that?'

She nodded her head.

'Then why the deuce don't you believe in *us*, and have the courage to take the risk with *us*, and see *us* through?' he cried, incensed. 'Are we worth less than a damned newspaper?'

She gasped, swallowed.

'The newspaper is your life! Do you remember saying *that*?'

'I was wrong. Last Monday your life was more important to me than my own. It still is – if you will allow it to be so. Throw me back again into my bachelor pond and that's where I shall flounder – comfortably enough, I daresay! – to the end of my days. I have neither the courage nor the energy to try love again. God knows I never asked to be inconvenienced by it in the first place!'

And he drank down his port as though it were water.

The face opposite him was as old as Eve. Over its mirror a dozen impressions delicately shifted and flitted until a great tenderness overlaid them all. Then she smiled most beautifully and placed one hand on his, and spoke to his condition. Her foreign turns of phrase were so marked as to indicate the depth of her feelings.

'Why do you think I come to help you all that long time ago?' she asked. 'Oh yes, I believe in you and your *Northern Correspondent*, that is most certain. I do not throw my money down the drains! But there are always many investments. Do you not occur to think that perhaps I might also like you a little? Am I not a woman? Shall all my dealings be of the head and not the heart?'

He glanced at her hand but not at her, abashed in his turn.

'Do you know what I feel when I see you lying *wounded*,' she pronounced the word to rhyme with *grounded*, '*wounded* to the earth for my sake, that I do not suffer? Do you know what I suffer? Do you know what I think?'

Her eyes were dark pools of tears.

'I think, "How shall I live without him? What will this life be, without him?" '

'Naomi! Dearest Naomi!'

'No!' she cried. 'First *you* speak. Now *I* speak!'

She withdrew her hand. She had been wounded in her turn.

'You come to me in your beautiful new clothes, and I am like butter turned. You have thought of me so much that you take me out to a beautiful dinner – you cannot afford it, I know, I have done the books! – and you buy beautiful new clothes. . . .'

'I borrowed them!' Ambrose cried, exalted.

'Be silent! What do I care you borrow? What do I care? You do it for *me*. That is what I care. And then you talk of marriage and reason and this and that, and ask why I do not help you out. Only at the end do you speak of love, and then you say it is inconvenient!'

'But you were pretty damned cool yourself about. . . .'

'No more! I have enough talking. You have to say only one little small thing – that you love me. That is all. And you say it wrong!'

She swept back her chair. She drew herself up to her full height.

'Naomi!' Ambrose beseeched.

He was truly sorry, but could not help smiling.

She stared at him, enraged.

'Kindly escort me to home!' she ordered.

Her dignity, her anger, could no longer deceive him.

'Very well,' said Ambrose grinning. 'I shall most kindly to escort you to home.' He held out her mantle. 'Allow me!'

He put Charlie's top hat on at a killing angle.

'I have been remiss, madam, very much remiss. I shall now make full amends. The whole of Millbridge shall know how much I love you! I shall shout it in the street. I shall waltz with lamp-posts. I shall serenade you exceptionally loudly upon the steps of Thornton House.'

Naomi's face changed.

She said, 'You would not do such things? You would not!'

She could not help smiling. She tried to hide the smile. She caught Ambrose's eye and giggled. She struck him, not very hard, with the handle of her fan.

'You are disgracious!' she cried.

'Disgracious? I like that word! I love that word! Let's kindly to go and be disgracious all the way down the High Street! Waiter!'

He settled the bill with a flourish. He held out his arm with exaggerated courtesy. In amusement and apprehension she laid a gloved hand on his sleeve.

'Would you be disgracious enough to marry me?' he asked.

'Not until you are better behavioured!' she answered with some spirit, and he laughed aloud at the slip.

'I think we have both drunk far too much wine. What a sensible thing to do. Mr Tyler! Congratulate me!' he cried, as they entered the coffee-room. 'This lady has consented to become my wife!'

It was late. The mood was merry. They were local celebrities. Strangers and acquaintances cheered boisterously, and once again they had to push their way through a friendly and demanding crowd.

Outside the moon was high and all the stars were out. Ambrose stood in the centre of the Market Square and cried out exultantly to its uttermost corners.

'I love you!' And then, 'Naomi!'

The echoes in the square answered him.

'Love you. Love you. Love you. Naomi. Naomi. Naomi.'

She covered her mouth with her hands in horror, in rapture.

He took her hands away and kissed them reverently. He kissed her very gently and lovingly upon the lips. His boisterous mood was melting away.

At the top of the High Street he spread his arms and waltzed a yard or two ahead of her from lamp-post to lamp-post, embracing the waist of each as lightly and carefully as though it were a dancing partner, and ended at the steps of Thornton House, bowing low.

One emotion chased another out. Naomi followed him, laughing, protesting. Finally, in tender silence, she watched him.

On the topmost step of Thornton House he sang his four-line madrigal, but only to her, and very softly.

Not a shutter creaked, not a soul stirred. Simultaneously they reached out their arms, one to the other, to seal the alliance.

Marvelling they drew apart to see this new half of their future self.

'You will marry me, won't you?' Ambrose asked.

Slowly, solemnly, Naomi bent her head.

'I hereby promise,' said Ambrose, lifting up one hand, 'that I will in no way alter or encroach upon the perfect partnership we have enjoyed so far. And I have this to say to God or the Fates or whatever powers rule our destinies. So long as we are together, nothing can harm us. So long as we are good in ourselves, nothing can do us evil.'

He smiled at the bright darkness of her face.

'And what do you say, dearest love?'

But Naomi could only find an image rich enough for this

rich present from the rich past her father had renounced.

'Oh, it is like the seven-branched tree my mother told me
of. Like a tree full of stars and birds. And all of them are singing
and shining for us.'

Part Three

New Editions 1835–1843

Real Fingers

chapter seventeen

28 September, 1835

Ambrose sharpened another pen and looked suspiciously at the office clock on the wall. As he thought, it had stopped. Then he saw the hand pause and hang like a water drop, and fall from twenty-two to twenty-three minutes past five. He sighed, dipped his newly-mended pen in the ink, and resumed work.

Sir Richard Grey and his party of Whigs were swept into power on the Wings of Reform, and so far they have proved to be a busy but in some ways a disappointing government. Already we are seeing the effects of their disastrous Poor Law, which has turned the workhouse from a public charity into a public threat . . .'

On second thoughts he crossed this out, and began again.

In this modern age of industrial growth and expansion, the old-fashioned style – we will not say 'system' – of local government is insufficient. The finest reforms are rendered useless if they cannot be put into operation, and so far the Whigs seem to have provided us with a carriage and horses and forgotten the driver! However, their latest Act will put a coachman on the seat who can take our local politicians for a nice brisk gallop!

He had a happy burst of inspiration, and grinned as he scribbled, tucking the foot of one leg around the ankle of the other.

The Municipal Reform Act should make a considerable difference to our present Mayor and Corporation, who will henceforth be elected or rejected by the ratepayers, instead of voting each other in as usual. Moreover, our local government will have the legal power to undertake major improvements and developments, thus giving them no excuse to squander public money on banquets fit for the Romans and a new Town

Hall not quite fit enough for the Greeks. Finally and most cruelly, their accounts are to be audited – a state of affairs which will cause the stoutest heart to falter!

Now he was well into his stride.

Whilst we congratulate the government on this latest Act, might we suggest that they provide their new driver with a whip, and take a cut at the excessive powers wielded by our Justices of the Peace? Were these landed gentlemen both just and peaceful we should have no cause for complaint, but human nature being what it is some of them fall short of the ideal. Then we shall have Reform indeed! It will be interesting to see . . .

But his own interest faltered at this point. Ambrose laid down his pen in defeat and stared hard at the minute hand, which appeared to be unable to reach the hour. Then it laboured forward and, on the instant, St Stephen's clock chimed six, and a knock on the door announced Frank Ormerod, carrying the Friday-night mock-up.

Ambrose sharpened another pen, to convince them both that he was not wasting time. He spoke briskly.

'Just putting the finishing touches to the editorial, Frank!'

'No hurry as yet, Mr Longe.'

Ambrose said as casually as he could, 'Any news from home?'

Frank Ormerod shook his head almost in reproach.

'Nay, Mr Longe, you should know me by this time. If there was any news, I'd have sent Jimmy running up to tell you.'

Ambrose nodded, and pretended to examine the mock-up.

'The ladies got Page Seven done, I see!' said Frank heartily. 'I like that. Shows spirit *and* dedication. Under the circumstances.'

'Yes, Mrs Vivian was writing the fair copy at our house yesterday afternoon . . . Good God, Frank, this business has been going on since last night. Isn't that time enough?'

Frank Ormerod sat down, unbidden, and spoke kindly.

'I've had seven little 'uns so far, Mr Longe, and the first is always the hardest on both parents. After that, you take 'em in your stride like. Now, sir, you've been up all night and come out without breakfast. You didn't eat above a spoonful of hot-pot at dinnertime, and you might not be here for supper – supposing I was to send out for a jug of hot coffee and a pork-pie?'

'You're very good. Just the coffee, Frank, if you please.'

The head printer rose from his chair. He was sympathetic.

'If there's anything any of us can do for you, Mr Longe, you know you've only got to ask. It might sound funny for me to say so – being teetotal – but why not try a nip of brandy with the coffee?'

Ambrose smiled and said, 'If I started nipping brandy I'd end up drinking the bottle, Frank!'

'Ah, there is that! I'll be off, then. If you could let me have the editorial in the next hour . . .?'

'I'll see to it in no time at all. Thank you, Frank. And, Frank?'

'Yes, Mr Longe?'

'If the baby had come on Wednesday I could have stayed at home!'

The head printer spoke soothingly.

'Nay, you'd only fret yourself and them, at home, Mr Longe. You're best off here with us!'

'Still,' said Ambrose to the closed door, 'a Wednesday would have been more convenient!'

They had been married on a Wednesday the previous year. Their wedding, like their engagement, was originally intended to be a private affair but had become a public event.

They began with an idea most beautiful in its simplicity: an intimate ceremony at St Mark's church in early April, their four closest friends as witnesses, and a small wedding breakfast at the Royal George. They ended as chief actors in the smartest social event of the season, entertaining over two hundred guests, ordering Naomi's gown from Paris and postponing the date to late July in order to fit everything and everyone in.

It was not the fault of the ironmaster that his wife graciously improved on the original plan. Indeed, he protested with his usual vehemence. But Zelah said that Naomi had only come to Millbridge at his instigation; that she had no relatives in England and needed some fatherly friend to give her away; and that the gesture would have pleased Charlotte. At this the ironmaster knuckled under and offered to hold the wedding at Kingswood Hall.

Ambrose was all for declining the offer outright, but had his mind changed by Naomi, who pointed out that the ironmaster had given her help and advice when her father died and must not be snubbed; that such a public family reconciliation could harm no one and possibly benefit all of them; and that a refusal would hurt Zelah.

So on a fine day in late July, Ambrose found himself in the position of many a man before him. He was dressed in an expensive suit of clothes which would serve him only for rare occasions. He had become a necessary but unimportant part of a religious and social ceremony for which he had no patience. And he had to be polite to people whom he detested or despised.

Their early guest list had been composed of Hal and Mary Vivian, and Jamie and Dorcas Standish. The final invitations fetched a host of German Blüms from Berlin, all of whom wandered round England for an interminable time before going home again; an army of the ironmaster's daughters and their progeny, who stayed at Kingswood Hall for weeks and kept calling on them; the Howarths of Kit's Hill, who were deeply discomfited but dared not refuse, and arrived bearing unwanted gifts; the chief staff of both *The Northern Correspondent* and *The Lancashire Herald*; and a number of local dignitaries who had to be asked because somebody else was, and whom, in consequence, Ambrose would not be able to hound or insult for at least a month.

He saw the ironies of the situation, he believed that in years to come he would relish its humour, but there were times in those long months of preparation when he thought the price of marriage came too high. The fact that he had none of his own way made him mutinous, and though he could have left *The Correspondent* in the hands of his deputies for a week, he decided he was indispensable and would only take time off between the Tuesday and Saturday editions. In fact, the wedding spoiled their engagement. They managed not to quarrel, but as far as Ambrose was concerned he had lost the glory of that cold March evening, when all the stars were out and he waltzed with the High Street lamp-posts.

This time the knock on his door heralded George Howarth, carrying a can of hot coffee.

'Hello there, George!' cried Ambrose, with false heartiness.

You would have thought that George was a perpetually expectant father, the way that Ambrose and every member of staff on *The Correspondent* treated him. He responded in his usual fashion, a tone both awkward and laconic.

'How do you find yourself then, cousin?'

'Not too bad, George. And yourself?'

'Fair to middling,' said George, as he always did.

Very deliberately he set the coffee down on the carpet near the door, picked up a sheet of old paper, folded it in eight so that it formed a thick pad, laid it on Ambrose's desk, and stood the can triumphantly on top of it. Then he took a clean cup, saucer and plate from the small corner cupboard and placed them by Ambrose's right elbow. He found a sugar-bowl and a spoon, and two biscuits at the bottom of a blue Wedgwood barrel, which he also placed within reach. Finally, he stepped back and eyed the arrangements to make sure they were as they should be.

'The milk's in the coffee!' George said, quite unnecessarily.

Ambrose thanked him, and waited. Everyone always waited after George had spoken, because more information might be forthcoming.

The assault in Prospect Mine, nearly two years ago, had not broken his spirit or impaired his faculties, but it had robbed him of speed. The old George was down there, fathoms deep in the mine of his understanding; he simply took time to surface.

He had been brought up for dead in a leafless February. By the time Ambrose fetched him out of hospital the horse-chestnuts were flowering. So long had it taken him to heal. He had walked unassisted to the hackney-carriage on that fine May morning. True, he could not hear or see as well as he had done. He had a slight limp, his smile was somewhat gap-toothed, his mended bones would always plague him in cold weather. But his gaze was as straight and blue, his handshake as firm as ever.

'Well, cousin,' George had said, very matter-of-fact. 'I'm back!'

There was little enough to come back to, since his injuries prevented him from doing manual labour and he had no settled home, but Naomi found a solution which pleased all of them. Having surveyed Ambrose's bachelor apartment at 21 Middleton Street, she suggested that the maimed hero might occupy the rooms rent free for as long as he liked. This solved the problem of George, who needed time and space to come to terms with life; and that of the furniture, which was unsuitable for Thornton House.

So, with Ambrose's help and encouragement, George began to educate himself. He found study far easier than human communication. He rose as soon as it was light, and worked until dusk. He learned as though learning were food and he ravenous, but he would not accept total charity; he insisted on earning some sort of living. He was too old for an apprenticeship of any kind, so Ambrose employed him as an odd-job man for *The Correspondent*. Within a year George made a unique place for himself on the newspaper.

He was still learning, still adjusting, still slow in his responses, but sometimes Ambrose felt that George was simply coasting along while he thought the next step out. Then, when the time came to change course, he would cast everything and everyone aside and go his own way, whatever that way might be.

So now Ambrose waited for his next remark, which turned out to be in praise of Naomi.

'That,' said George, regarding his presentation of the coffee and biscuits, 'is how Mrs Longe would like it to be done!'

He burrowed a little deeper into his mind, and produced a richer gem.

'And if that's how Mrs Longe likes it, then that's how it *ought* to be done!'

'I couldn't agree more!' said Ambrose, and his memory wounded him.

He had behaved well during and after the marriage ceremony for Naomi's sake, and she was radiant. Not young and innocent as brides were supposed to be, but without doubt the queen of her occasion. But paradoxes seemed to be part of their lives, and the incident which gave meaning to Ambrose's wedding day marred it for her.

It had happened late in the afternoon, when they escaped the reception for a few minutes to walk together in Zelah's rose garden. Unaware, or careless of the fact that they could be overheard on the other side of the tall hedge, two strangers were discussing them.

'Well, I should say that the Longe fellow has done pretty well for himself,' drawled the man. 'He must have more common sense than I gave him credit for – and she far less! I wish I could persuade *my* chief creditor to marry me and cancel the debt, I can tell you!'

The woman's reply was impish, delicately malicious.

'Ah! but the lady is a thought past her youth, and ready to pay any price for a husband!'

There was a pause, as though the man drew on his cigar. Then he spoke again wryly, with a curious distaste.

'Aye, she's handsome enough now, but these daughters of Judah soon run to seed – and he always liked his freedom. When he's finished spending her shekels he'll leave her flat!'

Rarely did Naomi seem other than content with her world and herself, but in that moment Ambrose saw her stripped of all defence. Stricken, she let go his arm as if he had said the words, and walked rapidly away from him. Angrily, helplessly, cursing them and her and the whole ridiculous business, he hurried after.

The day was hot, her stays were tightly laced. He caught her up without much difficulty, grasped her firmly by the arm, and steered her towards a rustic seat in the Long Walk, but there he could not help feeling sorry. However unimportant the incident was to him, it mattered very much to Naomi. She was taking short, harsh breaths to prevent herself from crying. Her hands were shaking, and she clasped them together in an effort to control herself. Gently, Ambrose took them in his own, and rubbed them gently.

A group of sauntering wedding guests, also in search of air and space, fluttered towards them, uttering bird-like cries of astonishment and concern.

'My wife is slightly distressed by the heat!' Ambrose said factually, motioning them to keep their distance. 'I wonder if you would be so kind as to fetch a glass of iced water for her?' And, softly to her, 'Steady, Nim! Must keep up appearances!'

Immediately the flock wheeled, and swept off in search of servants, leaving them in momentary peace.

'Come on!' said Ambrose, coaxing his bride to her feet. 'There's a disused summer-house in the wood – unless they've repaired it in the last few years. We'll hide in there.'

She went with him passively, all beauty and majesty gone. The summer-house had been locked, was falling into decay. She waited in dumb submission while he put his shoulder to the door and forced it open. He found a clean old handkerchief in his coat-pocket and spread it over the mossy seat within. There she sat down, careless of her finery. Her satin gown gleamed in the dim light. Her eyes were fathomless, wells of sorrow.

'Now, what's all this nonsense over a bit of spiteful gossip?' Ambrose asked her outright. Adding, 'Yes, you can cry if you want to, but I should like you to explain such extreme behaviour!'

He spoke in a stern and deliberate way, to steady her. Some colour crept into her cheeks. She ceased to shake and gasp. She tried to speak. Then a cataract of tears fell, a tempest of sobs shook her.

He had never seen her cry before, and the spectacle filled him with amused tenderness. She wept like a child, in total abandon, in dark despair. He took a fine white handkerchief from his breast-pocket and proffered it with a grin.

'This is positively the last one I have!' he said firmly.

In a minute or two she dried her eyes, blew her nose, took a deep breath, and composed herself. She sat on in silence, head averted, and examined the border of his handkerchief as if it were a thing of great importance.

'Well, what a storm in a summer-house!' Ambrose said lightly, trying to make her smile. 'If you're going to take that much notice of every envious remark we overhear, we shall spend most of our married life mopping you up! You can't be a leading social light and marry a newspaperman without becoming public property, Mrs Longe!'

Her lips quivered, but he was glad to see that their corners promised to turn up rather than down.

'I suppose you're going to leave all the talking to me, as upon another notable occasion?' he continued.

She shook her head and swallowed.

'Surely you don't take such contemptible creatures seriously?'

'I am no longer sure!' said Naomi in truth.

207

His face changed. He paled in his turn. He spoke gravely.

'Go on, if you please.'

She smoothed the border of his handkerchief as though her life depended on every crease.

'At first, I do not think you marry me for convenience. I believe you care for me. But since we are engaged you turn from me. You are unkind in many ways. Now I wonder whether they speak the truth.'

He was amazed. He was deeply hurt.

'I, unkind?' he cried indignantly. 'What? After agreeing to all this nonsense and flummery? After betraying every principle I ever stood for? I, unkind? I am the kindest idiot on earth!'

She gave one last dry sob, and sat up straight. She was recovering.

'Two days honeymoon!' she cried accusingly. 'You give us only two days! No time to go away. No wedding tour. No nothing. Then pf! back to work. That is the extent of your affection!'

She was ceasing to be sorry and becoming angry. She spoke with tremendous sarcasm.

'Why do you not marry your newspaper instead of me?'

'Ah!' he said, and was silent.

Naomi looked sideways at him. His expression admitted everything, and regretted it.

He said equally truthfully, 'Very well, I have behaved less than generously in this, but I should have liked our wedding to belong to us rather than to be a party for everyone else.'

It was her turn to question her judgement, and she did this honestly.

'Then I, too, made a mistake, but I thought that this would help you – with your uncle the ironmaster, with your newspaper. And I do love the Aunt Zelah, and also I like the idea of my grand wedding! But I would rather have a little wedding and not quarrel!'

'My dearest girl, it was not your fault. We should have talked this out. Heaven knows why we did not!'

'We listened to everyone but ourselves,' said Naomi wisely, 'and that is why we did not!'

He nodded. She smiled.

She said, 'Next time we are married, Mr Longe, we shall discuss the matter at great length!'

Gracefully she rose and shook out her gleaming gown, smoothed her coronet of hair. She was herself again. Her eyes demanded compliments. He answered her unspoken question.

'Yes, you are beautiful, and I love you very much.' Then, in his own defence, 'I would not have been so inconvenienced, else.'

Her upraised hands called on her usual witness.

'*He* is inconvenienced!' cried Naomi to the god of her fathers.

She was not serious, and he knew it. The decayed summer-house became a place of understanding, of reconciliation.

'I daresay they *could* manage without me for a week. Yes, I shall take a week off as soon as I can arrange it, and we will have a late honeymoon,' said Ambrose, thinking.

He jumped up, dusted himself down, and asked, 'Where would you like to go? Name your place, madame!'

He was thinking of Blackpool, of Southport, of Lytham St Anne's.

She replied instantly, 'Oh, Paris, of course!'

His face fell.

He said, 'That will take a fortnight! Well, it can't be helped.'

She laid her problem before heaven again, piteously.

'Why is he so cruel to me?' Then, as he caught her hands and turned her to face him, 'What are you doing?'

'I am trying to kiss you,' Ambrose said reasonably, 'and you will keep talking to someone else!'

She laughed. She left heaven to its own devices.

'I give you back your kiss!' she cried, doing so. Then gave him another, and said, 'That is interest, Mr Longe!'

'What? Seven and one-eighth per cent?'

'Do not be impudent. Please to kiss me again.'

In a while he said hopefully, 'I say, Nim, would they mind if we went home now? We haven't got much of this honeymoon left!'

She shook her head, and then nodded, between kisses.

St Stephen's clock struck seven. Ambrose's coffee had long since grown cold. He stared at his unfinished editorial without seeing it. He saw, instead, two Naomis.

The one slept deeply, splendidly, after love-making. Beneath the mantle of black hair her flesh glowed, luminous as pearl. The other was heavy and unbeautiful with child. She frowned and gasped over each pain, humble in the face of her torment.

He had never understood why the love of man should cause woman so much suffering. Such a chasm yawned between the bride-goddess on her pedestal and the breeding animal crouched in its trouble. Yet Naomi accepted both images, having inner knowledge of the mystery. It was he who questioned and fretted, he who wanted to know what could not be explained.

Bob Bullock knocked at the door this time, and Ambrose reached guiltily for his pen. Then he put it down again, tired of pretence.

'I don't seem able to finish this, Bob.'

'Here, let me have a look at it, Mr Longe.'

The overseer read it through, illustrating its effect on him with nods and chuckles, and laid it on the desk.

'It *is* finished, Mr Longe. You've just got to cross out *It will be interesting to see*. That's all.'

'But what was interesting to see? I can't remember. It must have been something.'

'Well, it don't matter,' said Bob sensibly, 'and it ain't necessary! This'll do us nicely. We'll manage the rest. Charlie can check the mock-up. He's got quite an eye for detail.'

He looked very kindly on Ambrose's rumpled appearance.

'If I was you, Mr Longe, I'd go home now,' said Bob.

Ambrose consulted the clock for the thousandth time that day. Fifteen minutes past seven.

'They were going to send Joseph with the carriage when anything happened,' said Ambrose. 'It's a long time to wait. It's a cruel business. You don't think she'll die, do you, Bob?'

Women did die. Bob's first wife had died ten years ago.

'Nay, don't mither yourself. Let me get Jimmy to call you a hackney-coach. There's only one road between here and the High Street. If your man does come you won't miss him.'

'Thank you – and the editorial is all right, is it?'

'Bang up to standard, Mr Longe. It's finished, sir. It's finished. You can go home now.'

Ambrose's nerves were playing the devil with him. The phrase troubled him. *It's finished. It's finished.*

Naomi is dead, he thought, and they're afraid to tell me.

As he stepped into the hackney-carriage an empty hearse passed him, jolting home to the Doles, and all the way up the High Street he imagined the knocker of Thornton House swathed in black. In his mind's eye he pictured Dollie drawing down the blinds. He saw himself wearing his wedding finery to the funeral.

The sound and feel of the carriage wheels was suddenly thick and soft. His heart thundered a warning in his head. He stared down at the cobbles and up at the front of his house, afraid.

As in the case of all serious illnesses the servants had laid straw in the road to muffle the noise of traffic. The lion's head knocker had been muffled too, but not in black. A yellow duster was tied round his eyes. He wore an air of forlorn dignity. People were walking more slowly as they passed by, looking up at the windows. One or two even lingered, watching, hoping to be the first to hear news of any sort.

Ambrose paid the driver and took the steps two at a time.

His home had been in an unusual state of noise and confusion that morning. Now it seemed unnaturally quiet, and he had forgotten his key. Reluctantly, he lifted the lion's head.

At that moment Joseph opened the door, wearing a great-coat. He was merely startled to see his master, but Ambrose read the surprise as terror. He could scarcely frame his question.

The manservant, reading his expression, took the liberty of placing a reassuring hand upon his arm and brought him safe inside.

'All's well, sir. All's well. I was just coming to fetch you.'

Ambrose's lips repeated, 'All's well,' but no sound came forth.

Joseph now spoke more slowly and clearly as though his master were deaf.

'You've got a son, Mr Longe. Born just after seven o'clock.'

Still Ambrose's lips repeated the words, and no sound came.

Joseph sat him down in a hall chair and called the maid. He brought Ambrose a glass of aquavit. He spoke to the girl in quite a different tone from the one he used to his employers.

'You stay here. I'll go and tell them he's home, Dollie!'

The maid now took over the task of conveying information.

'Mrs Longe is pretty comfortable, sir. Mrs Vivian's been with her all day, and doctor's been here since luncheon.'

Ambrose had been washed up safe, as it were, on to the shore of life. He felt perfectly calm and well, but his head and limbs were numb and he had some difficulty in comprehending the situation.

'Can I get you anything, sir?' Dollie asked.

He shook his head. She remained standing by him as if he had to be watched. In another moment Jamie Standish tapped him briskly on the shoulder and delivered his message intimately into one ear.

'A perfectly straightforward case. No complications. Six weeks in bed. Your son is healthy and strong. You can see them both in a wee while. The girl is just tidying everything up.'

Ambrose drank his aquavit in one swallow, and contemplated the empty glass.

'I'm quite done up!' he said, with immense astonishment.

'Aye, well, you will be. I've always said the husband suffers most!' said Jamie in dry amusement. And to the watchful maid, 'Go and see if they're ready, will you, Dollie?'

The maid, who had smiled at the state of Ambrose in his new clothes, now smiled at the state of him in his new fatherhood, and whisked smartly upstairs.

Ambrose tried his legs and found they would hold him. He straightened his brown coat and cream waistcoat, and adjusted his stock. Joseph reappeared and offered him a comb.

Down the stairs came the maid, followed by Mary Vivian, who pressed his hand and kissed his cheek and nodded in a friendly fashion without speaking. They all seemed to be treating him like he treated George Howarth.

'You can go up whenever you like, sir,' said Dollie.

Ambrose stood there, nonplussed.

'I'll call in again at ten o'clock this evening,' Jamie said, addressing Joseph, as being the most sensible person present.

The maid fetched two armfuls of outdoor clothes, and helped first Mary and then the doctor into them.

'I'll be taking Mrs Vivian home then, sir?' said Joseph civilly.

Ambrose did not hear him. He had decided to mount the stairs, counting them silently as he went, to prevent himself from stumbling.

He opened the door of their room and saw Naomi propped up against a mound of pillows, holding their child. He closed the door on the incomprehensible world outside. He found his way to them, and sat humbly at the side of the bed. He crossed his legs and clasped his knee, in an effort to seem at ease. He could think of nothing to say that did not seem to be superfluous.

She had been to a far place, somewhere that he would

never know. Her voice came from there, deep and soft, immensely comforting.

'Ah, my poor love. My dear love. Ah, my Ambrose. Come, sit closer. Come, sit here with me.'

Then he knew that his day had been as terrible as he suspected. Cautiously, he perched on the side of the bed. Carefully he embraced her, and closed his eyes that he might sense her more completely. She felt warm and whole. She had survived. Women were surprising creatures. She might have died, and here she was discussing names for the creature that could have killed her.

'You are sure you do not wish him to be called Ambrose after you?' Naomi asked, making certain of this vexed question.

Ambrose shook his head.

'Or Tobias, after your father?'

He shook his head again.

Naomi sighed, but not unhappily. She smiled.

She said, 'Then may we call him *Nathan*, after *my* father?'

Ambrose nodded. He did not care, so long as she was safe, so long as he could stay with her in peace. With her free hand she stroked his head. She murmured endearments to both husband and son.

Utterly content, Ambrose opened his eyes and saw a pink and frowning face only inches from his own. One minute hand was tucked beneath its chin, the other spread out fan-wise over its shawl.

'Oh, look!' said Ambrose, amazed, entranced. 'He's got real fingers!'

A New Era

chapter eighteen

Wednesday, 21 June, 1837

This world of three families and three houses was a magical one for the children, and each year it grew larger.

Superiority of age set Philomena and Santo Vivian apart from the rest. She, at fourteen, was attending Miss Partridge's School for the Daughters of Gentlefolk in Millbridge, and was full of condescension. He, well into his ninth year, took lessons at the rectory with Jarvis Pole and would become a weekly boarder at Millbridge Grammar School in the autumn. But the four younger ones had arrived almost upon each other's heels and grown up in each other's company, so they did not mind where they congregated. Between Thornton House, Beech Grove and the Old Hall at Brigge there was daily communication. In each home there was a nursery and playroom, and the young visitors fetched their nurses with them. Should a major crisis arise, each child knew that the judgement of an aunt could be trusted as implicitly as that of a mother, and they delighted in their presiding hostesses for entirely different reasons.

They found Dorcas Standish a soothing influence, because she was gentle and never scolded them, and each visit was exactly like the last. On the other hand it was tremendous fun to be with Mary Vivian, in spite of her quick tongue, because she lived in the middle of constant drama and anything might happen. Whilst Naomi Longe entered into the very heart of their childhood, glorying in their triumphs and sorrowing over their downfalls as though she were one of them.

Scarcely eleven months separated Alice Vivian from Cicely

215

Nathan Longe appeared, and six months later Matthew Standish joined the group. Now Matthew was toddling, and the cradle in the corner of the nursery stood empty, but only for a little while.

In the background, only available for events of staggering importance, were the heads of the three families. And, like their wives, each of them appealed to the children by reason of some special gift or idiosyncrasy.

Jamie Standish was the most feared and respected because he presided over the issues of life and death, but he redeemed this rather sombre image by doing conjuring tricks at parties.

Hal Vivian was the most handsome, admired by the little boys, adored by the little girls, and he created marvellous mechanical toys. His only fault, if fault it could be called, was that he never allowed any child to play with them.

Ambrose Longe was the most fun, with his thin brown face and quizzical brown eyes, and his talent for outrageous surprises. On Nathan Longe's first birthday, the previous September, Ambrose had brought an organ-grinder right to the front door of Thornton House and fetched the children out upon the pavement for their own private concert.

The man wore an ingratiating smile but his eyes did not smile.

He wound out his tinkling tunes to the circle of rapt faces, and made his monkey caper for them. Afterwards each child was allowed to put a penny in the creature's outstretched military cap and shake its small cold paw. The monkey shuddered in his red jacket and stared at them with piteous human eyes.

'Why does he shiver so?' asked little Alice Vivian, concerned.

'Because he comes from a hot country, far away,' Naomi had replied, 'and he feels the cold, even in his warm jacket.'

Then Alice found a sweet in her apron pocket and held it out, but the monkey nipped her fingers in his anxiety to get it, and she was frightened of animals for a long time.

*

On this first day of summer the children all met at Beech Grove, though it was actually the turn for Thornton House – as three-year-old Alice was quick to point out, when the Vivians' carriage stopped at the beginning of the High Street.

'On to the end!' cried Alice, pointing her finger towards the upper part of the town. 'On to the end!'

This battle-cry being ignored, she lay on the floor of the carriage and refused to move.

'Get up at once, you naughty child!' cried Philomena. 'I'm going to be – *late – for – school*!'

She emphasised the last three words with three sharp smacks, which made Alice scream loudly and weep and kick. Whereupon Santo, who detested one sister and adored the other, thumped Philomena hard between the shoulder blades.

'Oh, do for heaven's sake stop quarrelling!' cried Mary, exasperated with all three of them.

Philomena sank down on the carriage seat, sobbing, 'I can't breathe, Mamma! He's stopped me from breathing!'

'Nonsense, Philly! Santo, get out immediately, sir! Your Papa shall hear of this! Alice, get up at once! Margery,' to the stout, young nurse-maid, 'help me to lift Alice.'

The Vivians' arrival was usually the opening comedy of the day, and since they were always late everyone else was there to watch.

Dorcas stood in the doorway of Beech Grove smiling, as dark and lovely as ever, holding the hand of her grave little daughter, Cicely. At her side, her old nurse Sarah Pratt prevented Matthew from throwing himself under the horses. Behind them, Nathan Longe was squirming along the hall tiles, trying to get away from his nurse, Gussie Purdom.

'I've had enough of you already, Master Awkward,' breathed Gussie, 'and the day ain't half started yet!'

She spotted the distraction and seized upon it.

'Oh, *look* at Miss Alice! Oh, *what* a naughty girl!'

'What? Where?' Nathan scrambled to his feet.

He was at once deeply struck by the spectacle of Cousin Alice being carried across the pavement. Her sturdy frame and close-cropped head gave her a boyish look and a strong will was evident in the set of mouth and chin, but what people noticed first was the beauty of her colouring: her amber hair and darker amber eyes, her bright pink cheeks and milky skin.

She had held on to anything and anyone which could prevent her from being removed. Now, in order to make matters as difficult as possible, she was playing dead. Her body was rigid, her arms crossed over her chest, crusader-style, her eyes squeezed shut. A blue hair-ribbon slithered down over one ear. From the crook of one elbow peeped a rag doll, dressed like herself in a sky-blue cotton frock, white frilled pantalettes and black slippers. Alice was a bonny child and big for her years. Her porters were flushed with exertion.

'Oh, what a very large parcel!' Dorcas said, smiling. 'Do put it down carefully on the mat.'

Still playing the game for all it was worth, Alice lay perfectly stiff and motionless.

'Ah, what a pity you didn't bring Alice,' said Dorcas sweetly. 'She would have so enjoyed the new garden swing.'

The child's eyes snapped open. She sat up, clutching her doll.

'It's not a parcel, it's me, Aunt Dorcas!' she cried, and smiled like the sun and tried to set her hair-ribbon straight.

Now Cicily giggled and tugged at Dorcas's skirt, saying, 'Not a *parcel*, Mamma. It's *Alice*!'

'Iss Alice! Iss Alice!' Nathan shouted, escaping Gussie again.

And he ran round and round until he fell down.

Matthew laughed very loud, throwing back his head which was as fair and fluffy as a dandelion clock, drumming on Sarah Pratt's stomach with his heels, repeating the phrase as nearly as he could.

'Iss Ice! Iss Ice! Iss Ice!'

'Hush now, my beauty!' said Mrs Pratt comfortably.

218

Nathan scrambled up again, dodged Gussie, and pretended to be a spinning top.

'Do you know, it exhausts me even to *look at* that child!' said Mary factually. 'What are you doing with my portfolio, Philly?'

'I thought you'd forgotten it, Mamma,' said Philomena, demure and sly, 'so I picked it up as we came out. Aren't you going to work on your next article with Aunt Naomi? You said you wanted to see her!'

She knew very well what was afoot.

'Give it to me,' said Mary, snatching it back, 'and *hush*!' But the remark had been noted, and immediately all was bedlam. Alice ran towards her, crying, '*I* want to come with you and see Aunt Naomi! I said so. I said so.'

Nathan, who had suspected all along that something was being kept from him, stopped spinning and said pitifully, 'Mamma! *Mamma*!' and burst into loud sobs.

Cicely's eyes filled. Matthew wept in sympathy. Tears poured down Alice's cheeks, and she and Nathan clung to Mary's skirt and begged to be taken with her.

Santo's tact and good humour came uppermost. He was a hero in the younger children's eyes, and he knew it.

'Aunt Dorcas!' he said loudly, over the squall. 'Aunt Dorcas, don't you think we should try the new swing?'

'What an excellent notion!' said Dorcas quickly.

Alice and Nathan paused in mid-sob to consider this offer.

To Mary, Santo whispered, 'You go and take Phil to school. I can walk up to the rectory.' As she hesitated, he added, 'And I say, Mamma, you might drop in on Uncle Jarvis and tell him why I'll be a bit late!'

Then he began to tickle Nathan until the little boy rolled on the ground, laughing and calling for mercy.

'Who's going to have the first swing?' cried Santo.

Alice's tears dried visibly on her cheeks.

'Me!' she shouted, letting go of Mary's gown.

Matthew recovered, steadied himself by grasping Mrs Pratt's hair, and cried, 'Me! Me!'

Graciously Santo held out both hands for the little girls to clasp. Over his shoulder he spoke to the giggling Nathan.

'Come on, you! Stop fooling around!'

Followed by Dorcas and the three nurses, the children poured out into the garden of Beech Grove.

'Bless you, Santo!' said Mary under her breath.

Philomena said sourly, 'He's only doing that to dodge the first lesson. He hasn't learned his Latin!'

'Get into that carriage!' said Mary grimly, 'and don't dare say another word, Miss!'

Alfred whipped up the horses and they proceeded along the High Street and into Market Square at a brisk trot. Philomena, deeply offended, was delivered up to another day's ladylike schooling. Then the coachman turned into Rectory Lane and waited while Mary made her son's excuse, then finally drove her back to Thornton House. There, the Longes' carriage stood outside, with Joseph on the box, waiting. The manservant touched his hat to Mary and nodded to Alfred.

'We're in a bit of an upset this morning, madam,' he observed.

'I'm afraid it's going to be one of those difficult days, Joseph!' she replied, and ran up the steps and lifted the knocker which was not yet muffled.

Ambrose opened the door himself, crying, 'Thank God you've come. Naomi is being very brave, but we are all at sixes and sevens. I had forgot how awful it was.'

'Oh, my dear, don't fret,' said Mary kindly. 'Truly, it looks worse than it is. Is Jamie here?'

'He came and went,' cried Ambrose indignantly, 'saying he would be back this afternoon. What sort of medical attendance is that?'

Mary concealed a smile.

'He knows it will be hours yet. Had you not better go to work?'

'I was working until three o'clock yesterday morning, getting the Tuesday paper out,' he replied, in some exasperation. 'I arranged to stay at home today, so I could take Naomi for a drive. Why are babies so inconvenient, Mary?'

'Because Eve listened to the serpent! Now, Ambrose,' in a brisk voice which reminded him of Charlotte, 'you will only distress yourself and us if you stay here. Go to the office. I'm sure you will find something to do, and we shall send news as soon as there is any.' He hesitated, and she gave him a friendly little push. 'Go now. Do as I say. You know it is sensible advice.'

He took his top hat from the hall table and clapped it absentmindedly on the side of his head. Still he lingered, grumbling out of fear.

'And then there is King William dying or dead. We waited until the last possible minute before printing, in case a message came through. At least *The Herald* hasn't got it this morning, but if he dies now the damned *Post* will scoop it for Thursday. I tell you, there's no justice in the world, Mary.'

'Dying or dead, indeed!' she said contemptuously. 'The King has been ill before and lived. He is an old man who suffers from asthma. I used to have that, and believe me I thought I would die of it every time. Besides, nobody wants a young girl on the throne who can't say boo to a goose. Don't you worry, Ambrose. The doctors will keep him alive as long as they possibly can. Go to your office.'

He passed one hand over his face. His voice and manner changed.

'I don't give a damn about King William and the news,' he said. 'I'm just sick with fright over Naomi.'

Mary patted his arm and kissed his cheek.

'You're a good girl,' said Ambrose.

He took his top hat off again, and put it back on the hall table.

'I'll come with you and say goodbye to her first.'

He followed Mary up the broad staircase, saying plaintively, 'Why didn't they arrange it so that childbirth was painless?

Why let a woman suffer so? I don't believe all that nonsense about Eve . . .'

Millbridge borough council, in its new form, seemed pretty much like the old one. They were still mean with the Poor Rate, still liberal with civic banquets and pageants, still concerned with private profit rather than social improvement and still obstinate over the question of public hygiene. Jamie Standish, six years older and shrewder and tougher than at the time of the cholera epidemic, waged constant war on them. He would have preferred quicker results, but since he could not galvanise them into action he intended to wear them down to submission.

He was concerned with a far more urgent medical matter that June morning than the coming birth at Thornton House, though he left Naomi as comfortable in mind and body as he could. He had bullied an immediate appointment out of the council, to report a bad outbreak of fever in that part of Millbridge known as 'Back o'Beyond'. Now he sat in the outer chamber waiting, while they discussed important business.

'But we don't know for sure that the King's dead yet. There's a lot of difference between hard news and rumour,' said one councillor.

'No, but it's best to be prepared, ain't it?' replied another.

'Only we don't want to be in any way disrespectful to his sick majesty, do we?' asked a third.

'Ah, but preparation ain't disrespect, and how does that saying go? The King is dead, long live the King!'

'Only it won't be a king, will it? It'll be a queen!'

'Nay, never. They're not going to let a chit of a girl rule a big country like this.'

'She's the heir to the throne, and who else have we got?'

'Besides, it wouldn't be her as ruled. It'd be that mother of hers, and that Conroy. We'd have civil war in a month!'

222

The Lord Mayor said, 'Let's stick to the point, shall we? Other matters are pending.'

'Aye, we're in for a dose of Dr Standish!'

'He's a right bulldog, that one. He never lets go.'

'I wonder what bee he's got in his bonnet this time?'

The Lord Mayor cleared his throat, called for attention, and began to read his notes aloud.

'The question before us is that of our beloved King William's illness, which if it should prove fatal, though we hope he will be with us for many years yet, would give rise to us having a Proclamation Ceremony for the new monarch. This requires a good deal of planning and considerable expenditure of public money, and in the event of good King William's demise we don't want to find ourselves in a mess because we haven't worked it all out.'

'Quite right!' cried an alderman. Then added, 'How long will he have been on the throne, now . . .'

A mottled hand was raised, followed by a mottled countenance.

'Two questions, Mr Mayor. When King William was proclaimed we held a civic banquet at the Royal George. First, are we having the dinner at the Royal George again?'

'Where else is there that's half as good?'

'What about t'Fox and Grapes at Medlar? That's a grand place.'

'Nay, why not try the Iron Duke at Kingswood?'

'Eh, don't talk so daft. If it's a Millbridge ceremony we stop here. We're not piking off down the valley for us roast beef!'

The mottled man cried indignantly, 'I haven't asked my second question yet! Last time, Mr Mayor, the ceremony was proclaimed in six different parts of the town in front of six different inns, which gave the landlords a lot of extra custom. Now, isn't it only fair that the procession takes a different route this time?'

'What, round by six of your beer-taverns, Dan?'

A shout of laughter interrupted the proceedings.

An alderman said, '*I* vote we ask the Bard of Coldcote to write a coronation poem! He writes grand verse, does Harry Ramsbottom.'

'Oh, there's plenty of time for that. They won't hold the coronation for above a twelvemonth.'

'Mr Mayor, Mr Mayor! Last time the ribbons and favours were all purchased from Buckley's, which caused quite a bit of bad feeling among other haberdashers in the town. Wouldn't it be better if . . .'

'Let's sort out the procession first, shall we?' said the Mayor, beginning to lose track of the discussion. 'We can talk about the rest of it later.'

He found the right place in his notes, adjusted his spectacles, cleared his throat again and read in a tone of hushed importance.

'Now, first of all, there'll be the Beadle – on 'orseback. Then a company of Javelin Men. Followed by New Town Brass Band . . .'

'Why are you having New Town? Wroughton's the best band in the valley. You should ask *them*!'

'And what's wrong with Field Mill Brass Band I'd like to know?'

'Eh, I thought you were supposed to be at home, Mr Longe!' said Frank Ormerod, coming into the office with a paper in his hand.

'I thought you told me that I would only worry about the first child!' Ambrose replied, turning the joke on himself.

'Well, I'm glad you're here. I was going to send you this!'

And he put a scribbled message on the desk.

'How reliable is this information?' Ambrose asked, alerted.

'It's reliable. Come through last night from one of our business contacts who was in London yesterday. He says the King died early on Tuesday morning, and the little lass was Queen before breakfast. But that'd be too late for the morning papers.'

'But not for special editions, and not for evening papers, eh?'

'No. Mind you, they'd miss the express mail to Manchester, and we don't know when they'd catch the next coaches coming north, or which routes they'd be on.'

'Frank, get Bob and Charlie and George up here. We're going to set up a single-page special edition!'

The four men sat round Ambrose's desk, firing off ideas.

'Headline – KING WILLIAM IV IS DEAD!, and a summary of the monarch and his reign . . .'

'On the other side, LONG LIVE QUEEN VICTORIA! and a general portrait of the new monarch . . .'

'A black border, all the way round the front page . . .'

'Play the idea of a girl queen for all we're worth!'

'Aye, but tell them she's got an old head on young shoulders, though. Wise for her years, and that!'

'Yes, and keep her mother and Conroy out of it. No politics.'

'We can set up the whole thing now, short of putting the date in. Then, whenever the official news comes, we can print it!'

'Aye, and unless Sam Pickering knows as much as we do, and is as quick off the mark, we'll beat *The Herald* to it and stop *The Post* from stealing a march on us!'

'And tell Jimmy from me,' said Ambrose grimly, 'that if he isn't waiting on that pavement for every blessed mail-coach that comes through from *anywhere* I'll box *both* his ears!'

Naomi had been up since six o'clock, trying to creep from their bed without rousing Ambrose, but bulk and weight made her clumsy and he was awake in an instant. Unlike the first birth which had been protracted, her pains were quite strong and came every few minutes. She would have liked to concentrate on them by herself in peace, because the slightest gasp or grimace troubled her husband so much, but he would neither leave her nor go back to sleep. So she kept him occupied as best she could in giving orders to the servants who were already up and about, and in writing messages to Joseph to deliver to Jamie and Dorcas Standish and Mary Vivian.

At eight o'clock Nathan was brought to her, as usual. She supervised his breakfast of bread and milk and played with him for a while, managing to conceal the fact that she was in some discomfort. At nine o'clock Joseph took the boy and his nurse down to Beech Grove. Dr Jamie came and went. By the time the hall clock chimed the three quarters before ten Ambrose was in total disarray, and Mary's arrival and decision came as a god-send to himself and everyone.

The front door closed behind him. The household became quieter. The two women smiled at each other in mutual understanding.

'He is so good and so loving,' Naomi said ruefully, 'and he suffers so for me and so much wants to help me.'

'You have missed the next word out,' said Mary mischievously, untying her bonnet strings. 'It is *but*!, followed by a long pause!'

'Ah! you are a naughty one!'

Then Naomi turned to the parlour-maid, saying, 'Dollie, I am very well, and Mrs Vivian will stay with me. Go downstairs and say that I wish everyone to continue their normal duties until Dr Standish comes this afternoon. If Cook would step upstairs in half an hour I will discuss the day's menus with her. In the meantime Mrs Vivian and I should like some tea.'

The maid bobbed a curtsey and departed, taking Mary's bonnet and summer mantle with her.

'Now tell me truly, how are you feeling, my dear?' Mary asked.

'I tell you the truth. I think this one will be much quicker than the last. I think that Jamie has much on his mind this morning and does not believe me how strong the pains are.' She stopped and gasped and rubbed her back. 'Oof! That was such a one!'

226

'Gracious me!' said Mary, both fascinated and disturbed. 'Ought we to send for Jamie to come early, do you think?'

'But I do not know where he is!' Naomi cried dramatically. Then she shrugged and smiled. 'And I do not care a tuppence, either!'

'Lord above, Naomi! Should you like to lie down?'

'No, I wish to walk around. It takes my mind off the pain. When I lie down I must give myself up to it.'

Mary took her arm and they sauntered sedately round the room, stopping whenever Naomi had a contraction.

The morning routine of Thornton House rolled peacefully on. The scullery-maid scrubbed and whitened the front doorsteps. The boot-boy whistled over his daily tasks in the yard. Dollie brought a tray of tea-things, set her mistress and the room to rights, and then retired to the linen room to sew. Mrs Bagnall, the cook-housekeeper, mounted the stairs full of helpful suggestions and went down again prepared for any culinary emergency. Joseph took the carriage and horses back to the George, and afterwards cleaned silver in the kitchen. The long clock in the hall marked the passage of time. The two women were very quiet and tranquil together. The luncheon hour passed.

Then Naomi's face changed. She cried, 'Oh, I must lie down!'

And this time she crouched and panted over the pain like a dog that is short of water.

'Lor!' cried Mary, turning pale. She sat Naomi carefully in a chair, ran to the door and called the maids. 'Dollie! Quick!'

Naomi pressed her hands down on the arms of the chair and held her breath. A fine film of moisture gleamed on her skin. She groaned and panted and groaned again.

Mary found herself suddenly in charge of a situation at which she had expected to be an onlooker. The maid removed the warming pan and turned back the sheets. Together they helped Naomi into bed.

'Dollie, where can we find Dr Standish?'

'Mary, hold my hands! Hold my hands!' Naomi cried.

She hauled on Mary's wrists without mercy, forehead furrowed with effort, bowing over her travail, then lay back on the pillows. The roots of her hair were wet with sweat.

'Don't worry, Naomi, I'm here!' Mary told her, with tremendous misgivings. And to the maid, 'Dollie! Run downstairs and fetch hot water and towels. Tell Joseph to find Dr Standish – or any doctor – or any midwife – or anybody! Oh, and ask Mrs Bagnall if she knows anything about babies being born!'

Naomi laughed weakly, and two tears trickled down either side of her nose. She was taking short, timid breaths, as if afraid the pain would catch her on a long one.

'Oh, my poor Mary. I am so sorry.'

'I don't mind really,' said Mary, rubbing the places where Naomi had gripped her. 'In fact, I'm quite enjoying it. Only I should like Jamie to come fairly soon.'

'Again!' cried Naomi, signalling the onslaught of pain. 'Your hands. Give me your hands.'

'Oh dear, oh Lor! Where is everybody?'

'Madam,' said Dollie softly at her side, concerned but never forgetting her manners, 'Cook says she's the eldest of fourteen, and though she's no expert she can help.'

Naomi's latest groan took more breath than she had got, and still the pain demanded more. She breathed in and screamed out.

'Fetch her!' Mary said peremptorily.

Cook arrived very quickly for such a fat, short woman, bearing the kitchen scissors and a length of twine. She brought her face down close to Naomi's and spoke with the utmost consideration.

'Excuse me, madam, but I'll have to take a few liberties.'

'Oh, never mind that, Mrs Bagnall!' cried Mary impatiently. 'Having a baby takes every liberty a woman can put up with!'

'I'll be outside if you want me, madam,' said Dollie, retreating.

'It is here again!' cried Naomi. 'Oh, and again!'

'Lie on your back, madam, and fetch your knees apart,' said Mrs Bagnall. She threw back the sheets. 'Ah! We'll have somebody else with us in another minute or two. See, the head's crowned, Mrs Vivian.'

Mary stared open-mouthed at Naomi's splendid ivory thighs and the wet, dark head between them. The soreness of her wrists was forgotten. She had never seen a birth before and, though she felt she should have been disgusted, she was not. Perhaps too many generations of farmer's wives lay behind her for her to play the lady.

'Now, madam, we're nearly there,' said Cook to Naomi, 'and I don't want you to push no more. Nature'll do the rest on her own. You hold back as long as you can, and screech out when you have to. Now, Mrs Vivian, when madam pulls on *you*, you pull on *her* to take her mind off what's happening.'

'Very well, ' said Mary resolutely.

So she and Naomi hauled that little life on shore together with Mrs Bagnall directing them like some ancient mariner.

Naomi gave three loud, short screams. Mary saw the dark head convulse, the shoulders squeeze through, the body slither and leap like a fish, and Mrs Bagnall received a fine, large boy. The infant waved his fists, made water and yelled with shock.

'Another son, Naomi. Another son,' cried Mary, shaking her hands and kissing them.

They heard voices and footsteps on the stairs.

'Too late!' Mary shouted joyfully. 'We've done it without you!'

As Jamie Standish hurried into the room, full of apologies.

Naomi said, 'This one I should like to call Tobias, and again I ask you to be the godmother, my dearest Mary, because he was born by you. And I love you and thank you a thousand times, for what should I have done without you?'

Mary felt her eyes smart, knew she was near tears and

laughed them away. Reverently she held the newly-washed and shawled infant in her arms: light-heartedly she shook his scarlet fist.

'Hello, Toby!' said Mary. 'Welcome to the world!'

If it was any of them now, it was the two o'clock Leeds Mail en route from Liverpool. Jimmy was hopping up and down on the Middleton Street corner, waiting for the incoming coach and exchanging appalling threats and insults with the office-boy from *The Herald*, who was obviously on the same mission.

Then Ambrose Longe appeared, fresh from overlooking the special edition. The two lads quietened down and greeted him in subdued and civil tones. With everything done that could be done, with the prospect of confirmation only minutes away, Ambrose could not have stayed inside if they paid him. He stood with Jimmy on the corner, arms akimbo, in his shirtsleeves. His only concession to street-dress was to clap his top hat on one side of his head.

In another moment or two, caressing the ends of his moustache, looking sideways out of his sharp green eyes, came Sam Pickering, equally curious, to stand on the opposite corner and nod at his rival.

They heard the hooves and wheels of the Liverpool coach long before it reached the crossroads. They heard the ecstatic whine of the horn. The Leeds Mail drew rein only sufficiently to slow down and make sure nothing was coming the other way. Then as the guard threw two bundles of London newspapers on to the pavement, he bawled his news as he had bawled it at every passing stage over the last sixty miles, and would bawl it across Yorkshire.

'He's dead! The King's dead! God save the Queen!'

It was as though Cornmarket had been frozen in mid-action and rendered dumb, but only for a few shocked seconds.

Then Ambrose whipped off his top hat and waved it in the air, shouting, 'Long live Queen Victoria!'

The cry was taken up by those around him, and people

began to run up and down the street and into shops, passing the news from mouth to mouth. The driver of the Mail never took his eyes from the road. Dedicated, a master of his moment, he flicked up the lathered team and rattled off to the Royal George with the message of a lifetime.

Sam Pickering saluted the passing of the old monarch and the accession of the new one with the rest of them, and disappeared quickly into *The Herald* building. Clearly he had been as well informed as *The Correspondent* and had reached a similar decision.

Ambrose, about to follow his example, was transfixed by the sight of Joseph driving the carriage towards Middleton Street at a stately trot. Filled with hope and fear, completely forgetting the exaltation of a moment ago, Ambrose began to run towards him.

At the same time, Joseph's attention was diverted by the guard of the Leeds coach yelling his news as they passed each other. So he did not see his master until Ambrose was alongside, calling, 'News! What news?'

The manservant smiled. There was so much news. He was strangely stirred and moved by all of it. He replied heartily, frankly.

'No need for alarm, sir. All safe and well. Master Tobias Longe, sir, was born a little after one o'clock this afternoon.'

He could not help adding, 'So we've got a new queen, sir?'

'So we have!' Ambrose said. 'So we have.'

He rested his hand on the horse's harness. All about them was chaos, but in his centre he was still and smiling.

'Toby, eh?' he said. 'Well, God bless me. And my wife is well?'

'Very well, sir. Sitting up drinking tea with Mrs Vivian when I left, sir. Right as ninepence.'

Ambrose looked around him. Jimmy hung about on the pavement, reluctant to leave the scenes of triumph. He beckoned the boy.

'Fetch my coat from the office, Jim. And, Jim, tell them

that my new son is called Toby Longe – that'll mean something to one or two newspapermen among 'em. And, Jim, tell them to get on with that special edition and send a copy up to me at Thornton House this afternoon. You've done very well, Jim. Here's sixpence for you. Now run as fast as you can because I want to go home.'

'Yessir. Thankee, sir. Congratulations, sir!'

Ambrose clambered into the carriage with legs of lead. Joseph walked the horses down to the crossroads and turned. Out from the office ran Jim, followed by most of *The Correspondent*'s staff, all smiling and waving and shouting good wishes across the street.

In both buildings, the presses began to print out their tidings of national sorrow, and national joy.

Who Goes Home?

chapter nineteen

Much had happened in the past three years, and this meeting, held regularly every Thursday evening in a room above Pendleton's in Croft Street, was one such phenomenon.

The Oddities Club was a group of local professional and business men which had begun with less than half a dozen members and still scarcely numbered twenty. Once a month, each member was allowed to bring a guest at his own discretion. Mostly these passing visitors caused no particular stir and were ushered gently forth from the magic circle. Occasionally, a sparkling choice would prove to be a future Oddity. But woe betide the member whose guest proved to be a bad mistake, for his power of invitation could be temporarily suspended.

The club's rules were entirely those of sociability and style. A fellow had to be out of the ordinary and to contribute something of value to the general conversation. There was no chairman, no committee, no annual fee, no accounting. Their evening's food and drink amounted to less than two shillings per head. And since most of them were family men, they met at seven o'clock sharp and departed no later than eleven.

Pendleton's had been chosen partly for its convenience and largely for its own originality. Old Walter had departed this life soon after the club was formed, but Pendleton's did not change a jot. The patron's eldest son, known as Young Walter though he was close on fifty, saw to their comforts personally. And since club members were never drunk or rowdy, though often high-voiced and heated in argument, the old chop-house cherished them and was proud of this connection.

Ambrose Longe and Sam Pickering were the only

newspaper editors so far and, though Arnold Thwaites yearned to be one of them, he knew he would not be asked.

George Howarth was there in his radical coat, introducing radical friends. So sound was his judgement that none of these self-taught and articulate working men had failed to gain their admiration, if not their complete acceptance and agreement.

Jamie Standish and Harold Bailey were the medical experts, and they too could dig up some extraordinary acquaintances, including one gentleman who swore by the healing powers of electric shocks and had them jumping all over the place.

Hal Vivian was there tonight, as Ambrose's guest. He had been present on other occasions, was regarded as an honorary member and would have been elected long since except that his frequent absences forbade this. But when he did turn up he was always worth waiting for, because he treated his audience as though its knowledge was as great, its visions as wild and brilliant as his own.

That evening they had demolished a saddle of mutton between them, with redcurrant jelly and boiled potatoes, and done justice to a currant pudding with custard sauce. Now bottles of claret were set on the table and clay pipes brought for those who wanted them, and conversation of a sociable sort was in order before they began serious discussion.

Ambrose fetched out a fine cigar case and offered it round. Time had been kind to him, marriage suited him. He still looked remarkably young for his age. He still wore his top hat at a dashing angle. He was still slim and elegant. Like many of the male Howarths, he did not go bald and his hair grew as thick as ever, though its nut-brown warmth was giving way to steel. But his shabby inconsequence had gone. He was an advertisement for his tailor's excellence. His wit had matured. His opinion carried weight. His judgement was respected.

Mind you, as a father of three sons, and the husband of a lady financier with a will of her own, he had learned a thing or two in the past few years, and often with difficulty. Yet he had no quarrel with life on this midsummer evening, with the last of the day's sun coming through the thick glass window panes, and the first spirals of convivial smoke rising.

'Is Mrs Longe keeping well?' Sam Pickering asked politely.

For Naomi, newly-risen from childbed, must be accorded their first respects.

'Never better, Sam. I was brought to book this morning, in both senses, for failing to pay the butcher's bill. Well, Lord knows,' said Ambrose, deliberately courting their amusement, 'I suffered enough when young Jack was born, without bothering about bills. But at any rate, I knew Naomi was completely recovered when she came down to breakfast for the first time in six weeks, and straightway pitched into me about the butcher!'

They all laughed.

'And how is young Jack?' asked Sam, with a dry smile.

'A pestilential young rogue like the other two. I shall never be able to discipline them. Naomi won't allow it for a moment.'

'Is *Jack* a family name?' asked Hal Vivian, who had already been told several times by his wife, but never listened.

'Aye, in a manner of speaking, ' said Ambrose. 'I named the lad after my old teacher and first mentor, Dr Jack Ackroyd, who was headmaster of Millbridge Grammar School in my day, and one of the noblest and bravest men I have ever known.'

'Hanged, drawn and quartered at Lancaster Jail in 1812 for Luddite activities,' said Sam Pickering provocatively.

'Aye, well, he was not the only honourable man to be hanged,' Ambrose replied, firm and easy. 'The gallows, like every other institution, has its aristocracy.' He declined to be drawn on the Luddite question, and turned the conversation to his guest. 'By the by, what does your boy think of the old grammar school, Hal?'

The Cornishman smiled, and said, 'What most boys of eleven think of school – he wants to leave it!'

'Nay, he must stick to his learning!' said George Howarth.

The Cornishman's handsome face, usually withdrawn, was lit with pleasure. He loved his son, and Santo worshipped him.

'Oh, he knows that well enough. I shall apprentice him to my firm in another three years, and then we can be engineers together.'

'I hear your elder girl is off governessing in the Lake District,' said Sam Pickering, curious.

The Cornishman was fond of his daughters, but they did not interest him. He had to think about this.

'Oh yes. Philomena. Well, not exactly. She is staying with the family of a former client, and teaching three young children. They pay her pocket-money but of course she is treated like one of themselves.'

Since further explanation seemed necessary, he added reluctantly, 'She is only sixteen. Too young to go out into the world, and yet wanting a little adventure. So Mary and I thought of this idea. She went off last month, as cheerful as you please, and writes to us twice a week. She seems to keep pretty well, but complains about the damp.'

No one commented. Everyone thought privately that the damp would prove to be stronger than Philomena's sense of adventure, though, Lord knows, Lancashire was wet enough.

'I see that Alice is ruling the children's roost these day,' said Ambrose. 'I took it upon myself to deliver Nat and Toby to Beech Grove yesterday, having the morning off, and by Jove she had them organised in less than half a minute. They were lions with me on the way there, and lambs as soon as they caught sight of Alice!'

They all laughed again. Ambrose's face softened.

He said to Jamie Standish, 'I like your little Cicely. Lord, how she reminds me of my sister at that age. She even has a look of her. A quiet, pretty face, a docile demeanour – but she can handle people and situations like an adult, and misses nothing that goes on.'

'Aye. Aye,' said Jamie, well pleased. 'She's a dear lassie,

and she and Alice are as close as finger and thumb. Which is a good thing, because your lads and mine all stick together.'

'What a trio of villains they are!' said Ambrose, grinning. 'And in a year or two young Jack will be as bad!'

The other married members then gave proud evidence that their wives were women to be reckoned with, their daughters sweet-natured and beautiful, and their sons limbs of Satan. Meanwhile, the bachelors, having no family to boast about, looked knowing, as if to say, 'Ah! You don't catch *us* so easily!' – an opinion once held by every husband present, and long since extinguished.

A slight pause ensued.

Ambrose cleared his throat and said, 'We are able to have our friend Hal Vivian with us this evening for two important reasons. The first, as you will have guessed, was the opening of the railway between Preston and Lancaster. The second is his latest news, which concerns us closely, both as residents of this valley and members of this club.'

The glow roused by talk of his son had not quite left the Cornishman's face. Now it was illumined by another passion. He spoke lightly and amusingly, but the feeling beneath the tone ran deep.

'Sirs, I am uncommonly delighted that such odd news as this should first be shared with the Oddities! Indeed, apart from my own family – who have some natural curiosity in my future activities – no one else has yet heard of my latest project!'

He then asked whether all their glasses might be filled, and begged permission to give a toast. When this was done he stood up and raised his own glass. His build and stance, his dynamism, and a certain arrogant tilt of the head, reminded them of the ironmaster. Sam Pickering fingered his moustache. The shadow of a smile lay on his mouth. He had already heard the news, not from the son but from the father. But would keep his mouth shut.

'Gentlemen! We are on the eve of commencing work

on the greatest single industrial and social development that Wyndendale has attempted so far. A network of lines and stations which will radiate from Millbridge into Yorkshire, Lancashire and Cheshire and connect us to London itself. I give you – The Pennine Railway!'

The effect on the assembled company was tremendous. They had been expecting something in the nature of a new, fast steam-locomotive. The idea of a railway network on such a grand scale, with Millbridge as its centre, was staggering.

As one man, they jumped to their feet, crying, 'To *The Pennine Railway*!' And downed their claret as if it were water.

For a second time Hal Vivian asked that their glasses be charged.

'And I should like you to drink also to the man whose vision, experience, courage and generosity have made this possible. Gentlemen, I give you *The Ironmaster*!'

'To *The Ironmaster*!'

'Good health and long life to him!' said Hal Vivian sincerely, and drank his wine with reverence.

Everyone realised that father and son must have made up their differences to some considerable degree, and they exchanged covert winks and smiles as they toasted William Howarth.

Then they sat down again, silent and slightly stunned by the news, and as no one offered to speak Ambrose stepped into the breach.

'Would you like to tell us a little more about this project, Hal?' he asked. 'Does this mean that you will be directing operations from the valley? If so, what happens to your Manchester business? And have you brought any maps or plans to show us? I know we should all like you to flesh the idea out.'

'Hear, hear!'

'We'd best have another bottle or two to help us on!'

'I have no maps or plans with me,' said the Cornishman, smiling, 'but I can draw you as many as you please, if someone would be good enough to fetch me pencil and paper.'

These being brought, and a space cleared before him, he sketched a rough triangle, saying simply, 'Our country, gentlemen!' Then he marked the main cities and towns, and indicated railways already built or in progress by means of hatched lines. This done, he circled Millbridge and drew arrows darting from it in all directions.

'These are our intended railway lines. Some connect us to other lines. Others simply break new ground. It is an immense project which will cost a vast amount of time and money. But do you see, gentlemen? York, Leeds, Liverpool, Manchester, Chester are within our grasp for purposes of business and pleasure. London is already making sure that she can reach and be reached, so quick and easy access to the capital city – and all its advantages – is only a matter of time. Coastal resorts and ports will be mere hours away.

'And we are only part of this enterprise. Railways will cover the entire country. Taking a long view, gentlemen, the British Isles could be in everybody's reach within the next decade! Northumberland here. The Lake District there. Scotland and Ireland. The giants of the age are at work. George Stephenson, chief engineer of the London to Birmingham line. Isambard Kingdom Brunel, chief engineer to the Great Western Railway. Gentlemen, the Age of the Railway is upon us – and let me assure you that Wyndendale is holding a first-class ticket!'

George Howarth leaned forward, hands clasped between his knees, half-smiling and half-frowning.

'Then we've seen the last of the stage-coaches!' he remarked.

That gave them pause. They had been brought up with coaches. Even nine miles of railway line through the valley had not superseded this method of transport in their minds. To imagine the highways without their swaying cargos of passengers, luggage and mail was unthinkable.

Every man present had known the excitement of

239

drumming hooves and rumbling wheels on a fine or frosty morning, the wild halloo of the horn, and the road to adventure opening out before them. Had they not trusted their goods and their lives to the coach-drivers? Those kings of the highway, who kept solitary vigil on the box in hours when even the guard dozed, who took a surreptitious swig of brandy to wake them, who knew every valley and hill and pothole in the road between London and Carlisle.

How would folk correct the High Street clocks when they could no longer hear the Royal Mail rattle by, proudly on time? What would become of that noble hostelry, the Royal George, without its rambling stables full of horses, its ostlers able to unhitch a lathered team and fetch out a fresh one in a matter of minutes, its bountiful tables and bustling maids by means of which twenty travellers could be refreshed and back on the road in less than half an hour? What of the coaches themselves? The Mercuries, Diligences, Dreadnoughts and Flyers, rolling under the massive arch into the courtyard, bringing with them the air of great events.

Gone, all gone. Set the old driver in the chimney-corner, let him smoke his pipe and drink and dream. Break the coaches up for firewood. Turn the horses out to grass. The age of the railway train is upon us, and Millbridge is holding a first-class ticket.

'We shan't need horses, either!' said someone else, awe-struck.

And if horses were redundant then so were farriers, saddlers, harness-makers and so on, down to the farmer selling hay for fodder.

'And if the railways can carry goods faster and cheaper, they'll take trade from the canals. . . .'

'And who'll pay turnpike tolls when they can travel by rail?'

Even the Cornishman was silent for a few moments.

'And the drovers,' George added quietly. 'The drovers'll be finished, and all. Them goods wagons can transport cattle.'

But he was the only man present who had personal experience of drovers. The only one who, in his boyhood, had heard the shout from the far fields which made everyone on Kit's Hill farm stop in the middle of their work and hurry out, to stand and shade their eyes against the sun and look up at that dark cleft in the Pennine hills.

'Dro – o – o – vers!'

How George had scrambled up and run with his gaggle of brothers and sisters to watch the black river of cattle pouring down through the Nick o'Garth which divided Yorkshire from Lancashire. Come from Scotland perhaps, weeks away over the ancient drovers' roads, plodding mile by patient mile.

How he had run and run that he might be the first to open the gate into the Ha'penny Field, where cattle would stay overnight, sleeping and grazing, where the drovers' dogs curled into small pits and kept guard. And he had perched up on the stone wall to see the tired beasts counted in. 'Yan, teyan, tethera, lethera, dic . . .'

Then to squat at the back of the farmhouse kitchen that evening, keeping mouse-quiet so that he shouldn't be sent to bed. Waiting for the old drover to light his clay pipe and lean back in his chair. Becoming part of the drovers' tales. Seeing in his mind's eye the endless road stretching ever before him.

Gone, all gone. With the drawing of a map.

'We must change with the times,' Hal Vivian reminded them, cool and sensible, for his visions were more splendid than these.

Yes, they knew that. They accepted it, even gloried in it. They must and should and would progress. And yet, and yet. Just for a moment they must pause and look back.

For most of them the coachman mounted his box again and they sat by his side. The ostlers pulled off the cloths. The guard blew his horn. Out of the hostelry yard they rolled in their pride, trotting sedately down the busy street, the envy and interest of all. Past the crossroads, through Lower Town, and over the bridge. Then the last wonderful, stomach-turning pause. The final wind of the horn. And they were off, galloping like the devil down the Turnpike Road.

In the ears of one man alone rang that cry from the windy fells of the past.

'Dro – o – o – vers!'

As might have been expected, Naomi and Mary were hobnobbing over the supper table in the parlour of Thornton House, for this was Naomi's first day up after Jack's birth, and the two women were celebrating her liberty.

'What a relief it is to have one's body to oneself again,' said Mary, accepting a slice of cold boiled ham. 'All those months full of little miseries, and having to wear shapeless gowns, and then to go through purgatory. I am sure that if men had to do it the population would shrink overnight! Naomi, I hope you are not going to have any more children – at least, not for a long while.'

Naomi shrugged magnificently. The Lord, whether Christian or Jewish, would provide as He thought fit.

'Oh, fiddlesticks!' said Mary, divining the shrug. 'You know perfectly well what I mean. I don't intend to have any more babies if I can help it. And it is a perfectly simple and harmless method. You simply put a little sponge – inside yourself, you understand – then afterwards, you take it out. Look at me, my dear. I haven't been pregnant again since Alice was born!'

'But I have never heard of respectable women doing these things,' Naomi protested. 'Only your Flawnes Gardens creatures do such things.'

'Well, Aunt Cha used the sponge – it's a French method – and she was married to Toby Longe for eight years and only had two children by him and none afterwards. And don't tell me that Jack Ackroyd visited her every night just to discuss politics because I won't believe it!'

The mention of Jack Ackroyd brought Naomi's thoughts

back to her latest nursling, who was sleeping in deep content in his bassinette at the side of the hearth.

'Ah, my jewel,' she murmured.

'Naomi! Please attend to me. This advice is for your own good. Aunt Cha advised me to limit my family, so that I could give time to myself and my husband. Otherwise one becomes nothing better than a breeding animal! And Aunt Cha was always right. Besides, I'm sure Ambrose doesn't want a big family. He looks bewildered already!'

Naomi protested, 'But I am sure he would like a daughter. And so should I. And I would call her Jessica Mary.'

'That's all very nice, but you don't want her yet a while.'

'I don't think that Dorcas does these things.'

'She must do something,' said Mary practically. 'She's only had Cicely and Matthew so far. Perhaps they abstain?'

'No, I do not think so. There is no strain between them.'

'Abstinence used to be the only method, apart from the man interrupting himself.'

'I do not like those methods either,' said Naomi seriously.

'Perhaps Jamie uses something. You know. . . ?'

'Mary! Mary! How do you come to hear such things?'

'I've got a good nose for news. Ambrose says so. Anyway, you just remember that you could be enjoying life instead of having babies!'

Naomi sat back, eyes half-closed, and contemplated the fire-screen. Life had nothing more to offer her at the moment. She turned the conversation away from herself to signal that the subject was closed. Yet kept it in the same key, to show she was not offended.

'The Queen has been married almost five months now. I wonder whether she will have a prince first?'

Mary's thoughts scurried in another direction.

'Oh, don't you think Prince Albert handsome? I do. So manly and so chivalrous. No wonder she's head over heels in love with him. My goodness, I'd be the same.'

243

Naomi smiled on her friend with deep affection.

'Well, you will have your own handsome husband living at home again soon, as director of the Pennine Railway project.'

'So I shall! Late for supper instead of late for the weekend!' said Mary cheerfully.

She still loved him, but had learned not to worship. They were both happier in consequence. Besides, Mary had interests and ambitions of her own these days. She was the whole of Page Seven, since Naomi had abdicated in favour of motherhood.

'The Pennine Railway is an excellent investment,' Naomi said.

She spoke with faith, out of experience. She had invested in it heavily. Motherhood had not curbed her taste for finance.

'How is Ambrose taking your proposal for *The Correspondent*, by the by?' Mary asked.

'He has said nothing, one way or the other. And I have been otherwise occupied,' with a graceful gesture towards the bassinette. 'But it is not a matter of choice. It is a matter of common sense. We can no longer run *The Correspondent* as a little family concern, with Ambrose as editor and me as financier. The circulation has reached six thousand, and is increasing. The newspaper is ready to become a public investment. Ambrose does not like the idea, of course, but he will be troubled as little as possible. I shall make sure we own the major part of the shares, and keep an eye on the financial side still. The ironmaster is advising me, and he is very sound. So – in another month or so . . .'

'Lord above! What a far cry from the old *Clarion*!'

Little Jack Longe clucked and rustled in his warm nest.

'Ah, he is waking up,' Naomi murmured, bending over the bassinette. 'I must feed him.'

'And that's another thing,' said Mary. 'You can't get wet-nurses as easily as you used to! When I was a child, nearly every poor woman in Garth village had a squire's baby at one breast and her own at the other! Now they all go out to work in factories, and women like us have no choice. If we're not dead or invalids we must turn into cows!'

'But I prefer to feed him myself. I do not want a wet-nurse.'

'You're like Aunt Zelah. She fed Tabitha, but Uncle William wouldn't allow it after that. The rest of them were wet-nursed – and so were all mine.'

The infant opened his eyes and smacked his lips. Life was a series of surprises, but one or two facts were beginning to connect. He was hungry. He opened his mouth and yelled hopefully. He entered the land of milk and honey. His cup of content ran over.

For the ironmaster that evening, staying late at the House of Commons, life was at a high peak, and most resolutely did he put away thoughts of old age. Seventy-six last week and never felt better or more vigorous. Never felt happier, either. Not long now before Parliament went into recess, and then he and Zelah could go home to Kingswood Hall for the summer. Hal was winding up his affairs in the Manchester office, ready to join him in August. Then the two of them could begin on the most ambitious project of both their lives, and William's own life would change accordingly.

Of course, he would not rush matters, or let anyone down. He would serve his party until the next election. But he would not stand again for Parliament. Let a younger ... let another man take his place. Then he could go back to Lancashire for good. Concentrate his energies on the Pennine Railway. Be on the spot.

The day had been long and humid. The Thursday night debate had lasted longer than usual. Afterwards he had spoken a word into one or two influential ears, and drunk rather too much wine, and still his day was not done. He must write a line to Hal, to tell him that all was well, before he went home to Zelah in Queen Anne's Gate.

He and his son were closer now, more friendly and trusting

than they had ever been. But he must go carefully, he knew that. He must not dominate or interfere, must not scare the boy away with his love.

For he thought of the Cornishman as a boy still, though Hal Vivian would never see forty-seven again.

So the ironmaster mused over a blank sheet of paper, the ink drying on his pen, trying to find the right words and the right way, until it grew late.

'Who goes home?' came the call from a group of colleagues.

He answered loudly and cheerfully, 'Not yet awhile, I thank you. I have a letter to write.'

'It's near midnight, Will! Too late to be on the streets alone.'

'No matter!' he replied, but less graciously, for he did hate to be interrupted and the words were escaping him.

'Make sure you are not the last to leave, Howarth!'

'God damn it!' cried the ironmaster testily. 'I have been looking after myself and a host of others for six-and-seventy . . . longer than I care to remember. I shall keep to the lighted streets and be perfectly safe. Now leave me be, I pray you, and good night to you.'

In quiet contemplation, he found the paper consoling. It invited him, almost, to bare his feelings. After all, if he was honest with himself he had nothing new to write about. He only wanted to talk to Hal. So why not, for once, stop pretending that this was business and jolly good fellowship and say what he felt?

The lamplight soothed him, keeping the dark at bay, luring him into the past. He leaned back in his chair, remembering Kit's Hill – not as it was now, a rowdy, shabby farm-house, but in the days of its dignity. Why, if he half-closed his eyes he could picture them all this minute in the kitchen. His father smoking a pipe, Charlotte sitting at his feet and dreaming in the firelight, young Dick on his father's lap sucking a thumb,

246

and the goddess of all their childhoods, their mother Dorcas Howarth, presiding over them.

She sat very upright in her high-backed chair, a copy of *Robinson Crusoe* in her hands, reading aloud to family and servants. Old Betty Ackroyd was knitting a stocking, and comely Nellie was darning one. Tom the carter carved a wooden christening spoon. The scullery maids stoned raisins for the Christmas pudding. And he, William, sat at his mother's feet, and absorbed her presence. A rustle of silk, a faint sharp scent of lavender, smooth black hair and quick black eyes like his own, a clear voice. But, above all, a sense of her steel. You could kill Dorcas, but you could not diminish her.

Lamp and paper swam. The ironmaster was an old man full of tears. He picked up his pen and wrote very simply and quickly.

My dear son,

Who had never dared call him anything more tender than *Hal.*

My sin in fathering you, if sin it was, caused you and your mother – who was beloved of us both – much grief and hardship. For this I have a thousand times asked forgiveness of her in Heaven, and in a thousand ways tried to make it up to you since. I now ask you that there may be no shadow between us in the future, to forgive me as I know she has done. May God bless and keep you, my dear Hal.

Then he added briskly.

I look forward to seeing you in August. I shall be taking a back seat, of course, in your project, but will always be ready to help in whatever way you think fit.

He signed himself *Your father, William Howarth.*

He sealed the letter and left it to be posted for him.

The night was cool and silky after the sullen day. The ironmaster strolled out into Parliament Square and struck up towards Tothill Street for home. His heart and mind and conscience were clear. He even felt a little hungry, and looked forward to the plate of sandwiches always left in readiness for his return. He hoped Zelah had not gone to bed. They had been married for forty-five years, and only she could end the day properly for him: listening to his news, offering advice, giving her approval. Yes, he hoped she was not asleep. What time was it? He stopped under a gas lamp and took out his watch. Great Heaven! Past one o'clock in the morning! And again the past called to him, as he snapped shut the silver lid, for the fine old watch had belonged to his Great-Grandfather Wilde. Aunt Tib had given it to him when he was apprenticed to Bartholomew Scholes. What a long life *she* had had. Now how old would she have been back in '78? He reckoned it up on his fingers and was surprised. Not nearly as old as he had thought.

The quick cut into Queen Anne's Gate was dark but short. He could see Zelah's lighted window at the end of it. Undaunted, swinging his silver-headed cane, he strode into the shadows.

His reactions were almost as good as ever. He spun round, hearing the soft insidious swish of a blackjack, and turned to face them. The blow had missed him but caught his silk top hat, which fell and rolled a little way. The street was empty and silent, and he was too proud to shout for help. Where the devil were all those Peelers?

He backed against the wall, never taking his eyes off the enemy. The ultimate enemy. Four grinning youths encircled him. Envy, failure, poverty, greed and ignorance advanced upon him.

The cane would be no use to him. He threw it away. He squared up to them in boxing stance, as he had squared up to many a man in his younger days. Beneath the fine broadcloth coat his blacksmith's muscles swelled and tensed. Almost as good as ever.

'D'ye want a fight, grandad?' the leader jeered. He said to his fellows, jerking his chin over his shoulder, 'This old geezer wants a fight, lads!'

They laughed. They dropped their weapons. The Peelers would not be round here for forty minutes. They could punch and kick him to death. They moved in slowly, smiling, running their tongues across their lips like dogs.

248

God was good, William thought. He had a chance after all. They could have knifed him and run off.

'One at a time, gentlemen. Play fair!' said the leader, mocking the ironmaster, and on the instant threw a mean punch.

William dodged, swung a fist that could once drive a nail through a block of wood, and felled him. The youth squirmed on the ground.

God damn it, William thought infuriated, that whimpering cut-throat would have been out for the count twenty years since!

The other three hung back in sheer amazement for a second or two, and then abandoned all thoughts of fun. Two moved in together. The third picked up his weapon.

The ironmaster kept his head and timed his punches. He stopped them in their tracks, he left marks upon them, he forced their respect, but he could not overcome them. The blackjack sapped him viciously on one side of his head and he went down.

In a haze of blood and muddle he felt them take his watch and his money. Not very much money. Not worth a life, even an old life.

Alone, too weak to shout, he crawled to the end of the street and lay in an oblong of light which shone from their bedroom window.

The light gradually enlarged and enveloped him. He, on the other hand, grew smaller and smaller, and moved further and further away, until in the end he became an infant in his mother's arms.

Her glossy black head bent over him, her bright black eyes saw nothing beyond him. He had sucked each small breast dry and fallen away, swollen as a bee's bag. She talked to him. The sound came upon his ears like the sound of summer. And once again he was all the world to her, and she to him. And so the light went out.

A King is Dead

chapter twenty

In death as in life, the ironmaster insisted on holding the stage. Had he departed a few hours earlier his news could have travelled up with the parliamentary despatches by express mail, and reached Millbridge in time for *The Lancashire Herald* and *The Northern Correspondent* to print a handsome obituary in the weekend edition. As it was, he achieved far greater impact by arriving at half past six o'clock the following morning, when both editors were abed after their Friday night labours and their papers were already being distributed. His news value was too good to wait until mid-week, so nothing less than a special edition seemed adequate.

What pleasure the ironmaster would have derived from the way the guard of the London-to-Carlisle Mail jumped down and bustled into the Royal George to inform Benjamin Tyler. To have seen the venerable landlord throw up his hands in horror, and straightway send an ostler down to Thornton House with an urgent message, which would then be conveyed all over Millbridge, from Kersall Park to the Town Hall.

What delight he would have felt, at the sight of his nephew, hastily dressed and badly shaven, riding off breakfastless on a hired horse to break the news personally to other members of the family. How it would have gratified him to follow this shock wave down the valley and observe its effects upon high and low. To watch the way women nipped up their aprons and held them to their eyes, while men looked down and shook their heads and shifted their feet, in sheer wonder and disbelief.

How Mary's sobs would have touched him, and the Cornishman's remorse moved him. How the water would have sprung to his own eyes at the sight of brother Dick, hayfork in hand, quite unable to speak, tears coursing down his rough, red cheeks.

How deeply he would have appreciated the epitaph from one of his oldest workers, a retired puddler living in Gun Street, Snape.

'Eh! There's never been a master like him. Whatever shall us do without him? It don't bear thinking about!'

But in this ultimate event of his life the ironmaster could see and hear nothing. He lay cold and composed in his coffin, in the house at Queen Anne's Gate, hands folded in prayer upon his breast: a crusader borne home from victorious wars.

Five and forty years had William Howarth wielded dominion over an ever-growing kingdom, having a finger in every industrial pie in the valley, playing a major role in local politics, forming and heading important committees, supporting charities, founding two ironworks and a newspaper of some distinction, instigating a railway, creating the entire district of Wroughton, gaining industrial medals and awards in his own country and abroad. Finally, at the peak and pinnacle of his public life, representing Wyndendale in Parliament.

Only one honour was missing, folk would say. Why had he not been given a title? Why was he not Sir William Howarth, or Baron Kingswood, or something of that sort?

The answer lay locked in the ironmaster's still heart. No one would ever know whether this was a matter of personal choice or the machinations of powerful enemies – and he had many. Yet it must be said that he had never mentioned the seeming omission, let alone fretted over it.

Mindful that he practised what he preached, Ambrose dealt fairly with his employees. A twelve-hour day was considered reasonable, but twice a week their hours were considerably extended and their days distorted by printing the newspaper. So once the Saturday *Correspondent* was off the premises he gave them the rest of the weekend to make amends. This long break also saved fuel. The boiler fires, which produced steam to drive the presses, could be let out for thirty-six hours. Consequently, everyone was satisfied.

Today, those cooling boilers and tired workers were foremost in Ambrose's mind, but he could not turn aside for them. He felt that he must be the first to break the news to Mary and Hal, to Dick Howarth of Kit's Hill, to the manager of Snape Ironworks, and to the butler and housekeeper at Kingswood Hall. He could not have borne them to hear by default, or from the mouth of someone to whom the news was mere sensation. So he rode posthaste down to Middleton Street, and sounded the front door knocker like doom.

George Howarth was already up and about, despite the fact that he was not abed until four o'clock. Since the assault in Prospect Mine he had suffered cruelly from insomnia, and could rarely count on more than two or three hours' sleep a night. But he had learned how to turn this curse into a blessing, and much of his studying took place while others slept. So he was wide awake and limping downstairs in an instant to open the door.

For some time now, Ambrose had taken the precaution of keeping notes on all his uncle's past and present activities, so that an obituary notice could be set up quickly.

'George,' said Ambrose, bringing out his news in a rush. 'The ironmaster is dead. I'll give you all the details later. I'm off to tell the Vivians and the Howarths and his people.

'I want you to get hold of Frank Ormerod and Bob Bullock. Tell them to fetch in just enough workers to set up and print a news-sheet such as we did when King William died and Queen Victoria came to the throne. Right?'

Even as he was speaking, he thought, By God, the old boy is going out in style, like another King William!

But he must hurry on.

'Tell Bob they'll be paid extra time. Then find the ironmaster's file, and arrange the papers on my desk to form an outline of his life and works. Ask Charlie Ainsworth to rough it out. Open up the printing shop, order a firkin of beer from the Ship, and buy some bread and cheese and pickled onions. I'll be back in two or three hours.

'Oh! and, George, you'd best walk over the road and knock up Sam Pickering. I doubt he'll have heard, and *The Herald* is even more concerned in this than we are, with my uncle being the owner. He'll want to mark the event. Oh, and you can tell Sam what I'm planning to do. No need to cut each other's throats over a public matter like this. And tell him . . . tell him I'm sorry!'

'Right!' said George. He added, 'I'll have a bit of breakfast ready for you when you get back, cousin.'

Ambrose remounted the hired horse, and looked down at him abstractedly from the saddle.

'Where does Bellamy the boilerman live, George?'

'I don't know, offhand. He changed his lodgings not long since. Harry Pycroft'll know. The new office-lad. Bellamy's his uncle. Harry lives at number forty-five, The Doles, just off Newmarket Street.'

For Jimmy, *The Correspondent*'s first office-boy, had recently been promoted to a seven-year apprenticeship as a letterpress printer. His rival was similarly occupied at *The Herald*. And now a new pair of small urchins stoned or snowballed each other from opposite sides of the cross-roads.

'How's Mrs Longe taking it?' George asked.

'She's crying,' said Ambrose, turning the horse's head towards Lower Town. 'Crying her eyes out, George.'

Ambrose interrupted the Pycrofts just as the family was about to partake of breakfast, but they felt deeply flattered by his presence.

They were a very large family for such a small terraced house, so many that Mrs Pycroft was forced to arrange their meals in shifts. And though, on such short acquaintance, she would be unlikely to tell Ambrose where The Doles' communal privy was situated, his nose needed no information. Its stench, on that warm summer morning, was quite penetrating.

Mr Pycroft had already departed for Green Lane cotton-mill, but the rest of them were there. A baby sucked vigorously at Mrs Pycroft's breast, four children sat at the table eating, four others stood round awaiting their turn, and the rest lay abed until they were called: six-year-old Harry being among them. But Mrs Pycroft knew what was due to a person of Ambrose's importance. With the baby still clinging limpet-fashion to her bodice, she screamed Harry's name up the steep staircase which divided one room from another. The boy tumbled down in seconds, and stood in awe before his master, wondering what crime he could have committed which warranted a personal visit.

However, on being told his errand and given a penny, Harry was greatly reassured. Furthermore, Mrs Pycroft put his breakfast into his hand, and threatened to box his ears if he wasn't quick, to show Ambrose that nothing in the way of nourishment or good manners was wanting in her establishment. And, since the lad slept in the vest and shirt he wore by day, and owned no shoes at the moment, he needed only to put on a pair of patched trousers.

The whole family assembled on the doorstep to watch Ambrose ride away, and to show their neighbours what sort of company they kept. Then Mrs Pycroft gave Harry a push, and the lad trotted off barefoot down the narrow street, holding a slice of bread and dripping in one small dirty hand, and snatching large and delectable bites from it as he ran.

The mayor and council were in active disarray. They had held an emergency meeting in the panic of the moment, without being in full possession of the facts. This was not unusual, and they had overcome any embarrassment by falling immediately into argument over the question of precedence in the iron-master's funeral procession.

Until an alderman said, 'But suppose the family wants a private funeral? And they might bury him in London, come to that! It's no use talking about beadles on 'orseback, Fred, if he's not coming here!'

'Nay, he must lay in Garth churchyard with the other Howarths,' said Dick firmly, wiping his cheeks with his shirt sleeve. 'There's no question of that. There's generations of us there already. That's where Mother and Father lay, and where I'll lay when my time comes. And that's where our William belongs.'

'I think,' said Ambrose gently, 'we must wait to hear his wife's wishes on the matter, and even perhaps his own. The ironmaster may have left particular instructions.'

But Dick would have none of it. His tears welled up again and again, however often he wiped them away. No, he shook his head from side to side like a beleaguered bull, and would have none of it.

'Nay, our William must lay in Garth churchyard, our Ambrose. Along with the rest of the Howarths.'

Back up the valley Ambrose rode, leaving the ironmaster's kingdom in disarray. The vastness of his uncle's empire, the complicated procedures which would be required to dismantle it, the ramifications of legal and personal detail, even that first question of his funeral, were assuming nightmarish proportions. One man had died, and a little world shuddered to its foundations.

To act as family messenger had been natural and right, but as the morning progressed Ambrose realised that he was being regarded as the family's chief representative. Of course, William's children by Zelah were all daughters, his natural son Hal Vivian could not be publicly acknowledged, and Dick Howarth didn't count. Poor Dick. So people were bound to turn to someone, though, God knows, he had never coveted or courted the position. He wondered how on earth his aunt was managing, all by herself in London, needing to make great decisions when her strength had been sapped and her judgement possibly shaken by events. Should he not go to her? But how could he, without knowing what she planned to do?

My God, Ambrose thought, I hadn't realised how much we relied on the old boy to lead the band. Now *I'm* leading the band, instead!

Sam Pickering was waiting for him when he got back, standing with his hands in his trouser pockets, staring down from the window into the hurly-burly of Middleton Street. On him, too, a portion of the ironmaster's empire was resting, and proving to be as heavy and uncomfortable as the weight upon Ambrose's shoulders. His green eyes had lost their cool complacency. His hair seemed to be thinner, his drooping moustaches greyer. Even his greeting had lost its bite.

Ambrose told young Harry to fetch them a glass of beer apiece.

'How are you doing, Sam?' he asked.

'Badly,' Sam replied, with the utmost honesty.

'What's your position with *The Herald*?'

'I don't know. He always said he'd see me right. But what does that mean?'

Ambrose shrugged.

'Are they fetching him home?' Sam asked.

'You're about the hundredth person to ask me that this morning, and I still don't know. I called in at the Old Hall again, on the way back, to see if Hal Vivian had heard from my aunt, but he hadn't. So until I have some hard news, we're stuck.'

'Mrs Howarth will have written to you, surely?'

'Not necessarily. Hal is his son, after all. Mary says she'll ride up here at once if they have news.'

'Ah, Mrs Vivian's quick off the mark!' said Sam, smoothing the ends of his moustache. 'She'll let you know.'

'Can I help *you* in any way, Sam?'

'Not really. We're putting out a special edition, like you.

I daresay we've got the same information as each other. I just came over to . . . well, I just came over. I'd best be off back.'

'As soon as I hear anything . . .'

'Aye. Thankee. I'll do the same for you if I hear anything. How's Mrs Longe keeping, by the way?'

'Very well – apart from this news, of course.'

He recognised a solitary carelessness about Sam Pickering which had once been a mark of his own bachelorhood.

'You should get married, Sam!' he remarked, with dry humour.

The beginnings of a smile glinted in Sam Pickering's eyes.

'Why?' he answered, equally dry. 'Do you think I haven't got troubles enough?'

The Manchester Mail brought Zelah's letter at teatime. In the first hours of shock and grief she had managed to compose herself, to sit down at her desk, and write to Ambrose as the official head of the family, to ask if he would take responsibility for his uncle's funeral. She recommended Tom Hadley, the ironmaster's secretary at Kingswood Hall, as being the person best able to assist him.

Zelah was bringing the body home on Sunday by private carriage, and hoped to arrive sometime on Monday evening – please to tell the housekeeper. The ironmaster was to be buried in Wroughton, among his people. The funeral would be a public occasion. And would Ambrose fix a day, late the following week, which would fit in with his own commitments and give everyone time to prepare?

On that day, Zelah wrote, all industries, shops and schools in the district were to be closed so that the ironmaster's people would be free to mourn him, and public refreshments should be provided. These were the main stipulations. Otherwise Ambrose was to conduct the proceedings as he thought fit and proper.

She apologised for all the trouble this was bound to cause

257

him, but expressed herself as being fully confident in his abilities and sure of his compassion. She added a postscript for Tom Hadley which read like shorthand – something to do with an invitation list – and another which said she was writing to Hal Vivian, to Dick Howarth, and to Sam Pickering.

She signed herself simply, *Thy friend, Zelah Howarth.*

Ambrose went to the top of the stairs and shouted for Harry, who took them two at a time, shining with willingness.

'Harry, I want you to run up to my house and give this letter to Mrs Longe. Tell her I'll be home late, and not to wait dinner for me. And ask Mr Bullock if he'd be good enough to step up here, as I'd like a word with him.'

Frank Ormerod came in at that moment, carrying the proofs of the special edition. Ambrose sat down and checked them through. Bob Bullock appeared soon after, and stood talking quietly to Frank for a few minutes while they waited.

'Good!' Ambrose said finally. 'I don't know what *The Herald* have in mind, but they won't better this!'

The news-sheet was bordered in black, like a giant mourning card, and headed – WILLIAM HOWARTH. M.P. – A MAN OF THE PEOPLE.

The opening line of the paragraph proclaimed – *A King is Dead.*

'See this through for me, will you, Bob?' said Ambrose. 'Then you can pay the men and shut up shop. I'm off down to Kingswood Hall again. Tell George . . .'

I've spent all day, he thought wearily, telling somebody to tell somebody else to do something.

But the weight of responsibility was being lifted at the prospect of action. He had always responded well to crises.

More cheerfully than at any time on that strange day, he said, 'And tell George to fetch round that miserable piece of horse-flesh I hired from the Royal George – if it's still breathing!'

*

At first it might seem that the ironmaster, in dying, had robbed himself of the honours due to him, for no one else was half so good as he at organising state occasions. But a breath of his genius was infusing Ambrose, as that gentleman rode thoughtfully down the Black Road to Wroughton. He was remembering William's public celebration of the victory at Waterloo, on the day that Charlotte's Will was read. At that time Ambrose had been too sad and confused to enjoy himself, but nevertheless his reporter's mind had recorded the event faithfully and in surprising detail.

Of course, he thought, we can hardly hold such frivolities as a fairground, and have wrestling matches and so on. Still, the roast ox would be quite appropriate for the crowd. We've got to feed them on something. And Wroughton Brass Band could play sacred music. Wait a bit! Wasn't there some sort of a choir? And didn't a giant of a fellow from the foundry sing a solo, and my uncle asked him to sing again?

'Isaac Lawler!' said Tom Hadley triumphantly, remembering. 'That was Isaac Lawler! He must be all of fifty now. Well, that applies to a good few of us, Mr Longe!' Passing a hand over his thin hair. 'But he's still in voice as you might say. Wonderful bass! Never heard such a bass in all my life! Of course Wroughton Choral Society was in its infancy then. They've made a big name for themselves since. They sing Handel's *Messiah* every year, just before Christmas, in our biggest church. St Luke's at Kingswood . . .'

He went off at a tangent, saying, '. . . that's where Mr Howarth will be buried, of course. Oh yes, he had a mausoleum made ready there, years ago. A family vault. But, bless you, sir, who's to use it? Excuse me putting it that way, Mr Longe. No offence meant. But who's to use it? His daughters will be buried with their husbands! His line has died out.'

The thought of Hal Vivian hung between them, but was not voiced.

'Anyhow, I seem to have got off the point,' said Tom. 'Where was I? Oh yes, Wroughton Choral Society and the *Messiah.* People come from twenty miles round to hear them, you know. Of course, hymns are more usual at a funeral. Still, it's sacred music, isn't it? And Mr Howarth always liked a good choral work. It seems only right.'

A festive air was beginning to invade the solemnities. Tom Hadley re-read Zelah's message to him and pursed his mouth.

'Now, Mrs Howarth is asking quite a lot of us with regard to the invitation list – which you might say is our Number One Guest List. Some of them will never get here on time. However, I'll do my best. What day were you thinking of, Mr Longe?'

'I'm prepared to go as far as Friday morning, but no later,' said Ambrose firmly, mindful of his weekend edition.

'Then should we say Thursday, which is time enough, and gives you just that little bit of leeway?'

'Thursday it is!' said Ambrose, satisfied.

'Now, should you like a bite of supper, Mr Longe? It's past nine o'clock. We could lay you a place in the dining room, and I'll have mine here in the library and carry on with the arrangements.'

'Well, I don't want to sit by myself at the head of twenty feet of polished mahogany,' said Ambrose sensibly. 'Suppose we both work over supper in here? There's plenty for us to do.'

Tom Hadley's face brightened.

'If you're agreeable, sir, nothing would please me more.'

He shuffled the pages of the guest list neatly together, with hands which shook slightly.

'Mr Howarth and I often have a working supper together at the end of the day, when he's here,' he remarked. 'I always look forward to him coming back from London.'

Then he remembered that there would be no more working suppers with the ironmaster, and fell silent.

*

The task Zelah had set them was prodigious, especially as so much had to be accomplished in so short a time.

'I shall just have to stay here until I know we've sorted it out!' said Ambrose. 'Can someone take a message to my wife?'

That evening, and for two days afterwards, a stable-lad rode to and fro between Wroughton and Millbridge, keeping all parties in touch with progress. Ambrose and Tom Hadley went to bed late and rose early the following morning. By supper-time on Sunday they had structured the occasion and sent their orders to *The Herald* and *The Correspondent*, who worked through the night, printing invitations, travel directions, hymn sheets and schedules. By seven o'clock on Monday morning the Carlisle Flyer had borne their mail away, and another day's work began at Kingswood Hall. But they had so much help and sympathy. Everyone was eager to be part of the ironmaster's final public appearance, anxious that it should be his best.

On Monday evening a private carriage arrived in the cool sub-dued twilight. Down stepped Zelah, white of hair and face against her inky mourning, but composed and tranquil. Then four of the workmen from the estate lifted the huge coffin carefully, and carried it reverently. A bier was standing in the middle of the entrance hall, at each corner of which stood an immense church candle in a silver sconce.

Zelah followed the coffin, taking off her gloves, having a word and a handshake for everyone, a kiss on the cheek and a smile of thanks for Ambrose. Then the lid was removed, and they stood together arm-in-arm in silence.

Like a king in state, thought Ambrose. Like a king in state.

William looked amazingly dignified. The art and craft of the best embalmers in London had made sure that he was presentable, though his head had been turned a little to one side on the satin pillow to hide the splintered bone, and there were faint shadows on his hands and face, suggesting bruises

261

cunningly concealed. But his expression was proud and valiant still, his mouth firm and unafraid.

When Zelah had looked her fill she turned to Ambrose and spoke in a practical way, without self-pity.

'Now, my dear, though it is growing late and supper is ready, I cannot sleep or eat. So wilt thee tell me what thou hast done so far? Poor Dick and our dear Hal have been much in my thoughts.'

Dick Howarth and Hal Vivian were only two of many delicate but important details which concerned them. For it should have been one of them, and not Ambrose, who took the ironmaster's place and gave help and comfort to his widow, but this was not possible. So they must find a way to honour the family relationships without embarrassment on either side. In the end Ambrose hit upon a neat solution. He and Dick would escort Zelah between them, to and from the church. Hal and Mary Vivian, with Naomi, should lead the procession of relatives. Then as coffin-bearers, he and Dick would be at the head, Hal Vivian and Sam Pickering at the foot.

'And at the reception?' Zelah asked.

'You receive the guests, and shake them by the hand. Dick and Naomi and myself, and Hal and Mary, stand just behind you and bow.'

Then Zelah smiled and touched his cheek and said, 'I have always loved and admired thee, Ambrose, and I knew thee would help me.'

For the whole of Tuesday the ironmaster lay in state while his people filed silently round him, holding their children up that they might see the great man. Then at ten o'clock, the front doors of Kingswood Hall were closed on the last of his viewers, to be opened again for the first of his daughters and their families.

There had not been such an assembly in Wyndendale since Ambrose's own wedding, six years previously. Despite Tom Hadley's doubts, the response to invitations was astonishing.

Every available room in houses belonging to the family, and in every decent hostelry from the Royal George in Millbridge down to the Iron Duke at Kingswood, was occupied by distinguished mourners.

Thursday morning's mist heralded a fine, hot day. A concourse of carriages moved off towards Wroughton and jammed the main road for miles. At the Hall they nailed down the lid of the coffin and placed it in a fine glass coach and heaped it with flowers.

Even the time of year is right, thought Ambrose. He couldn't have planned it better!

And Zelah, smiling, looked up at the cloudless sky.

'Well, thou hast a fine day, my love!' she said to herself.

The procession was waiting for her. Gracefully she veiled herself and accepted Ambrose's proffered arm. Gracefully ascended into the waiting carriage. Gracefully bowed her head to indicate that the procession should start. And the ritual began.

Ambrose had always hated funerals, but the sombre magnificence and dignity of this one enthralled him. The ebony gloss of the horse's coats. The silver harness and sable feathers. The rhythmic pace and grace of carriages and walking mourners. He had not realised there were so many shades of black, or that materials could produce such a range of lights within them. The coal-black brilliance of silk, the thick, soft, sooty black of velvet. The hard, bright black of jet necklaces and earrings. The lace and lacquer black of fans. A nocturne of black as far as you could see, with only the sad pallor of faces to relieve it. The hushed trot of hooves, the hushed roll of wheels. And all along the route the silent people, each wearing a symbol of loss, even if it were no more than a mourning band of dark ribbon, holding their children shoulder-high.

Then Wroughton Brass Band struck up the Dead March from *Saul*, with a weight of experience and authority far beyond that first thin sound, twenty-five years ago. Pomp was in the

263

brass. Pomp and power. How the ironmaster would have loved it. How he would have hummed the tune in the back of his throat, and tapped his knee in time, and wiped his eyes and shaken his head at the splendour of it all.

And it is for you, Ambrose thought. It is all for you. We have done our best. For you.

The pageant unfolded effortlessly, as though the occasion were pre-ordained. No amount of rehearsal, had rehearsal been possible, could have guaranteed this. Perfection is not to be achieved, but can be bestowed.

St Luke's Church was so large and splendid as to resemble a cathedral. Surely any sound would be lost up there among the timbers? But, no. The acoustics were excellent. And the vicar's voice, which was light and clear, came over like some angelic message, bringing them the promise of a new heaven and a new earth.

Then Wroughton Choral Society began very softly and gravely to sing 'Since by man came death', and Isaac Lawler followed them, also very grave and soft. For behold he would tell them a mystery. They should not all sleep but they should all be changed.

The great bass voice gathered power and momentum. It swelled forth. 'In a moment. In the twinkling of an eye.'

And fairly thundered to the rafters. 'At the last trum-pet!'

Up went the silver trumpet of Eli Hardwick, and he and Isaac Lawler poured out their message of hope, the one complementing the other, until the wrought-iron chandeliers hanging down the middle of the church gave forth a faint resonance. And the eyes of the congregation were wet, and their hearts were exalted. For they knew that the corruptible had put on incorruption, and the mortal had put on immortality.

Naomi was silent on the way home. Her emotions had been spent. Her vitality had drained away and left her clothes to mourn for her. She sat pensively in their private carriage and clasped her husband's arm, and would have liked to put her head on his shoulder, but the streets were full of people and everybody was looking at them.

Ambrose, though his body touched hers sympathetically, though his heart was warm and strong for her, had his mind elsewhere. His spirit rejoiced. He had achieved a triumph that day, for himself and the ironmaster, something which turned grief into glory. And the music had reached deeper still, spoken to him without words, enabled him to understand something which could not be put into words. Still, he tried to express what he felt, because words were his tools.

'I can't possibly respect that abominable old Jehovah of yours, Nim!' said Ambrose lightly. 'And Christ was a good man wasted. Why hang on a cross for such a pack of wolves and fools as we are? But I suppose Handel knew something that I don't.'

Her sombre eyes looked through and beyond him. Her mouth moved as if about to defend that God of her people, whose mercy was infinite, whose justice was terrible, whose strength was her shield and buckler. Then she remembered that this was Ambrose, who understood more than he knew. So she squeezed his arm and smiled and said nothing.

He looked at her sideways and decided she needed cheering up.

'I simply can't believe in God!' said Ambrose provocatively.

But Naomi had no energy to bandy words and ideas with a man who used them so much more cleverly than she did. Unwittingly, out of fatigue and loving kindness, she delivered a *coup de grâce*.

'Never mind, my love,' said Naomi soothingly. 'After today, He believes in you.'

A Domestic Interlude

chapter twenty one

March, 1842

'The good that men do lives after them,' Ambrose quoted sarcastically, over his weekend edition of *The Lancashire Herald*. 'The evil is oft interred with their bones!'

'*Now* what is wrong?' Naomi asked, somewhat impatiently, for Ambrose in off-duty hours could be infuriating.

He had left home at eight o'clock on Friday morning, returned and crept into bed just before daylight on Saturday, slept until the middle of the afternoon, and was partway through a meal which could neither be called breakfast nor luncheon, and would certainly spoil his appetite for dinner. His tasks were over until the morrow. Hers were not and the household routine had been dislocated. This did not occur to him. Long ago she had said she did not mind what hours he kept. He presumed she still felt the same way. Even his state of dress was relaxed. His tasselled cap matched his ruby velvet smoking-jacket. He wriggled his toes contentedly in leather Turkish slippers.

On a small round table by his elbow was laid a plateful of cold roast beef, a saucer of pickles, two rounds of hot buttered toast and one of the children's rice puddings from their midday meal, garnished with a tempting spoonful of strawberry jam.

Meanwhile, Naomi presided over the tea-things by the hearth, endeavouring to turn the frayed edges of her temper. She had miscarried a baby two months since, and the physical and emotional misery of the experience still plagued her.

'My dear Nim,' said Ambrose heartily, unmindful of the way her brows were drawn darkly together, 'you had best put in your bid for a Millbridge Concert Hall before the ironmaster's public bequests are squandered on a new council chamber and half a dozen civic banquets! Oh, I know what you are going to say!' Waving his hand to still her protests. 'The bequest is legally tied up, and no one can touch it except to fulfil the purpose for which it was intended! Balderdash! You know as well as I do that if it were tied in a dozen Gordian knots those scoundrels on the Council would find a way to cut them!'

Whereupon he held out his cup for a fresh infusion, without either looking at her or asking her, and continued to amuse himself.

'Cast your vote, my dear, cast your vote, ere the Howarth Foundation is frittered away!'

Instead she cast the sugar tongs back into their basin and folded her arms. After a while Ambrose became aware that nothing was happening, laid down both cup and newspaper, and peered at her over his reading spectacles.

'*Now* what ails you?' he asked.

'Oh, nothing, of course!' she replied, implying everything.

His own nerves being in excellent condition, he was puzzled to know what he could have said to annoy her.

'Surely, you're not fretting about the Millbridge Concert Hall?' he asked, amazed.

'No, no!' she cried sarcastically. 'Why should I care? Have I not been music critic on *The Correspondent* for years of donkeys . . .?'

'The phrase is *for donkeys' years*, Nim . . .'

'Do not interrupt! Have I not looked over properties and tried to find suitable sites? Have I not said I will raise money, and make a generous personal contribution, if only they will meet me halfway, if only they will help me just a little – with a grant, with a building? Even just to show enthusiasms? And why did your uncle not consult with me, if he was going to leave money for cultural purposes? Why did he mention a *theatre*?'

'What's wrong with a theatre?' Ambrose cried. 'If we have a theatre in Millbridge we can attract some decent companies

267

here instead of making expeditions to Manchester.'

'No, no. Do you not understand? It is easier to move mountains than to move these councillors. If they build a theatre with your uncle's money they will never help to build a concert hall. They will think they have done enough!'

Her tone was high but gave no warning of the tears which suddenly ran down her face.

She began to sob, saying, 'I am sorry. I am so sorry. But I cannot help it. I cannot help it.'

Ambrose sighed, and came over to comfort her. He was growing a little tired of these scenes.

'I was only teasing, Nim. There's not the slightest reason why Millbridge shouldn't have both. Besides, why not raise all the money yourself, own the theatre, and pay yourself back from the profits?'

It was an unwise suggestion.

'Why not? Why not? For a thousand reasons why not!'

'Just give me one of them!' he said, speaking more sharply.

'Because for one reason I have just invested a great deal of capital in new type and new machinery for your newspaper!'

'Now that is an unfair statement,' said Ambrose, pointing his finger at her. 'There was no other way. We have doubled the reading-matter and the number of advertisements – and with that blasted stamp-duty sitting on top of us, we can only fit it all in with smaller print and closer columns. Our circulation has doubled again, so we need bigger and faster printing presses. I explained it all to you, and you offered to lend us the money. If you couldn't afford it we should have borrowed capital elsewhere. Besides, you'll get it back in no time. Last year we cleared Lord knows how many thousand pounds of profit!'

'Five thousand, eight hundred and thirty-six pounds, thirteen shillings and fourpence three farthings,' she replied automatically.

He started to laugh.

'It is not funny!' she cried.

268

'Yes, it is, Nim. Very funny. Lord, fancy remembering a sum down to the last farthing! Anyhow,' sobering down as he saw she was now doubly wounded, 'we've made a profit. As far as I'm concerned you can spend every penny of it on a concert hall. I know what this means to you, and I approve. I'll sign whatever I have to, to make it legal.'

'Oh! Oh! Oh! You are impossible. You understand nothing. Profit is not pocket-money. We have share-holders. We have . . .'

'Oh, go your own way then,' he said, annoyed, returning to his chair and picking up his discarded newspaper. 'If I don't understand anything I may as well not try to help.'

Naomi smoothed her skirt with trembling hands. The silk squeaked softly beneath her wet fingers. She could not stop.

'And why did your uncle leave money to Mary, and not to you?'

'He left money in trust for our children, damn it!'

'And have you heard how Mary proposes to spend her legacy? I could not believe, when she told me. Such a ridiculous notion!'

Ambrose lowered the newspaper.

'I think it's an excellent idea.'

'What? A ladies' magazine? Who will buy it?'

'Mary has actually knocked on the door of every lady in the valley who is able to afford such a luxury, and found sufficient numbers willing to subscribe to such a project.'

'Yes, at first! But what then? Supposing it fails?'

'Then she's spent her legacy on something she enjoyed doing. Hang the consequences! I admire her for it. I'll tell you something else. Mary may not be a financial expert but she's a shrewd business woman and a damned good journalist. She'll make it pay. You'll see.'

Then he vanished behind *The Herald* again. Naomi looked at him sorrowfully. She dried her eyes and cheeks. She wiped her fingers. Her nerves had betrayed her into unwonted peevishness.

Trying to make amends, she asked, 'What of her work on *The Correspondent*? It will be difficult to replace her. Must she not give up Page Seven?'

He took this as an implied criticism.

'Oh, it will be a long while before we need think of that, and she won't let us down. Never underrate Mary!'

Naomi answered quietly, 'I do not underrate her. She is my friend. I only ask.'

Then she rose and went out of the room to cry in peace.

Left by himself, Ambrose threw the paper down. He poured himself a cup of cold tea and drank it and grumbled at it. What was a fellow to do at four o'clock on a Saturday afternoon in Millbridge?

Dollie knocked on the door to see if he wanted anything else. A muffin bell sounded beneath the window. Ambrose put the two facts together and his face brightened.

'Have the boys gone out to Kersall Park, Dollie?'

'No, sir. It was too windy today. They're in the nursery with Mrs Purdom. I'll be taking their teas up shortly.'

'Well, Mrs Longe is resting, and I haven't seen them for a couple of days. Why can't they come down here and have tea with me? Then Mrs Purdom can have hers with you in the kitchen.'

Dollie considered this enticing prospect. Bringing up the Longe boys was no sinecure.

'Well, sir, I don't see why not.'

'I don't either. So hurry up, there's a good girl, or we shall lose him!'

'Lose who, sir?'

'The muffin man, dammit!'

Ambrose threw up the sash window of the parlour and leaned out, calling, 'Hey, you there! Wait a moment, will you?'

Dollie ventured to say, 'I think the children might be a bit young for muffins, sir.'

Plain bread and butter was the order of the day, and

a slice of plain sponge cake if all the bread and butter had been eaten.

'Rubbish. No one's too young for muffins. They're very wholesome. Do you want some in the kitchen?'

'Well, sir, it would be nice.'

'How many do we need for all of us?'

'A dozen would be enough, sir. One apiece.'

'Nonsense. Fetch two dozen. That's two apiece for all of us. Here's a florin. Run out and get them, will you, Dollie? And tell Mrs Purdom to fetch the boys down here, and then you can forget about us. We'll toast our own on the parlour fire. I shall want hot fresh tea for four of us, four toasting-forks and plenty of butter.'

'The children only drink milk, sir, and Master Jack shouldn't have a toasting-fork. He's only two. He might stab himself with it, or fall into the fire . . .'

'Be off with you, girl. The fellow's waiting!'

'Yes, sir!' said Dollie, accepting anarchy.

And she ran briskly down the front doorsteps, florin in hand, and returned with an apron full of floury delicacies.

In another few minutes, just long enough to have their faces and hands washed and their hair combed, down came Ambrose's three sons, shining with pleasure. While Gussie Purdom, all gratitude and hypocrisy, dropped a deep curtsey.

'Here's kind Papa, then. What do you say to him, boys?'

They stood solemnly in line, hands clasped behind their backs, heads well up, and spoke in unison.

'Good afternoon, Papa!'

'Oh, never mind that!' said Ambrose. 'Let's not pretend you've got any manners. Go and eat your muffins in peace, Mrs Purdom, and leave the devils with me.'

Gussie would have preferred her employer to play her game, but as he did not she gave a stiff smile, and made a stiff curtsey, and disappeared to enjoy herself in the kitchen.

As soon as the door had closed behind her the three boys

flung themselves on Ambrose, shouting for joy. There was no doubt as to their parentage. They were all nut-brown lads, with hazel eyes and curly heads, and an air of mischief. But they possessed a knowledge of domestic politics which Ambrose had always lacked. As soon as they heard Dollie's knock on the parlour door they stopped in mid-action, in mid-syllable, and became quiet and well behaved.

Dollie was not deceived. She looked at them meaningfully as she set down the loaded tray, and began to clear away the remains of Ambrose's meal.

'Leave the pudding,' said Ambrose. 'I'll have that later.'

'Why?' said Toby curiously, 'Do you *like* it?'

'Yes. Especially with jam on it.'

'I don't,' said Toby. 'Even with jam.'

He was not yet five, and still liable to social lapses.

'I expect that was my pudding what I left,' he remarked.

Nathan, now six-and-a-half, nudged him to silence and nodded in Dollie's direction. Only Jack, too young to play the diplomat, pointed to the tower of muffins and said hopefully, 'Who's them?'

'Hush,' Nathan replied. 'They're all for Papa.'

Dollie pursed her lips to prevent herself from smiling, and closed the door behind her.

Pandemonium broke loose immediately. Toby grabbed the muffin-dish and the tower toppled. Jack stabbed his finger on the prong of a toasting-fork and stumbled over the fire-irons. Nathan had to save him because Ambrose was too busy catching muffins.

'Stop!' roared the patriarch.

They froze to attention.

'If you don't obey my orders,' Ambrose threatened, 'I'll hand you right back to Mrs Purdom and tell her what you did. And,' he added with relish, 'as this will interrupt her tea in the kitchen she'll be very cross indeed!'

Jack swallowed a sob. He was afraid he was bleeding to

death, but he would not endanger their treat. Mutely, he held out his finger.

'That's only a scratch,' said Ambrose, and tied it up with a piece of tape from Naomi's sewing basket.

'Now!' he cried, dusting the fallen offerings with the cuff of his smoking jacket. 'We are going to do this in an organised fashion. Have you ever toasted muffins before?'

They shook their heads. They stared at the unshielded and forbidden fire, fascinated.

Jack tugged at his father's sleeve. He stammered with excitement.

'I– I– I– han't *ate* a muffing. Never.'

And he shook his head from side to side emphatically.

'You haven't ate a muffing never? Well, you're going to eat two today! What do you think of that?'

'Mrs Purdom says they'll give us stomach-ache,' Toby remarked.

'Shut up, you fool!' Nathan whispered.

Ambrose pretended not to hear.

'Kneel down on the hearthrug, here,' drawing an imaginary line with the toe of his Turkish slipper, 'and don't move any further forward. Here's a fork each. No, Jack, hold it by *that* end. God help me! Here's a muffin each. I'll put them on – *I'll put them on!*'

'Do as you're told,' whispered Nathan to his brothers on either side, 'or we'll be back upstairs on bread and butter, with blooming old Mrs Purdom yelling at us!'

'Now hold them out to the red part of the coals, and I'll tell you when they're done. Keep your toasting arms stiff. No weakening!'

Scarlet-cheeked, tongues held between teeth, the three boys toasted a muffin apiece, which Ambrose split and buttered lavishly.

'Aren't you going to scrape some of it off, Papa?' Nathan asked, amazed at this extravagance.

'Certainly not. Ready for the next round?'

They marshalled their forks and nodded.

Stacked one on top of the other, the muffins oozed butter into the bottom of the dish. Tea steamed invitingly in the silver pot. Tactfully, Dollie had brought a large earthenware jug full of milk.

'Should we sit up at the table, Papa?' Nathan asked.

'No, better not. You'll only smear the cloth. Sit on your handkerchiefs on the rug, and watch out for melting butter.'

He tied a large dinner napkin round each small neck. They sat cross-legged, grinning at each other complicitly.

'Who wants tea?' he asked.

'Me! Me! Me!'

He poured out three mugs full of milk and coloured them faintly.

Jack drank his mug right up and lost his breath. Ambrose was privately alarmed, but Nathan and Toby had seen it all before.

Jack came up for air, whispering reverently, 'I do *like* tea!'

'Who wants jam?' asked Ambrose.

They thrust their dripping muffins forward, unable to believe their luck. They ate until they could hold no more.

Ambrose ate with them, and finished off the cold rice pudding.

They watched him, entranced.

'What shall we do now, Papa?' Nathan asked, and hiccupped.

'What about a walk in Kersall Park?'

'Mrs Purdom said it was too windy,' Toby reported.

'Well, I expect it *was* too windy earlier on,' said Ambrose diplomatically, 'but it's all right now.'

Nathan and Toby looked at each other. They would not have considered their nurse, but their father was so unpredictable that it seemed wise to look after him.

'You'll have to carry Jack some of the time. He's too little

274

to walk all the way. *She* gets fed up with him,' said Nathan.

Jack was deeply troubled by this confession on his behalf.

'No bother. He can ride on my shoulders,' said Ambrose airily.

'Hooray!' shouted Jack, jigging up and down.

'Let's find your outdoor clothes, then. We can manage that by ourselves, can't we?'

'They're in the hall cupboard,' said Toby. He added, 'Me and Nat can put ours on, but Jack can't.'

'You're about as much use as a two-legged stool, aren't you, Jack?' said Ambrose, grinning.

The child nodded solemnly, and looked puzzled when his brothers shouted with laughter.

'Come on, then. We'll take the muffin we couldn't eat, and feed Lord Kersall's ducks for him!'

He squatted on his haunches to tie Jack's woollen muffler round his neck, and said, 'By God, I am full!'

'By God, so am I!' Toby cried. 'By God, I am!'

Nathan began to giggle and punch his brother, shouting, 'Don't swear! You mustn't swear!'

While Jack cried, 'Ha! Ha! Ha!' and held his sides, in imitation of Mr Tyler from the Royal George.

The kitchen door opened quietly, surreptitiously.

'Come on! Let's hop it before we're caught!' Ambrose whispered.

One by one, fingers held to lips, they tiptoed across the hall and out into the blustery High Street.

Naomi woke, sensing that someone was in the room, and pulled herself up into a sitting position. It was already growing dark. By the window, Ambrose turned to smile at her apologetically.

'The lamp-lighter's on his way down the street. I was just drawing the curtains, Nim, so that the gas lamp wouldn't shine in your eyes. Stay where you are, and I'll order some tea.'

She was as anxious as he not to bruise the tender shoots of reconciliation, and chose her words carefully.

'Yes, I should like some tea, my love. But what time is it? I must go downstairs. The boys always come to the parlour to spend an hour with me at five o'clock. They will wonder where I am.'

'It's half-past-six already. Nimmie, Nimmie!' As she started to get out of bed. 'Stay there in peace! The world won't come to an end. A clock is only as important as you allow it to be. The boys know where you are. They're sitting outside on the landing.'

'So quietly? But Mrs Purdom . . .?'

'Mrs Purdom is screeching with laughter in the kitchen, having been given the rest of the afternoon off. They've been with me.'

'But she likes to take them off to bed at six o'clock.'

He came over and held her hands in his.

'Nim! When you've drunk several cups of China tea, and eaten a few small, rich cakes, and you're feeling quite yourself again, I want to discuss Mrs Purdom with you. Until then, she is taking orders from me. Now, can the boys come in and sit on your bed? They've had enough of me for the moment, and they're rather anxious for you – particularly the heroic Jack, whose short legs have toiled for miles!'

She held her tongue. She kissed his cheek. She nodded. He turned her hands over and kissed the palms. They dared to look directly at each other, to smile and feel the world come right again. He walked over to the door and opened it.

'Line up!' said Ambrose cordially but firmly.

Delicate shuffling noises indicated that they had done so.

'Now, come in very quietly, because Mamma is only just awake. If I hear anyone raise his voice he goes straight out again. All right, Nat, lead the way. Quick march!'

'Oh, my boys,' Naomi whispered, as they stood in a hopeful row, and did not know whether she should laugh or cry.

They smiled shyly at her, their eyes saying what they could not and would not have put into words.

'Come, sit on the bed,' said Naomi fondly. 'Ah, my Jackie with the short legs!' As he mountaineered up the satin slope into her arms. 'Come, Nat, come, Toby, sit here. One on each side of me. Now tell me what brave things you have all been doing . . .'

Ambrose heard the exalted babble of replies, and something which had become rare in the last few months, Naomi's deep, rich laughter.

This evening he intended to absolve her from the demands of the household. He ordered a light supper for her and wine for himself, to be served in their bedroom at nine o'clock. When the tea-tray was ready he took it from Dollie and sent her away. He sat on the bed with the boys, and insisted on a share of the conversation. Not until long past seven o'clock was an obsequious Gussie Purdom allowed to remove her charges, curtseying all the way as if in the presence of royalty.

Husband and wife looked long and lovingly on one another.

'But what an amazing man you are!' cried Naomi.

'Not really. I couldn't do it day in, day out, as women do. I thoroughly enjoy myself for a while, and so do they, but that's enough for all of us. Nim, about Mrs Purdom . . .'

'Yes? You don't like her? I think her a little strict at times, but then you said that *I* was not strict enough!'

'It's nothing to do with discipline. I dislike the way she scares them with superstitious nonsense, forces good manners on them outwardly, and doesn't care what goes on in their hearts and heads. They're decent little chaps, and they stick together like good 'uns. But if she can break down that fellowship she'll turn them into cowards and hypocrites. We must get rid of her as soon as possible.'

'But what reason shall I give?' cried Naomi, distressed. 'She is honest. She does what she thinks is best. She works hard.'

'Oh, there's no need for you to shoot my bullets. I'll give her notice, and I shall tell her why I'm doing it, too. But I'll play fair with her – a month's wages, and a carefully worded reference about being honest and hard-working and doing her best. Intelligent parents will see through that one. As for the rest, let's hope their children have thick heads and thick hides. It isn't really ethical to pass her on to anybody else, but I can't take away her livelihood.'

'Ah! What a great inconvenience it is for you, to bring up a family!' cried Naomi, mocking him. Then she was serious again. 'But how soon will you do this.'

'Not until we've found someone suitable to take her place. We need a good-hearted, wise and sensible woman like the Standishes' nurse, Sarah Pratt.'

'Mrs Pratt is an old family servant. She has been with the Poles or the Standishes for nearly thirty years.'

'Family servants have to begin somewhere. We'll find one. Now, Nimmie, there's something else I have to say – which you're not going to like. No more babies.'

'Oh! Just one more. I shall be very well soon. And I do so want us to have a daughter.'

'There's no guarantee we shall ever have a daughter. You could go on for years, Nim, producing young hellions.'

'You like them, though!' Coaxingly, stroking his cheek. 'You do.'

'Never mind that beguiling nonsense,' said Ambrose firmly. 'Three babies and two miscarriages in eight years is enough for any woman. Besides, if you really admit the truth you're only angry about Mary's magazine because you'd like to do the same sort of thing. I remember Mary having a few tantrums when she was festooned with infants.'

Naomi started to contradict him. Then stopped, and thought.

'Keeping an eye on *The Correspondent*'s accounts isn't enough for you. You should think seriously about bullying the entire valley into building a concert hall. Think about your own music, too.'

'I am nothing. Nothing. I play a little, that is all.'

'Well, I don't know enough about music to argue that point with you, but I think you play beautifully. And I rather liked having my own private concerts on Sunday evenings. The only thing that's happened to the pianoforte recently is that its lid has been dusted.'

Her smile admitted that he was right on all counts.

'Just remember, Nim. Our future motto will be *Abstinence makes the heart grow fonder*!'

Naomi continued to smile, but this time enigmatically.

A Man of the People

chapter twenty two

The suburb of Flawnes Green had borne a name for forbidden pleasures since the turn of the century. No decent woman would be seen in the vicinity of Flawnes Gardens, and in the darker district of Lower Flawnes the police took care to walk in pairs by night. So cynics were amused when the Mayor opened this latest public recreation ground, and innocently named it Flawnes Pleasure Park.

It was not the first people's park, of course. Lord Kersall and the ironmaster, among others, had bestowed gifts of enclosed land upon their subjects. But this one had been bought with public money and created by the Borough Council, and it belonged to the people. The poorest folk could enter its iron gates with a feeling of ownership rather than a sense of obligation, and the pleasures of this park were generally light-hearted and innocent.

On weekdays it provided somewhere for children to play, while their mothers or nurses sat and gossiped. On Sunday afternoons, when they had worshipped their God and eaten their dinners, whole families sallied forth to enjoy themselves: parents sauntering arm-in-arm along the cement walks with their dogs on a lead, their children running ahead of them bowling hoops or dragging toy horses on wheels, and everybody keeping off the grass. There were kidney-shaped beds of flowers to admire, a new sundial made to look old, an ornamental iron drinking fountain, a pond on which ducks swam and boys could sail their boats, and best of all an iron bandstand surrounded by iron chairs, where Millbridge and District Brass Band played light music between two and four o'clock on summer Sunday afternoons.

Very smart in his dark-green uniform with imitation silver buttons, the park-keeper also strolled along the paths on a constant tour of inspection, nodding respectfully or familiarly to those he passed. He it was who held the keys to those wrought-iron gates forged at Belbrook Foundry, and with them he ceremonially opened the park at nine o'clock each morning, and locked it at dusk.

Yet even here, where there should have been perfect democracy, people divided instinctively into classes. On this fine and breezy afternoon a group of handsome lads were racing their sailing ships from one side of the pond. On the other side a huddle of ragged urchins kept themselves and their lump of whittled wood out of the way. Shabby families did not take advantage of the three benches under the trees. They sat further up the Long Walk on a roughly-grassed slope. No well-bred adult or child used the drinking fountain. Even the chairs round the bandstand were split into rich and poor sections. No one intended this. It seemed to be the natural order of events.

Today these self-imposed rules were being violated. For an elegant gentleman in a chocolate-brown coat and fawn trousers was sitting by the side of a working man, apparently from choice. Occasionally, one or other of them glanced towards the boys at the edge of the pond to make sure all was well, but otherwise they were absorbed in a conversation which had reached some crucial point for both of them.

'What I've got to tell you, cousin,' said George Howarth slowly, 'is summat as grieves me just as much as it'll grieve you. I've pondered for a long while, and wished things might be different, but there's no other way out. The only thing as fears me is that I shan't make myself understood.'

'Oh yes, you will,' said Ambrose cheerfully. 'I've always said you had a gift of expression that any journalist would envy.'

His tone was light, but the way in which he stabbed a little hole in the rough turf with the ferrule of his cane showed his unease, and he looked sideways at his cousin as he spoke, trying to read his expression.

George, on the other hand, gazed into the distance, his eyes very blue and steady. He had always appeared to be older than his years. Now in his thirties, his countenance had weathered to the texture and colour of an old red apple. His body had shrunk, his hands were gnarled. From a distance, one would have taken Ambrose to be the younger man. On closer inspection, however, the steel in his hair and a certain steely self-containment told another tale.

'Crack away, George. Give it to me short and straight.'

'I'm leaving,' said George briefly. 'Leaving *The Correspondent*. Leaving my rooms. And leaving you, and all, cousin.'

The ensuing pause said more than words could have done. Neither man looked at each other.

Then Ambrose said thoughtfully, 'That's a bit of a facer!'

'Aye, it is, that. And you've got the right to know why, cousin, because nobody in this world has done as much for me as you have. It's not ingratitude. I know the value of you, cousin – no man better. But it's time I were piking off afore I lose sight o' myself.'

Ambrose dug away at his little hole in the turf, disturbed.

'Where are you going, George?'

'That's summat as I don't exactly know myself.'

'As far as I'm concerned, if you've nowhere particular to go, you can stay where you are – hang the job!'

'Nay, that wouldn't be right,' George replied decisively.

Ambrose accepted this with a sorry little shrug.

'How are you going to earn a living?'

'I'm going preaching, cousin, round the countryside. I shan't ask nowt more than a night's lodging and a share o' bread and cheese.'

'Preaching the word of God?' Ambrose asked, amazed, for he had never thought of George as being religious.

'Nay, cousin. Preaching poor man's justice. I've sat on my backside wi' a full belly for long enough. I'm going back where I ought to be – along wi' them.'

Now both men looked at each other directly.

'I know you're a dedicated Chartist, George,' said Ambrose carefully, 'but I shouldn't rely on them for financial support or political success. Their fortunes have fluctuated enormously. I'm sure they'd be glad of your help, but they can't even pay their lecturers, let alone keep you. Besides, revolutions favour men who have a taste for power rather than men of honest conviction.'

'Aye, I expected you to take that line,' George replied. 'It's what I said right at the beginning, cousin. We're chalk and cheese, thee and me. We may be aiming at the same goal, but I'm on t'other side o' the street – like them lads, over there, sithee?'

Ambrose saw his three sons and Matthew Standish on one side of the pond, and the unknown boys opposite. They could have been a different species.

'I know and deplore social injustices as much as you do,' he replied energetically, 'but you can't accuse *The Correspondent* of laziness or complacency. Look at our efforts over the last nine years. Every campaign we have launched has brought results. I'm not so stupid as to think that the country is governed according to my editorials, but I know they make a contribution, however small, to social reform.'

He prodded a little hole in the turf to mark each achievement.

'First. We've opened people's eyes to the inhuman features of our workhouse system.' He brightened momentarily with humour. 'Mind you, I think we should acknowledge the help of Mr Charles Dickens with regard to that. I daresay more people read *Oliver Twist* than read *The Northern Correspondent*!'

Then he was serious again.

'Second. The Coal Mines Act has prohibited the employment of women and children underground, and the employment of any child under ten years old, and forbidden anyone under the age of fifteen to be put in charge of machinery.

283

'Third. Factories. Owners are no longer allowed to employ any child under the age of nine, and no child is allowed to work at nights. Young people's work hours have been drastically reduced, and we're campaigning to reduce them further. We want a limit set on the hours that women work as well.

'Fourth. Education. We've worked hand-in-glove with Edwin Fletcher of Millbridge Grammar School on this one. In Lower Town, this moment, we have a public reading room, we're building a Mechanics Institute, and we're campaigning for a workmen's library. Hand-in-glove with old Jarvis Pole of St Mark's, we have helped to raise money and interest in local Sunday Schools, where children are taught to read and write free of charge – my mother would have been pleased about that!

'Fifth. Public health. We've been playing bully for Jamie Standish all the way along, persuading them to resuscitate the old cholera unit and turn it into a fever hospital. I grant you, they're taking their time over that as usual, but it is on paper at least. Oh, and we're still after them to improve the drainpipes.

'Finally, and however humbly, take this park as an example of our muscle-power. *The Correspondent* was responsible for voting in the local councillor who suggested it, and backing him all the way. We're infiltrating quite a few men of action and good conscience into the Borough Council these days. We *do* progress.'

Then he turned to his silent cousin and said, 'All right, George. Add that lot up! And tell me whether this isn't a better country to live in than it was nine years ago, and whether it isn't a fair achievement on the part of a provincial newspaper!'

'Aye,' George replied gently, and actually put his hand over Ambrose's hand to soothe him, and patted it. 'But we've nobbut scratted the surface, cousin. It's not enough, and it's not fast enough. And you're looking at it from the outside, instead of feeling it like a knife in your guts. Look at them lads of yours, and say this to yourself.

' "The workhouse sold my Nat to a chimney-sweep when

he were seven year old. He were feared to climb, so the sweep lit a fire behind him to make him go, though the sores on his knees and elbows were raw. He got stuck on an awkward bend, and choked to death.

' "They sent my Toby down the mine when he were six, to work thirteen hours a day, opening and shutting ventilation doors. He used to sing to keep his spirits up. He were feared of rats in the dark. He ate candle-ends because he were famished. He tried to run away, and tumbled down a shaft.

' "They set my Jack to wind cotton bobbins in the mill twelve hours a day. He were only four year old. His eyes smarted and his body ached. When he got drowsy they beat him, but one day he dozed off in spite of them and fell into the machinery." '

'For God's sake, George . . .!'

'Aye, now it comes close to home, don't it? It's not just some poor woman dragging a three-hundredweight wagon along a tunnel until she tears out the unborn child she's carrying, it's *your* wife.'

Ambrose put up his hand, to indicate that he should stop, that the point was taken. But George had not yet done.

'Even your notion o' time is different. You can afford to wait, cousin. You're well-housed and well-fed and well-content. What's nine years to you? But to a clemmed and famished babby, nine *hours* is too long to wait for the milk that'd save it.'

The tears were running down his face. He wiped them away fiercely, unashamedly.

'You talk about progress and achievement. If this country is so good to live in why are poor folk emigrating, facing the misery of a voyage in steerage, and the unknown when they stumble on shore? Over one hundred thousand this year, and more and more every year that's counted. You talk on Acts o' Parliament as though owners said to theirselves, "Oh, dear me. I've been a bad lad up to now, but on Monday morning at six o'clock sharp I'st be a good employer." Rubbish! They'll cheat and lie and cover up until they're threatened wi' summat more than moral pressure. Folk are dying, cousin, for lack o' work. Them as can't work can't eat, sithee! And there should be more to life than working and dying, any road. More than a bowl o' charity soup served on a street corner, as if you was a beggar by nature.'

He looked back into his childhood, and spoke from it.

'I'm not saying it weren't hard, and it weren't poverty-stricken, but when we had the land we had us self-respect. Now, we've lost the common where we grazed us animals and collected us firewood. We've lost the tied cottage and the patch of earth where we grew us vegetables. We've lost us neighbours and the village we was born in. The very air we breathed has turned to smoke. We've been sold into slavery as surely as if we was black men. We have to sign us lives away, and take low wages and long hours and ill-treatment, and if we run off they can put us in prison. I'm not talking about yesterday, cousin. I'm talking about now! It's still happening.'

Like his grandfather before him, his face had reddened, his eyes become a deeper shade of blue, as he warmed to his argument. Now he stood up abruptly, and thrust his hands in his trouser pockets, composing himself. Then he spoke quietly and emphatically.

'I *canna* stand by and look on. I'm no middle-class radical, as can eat a good dinner while they're clemmed. What happens to them, happens to *me*. I'll fight for them as best I can. I'll die for them if I must. I'll put my arm round them and cry wi' them, if I can do nowt else. But I'm *one* of them, cousin, and that's where I belong.'

There was nothing else to say. Ambrose got up slowly from the grass. He put his hand on George's shabby shoulder, and patted it. He nodded encouragement and understanding, and George nodded abruptly back. Then Ambrose walked down the slope towards the group of shouting boys, who would never be robbed of their childhood.

Gifts and Little Voices

chapter twenty three

December, 1843

The ironmaster's Will had been a masterly affair, whose influence like his dominions was far-reaching. Only now, more than three years after his death, were the last odds and ends of his vast estate being wound up. He had forgotten no one. Even the act of passing them over – as with Ambrose, whose children benefited in his stead -- had been the product of long and deep thought.

For lack of an acknowledged heir the ironmaster's empire must be sold piecemeal, and the proceeds divided among his descendants. Mind you, with six married daughters, over thirty grandchildren, and a fourth generation already under way, he had more than enough family to satisfy. And after them came close connections in all the ways of his life: old workers and faithful servants, who must be remembered and rewarded according to a delicately adjusted scale of merit and importance.

Besides personal legacies to Hal and to Mary, he left in trust a generous sum of money for the construction of the Pennine Railway. Sadly, he could not bequeath his experience, which would have been even more valuable. Hal Vivian was a passionate and dedicated, but not a businesslike or politic man. Still, the ironmaster had done what he could while he was alive. In dying, he must loose his hold of events and let them take their own course.

While doubting Sam Pickering's ability to rise to lofty heights, he nevertheless held him in great respect. So he left the fellow sufficient shares in *The Lancashire Herald* to assure him of an income for life and a voice in the running of the news-paper, but not enough to give him the whip-hand, and Sam continued to act as editor. Here again the investment suffered from the ironmaster's absence. *The Herald*'s committee was com-posed entirely of sound Tory businessmen, none of whom pos-sessed his breadth of vision. Whereas it had once reflected the many facets of William Howarth's character, it was now becoming a provincial mouthpiece for the Tory Party. That didn't worry Sam, of course. He was always a loyal Party man.

On this late winter afternoon, sharing a hackney-coach with Ambrose on their way to Kingswood Hall, he was content with life. For the Hall was sold at last, and Zelah Howarth had invited them for six o'clock, to fulfil the ironmaster's final request. Each was to choose some small personal object, by which they would remember him.

'So the old man still holds out an iron hand!' Sam remarked, in rare good humour, and offered Ambrose a cigar.

In the last twelve years his work had fulfilled and mellowed him. His grey moustaches no longer drooped, but curved upwards, short and crisp and neat. The barber had parted his hair on the left side and brought some of it forward in curls over the ears, while cleverly sweeping the rest across the thin part of his crown. His green gaze was just as sharp but more tolerant. He had not married, and continued to live comfortably in his bachelor apartment at 38 Cornmarket.

'Aye, still holds out an iron hand!' Sam repeated indis-tinctly, cigar in mouth, bending over for a light.

Ambrose struck several matches, each of which sputtered and flared and stank of sulphur. A few lost their heads and soared across the hackney-coach like miniature rockets, and had to be beaten out before they burned the upholstery.

'You take your life in your hands with these things!' Sam joked.

'I think we're nicely on fire now!' Ambrose replied, in the same vein. Then, more seriously, 'And you must admit that they're a damned sight more convenient than a tinder-box.'

The two men settled back in their seats to smoke and talk.

'Mrs Longe keeping well?' Sam asked civilly.

'Remarkably so. Considering.'

'When's the latest addition expected, then?'

'Sometime in mid-January. Not yet, thank heaven!'

Ambrose was notorious for his sufferings when Naomi gave birth.

'A little bird told me that this would be the last of the family,' Sam remarked, looking at his companion keenly.

'I think that little bird's name must have been twittering Mary Vivian!' Ambrose replied good-humouredly. 'Well, I think that four children are enough for anybody, don't you?'

'As far as I'm concerned, it'd be four too many!' said Sam, grinning. 'Aye. Mrs Vivian's got a ready tongue for any occasion!'

'I take it that you no longer wonder why I handed the production of her magazine over to you?'

Sam shook his head from side to side, saying, 'I knew it wasn't for charitable reasons, at any rate!'

'Oh, quite. How are you both working together?'

'In fits and starts, as she gets better and better ideas! Still, it should be interesting. *The Herald*'s done a variety of jobbing work, but we've never printed a ladies' magazine before. It's taken a while to get it all together, what with Mrs Vivian's notions and our technical difficulties – for instance, we shall have to hire girls specially to paint the colours on the front cover, at five shillings a week apiece! But I've talked to her like a Dutch uncle, and we both know where we stand. As long as she pays us on the nail we'll print *The Lady's Hour.* As soon as the bills start mounting up we stop!'

'Precisely. I thought it would be easier for *you* to throw out the project than for *me* – related as I am twice over, with Mary being Naomi's best friend as well as my blood cousin!'

'Don't you hold a lot of hope out for it, then?' Sam asked, interested. 'I've got quite a bit of faith in Mrs Vivian, myself.'

'Oh yes, I'm inclined to back Mary's flair and judgement. But there's always a chance, isn't there, that it won't catch on?'

'Aye, I'll give you that.'

'Personally, I think she'll make a go of it. But it's still best that *you* print *The Lady's Hour*!'

Sam grinned round his cigar.

'We'll have you crying your eyes out because you didn't take the job on yourself!' he remarked, with tremendous satisfaction.

'I shall be the first to congratulate you both.'

'I don't doubt that,' said Sam drily. 'You was always stylish. But that don't mean you won't curse yourself in private!'

Zelah Howarth came forward gracefully to greet them. As always Ambrose felt her serenity erase his cares. So must the ironmaster, he reflected, have bathed and renewed himself at this fount of inner peace. No wonder the old bastard had lasted so long and done so well!

'Welcome to thee both,' cried Zelah. She gestured at the assembled company. 'As thee sees, we have quite a gathering.'

They had both been present when that document which Ambrose dubbed *The Iron Will* was read, three years ago. Today they were part of a crowd of minor legatees, since William's immediate family had chosen their private mementoes of him long since.

'It is my last reception here,' said Zelah, but there was no sadness in her statement. 'Tomorrow, Anna and I set up house in the village near my old home of Somer Court. My nephew, John Scholes, is ironmaster there now. We shall have all my Warwickshire relatives around us, and many old friends of Quaker and other persuasions. I do not feel that I am going away, Ambrose, but that I am going home. And Tom Hadley, who hath given us such strength and support, is staying behind to close the house before he takes up a new appointment.'

Servants were moving in and out of the little throng with

trays of sherry and plates of assorted sandwiches, cakes and biscuits. The refreshments were light, but had been prepared and presented with a delightful attention to detail. These exquisite mouthfuls would not spoil one's appetite for dinner, and yet they staved off the hunger which a man was bound to feel when his last meal had been eaten at noon. Even the air of this occasion was light and leisurely, although upstairs the maids were still packing personal luggage, boxes stood in the entrance hall, and most rooms were empty of furniture.

'My dear Aunt Zee, you always do everything so beautifully. When you leave here, more than forty years of lavish hospitality will go with you! Who can imagine Kingswood Hall without the Howarths?'

'Thee should not dazzle me with worldly compliments, Ambrose,' Zelah replied, smiling. 'Remember that I have been accepted into the Society of Friends once more, and am now a plain Quaker!'

'Nonsense. The adjective *plain* could never be applied to you under any circumstances!'

She laughed, and touched his hand affectionately, and turned away to welcome Hal and Mary Vivian, who had arrived rather late as usual.

'And that's another thing,' said Sam at his elbow, popping a miniature sandwich into his mouth and washing it down with sherry, 'Mrs Vivian isn't the most punctual person in the world!'

'She's punctual when she has to be! Hello there, Mary, we're tearing your professional reputation to shreds!'

She laughed, wrinkled her nose at Ambrose and shook hands with Sam Pickering. She was watching her husband greet Anna Howarth, and a certain tenseness in her expression betrayed jealousy.

'Don't be a goose!' Ambrose whispered, taking her arm and leading her away. 'It must be twenty-five years since they were engaged, and Anna's the nearest thing to a saint that I've ever come across.'

291

'I don't care,' Mary whispered back furiously. 'Hal and Anna only broke that engagement because they found out that Uncle William was father to both of them! It still makes me feel that my marriage is an accident rather than a proper intention!'

'That's a trumpery notion, better put in the silly mind and mouth of a languishing literary heroine! By the by, when does *The Lady's Hour* burst upon our waiting world?'

Mary was animated and vivacious in an instant.

'The first issue will be out in February.'

'Then you'll be busy throughout January? Naomi will have to produce the baby without you for once!'

He spoke teasingly, but felt alarmed. He relied on Mary. She started to say something and changed her mind.

'What's up, pisey cat?' Ambrose asked, knowing her. 'Oh, and that reminds me – I'll thank you not to discuss my personal affairs, Miss! I have just heard from Sam Pickering that this infant will be our last. Very obliging of him, I'm sure, but it's none of his business. I didn't know you gossiped with *him*!'

Flustered, Mary began to protest and explain at the same time.

'Why, you said so yourself only last week. "This is the last!" you said. In front of him and three others. It was a casual . . .'

Zelah, coming up to them unnoticed, squeezed her arm.

'There is a messenger in the hall for thee, love. Ambrose, my dear, would thee like to take Mr Pickering into the library and choose thy gifts? If thee doesn't lead the way everyone will be here for dinner, and only members of the family are invited to that!'

Mary promptly vanished. The two men accepted another glass of sherry and strolled into the library, where Tom Hadley stood by the long table ready to be helpful. Ambrose had the feeling that these handsome little knick-knacks had already been allocated, but he did not care, it was not important.

Sam Pickering's green eyes were fixed on a handsome glass paperweight. His hand moved tentatively, acquisitively, forward. His choice was not questioned. Satisfied, he pushed it into his jacket pocket, gulped down the rest of his sherry, and was ready to leave.

'I don't want anything,' said Hal Vivian, in Ambrose's ear. 'Aunt Zee has been generous enough to me already. But Mary would like something, I know. Where is she?'

'A message came for her, and she darted off.'

'Oh, yes! Probably to do with the magazine. Let me see . . .'

'Would Mrs Vivian like Mr Howarth's leather blotter and his silver inkstand, sir? Being a literary lady,' Tom suggested.

'Excellent idea!' said Hal. 'Come, Ambrose, you must have something. You didn't benefit directly.'

'I did, actually. Aunt Zee gave me first choice of his library. I have done rather well and now have a modest library of my own!'

Tom spoke confidentially in their ears.

'Mrs Howarth and I rather thought that Mr Longe would like the silver desk calendar. It's an ingenious little article. You can change the date and day and month quite easily.'

'Oh, thank you!' Ambrose cried obediently, and accepted the gift.

So it *had* been sorted out beforehand. He thought so. Well, you could hardly have a scrimmage for bequests. Too undignified.

One by one people were guided to their choice. The crowd thinned out rapidly, and finally became a few old friends gathered together for the last time in this great house. The end of another era. The long shining table and chairs in the dining room stood in empty state. Five places had been laid on a round table in the breakfast room.

'Where on earth is Mary?' Hal asked, as they went in to dinner.

'Oh, she was called away on an urgent matter,' said Zelah, smiling. 'She said she would see thee at home later, and that we were to eat without her. Come, Hal, thee shall sit next to me. Ambrose, pray sit over there. Tom, wilt thee sit next to Anna?'

'It's a pity Naomi couldn't be here too,' Ambrose said, feeling that her presence would have completed the occasion.

Zelah's smile understood, agreed with, and consoled him.

'Now, Ambrose, wilt thee play host for me?' she asked.

He did so most gracefully, although he could not help feeling that a ghostly ironmaster was despising his efforts.

It was almost midnight before he paid the driver of the hackney-coach and negotiated the steps of Thornton House, fumbling for his keys. Joseph opened the door while he was trying to find the lock, and helped him off with his overcoat, remarking on the cold. As if to remind him that servants should not be kept up, the long clock in the hall chimed twelve strokes quite distinctly.

'Am – am late?' Ambrose said, astonished at the passage of hours.

'Not at all, sir,' said Joseph reassuringly. 'In fact, sir, I should say that you were right on time.'

This remark struck Ambrose as being very strange, but he realised he was slightly the worse for the ironmaster's best claret and he endeavoured to understand it.

'Wife not – stayed up – I hope?'

'Oh no, sir. Mrs Longe retired quite a while ago.'

Upstairs, a bedroom door opened and closed quietly.

'There. Woke – woke – woke her!' said Ambrose penitently.

And was utterly confounded to see Mary Vivian coming downstairs.

'S'wrong?' he cried, alarmed in an instant.

'Nothing's wrong, you old silly!' said Mary, slipping her arm through his, and smiling. 'I dropped in to see Naomi, as I was in Millbridge, and stayed with her until you came home. That's all.'

'Should I bring some coffee, madam?' Joseph asked tactfully.

294

Mary nodded, and smiled even more broadly.

But Ambrose was afraid, and started up the stairs, holding tightly to the banisters whenever he could find them.

'Come on, you old lush!' Mary said, taking his arm, and giggled.

He would have told her to mind her manners, but claret and apprehension had rendered him wordless.

Their room was quiet and candle-lit. A most beautiful fire blazed on the hearth and sent shadows leaping on the walls. He heard Naomi laugh softly and say, 'So!' and could have wept with relief.

'Thought – something – wrong!' he said, putting out his arms.

'Steady a minute, Ambrose!' Mary ordered. 'You're facing the wrong way.'

The stifled laughter of both women roused his pride and steadied his legs. He took a mental grip on his mind and tongue.

'Sorry – Naomi – bit too much – to drink.'

He focused on her smile. She was sitting up looking very splendid and triumphant, and her baby lay in her arms.

Ambrose turned stone-cold sober.

'Your daughter, Jessica Mary, Mr Longe!' said Naomi, smiling.

He moved forward like a dreamer, and put his forefinger into the little pink palm. Jessica's eyes opened. Her fingers closed round his delicately. She went back to sleep again. He was incredibly moved.

'Why – you're the only one who's – caused me no grief,' he said to himself. 'No grief at all.'

The two women exchanged smiles over his head. He was bemused.

'I thought – she wasn't expected – for a few weeks, yet.'

'I told a little lie,' said Naomi soothingly. 'You always suffer so. It was better that you should not worry.'

'Oh, stuff!' said Mary frankly. 'I've been on tenterhooks for the last week, praying she wouldn't arrive in the middle of the night. We didn't want to cope with you as well as the baby!'

He was too amazed and happy to be hurt, but Naomi looked at her friend reproachfully and said, 'Mary! Mary!' in a low voice.

Unrepentant, Mary went on, 'But the message came this afternoon when we were at Kingswood Hall. So I told Aunt Zee to keep you as long as possible, and it's all worked out beautifully.'

He had not listened, looking and looking at his daughter. He put a finger in the other palm, and again her dark-blue eyes opened and fixed on his face, her fingers closed softly round his own, and her mouth wavered into the semblance of a crooked smile.

'She knows me,' said Ambrose. 'Do you see how she smiles?'

Even Mary was not so cruel as to say that it was wind.

Ambrose woke up by degrees in the spare room bed, filled with relief and joy at the thought that Naomi was safe, and the child born. Then, happy as a boy with a box of treats ahead of him, he recollected that this was his day off, and he had promised to take his sons out to see the Christmas shops. And treats lay inside treats, like Chinese boxes, as he realised they could enjoy Christmas together without the threat of Naomi's ordeal hanging over them. Until at last all these thoughts demanded immediate action, and he sprang out of bed and reached for his dressing gown.

As he stuck each foot into a cold slipper the long clock chimed seven. He felt astonishingly well, and set it down to the excellence of the ironmaster's claret and his own high spirits. The fire had burned out, and already the room was chilly, but sunlight pierced through chinks in the curtains with a peculiar brightness, and the early morning sounds had a muffled tone. He drew the curtains apart, and again his heart lifted as if he had been Nat or Toby or Jack. Snow. Thick, soft, white snow, almost unmarked as yet. Just a single trail of footprints along the pavement, and a double line of coach wheels in the road. Lord above, what a day it would be! They could go tobogganing on Kersall Hill. Go snowballing. But first of all, first and most important . . .

He padded quietly downstairs to find Dollie, was reassured as to the condition of mother and child, and taken tiptoeing in to Naomi with the morning tray. They were very quiet and happy together for half an hour, drinking tea and talking a little in low voices, and watching the sleeping infant. Then Ambrose went to the nursery for the boys so that they too could hang over the bassinette.

But three-year-old Jack stroked the baby's silky black hair when no one was looking, and experienced two terrible emotions at once. Simultaneously, he loved her so much that he wanted to die for her, and he hated her so much that he could have killed her. Overcome, he scrambled into his mother's arms and sobbed with frustration.

'You know I love you?' Naomi whispered into his hair.

She held him close until he was restored again, and then she dried his eyes and made him laugh instead.

Entwhistle's Toy Shop, in Market Square, had been built the previous century and bore the hallmark of elegance belonging to that era. Two elegant barrel-shaped windows were set on either side of a dignified front door, and just beneath the fanlight – in letters of gold on a black ground – Benjamin Entwhistle was rightly proclaimed to be a Toy Maker and Toy Supplier of Distinction. There was hardly a moment of the day when some small face was not pressed against one of his window-panes. And at night, when the street-lamp shone into the shop, adults could be seen standing there entranced, staring into the depths of their childhood.

There was no snobbery about Entwhistle's. They imported toys as well as making them, and you could buy anything from a whip and top to a fully-furnished doll's house. The ground floor held a selection of small appetisers for all ages and both sexes. The first floor was a feminine, and the second a masculine province. The third floor housed an astonishing collection of specialist and mechanical toys. In the basement workshop Benjamin pursued his own fine craftsmanship. In the attics, he and his mother and sister made a cramped but cosy home.

Ben Entwhistle was a strange fellow, half-child himself, and some said half-touched, but perhaps that touch was of genius. In the world of toys and children he was entirely at home. As to the world outside, his womenfolk dealt with that, though he liked to greet new customers and old favourites. Up he would climb from the basement, with paint on his fingers, wood shavings in his hair, and an ingenuous smile on his face. He always began each friendship by saying, 'Good day, young sir,' or 'young miss', 'Do you know my name?' And when the child, having been coached beforehand, whispered shyly in his ear, 'Mr Entwhistle!' he always said, 'Not quite. Listen to me! Mr Ent . . .' And then he whistled two notes, and said, 'Now *you* do it!'

As they grew older they found this embarrassing, but he seemed to know that, and did not trouble them once they were eight or nine.

So now, having shouted and snowballed their way up the High Street, Ambrose's three sons pressed their noses against every available window-pane before entering to choose the gifts which would be theirs on Christmas Day.

'Papa,' said Nathan, 'should we choose a Christmas present for the baby, too?'

'What's its name?' Toby asked.

'Jessica Mary,' said Ambrose.

'I don't think much of that!' Toby observed judiciously.

'I don't neither,' echoed Jack loyally.

'It doesn't send me into a rapture!' Nathan remarked, who was inclined to pick up expressions from Mary Vivian.

'Well, never mind,' said Ambrose, squashing the argument.

A small silvery bell over the door tinkled as the boys filed in. They doffed their flat peaked caps and bowed their heads.

'Good morning, Mrs Entwhistle!' they cried in unison, to that stout and dignified lady sitting behind the till.

'Good morning, young sirs,' she answered, very correct.

They then greeted Miss Entwhistle, who was thin and wistful.

The old lady lifted a stout walking stick which leaned against her chair, and knocked the floor thrice to alert her son.

Jack hid behind Ambrose, and tugged the sleeve of his overcoat.

'What's wrong with you, you idiot?' Ambrose whispered.

Jack whispered back, 'He'll want me to whistle his name, and I can only blow.'

Toby pulled himself up on his toes so that his face was level with Mrs Entwhistle's formidable countenance, and said, 'We've got a baby sister this morning, called Dessima Rary.'

She looked at Ambrose for confirmation, and replied amiably, 'Have you indeed, young sir? That's very nice.'

'Oh, very nice!' said Miss Entwhistle, and clasped her hands.

'I suppose we'd better give her a doll for Christmas,' said Nathan, who had previously ignored the existence of such things.

'Good day, Mr Longe,' said Benjamin, appearing bit by bit up the basement stairs. 'Good day, my young friends!' to the boys.

Nathan and Toby answered obediently, 'Good morning Mr Ent . . .' and whistled two good clear notes.

'I told you!' Jack whispered into the waist of his father's overcoat.

Tactfully, the Entwhistles affected not to notice his lack of response, and he was able to come out shortly afterwards, undisgraced.

Then the old woman preened herself behind the till,

saying in a tone of great importance. 'These young gentlemen have a baby sister, Benjamin. What do you think about that?'

He threw up his hands to heaven, amazed. He rounded his eyes and opened his mouth in astonishment. The gestures were as eloquent as those of a clown or a mime, and went straight to their hearts.

'Oh, what a day for celebration!' cried Benjamin. 'And by what name are you going to call this pearl of a princess?'

Nathan spoke up, as the eldest son.

'We don't like her name very much,' he announced frankly.

'But we want her to have a present, just the same!' said Toby.

'Because we love her a lot!' Jack explained, and added in a deep voice, '*I* don't! I *hate* her a lot!'

As horrified as they, he cried, 'That's not me saying it. That's my Little Voice and he's a very naughty bad boy indeed!'

'Indeed, he is!' said Mrs Entwhistle deeply, 'and should be shut in a dark cupboard and fed on bread and water.'

'No, he shouldn't,' cried Nathan, contradicting an adult in his excitement, 'he should be chained up in prison and starved to death!'

Toby shouted, 'No, he shouldn't. He should be *poisoned* and . . . and . . . made to walk the plank . . . and . . .'

Ambrose cuffed all their heads and spoke up authoritatively.

'Now, Mr Entwhistle, incredible though this may seem, these boys have been very good all year and deserve specially nice presents on Christmas morning. So if we promise that they will be Extremely Quiet and Polite – *unless they want to be taken home at once!* – may they choose a gift each?'

'By all means, sir. My sister will be delighted to help you.'

Ambrose leaned forward and said something in his ear.

'Oh yes, sir. I hadn't forgotten. It arrived yesterday. Seven shillings and sixpence. And a good selection – like you asked.'

Order and honour restored, the three boys spent a wonderful hour on the second floor, from which they emerged with a noble fort and a battalion of lead soldiers, an ornate brass bugle and drum, a set of building bricks with pictures on one side and alphabet letters on the other, and a Jack-in-the-box.

Down the narrow stairs they filed, to have the gifts approved by Mrs Entwhistle, ceremoniously wrapped, and put away to be delivered on Christmas Eve. A very large and mysterious brown paper parcel was then produced for Ambrose. The boys knew better than to remark on this, but Toby spoke up on another issue.

'What about Cressima Dairy's doll?'

Miss Entwhistle said gently, 'Oh, your sister will come and choose that for herself when she is bigger.'

'No!' said Toby, going scarlet. 'She has to have a present!'

'It's not fair to leave her out, Papa,' said Nathan.

Jack shouted, 'Cressa Rary's doll!'

Ambrose said, 'We seem to have forgotten my daughter. Lead us to the dolls, Miss Entwhistle.'

Previously, the boys had scorned any thought of the first floor. Now they were led into its sacred precincts and asked to stay by the door.

Miss Entwhistle went over to a deep box without a lid, rummaged inside, and held a up a calico doll for approval. Their silence answered her. Unperturbed, she rummaged in another box, and fetched out a jointed wooden doll with round red spots for cheeks and painted black hair. Again, all stared at it dumbfounded. A papier mâché creature with startled eyebrows also failed to move them.

Nathan said as politely as he could, 'We mean – a *real* doll.'

Miss Entwhistle looked to Ambrose for guidance.

He said sympathetically, 'Could you show us your *best* dolls?'

'Very well, sir, but would the young gentlemen not touch anything as we pass through, if you please?'

Gingerly they tiptoed after her, through a lane of fragile china tea-services to an inner sanctum. She unlocked the big glass case.

'I can't hardly *breave*!' gasped Jack, holding his stomach.

But Toby pointed to a sultry beauty on the top shelf, and said, 'There she is! There's Chessima's doll!'

Ignorant males though they might be, they all recognised her. Her translucent wax face was full of character, her blue glass eyes looked grandly upon them. Her fashionable bonnet and gown were beautifully made, and generously trimmed with lace. Had they been of the feminine gender, Miss Entwhistle would have been delighted to show them the doll's kid limbs clad in silk stockings, her chemise and petticoats and pantalettes. This being out of the question, she held the gown tightly round the doll's ankles, and lifted her down reverently, showing only the tips of her leather slippers. She was a large doll, perhaps eighteen inches long. Her hands were modelled of wax.

'This is my favourite, too!' Miss Entwhistle confessed shyly. 'She was made in Waltershausen, in Germany, by a wonderful doll-maker called Herr Kestner. I think of her as being *Isabella* – only in play, of course!' she added hastily, full of confusion.

'Why can't we call our sister Isabella?' Nathan asked. 'That's a pretty name.'

'I'm going to call her Isabella anyway, and no one can stop me!' said Toby belligerently.

'I *like* Isabella!' said Jack, and in a deep whisper, 'I *hate* Isabella.' Then louder, 'That's not me, that's my Little Voice!'

Miss Entwhistle dared confide the price to Ambrose.

'Never mind!' said Ambrose, philosophical to the last. 'Wrap the lady up. Home, boys!'

There was such excitement after tea that the monthly nurse found it necessary to remind them not to be noisy, for Mamma's sake, before she disappeared to the kitchen for a gossip. Joseph moved the furniture away, and fixed up an old white sheet on one wall of the nursery. The children's table was moved to the opposite end of the room, and their chairs placed in audience. He lit a candle to show him his way, and drew the curtains against the winter evening.

'Now everybody is to keep looking at the sheet, and nobody is to turn round!' called Ambrose from the door of the nursery, holding the mysterious parcel.

The three boys held their breath, trying to guess what was to come. Metallic bumps and clinks. The scratch and flare of matches. A smell of hot oil. Then a light focused and shone upon the sheet.

Ambrose said, 'Who would like to see the Swiss mountains?'

And there before them, out of nowhere, came a wonderful grey-green snow-capped Matterhorn against a bright blue sky, with little red climbers toiling up its face.

Nathan clapped both hands over his mouth. Toby shook his head from side to side violently. And Jack held his sides and said, 'Ha, ha, ha!' Then with one accord they ran towards the picture to grasp its reality. The mountain rippled as the sheet moved. The colours ran over their arms and faces. They shouted and jumped for joy.

They sat carefully round the edge of Naomi's bed, clad in their nightshirts, and watched Jessica sleeping in the bassinette. At their request, Isabella had been placed next to her for a few minutes. Infant and doll were almost the same size. The boys looked on both of them with a satisfied and proprietary air, before returning to the task of educating their mother.

'It's called a magic lantern,' cried Jack, trying to explain the wonder, 'because it's – it's – it's *magic*!'

'You didn't think of calling Jemmasirary *Isabella*, did you?' said Toby pityingly. 'You ought to of asked us, didn't you?'

Nathan was puzzling over the question of justice.

'Mamma, you know we get smacked if we swear? Well, when the matches burn his fingers, Papa always says "God dammit!" He does. He always says, "God dammit!" '

'That's *his* Little Voice!' said Jack.

Part Four

By-Lines 1847–1850

Threats and Promises

chapter twenty four

Ambrose laid down his pen and looked up at the clock on the wall of his office. This Thursday was notable for two events: one being his birthday, and the other the first meeting of the Oddities Club since typhus fever struck Lower Millbridge. That morning's breakfast had been a festive affair, with Naomi and the children bestowing gifts upon him. That evening he would dine with good friends, and celebrate the passing of an epidemic as savage as the cholera.

Outside, there was such a fog that the haloes of the gas lamps seemed smeared. But inside, his own lamps provided a certain amount of warmth as well as light, and emitted a soft hissing sound which was distinctly comforting. The major source of heat came from the fire in the grate, which the office-boy replenished with coal every few hours.

Ambrose had most sternly resisted Naomi's attempts to make a second home of this room, turning aside offers of velvet curtains and Axminster carpets, a clock in a glass dome, and water-colours of the Lancashire countryside. So it was a plain and businesslike place, furnished with deep buttoned leather chairs, a broad pedestal desk, and mahogany shelves and cabinets, in which a man could work and talk and sit undistracted.

He loved this season of year. He felt that his mother must have been happy, carrying and bearing him, for him to walk so lightly through life: so lightly, and for such a length of time. He had been born, Charlotte told him, just before six o'clock on a foggy London morning, and then wrapped in a soft cloth and

307

a piece of old blanket and laid in her arms. But as soon as the local church clock struck the hour he had widened his eyes and moved his head, to stare at her in wonder.

Now St Stephen's clock began to chime a different hour in another century and a new age. And Ambrose said quietly to himself, with the same wonder which must have seized him when he entered the world.

'Good Lord! I am growing old!'

It seemed to him that life was having a joke at his expense, to put him in such a harness.

He added, lest the fates be misled by this admission.

'And I have never felt better!' Then to the knock on the door, 'Come in!'

Frank Ormerod had put on a great deal of weight in the past fourteen years, and the climb up the stairs always robbed him of breath for a minute or two. So he usually wrote his opening comment on a sheet of paper, and put it in front of Ambrose for consideration. Most of the time it was a routine remark. Today it was a bombshell.

'I have confirmed that W. H. Smith of London got *The Times*, *The Daily News*, *The Herald* and *The Morning Post* from London to Manchester the same day, by means of a special express train.'

'Happy birthday!' said Ambrose ironically.

Frank had got his breath back by now, and loyally echoed the sentiment. Adding, 'They sent them to Birmingham and Liverpool, too. Now, I don't know how you feel about it, but this worries me.'

'I'm not exactly delighted, myself!' Ambrose replied.

'Of course, the threat's been hanging over us for a long while now,' said Frank, 'but they've got the edge on us at last. Who's going to read *The Correspondent* on Tuesday and Saturday – with most of its outside news rehashed from London papers anyway! – when they can read *The Times* six days a week, fresh off the press?'

Ambrose leaned back in his chair, fingertips together, thinking.

'I'll give you one good financial reason, for a start,' he said, after a while. 'It costs our readers only ninepence a week to read all the news in *The Correspondent*. It would cost them half-a-crown to read *The Times* every day. So we come a great deal cheaper!'

'Aye.' Reluctantly. 'There is that.' He was unconvinced. 'But the Whigs are back in, and you know what they're like for reform.' Frank was strictly conservative in outlook. 'What if they lift the duty off advertisements and paper and reduce the stamp? Why, London dailies could be coming up on an express train at a penny or twopence a copy. And *then* we'd be out o' business!'

'Not quite!' said Ambrose. 'If they can publish daily at a penny or twopence then so can we. And why should Lancastrians care what happens in London? Most of them never go there. The Manchester and Liverpool markets are more important to a Lancashire businessman. And the rest of our readers want to know the local news.'

He looked closely at his colleague.

'You're in the doldrums today, Frank!'

'Aye, well, we're printing close on nine thousand copies an issue now. And that's not funny, by any account.'

'Oh, I see. It's prosperity that worries you!'

'Nay, it's not. And I'm not feared of responsibility, neither. But if you'll come downstairs and take a look, you'll see what we're up against.'

'I'll come downstairs and take a look anyway!' Ambrose said amicably. And as they descended to the lower depths, he added, 'Oh, and there's something else in our favour. I presume you checked the W. H. Smith news by Electric Telegraph?'

'I did. And that's another thing! You can't be sure that you're getting the information right. That Cooke and Wheatstone's machine ain't exactly fast and it's not always accurate. Remember the trouble we had, checking up, when they thought

309

the French King was murdered in the summer? Besides, telegrams come expensive – I'll bet Mrs Longe raises her eyebrows when she sees the bill!'

'Yes, but I hear someone's working on a new sort of teleprinter, which records the message in dots and dashes . . .'

'Aye. A chap called Bain. Let's hope it's an improvement.'

'Oh, come on, Frank, it's bound to improve. Look at the progress the telegraph system has made over the last four years. It was only good enough for railway signalling when they first started using it.'

The door at the bottom of the second flight of stairs divided the working from the thinking section of *The Northern Correspondent*. As soon as it was opened their ears would take the brunt of their Applegath-Cowper four-feeder printing press going full-steam ahead. Ambrose paused, with his hand on the door knob.

'Well, the Electric Telegraph will be our saving grace. So far London news has only been able to travel as fast as the London newspapers. But when news travels nationally and internationally by telegraph, we shall receive it at the same time as the London papers!'

Frank nodded reluctantly, for his real worry lay within himself. He felt he was slowing down, whereas the newspaper world was speeding up, and he wondered sometimes how he could cope with it.

'We'll manage!' Ambrose said cheerfully, answering the unspoken fear, and smiled, and opened the door.

In the past four years *The Correspondent* had already enlarged its offices by taking over the adjacent house. They were thinking of a new site and new premises altogether, but in the meantime Nos 21 and 23 Middleton Street were adequate. And Millbridge Electric Telegraph Company were occupying No 25, so they were next door to incoming news as well as publishing it.

The two men entered the composing room. The work of compositors had not changed fundamentally in four centuries.

Even in this modern industrial age new type was still hand-cast. Still the typesetter, holding his composing stick in the left hand, picked capital letters from the upper case of type, and others from the lower case, and set them in the composing stick to form sentences of looking-glass language. Carefully, he justified the margins, spacing individual letters so that the edges of the printed page would be even. And to and fro he walked across the room, putting each batch of lines into the galley tray, until it was full.

On the other hand, printing-presses had moved with the times.

An archway had been cut through the dividing walls of the two houses, and stacks of paper and stone jars of printing ink stood on either side of it. Beyond the arch the room was dominated by the Applegath-Cowper machine which resembled two four-poster beds standing on top of two others. It towered to the ceiling, dwarfing its minions who were working on different levels. The bed of type alone weighed three quarters of a ton, and the floor beneath it had been reinforced.

Rhythmically, mechanically, in the constant roar, four men laid four sheets of blank paper on to the flat bed of the press. And every three and half seconds four boys removed four sheets of newsprint. At top speed, four thousand impressions could be produced in an hour. Tonight, they were printing the outside pages of advertisements and entertainments. Tomorrow night, they would perfect the process by printing political and business news on the other side of the sheet.

The sound of the press moved Ambrose as much as Beethoven's Eroica symphony moved Naomi. It was simply a different kind of music. He stood watching and smiling, wholly entranced.

'It's not funny when we break down!' Frank bawled in his ear.

Ambrose shook his head in sympathy. It was not his business to cope with mechanical troubles. In any case, this was the finest printing-press of its kind they could buy.

'The old Napier still earns its living!' he shouted back. 'You can use that at a pinch!'

It was Frank's turn to nod. He put his mouth close to Ambrose's ear again.

'I suppose if we lived in America we'd be having one of them Hoe type revolving presses? They say it'll turn off eight thousand impressions an hour.'

'I daresay Applegath's eight-feeder rotary press will do the same when it's finished,' Ambrose yelled back. 'I hear that *The Times* is having one! They must be doing even better than I thought!'

'*The Times* is a national daily!' Frank reminded him, at top pitch. '*The Correspondent* don't need that sort of press.'

Ambrose thought, 'She will. But perhaps not in my lifetime.'

Aloud he cried, 'You're doing a grand job, Frank!' which was the encouragement the man needed.

They walked out of the room, and resumed their normal tones.

'And that's another thing,' said Frank, but his voice had lost its note of despair. 'I'll bet Sam Pickering's smiling like a cat with a saucer of cream over printing *The Lady's Hour* for Mrs Vivian. That magazine's never looked back. A good steady circulation, with a marginal increase. Very popular among the ladies in the valley. And to give Sam credit his Cornmarket Press do a lovely job, and all. I *said* right from the first that we should print it, Mr Longe!'

But Ambrose smiled and shook his head, and put his hand on Frank Ormerod's shoulder.

'Believe me, it would always have been too much trouble!' he replied, grinning.

An Hour with the Ladies

chapter twenty five

March, 1848

'Mrs Vivian, madam,' said Dollie, and retired to fetch the tea-things.

It was Mary, of course, looking particularly ravishing in a new ensemble. Having an eye, as well as an ear, for what interested both sexes, she had made herself into a fashionable living advertisement for *The Lady's Hour.*

'Oh, look!' her readers cried, seeing a new confection floating along on the other side of the road, 'there goes Mrs Vivian. You know – the magazine lady!'

Today it was a blue-grey satin gown, and a matching bibi bonnet trimmed with white feathers tipped in paler blue.

'My dear Lady Editor!' cried Naomi, embracing her.

'My dear Lady Director!' cried Mary, laughing, 'Goodness me, what famous people we are these days.'

'Yes, it is good,' said Naomi simply, 'and we are fortunate.'

'I don't know so much about fortunate!' Mary began, in her usual headlong manner. 'I do believe that the whole valley is being dug up for drainpipes! Do you know that Alfred had to stop the carriage in the middle of the High Street? And I could only reach the pavement by means of a *plank*, and had to pretend not to notice all sorts of insulting compliments from the navvies about my ankles! And it's no use complaining to Hal about those creatures. He worships them!'

Their remarks had not really displeased her, as Naomi observed by the dimple at the corner of her friend's mouth.

'Yes, they have rough tongues, but they are good workers,'

Naomi replied soothingly, 'and what is this little inconvenience compared to the risk of another epidemic? Think how many people died of typhus fever last year – even people with whom we were acquainted. At least, it made the Council do something about drainage and sewerage. And we are supposed to be having a better water supply, too. But Ambrose and Jamie are afraid they will only improve the Old Town, and leave the poor quarters just as they are.'

Public welfare not being one of her major interests, Mary said, 'I'm sure your boys love all the upheaval. I saw them just now talking to the navvies further down the street, with dear Mrs Lillie hanging on to Jessica and trying to stop Jack from falling into a huge hole!'

'They learn such terrible words from them,' said Naomi, and lifted her hands and eyes momentarily to the front parlour ceiling. 'Come on, my dear. Come by the fire. How well and how young you look!'

'At forty, my dear?' cried Mary, delighted. 'Still, I don't think that women age as quickly as they did, do you? My poor mother was dead at forty-four, and quite worn out. It doesn't bear thinking of! And yet I work shockingly hard, I can tell you. And so do you, I know, but you look handsomer than ever. Now, madame,' loosening her bonnet strings, and producing a large notebook, 'I have come to interview you, on behalf of our magazine readers, as the first lady in our series of *Wyndendale's Remarkable Ladies* . . .'

'Before we have tea?' Naomi asked, surprised.

'Well, *while* we have tea, then. I'm used to working *through* meals, these days,' said Mary importantly.

Amused, for she managed both her public and her private life without fuss, Naomi bowed her head. It was in her friend's nature to be the heroine of her own self-made dramas, and she had known and loved her too long by this time to take offence.

'Of course!' Naomi replied. 'I forget how busy you are!' There was a gleam of mischief in her eyes as she went on, 'I ask just one question of you before we begin. Why did you not ask Lady Kersall to begin your series? Socially speaking, *she* is the first lady in Wyndendale.'

'Oh, there's nothing remarkable about *her*, except for a title!' Mary cried scornfully. 'Our readers prefer to identify with someone like you, who is married to a man they can speak to in the street, and has a family to bring up and a household to run, and yet can envision the Millbridge Concert Hall and raise the money to build it. They want to think that *they* could wield that sort of public power and have that sort of inspiration. That *they* could persuade the great Jenny Lind to sing there on the opening night . . . Oh! I shall want details of her stay with you, by the by.'

Naomi lifted one hand to halt her friend's progress. She was amused by the way Mary rattled on, but would not allow her to embroider the truth.

'Jenny Lind did not stay *here*, my dear. I booked a suite of rooms for her at the Royal George – and visited her there, naturally, because we both have many friends and acquaintances in the music world. But she had a private supper here with us after the concert.'

'Oh well, that's almost as good. Can you remember what she wore – when she saw you on those private occasions, I mean? I have details of all the important ladies' gowns on the opening night at the Concert Hall, because Dorcas took note of them for Page Seven.'

'Yes, I believe I can remember,' said Naomi, amused again. Then she persisted, lightly, naughtily, 'But how you surprise me not to be interested in Lady Kersall! The stories in your magazine are all about proud and beautiful ladies with titles – or those who marry a title.'

Mary hesitated a moment.

'Oh, well. I admit that I did ask her first. But the wretched creature said she would have nothing to do with *Lady's Hour*!'

Naomi laughed aloud and clapped her hands.

'Mary, my Mary. What a – what a – Picey Cat you are!'

'Pisey!' Mary corrected her, with a grin. 'Ah, good! Here comes tea! I'm starving. I didn't have time for luncheon. Now, I hope you're prepared to answer a number of personal questions.'

'Of what nature?' Naomi asked dubiously.

'Oh, goodness me, nothing and everything!' said Mary, amused in her turn by Naomi's sudden withdrawal. 'How you choose your clothes, and which gown is a particular favourite – preferably one with sentimental associations. The recipe for some special continental dish, preferably one that Ambrose likes . . .'

'But I gave you all my recipes for Page Seven long ago!'

'Oh, nobody will remember that! Also, we want to know how you keep so healthy and beautiful. And have you any special beauty tips you can give us? Your German aunt's recipe for face cream would be useful, if you can bear to part with it to the general public.'

Naomi smiled, and said, 'No wonder Lady Kersall was reluctant! And do you want a few hints as to the buying and selling of stocks and shares, or how to add up a column of figures in your head correctly?'

'Oh, Lor'! No, Naomi. Nothing like that.'

'Your readers prefer to think that I create the Millbridge Concert Hall out of strüdel and face cream?'

'Now, Naomi, don't be so satirical!'

'They wish to pick the flowers but not to meet the gardener?'

'Naomi, you're being difficult. You know perfectly well that I should be out of business in an instant, my dear, if I started all that earnest stuff. *The Lady's Hour* isn't here to ruffle feathers but to smooth them down and point out the beauties of female plumage! And it *is* lovely to be a woman, of course, if you're lucky enough to be pretty and reasonably well-to-do, and find a nice, kind husband who loves you, and if you don't have too many babies or die having them.'

'And that is your only concern?' Naomi asked, eyebrows raised.

Mary discerned an undercurrent of criticism and resented it.

'Oh, it's all very well for Ambrose to publish social injustices abroad, and for my brother George to preach sedition and get put in prison for it, but they're men. They can do as they please. And even if I were a man I should be inclined to take Uncle William's point of view. I'm not a fool, and I see a great many things that I should like to alter, but I can't do that. So I cut life to my own pattern, as best I can, and look after those I love. And I persuade women that there is nothing nicer than being a wife and mother.'

'And that is what you believe?'

'You know perfectly well, Naomi, that if I stayed at home all day looking after my children – much as I adore them – I should go mad in five minutes! And I would truly rather die than drudge in poverty all my days. As it is, my dear, I enjoy life outside my home, and show other women how to enjoy life inside theirs.'

The interview had become too serious. Mary spoke more lightly.

'Mind you, most women are not like us, you know. Look at Dorcas! She simply adores daily life at Beech Grove. You won't get her yearning to run a magazine or finance a company, my dear. Not in a month of Sundays! An occasional contribution to Page Seven is her wildest limit.'

Naomi did not respond to this sprightly sketch of their mutual friend. Her voice was distinctly sombre as she replied.

'I wish you to tell your readers that to be a woman with outside interests of her own is not all ales and cakes. That it is hard work. That often I despaired. That often I was afraid.'

'Oh yes, I will,' Mary promised, already thinking of nicer ways to put this statement.

Naomi spoke even more sternly, to invisible readers who did not want the whole truth.

317

'I do not like *silly* women!'

'Oh yes, you do,' said Mary ruefully, impishly. 'You like me!'

'You are not silly. You are very shrewd. Very strong-willed. Very intelligent. You laugh and smile and chatter to cover up the fact that you get your own way.'

'Naomi!' Caught out.

'I wish you also to tell your readers that my views on the education of women are strong. My father educated me as good as a son. Jessica shall be educated as good as our sons – both Ambrose and I agree on this. We do not like the fashion for women to be taught parlour tricks, like dogs. A little music, a little art, a little writing of verse – and none of it done well.'

'Just as you please, my dear. It may not come out exactly like that, but you shall approve the copy before we publish it.'

Naomi regarded her with some irony.

'Yes, you will find a way to please all of us,' she answered, 'without offending any of us.' She shrugged. 'Well, who am I to complain? I have learned much about local politics in the last few years. What do you say? I have touched pitch with the hands and defiled them?'

'Oh, that's coming it a bit strong!' Mary said good-naturedly. 'You mean you've learned to manage people.'

Naomi sat thinking. Her face and demeanour changed.

'I have been rude to you, I think,' she said repentantly.

'No, you haven't!' Mary cried, ridding herself of the note-book, and coming over to clasp Naomi's hands. 'You've upped and told the truth as usual, and I love and admire you for it.'

The two friends searched each other's faces for signs of hurt or displeasure, and found none.

'Sometimes, Ambrose says I make a sermon!' Naomi admitted. 'But I tell him – if we cannot talk together of what we think and feel, how are we to know each other?'

'Well, most people prefer *not* to know each other!'

'Then I must continue to make a sermon!'

But she was smiling now, and Mary smiled back most lovingly.

Saying, 'Lor', Naomi! You do remind me of Aunt Cha!'

Knights Errant

chapter twenty six

April, 1848

Saints and martyrs, Ambrose thought, are uncommonly difficult people. Although their bravery and sincerity cannot be questioned, although their intentions are of the noblest, and their lives dedicated to the highest purposes, how very much easier it is to cope with ordinary sinners.

The letter which lay before him on his office desk was George Howarth's first communication in five years, and came from Wigan. The paper was poor and dirty, the handwriting too meticulous – the hand of a self-taught man who is afraid of less than perfection. His spelling was good as far as it went, but he still wrote as he spoke which was both a strength and a weakness.

> *Dear Cousin, Its me again. George Howarth. Ive been arrested for nowt more than standin int Market Place listenin to somebody else speak. This ant the first time Ive been in prison and Im feared theyll sentence me heavy. I know I piked off sudden-like but your the only one as can help and I have summat to ask you. Wilt come to Wigan and see me? Your cousin George.*

'Come in!' Ambrose called, hearing the double knock on the door. And as the customary slip of paper was laid in front of him, accompanied by much wheezing, 'Sit down, Frank. Where's the war?'

For Frank Ormerod had capped all the office's black jokes throughout February and March, by panting up the stairs and delivering first of all a note which read, 'Revolution in Paris,' to be followed at intervals of every few days by, 'Riots in Vienna,' 'Explosions in Bohemia,' 'Hungary declares itself an independent nation,' 'Austria under attack from all sides,' and 'War of liberation in Italy'.

This one read, 'Frederick William of Prussia drives Danes out of the duchies.'

'We seem to have a European revolution on our hands!' Ambrose observed. 'No wonder they've arrested George Howarth for standing in Wigan market-place!'

And he handed the letter to Frank, who pursed his lips and shook his head as he read it, and spoke with wry affection.

'The daft little pillock!' said Frank, handing the note back. 'So you're going down there to bail him out then, are you?'

'No, I'm going to see if they'll transfer him to Millbridge Jail while he waits for the Assizes. I can keep an eye on him here. I have a little influence with the law these days – I used to be on the other side of it when I was young!'

'Them Chartists!' said Frank, contemptuously. 'There was one time, back in the thirties, when I thought they were going to take the country over. But they've fizzled out like a lot o' spent rockets.'

'That's a good phrase,' said Ambrose absently. 'I must remember that one. They convinced our George, at any rate.'

'Aye, well. He's an innocent, isn't he? Our George.'

Ambrose said, 'It's ironic how life turns your best intentions inside out. Do you know I took him to that mass meeting on Kersall Moor, ten years ago, because I thought it might liven him up a bit.'

The torches, flaring against the night, had lent an air of magic to the occasion. In the crush of the crowd, hearing the old roll and thunder of radical argument, watching the rapt uplifted faces, Ambrose felt his political pulses race again.

Nearly fifty thousand working men were gathered there. Some of the older ones were carrying the banners they had borne at Peterloo, nearly twenty years before. And as each separate group brought forth its leaders and its hopes and grievances, it seemed for once as if all the radical streams were flowing together, to form one mighty river which would flood the nation.

And yet, though he waged constant war upon social evils, Ambrose tended to be more of a realist than an idealist where politics were concerned. He had lived too long and seen too much to believe that any single movement had the ultimate answer, or that any of its leaders might be Messiahs.

In his mind he heard Charlotte's voice saying, 'Beware of the emotions roused by torchlight and the dreams of fine orators!'

Then Ambrose came down to earth. He knew that tomorrow, and ten thousand tomorrows, would dawn bleak and cold for these listeners, who must return to the treadmill of their daily lives. The paradise of a fair day's work for a fair day's pay was far off, still.

But George Howarth, being a man of great heart and simplicity, was moved to tears and talked of nothing else on the way home. For a week or more, his passionate enthusiasm for the Chartists was a matter for private amusement among the staff of *The Correspondent*. He buttonholed anybody who would listen to him. He could quote the aims of their People's Charter off by heart. Then, as though the experience had proved too much for him, he went underground again.

At lunchtime, in Pendleton's Chop-house, seeing Sam Pickering sitting by himself at his particular table, Ambrose strolled over to join him, and ordered a bottle of claret for the pair of them. But no sooner had the wine been poured out than Sam spoke up with a grin.

'I hear George Howarth's in prison again!'

'How the devil do you know that, you old fox? I was just going to tell you!'

'Your office-lad's got a big mouth, and mine has big ears.'

'Do you pay them for the information?' Ambrose asked unkindly.

'I don't have to,' said Sam, and ate a mouthful of pie-crust. 'They wag on without an incentive. What's our George done, then?'

'He was arrested for listening to someone speak in the market.'

'He was arrested because he's a known Chartist,' said Sam, spearing a chunk of meat. 'The state of affairs in Europe is enough to frighten anybody. They're mopping up the people who might cause trouble here. *We* don't want a revolution.'

'The Chartists did. Oh, thank you, Albert. That smells good.'

'The Chartists are finished. And now the Corn Law's been repealed the Anti-Corn Law League's got nothing to shout about, either,' said Sam, mopping up his gravy with a piece of bread. 'I told you a long while ago that changes come at their own pace, in their own time.'

'Time doesn't mean as much to you as it does to a starving man,' said Ambrose, unconsciously quoting George.

'It's no good being high-minded,' Sam replied. 'You know as well as I do that the Chartists and the League were ambitious. They both wanted working-class support on a national scale. And there was no brotherly love beyond the Charter, neither.'

'They weren't all like that. Lovett was a sound man, and he had the support of the educated artisans and the liberal-minded middle class. He was the brains behind the Charter. But he had people like that rabble-rouser O'Connor to contend with, and an army of hungry workers who only asked for a pike in their hands, and promises of a three-hour working day, roast beef, plum pudding and beer forever!'

'Of course, you and O'Connor never quite saw eye to eye, did you?' Sam Pickering remarked slyly.

This was a nasty dig, for Fergus O'Connor of *The Northern*

Star had mounted a personal attack on Ambrose in his newspaper, calling him 'a bogus revolutionary', deriding his editorials as being 'the ineffectual bleats of a middle-class fence-sitter', and finally describing *The Correspondent* as 'a Tory Wolf in Whig's Fleece'.

'I wonder what *The Northern Star*'s circulation is now?' Sam went on, in a tone of idle curiosity. 'It was selling ten thousand copies a week before it had been going four months.'

Ambrose replied coolly, 'Well, it wasn't enough for our friend Fergus anyway. He wanted to hear the roar of the crowd. Words don't draw blood – at least, not at first hand. He did well to get himself elected to Parliament.'

'You aggravated the Anti-Corn Law people, too!' Sam remarked, being in an aggravating mood himself. 'I heard that Charlie Ainsworth was mobbed on one occasion.'

'He was turned away from a meeting and somewhat roughly handled. No bones broken. Some people don't like honest reportage!'

'Aye, well, I told you how it would be!' said Sam, picking his teeth reflectively. 'You can take an impartial view if you want to, but no one will thank you for it. You'll end up, as you did in this case, like the meat in the sandwich. Now the likes and dislikes of the radical press never affected our sales. Our readers are dependable.'

'Our sales weren't affected, either,' Ambrose replied shortly, 'We cater for *thinking* people who see both sides of the question!'

They had made their points for the thousandth time.

'Have a jam roly-poly on me,' Sam said, as his own portion came to the table. 'They're very tasty.'

Ambrose nodded, and poured them another glass of claret each.

'So what are you going to do about our George?' Sam asked.

'I'm getting him transferred to Millbridge Jail if I can,

while he awaits trial. Then I can deal with things on the spot.'

'Oh, you should manage that,' Sam remarked ironically. 'Being such a law-abiding and influential citizen as you are these days!'

As with all radical movements, the fortunes of the Chartists had fluctuated according to the economic climate. In the bitter winter of 1840 hidden cases of fire-arms were discovered in the Spinning Yarn, that old rebels' haunt on Swarth Moor. Whereupon the landlord was severely questioned, and revealed the names of half a dozen local men who were promptly arrested.

The affair was over in a matter of days, without further trouble. And George, who had been unaccountably absent during this time, turned up looking as if he had been sleeping in straw. He did not venture any explanation, and Ambrose did not need to ask any questions. George had evidently reached some conclusion on his own, and was following it up.

For a couple of years afterwards, as if aware that they had sailed a little too close to the wind, Chartists became peaceable, respectable. In the valley's parks, local members stood on wooden boxes of a Sunday and spoke like parsons of the brotherhood of man. Flawnes Green Teetotallers Association joined them. One Chartist was elected a member of Millbridge Council, and did an honest job until he was quietly voted out again.

In this milder climate George begged a private interview with Ambrose in order to admit his allegiance to the cause, and to say that he was proud of it. He also said that if Ambrose objected to his association with the Chartists – on account of Fergus O'Connor being rude to him – he was prepared to leave his niche at Middleton Street that very day. No offence meant, and none taken, but that was the principle on which he stood, and he wouldn't change it for nobody.

'Oh, shut up and get out, George!' Ambrose had told him, with great good-nature. 'You can swear allegiance to the devil as far as I'm concerned. It's your life, man, not mine.'

325

George hovered indecisively for a moment, and then turned on his heel and went.

But in the summer of 1842, as the Plug Riots spread across Lancashire into the West Riding of Yorkshire, Wyndendale had suffered its own brief revolt. For two days all the cotton-mills were stopped by workers pulling the plugs out of the boilers, so that steam-powered looms could not operate. Strikers picketed the iron mill gates. Bands of workers marched down the main streets bearing placards.

Ambrose was greatly relieved to see that George stuck to his post throughout the disturbances. He even dared mention the fact, wondering whether the flame of Chartism was burning low, but George dashed this hope immediately.

'Nay, this is nowt to do wi' t'Chartists, cousin. This is working folk driven to do summat by theirselves, because they're clemmed. And I'd have marched wi' them if I hadn't got other responsibilities, but I dursen't get involved as it is.'

Ambrose, relieved and surprised, under the impression that he was referring to his ties with Middleton Street, retired to his office with his mind at rest. This pleasant delusion was shortly to be shattered by the arrival of two police constables with orders to arrest George Howarth.

'But I can produce twenty witnesses, who will tell you that he was here throughout the rioting!' Ambrose cried indignantly.

'Yes, sir. But he's a regular known Chartist. He's treasurer of the local group. And we've been given orders to fetch in everybody that might have an interest in public demonstrations.'

'*I* didn't know he was their treasurer!' cried Ambrose, struck by the incongruity of the idea.

The constable interpreted this as a cry of outraged dignity, and replied soothingly.

'Well, you're not to blame for that, sir. You never know who to trust these days, do you? You'll be asked to give evidence, of course, seeing as you employ him.'

'I'll give evidence all right!' cried Ambrose, infuriated.

'Both in court and in the columns of this newspaper. He has done no wrong. And I want to speak to him before you take him away.'

'Whatever you say must be said in front of us, sir,' said the constable respectfully.

And all Ambrose could think of, as George limped into the office, and stared at the three men, was, 'I couldn't help you, George.'

His cousin's steadfast gaze forgave him his inadequacy.

George said practically, 'Under my mattress upstairs you'll find an old stocking, cousin. The money in it belongs to the Association.'

'Everything will be all right, George. Don't you worry.'

He watched him limp off between the two tall policemen: cap set squarely on his head, muffler tucked inside the breast of his jacket, though the day was warm.

'I'll speak up for you, George!' he cried.

But George never turned round.

He was sentenced to six months' hard labour in a House of Correction, from which he emerged silent and subdued. Later that spring he made his choice between Ambrose and the Chartists and took his leave of Middleton Street. Though they heard news of him now and again, there had been silence for the space of five years, until this letter came asking for help.

Ambrose sat on a hard chair in the visiting room at Millbridge Jail, waiting for George to appear. Obviously, those who designed this meeting place had no intention of making prison life inviting. The walls were varnished with dark-brown paint. The flagged floors were uncarpeted, the small barred windows uncurtained. Even the air seemed to have been imprisoned and sentenced for life.

The building had been twice enlarged since Charlotte Longe was brought here back in 1812, on a charge of treason. And the number of cells had increased considerably since

Ambrose was pitched into one of them on his first charge of printing and distributing a seditious newspaper, back in 1824.

Enlarged but not improved, Ambrose reflected. There was simply more scope for it to be inhospitable.

A burly warder brought his cousin in, handcuffed as though he were some particularly desperate criminal, and George limped gamely beside him. His hair had turned grey, but a sparse and dusty grey, not the distinguished steel of Ambrose's uncovered head.

With some difficulty, the warder manoeuvred himself and his prisoner into a couple of chairs at the other side of the deal table, and addressed himself to Ambrose.

'You can talk about the family and that, but no politics, no secret signs, and no speaking in a foreign language.'

Good God, Ambrose thought, what fools they must think we are. What fools they must be themselves. Imagine trying to give a secret sign in full view of a watchful third party. Think of talking sedition in French and hoping to get away with it.

Aloud, he said, 'I quite understand. Hello there, George.'

George Howarth's shoulders were bowed. His mouth was set in a thin sad line. But his eyes blazed out for an instant. He repeated the phrase he had used when he came out of hospital fourteen years ago.

'Well, cousin, I'm back.'

'I'm glad to see you,' said Ambrose. 'I've been looking into your case. I'm afraid you're an inveterate offender with a long record, George, but at least you weren't carrying arms. I'll do what I can.'

'You're not allowed to talk about his case!' said the warder.

George ran his tongue over his lips and spoke quietly.

'It's family news as *I* want to talk about, sir.'

The warder nodded, and looked hard at Ambrose, who made a great show of feeling for his handkerchief, clinked some loose change together inside his back pocket, and looked meaningfully back.

'Just keep it personal, so's I can follow what you're talking about,' said the warder, understanding, 'and you're all right for fifteen minutes.'

George dropped his eyes, ashamed.

'Well then, get on with it!' said the warder, nudging him.

'I made some good friends in Wigan, cousin. A miner and his wife. They took me in when I come out o' prison for the second time. They made a home for me, as I haven't had a home in years. I were uncle to their children. I could allus go back here, no matter what, and know as I was welcome. I was one o' them.'

Here he wiped his eyes with the cuff of his left sleeve.

'Well, he were killed in a fall at the mine, last summer. I felt I were obliged – nay, that's not the right word! – I were there and they needed me. I had a choice to make. I could go on wi' the Chartists as I had been doing or look after Alf's family. It were a hard choice, cousin, but I had to do what seemed right. I got a job at the coal face. I've been keeping them as best I could – but my best these days ain't much! And I've been keeping out o' trouble, too, as best I could – and I don't seem to have done so well at that, neither! Cousin, I were only standing there, and they come up and arrested me.'

Ambrose was experiencing all the emotions that George managed to arouse in him at once: astonishment, reverence, amused disbelief and sinking dismay. However, he accepted this new development, as he accepted all else about his cousin, as being somehow necessary.

'And that were why I asked you to come to Wigan,' George added simply, 'because that's where they are. Up here, I don't know what's happening to them, and Norah don't know what's happening to me.'

Ambrose had the same sensation of failure he had felt when he had made the pun about Prospect Mine in his article, and unwittingly told the bully boys where to find his cousin.

'Now I have to ask summat of you as I wouldn't ask for

myself,' George continued, 'but if I canna fend for them some-one else must. Cousin, will you see them right for money while I'm here? I'll pay you back when I get out, somehow.'

Now Ambrose came to life again, for this he could do.

'Good God, of course I will. I'd thought of that already. No need to pay me back, George. I shall consider it a privilege to help. How many children are there?'

'Only two. A grand little lad, going on eight, and a bonny little lass nigh on five years old. Like your Jack and your Jessie. But if there'd been ten of them,' said George stoutly, 'it would ha' made no difference to me.'

'I'm sure it wouldn't!' said Ambrose, and wanted to laugh, and wanted to cry. 'Would twenty-five shillings a week be all right?'

'Eh, they'll be better off without me than wi' me on that!' said George ruefully.

'Right you are, George! Now I can't do much about having you transferred back to Wigan, I'm afraid – it was a hell of a lot of trouble moving you here!' He caught the warder's eye and hurried on. 'If you'll give me the name and address I'll go and see . . .?'

'Norah! Norah Howarth. I married her, you see.'

Ambrose's mouth opened and shut.

He said, 'I thought you hadn't much time for marriage, George.'

'Well, it seemed only right. Once folk had got over Alf being killed they started to talk. She's a grand woman is Norah. I weren't going to have her name bandied about on account o' me.'

Ambrose copied the address down carefully in his notebook.

'Time's up!' said the warder, tired of the interview.

'Oh, by the way, where is your prison charity box?' Ambrose asked, turning to him and speaking casually, cour-teously. 'I have something to contribute.'

He stared round the hostile little room.

'I don't see it for the moment!' he remarked.

He took a sovereign from his pocket and placed it on the table.

'Perhaps you would be kind enough to slip this in for me?'

The warder palmed the sovereign and said in a conciliatory tone, 'I'll see to it, sir. Now, I've got to take him back fairly soon. Was there anything else before he goes?'

'Five minutes more?' Ambrose asked, eyebrows raised.

The nod promised him just five minutes.

He unhooked his pocket-watch and set it on the table before them so he could mark time passing, then addressed himself to his cousin.

'Now, George, why shouldn't I bring Norah and the children up here? We could settle them in your old rooms at Middleton Street.'

'What, leave all her folks and friends and come among strangers?' cried George. Then his face changed, and he said, 'Well, there's not a lot o' choice, is there? I know she'd be safe near you. And you canna go to and fro-ing to Wigan every five minutes. Put it to her, wilta?'

'We'll talk it over between us, and do what she feels best,' said Ambrose gently. 'And I had an idea about a job for you when you come out. A few of your old friends in the movement are opening one of those new Co-operative stores in Lower Town, in Newmarket Street, next year. I made enquiries, and they'd be glad to have you. Really glad. A lot of people like you, George. Remember that. And their aims are excellent. Good quality food at the lowest possible prices, and a dividend paid to each customer from the profits.'

'Aye, I know that. It'd be honest work. But I canna hump sacks.'

'No, but you could weigh up goods and serve behind the counter.'

George's face reflected conflicting emotions. Relief and

sadness, gratitude and disillusionment. He had risked all of himself and lived out his deepest beliefs, in order to come back to his beginnings and serve in a Co-operative shop.

'I haven't no choice, have I?' said George frankly.

'Well, it will do until something better turns up,' said Ambrose quietly, understanding him too well to feel piqued by the reply.

Several seconds of that dearly bought time ticked away. Then George lifted his head and smiled at Ambrose.

'Nay, I'd have to be a Turk to complain o' your goodness to me, cousin,' he said in his old warm way. 'It'll all be the same in a hundred years' time! I did what I thought were right, and I did what I wanted, and I'd do the same again. I've got nowt to complain about.'

He had forgotten the warder, the prison, even Ambrose. His eyes were very blue, scanning some far horizon they could not see. Chartism had failed him. He was hobbled by a wife and two children, whom he might not see for a year or two. He was nearly forty, and prison would not improve the health of a man who was no longer robust.

And yet, observing him, Ambrose could imagine George working for the Co-operative movement in a store as he had worked for *The Correspondent* at Middleton Street: willing, friendly, living mainly inside himself. He would weigh out the butter and flour and cheese, remember all the customers' names and have a word and a smile for everybody, but the deepest part of him would be resting and healing itself ready for the next move, whatever that might be.

And whatever it was, Ambrose thought, shaking George heartily by the hand, he would not complain.

He nodded benevolently upon the warder as upon one he would bribe many times, and the warder nodded curtly back. In one way they understood each other better than either of them would ever understand the little man standing between them.

'You're the last of the knights errant, George! Did you know that?' Ambrose cried, as his cousin was escorted away.

'The last of the knights errant!' Ambrose repeated to himself quietly.

Then he hooked his watch back on to its chain, picked up his silk top hat, clapped it on one side of his head, and left the room to glower by itself.

A Cruel Taskmaster

chapter twenty seven

September, 1848

The atmosphere in the council chamber at Millbridge Town Hall was a-flutter with consternation, as Jamie Standish strode up and down the room haranguing them, with his hands clasped behind his coat-tails. He was always hard on them, but had they known he was going to behave as outrageously as this they would never have allowed him in.

'You have learned *nothing* from experience!' Jamie was shouting. 'You always do *too little*, and *too late*!'

He paused and threw down a document before the Mayor, which skimmed perilously close to the end of that gentleman's nose.

'This communication, sir, which I received over a week ago – and which I have not so far been allowed to debate with you personally – is a *death warrant* to the poor people of Millbridge!'

He resumed his pacing, breath coming short and fast. He was so angry he could have hit the fellow.

The letter lay half-open on the long table. It was an official notice from the council that all the money in the Public Sanitation Fund had been spent. Until further meetings were held, and new financial arrangements agreed, they regretted that the new sewerage and drainage system could not be extended beyond the Cornmarket, and that the plans to build new reservoirs for a better supply of filtered water must be postponed.

Jamie Standish reached the window and automatically threw it open to allow fresh air into the room. Forty-six years ago his great-uncle had flung up every window on a hot summer day, to see if the stink from the street would drive the council's predecessors into laying down iron drainpipes instead of wooden ones. This afternoon the air smelled sweeter in the Old Town, and the weather was autumnal.

He spoke less forcefully now, and they listened because they were afraid of his temper and relieved by this more reasonable tone.

'I have been privileged to communicate with such public-spirited medical men as Henry Gaulter and James Kay of Manchester and with Robert Baker of Leeds. These names may not be known to you, gentlemen, but I assure you that they will be honoured in history when your own are very properly forgotten! I mention them so that you shall not think you are dealing with one eccentric doctor. There are many of us working and fighting for the betterment of public health.

'It is twelve years since I published my findings and figures for the cholera epidemic in Wyndendale. It is nine years since I published a statistical survey of general diseases in the town and environs of Millbridge. These theses were both proof and plea for the need of good sanitation and filtered water. I took care to give copies to each member of the council so that they might understand the reasons for sanitary reform and so be able to act upon my recommendations.'

He wheeled round and cried loudly, 'And – nothing – was – done!'

They kept silent, not even daring to glance at one another in sympathy. He continued, more quietly.

'We will pass over the innumerable occasions on which I have pleaded my case, backed by evidence of local epidemics. I will remind you instead that a few months ago the government passed two Public Health Acts, both of which stressed the urgent need to grapple with *all* endemic diseases. But even at that time, gentlemen, there was cholera in Russia again. *Cholera*, gentlemen. *In Russia. Again.*'

Still they sat mute and sullen and afraid.

'Of course,' Jamie continued, sarcastically, 'it was the national epidemic of typhus fever which finally drove the government to act. Typhus fever, gentlemen – famine fever, as they call it! – whose death toll among the poor in Millbridge last year was as horrendous as any cholera epidemic. If your own bowels had been moved in the same way, gentlemen, they might have been moved to compassion! But I digress!

'The Public Health Act itself gave you the power to create a local Board of Health in places where ten per cent of the inhabitants asked for one. I made it clear, at the time, where your duties lay. So did *The Northern Correspondent.* And yet you did not even ascertain public opinion on the matter. Once again – nothing – was – done!'

He dropped his voice to such a low pitch, and their silence was so absolute, that they could hear the faint belling of the curtains in the autumn breeze.

'Do you know *why* nothing was done, gentlemen?' Jamie asked softly. 'It was because you, or those who vote you in, own slum property. Because your financial interests, or theirs, are threatened by such reforms. And on such personal and transitory concerns does the health and well-being of *eighty thousand people* depend!'

He began his striding up and down again, and as he passed each member of the council, though he was a good yard away from them, each man shrank a little in his chair.

'When William Howarth, the ironmaster, died,' Jamie went on, almost conversationally, 'he was kind enough to leave me a handsome sum of money – partly because I was a relative through marriage, partly because I was the director of the most important hospital in this valley. He also left instructions that it was to be spent upon some form of medical research, in whatever way I thought fit.

'His generosity enabled me to buy a Lister microscope from London. The best available instrument. With the help of that astonishing microscope, gentlemen, I have been able to study the water we drink – and I can assure you that it is not a pretty sight at close quarters! I found that it contained mysterious and minute particles, unrelated to its usual *animalculae*. I eventually discovered that these were partially digested fragments of food from the intestines. And from this information I concluded, as I had often feared, that our drinking water was tainted – however subtly – with sewage!'

He delivered the next assault in hard clear tones.

'From my own research and observations, and from the work of other medical colleagues, I have reason to believe that typhus and cholera are modifications of one another. In most cases they are preceded by diarrhoea. And what we call summer diarrhoea, and also dysentery, are members of the same family. Now, what might be the effect, I asked myself, if we drank water in which there floated particles from the bowels of a person infected with one or other of the diseases?'

He stopped by the Mayor this time.

'I wrote a paper on that subject, too, sir, on which *The Lancet* was pleased to make favourable comment. Again, I gave you and the members of this council a copy. *You* told me confidentially . . .' – here the Mayor looked extremely worried – '. . . that you would use it to urge the immediate building of four reservoirs to supply the town and its environs with filtered water. Again,' and his voice rose to Olympian heights of wrath, 'nothing – was – done!'

He looked scornfully at the silent councillors round the table. He strode away. He came back, softer in tone and aspect.

'I think that there cannot be one of us here,' he said quietly, 'who did not lose someone dear to them in the cholera epidemic, sixteen years ago, who has not lost someone in last year's typhus epidemic. There can be *no one* – for the terror of it was all about us – *no one* who did not see how shockingly its victims suffered.'

Still sorrowfully, like a teacher chiding errant pupils, he

said, 'And yet you have learned nothing from these lessons. But I tell you that disease is a cruel taskmaster, and will set them before you again and again until you do something about it.'

He surveyed them without hope.

'Do any of you realise that the only thing we doctors know about cholera, for instance, is how to recognise it? That we can only try the same hopeful ineffectual remedies as we did in 1832? That we must endure it as best we may, and pray to Almighty God to have mercy on our souls? And that perhaps the prayer may be of more assistance than the remedies we apply?'

One or two of them said deeply, 'Amen!'

Jamie Standish seemed to have finished, and a rustle of relief went round the table. Now was the moment when he would ask them seriously to consider what portion of the rates they could put aside, in order to proceed with the Public Sanitation programme. They were all wondering how to placate him when he spoke up for the last time.

'I have something here which should interest you, gentlemen.' And he took a slip of paper from inside the breast of his coat. 'This information comes by courtesy of Mr Ambrose Longe. In the public interest, he has allowed me to give you news which readers of *The Northern Correspondent* will not know until the weekend. Unless, of course, by then, you will have thought fit to do something about it – however belatedly.'

He laid down the slip of paper before the Mayor. It was a message from the Telegraph Office, received earlier that day.

'*First cases of cholera confirmed in this country. Details follow later.*'

Leper's Charter

chapter twenty eight

'I need your help and support, Ambrose,' said Jamie Standish.

He refused to sit, being too charged with nervous energy, and paced the office up and down as he talked.

'And though you may consider my proposals extreme, it *is* a matter of life and death,' he added.

Ambrose indicated that he should explain himself fully.

'I have made an ally of the cholera, in that Millbridge council are equally terrified of us both!' Jamie said, with some satisfaction. 'I mean to continue in that way. If I have *The Northern Correspondent* solidly behind me nothing can prevent my measures from being adopted. If I have not,' and here he regarded Ambrose with both hope and defiance,' 'then I must manage without you – fight you if need be.'

'Strong words!' Ambrose remarked lightly, but did not smile.

'Aye, well, you're no stranger to strong words yourself. Do I not recall a leading article in *The Clarion*, back in 1831, describing the first cholera circular as *a leper's charter*?'

Ambrose smiled faintly, and nodded.

Jamie halted by his desk, looked him in the eyes, and said, 'I am asking you and your newspaper to back a leper's charter of my own.'

Ambrose considered this proposition without relish.

'Allow me to imagine the sort of thing you have in mind,' he replied slowly. 'Everywhere stinking of chloride of lime? Relatives and close contacts of the sick isolated? Individual houses marked *Cholera*? Mass disposal of bodies in common graves? Stricken areas placed out of bounds? No favours granted to anyone, high or low? In short, a well-intentioned tyranny?'

At each enquiry Jamie gave an abrupt nod.

'If they had allowed me to deal with the typhus like that,' he said, 'I know I could have contained it better. I *know* it. We must learn from past experience in order to cope with the present, and to make the future possible. I should like you to see what Harold Bailey and I have devised, in case of cholera.'

And he unrolled a little chart and laid it before Ambrose.

'This is merely my portable terror-raiser!' he remarked with grim humour. 'Our real allies are two vast maps on the wall of the fever hospital – one of the valley, one of the town and environs of Millbridge. We shall put someone in charge of marking the outbreaks with flags, and taking down details, if Wyndendale suffers a second epidemic – as I fear it may.'

As you fear? Ambrose wondered. For there was little fear about Jamie. He was plainly itching for close combat.

'This is the one on which I shall base my paper. The town chart. The other simply serves as general evidence.'

Millbridge had been divided just south of her crossroads, at Cornmarket. The Old Town was marked *Houses supplied by Belmont Reservoirs*, and coloured a light fresh blue. Lower Town was a dull brown and bore the legend *Houses supplied from River Wynden.*

'I am expecting to prove a connection,' said Jamie, 'between cholera deaths and water supplies. Now, tell me how you feel about a campaign run by the pair of us.'

Ambrose was both enthralled and horrified.

'Take your time before you answer,' Jamie advised him. 'You're either for or against me on this – and I would say the same to my own dear wife. There are some issues on which a man must stand alone if need be.'

And now at last he sat down quite patiently, and waited.

Ambrose pondered the little chart, considering every possibility which might arise. Then he rolled up Jamie's terror-raiser and pushed it towards him.

'It's going to be hellish, and *The Correspondent* will back

340

you all the way,' he said quietly. Then with rueful humour, 'I can't very well refuse you, since we're right on the firing line – even though Middleton Street *is* on the fresh water side!'

Jamie wrung his hand until the bones hurt, and stuffed the scroll in a side-pocket, triumphant. He jumped to his feet.

'I'll let you know the next step as soon as I've seen the council again!' he said, prepared to tackle them straightaway.

'Oh, by the by,' he added, pausing at the door, 'how's George's wee family settling down?'

'As well as can be expected,' Ambrose replied.

Negotiations with Norah Howarth had been long and difficult. Primarily, she was afraid of uprooting herself and her children. They were part of a close-knit mining community and had never been outside Wigan in their lives. Also, the idea of living on Ambrose's charity, even though he was related by marriage, hurt her independent spirit. So she refused financial help outright. She said she could earn a few shillings by washing and cleaning, and would stay where she was and be beholden to nobody. Plainly, also, she was thinking she could manage for the few months her man was away.

Then, being considered a particularly desperate and hardened case, George was tried at the Lancaster Assizes and given a two-year sentence in Lancaster Jail. By herself in Wigan, Norah had no chance of communicating with him, for she could neither read nor write. Housed over the offices of *The Correspondent* she could rely on Ambrose to influence events, to keep in touch with her husband, and perhaps even take her to visit him once or twice.

Finally she was persuaded that any hope for George's future must lie in Millbridge, and that she could support herself and her children more easily by living rent free. In the end she agreed to accept a form of exile.

Joseph, the coachman, had long since ceased to be surprised by any of Ambrose's actions or acquaintances, so his face expressed no concern at the poverty of their surroundings or the purpose of their visit. He slowed the horses to walking pace and ignored the interest aroused by their arrival.

Curtains twitched slyly. Children stopped their games of hopscotch and marbles. As if by accident women appeared in doorways, to stand, arms folded over their pinafores, infants clinging to their skirts. Only one person did not stare at them or appear to notice their approach. At the far end of the street Norah Howarth continued to whiten her front doorstep with a donkey-stone.

'Stop at number fifty-three, Joseph,' said Ambrose, amused and sorry.

As the carriage drew to a halt Norah finished her work, rinsed and dried her hands, and rose to greet her visitors.

She was a sternly handsome woman, tall and gaunt as though life had worn her down with constant friction. She humbled herself before no one but her God. Her height and dignity triumphed over the drab gown and sacking apron. She held out a cold, red hand to Ambrose and spoke with brisk good nature.

'Well, Mr Longe, you can see what I've been doing, I reckon. I've been scrubbing through since four this morning. T'boxes are packed and t'childer are ready. I shan't keep you above a few minutes while I wash me and change me. Come on in.'

Ambrose could hear the children calling to him from the kitchen, where he rightly guessed they were marooned on the deal table, dressed in their best clothes, having been told not to move.

'They've had their breakfasses. Don't go spoiling them,' said Norah, as Ambrose felt in his overcoat pocket. 'You can sit you down on George's old chair. I'll just draw some clean water from t'pump.'

The two children watched her every move with absorption, as if it were a lesson in life. When she had gone upstairs with her bowl and flannel they turned their attention to Ambrose.

342

They were strangely serious little creatures. Eddy, the same age as Jack, had none of Jack's adventurous spirit. Amy, a contemporary of Jessica, lacked Jessica's spontaneity. Circumstances had been too hard for them to enjoy such a luxury as childhood. Yet there was something childlike behind their tight polite smiles, behind their wistful faces, which came to life for Ambrose. Still, their sense of what was right and proper always prevailed. They had heard Norah tell him not to spoil them, and they refused his proffered peppermints, though their eyes lusted after the paper packet as it returned to his pocket.

All Norah's furniture had been sold, since it would have cost twenty times its worth to move, and George's apartment was already fully furnished. Besides, she needed the small sum of money it fetched. So she had parted with most of her past. One of the boxes in her parlour contained clothes and bedding, the other held household utensils, a few ornaments and prints bought from the pedlar, and George's books. Amy nursed a homemade rag doll. Eddy was the proud possessor of a bag of marbles, some of which he was constantly dropping on the floor by accident.

Down came Norah in her Sunday black gown and her best black bonnet and shawl. She carried the enamel bowl with care, lest her finery be splashed. Two flaring red cotton roses were pinned to the crown of her bonnet, and she was obviously pleased with them. It was the first sign of femininity Ambrose had seen in her.

She gave him a nod, as if to say, 'I shan't be a minute!' and went out into the communal yard to empty and rinse the bowl. With ritual gestures, she put her scrubbing brush, damp cloth and donkey-stone neatly into the bucket, stood the bucket in the bowl, and placed it on top of the nearest box. For the last time she mounted the stairs, and returned with her working clothes neatly made into a bundle, which she placed on top of the second box.

'Right!' said Norah, with sombre satisfaction. 'I've done.'

343

She shepherded her children to their seats, and supervised Joseph as he stowed her belongings into the boot. The neighbours were still out, watching, and as soon as departure seemed imminent several women came forward to shake Norah's hand and wish her well. She acknowledged each of them with grave pleasure, thanked them for past kindnesses, and wished them well in turn.

Ambrose helped her into the carriage, amazed at her composure, and held himself in readiness for a burst of grief as soon as they turned the corner of the road. Norah's self-control never failed her. She did not glance round once at her old home, but set her lips so that they should not quiver, and looked steadily ahead of her as they trotted sedately through the maze of dirty streets.

At the turnpike road Joseph paused before giving the horses their heads, and Ambrose felt the customary surge of excitement as the broad highway unfurled its ribbon before them. Eddy and Amy sat primly, side by side, but their eyes shone, and they could have whooped for joy.

Ambrose watched Norah anxiously. Her lips moved. He leaned forward to catch the words with which she was comforting herself.

She was saying, finally and sadly, 'I left it clean, any road.'

Then Joseph clicked his tongue, flourished his whip and flicked the reins simultaneously. And they were off.

Everything had been done, with the utmost loving kindness, to make them feel at home, but they were cruelly isolated. To live at the top of a large office building among strangers, after the intimate community of a familiar street, is to be wholly disorientated. The very business of *The Northern Correspondent* confined them. Their only means of access was a back staircase, on which they could not linger since it was also used by the staff. Moreover, when the children did reach the pavement, they found themselves at hazard in Millbridge's busiest thoroughfare.

Apart from frugal shopping expeditions, and a Sunday

morning attendance at St Stephen's church, George's family were as surely marooned as if they had been banished to a desert island. And when local people spoke of them at all they referred to them almost contemptuously as 'them foreigners at t'news-papper office!'

Still, they did their best to mingle. Being on the edge of the Old Town, Norah found herself daily work in two or three of the big houses. She entered the children at a Dame School just off Newmarket Street, where, for a penny a week apiece, they began a very rudimentary education indeed. Again, Ambrose wanted to help. Again, Norah refused him. He continually went out of his way to find a solution to their problem, only to discover the truth of George's statement that they were as different as chalk and cheese. There was no common ground on which to found a friendship.

An afternoon call at Middleton Street from Thornton House proved to be purgatory for both sides, but it was worse still with the Vivians. Norah had been awed by Naomi but she took an instant dislike to Mary. No wonder, she said to Ambrose, that George never kept up with this sister. She were too grand by far! And Norah might have said more, except that she knew how close the two families were, and so desisted. Only to herself could she have been heard muttering, 'Lady Muck!' as she scrubbed doorsteps for a living.

But a visit from the Howarths of Kit's Hill was successful from the moment that Hatty panted up the stairs, hampered by two small scarlet-cheeked children and an ample basket.

'I hope you don't mind us dropping by, like!' cried Hatty cheerfully. 'We shan't stop if we're not wanted, but I come up to t'market with our Dad and Fred every Sat'day – and they're supping their pints at t'Red Lion!'

'Nay, come on in!' cried Norah, with a warmth she could not feel for the Longes and the Vivians.

These were the sort of relatives she expected George to have.

Eddy and Amy, intent on every change of her expression

as usual, also brightened, and looked at the smaller strangers with hope.

'I've got no oven here,' said Norah in apology, 'so I canna bake owt, but I've bought some bread and butter from t'Co-op and I'll brew us a pot of tea.'

It was not in the nature of a farmer's wife to come empty-handed. The large square basket on Hatty's arm contained just enough to ease life for this new sister-in-law, and not enough to put her under an obligation. On Norah's table Hatty set a clutch of eggs, a cold boiled fowl, a slab of butter, a wedge of cheese, a quartern loaf of home-baked bread, a round, heavy fruit cake, a large jar of blackberry jam and a small can of milk.

'Well, you're feeding us, aren't you?' said Hatty, arms akimbo. 'Any road up, I'm not carting these tu'thri things all the way back to Garth Fell! You'll be doing me a favour, taking them. They're nobbut what I've got left over from this morning's market!'

Her manners might leave something to be desired, but her sense of delicacy was very nice.

Then for an hour or so Hatty and Norah talked, and the four children played, and all of them regaled themselves at the tea-table, until the wheels of a farm wagon announced the arrival of Dick Howarth and Fred Tunstall. And up the back stairs came the heavy double-tread of boots, and round the door came two crimson faces to greet these new members of the family.

Neither man could be called a brilliant conversationalist. They were inclined to make do with grinning broadly, and shifting from one foot to the other, as Hatty made herself and her children ready for the long road home. But their goodwill and good humour was evident.

'Take care o' thysen!' Hatty said, embracing her sister-in-law. 'We'll come again next Sat'day, if we're welcome.'

'Eh, I'd like that!' Norah cried.

'And you must come and see us, and all, but we're ten

mile down t'valley. Still, what about having your Christmas dinners with us? Dad'd fetch you, wouldn't you, Dad?'

'Aye,' said Dick. 'I would that.'

'So there's plenty to look forward to,' said Hatty, always optimistic, 'and our George'll be out in no time at all. So good night, and God bless, and I'll see thee a-Sat'day – all being well!'

Without which greeting no God-fearing woman would have parted from any friend.

They managed several Saturdays, and the Christmas dinner, before a traveller was taken desperately ill at the Royal George overnight. Jamie Standish, called in by a vigilant landlord, diagnosed cholera.

From then until George's release some part of Wyndendale was always in quarantine. They did not have an epidemic as such. The outbursts were sporadic. So sometimes Norah could work and the children could go to school, and they could see their friends once a week, and sometimes they could not. They were fortunate in that they were never personally stricken, but unfortunate nevertheless.

Had you been standing in Middleton Street, practically any hour of any day during the two years that Jamie Standish fought the cholera, and glanced above the freshly whitened legend of THE NORTHERN CORRESPONDENT to the attic windows above, you would have seen two little faces pressed against the panes watching the world go by.

Perceptive as he was, Ambrose had never understood the relationship between Norah and George, nor realised how much Norah had suffered, until he brought the hero home in the autumn of 1850.

Wyndendale was rejoicing in this nut-brown season of the year as it had rejoiced in the green spring of 1833. Once more it had survived an onslaught of disease, and would put out new shoots of hope and promise for the future. Once more its medical officer had compiled a weighty document of facts against an

347

enemy of mankind, and proved to his professional satisfaction that ten times as many people had died of cholera in Lower Town as in the Old Town. Once more, *The Northern Correspondent* had taken an unpopular course, and stuck to its convictions in spite of public opinion, and been right to do so.

Therefore Ambrose helped George from the carriage with a feeling of satisfaction at a job well done. Having taken care of Norah, he thought it fair enough that Norah should now take care of George, and so lift a long-standing responsibility from Ambrose's shoulders.

So he was greatly astonished when she wrung her hands, and broke down as little grey George limped towards her. The two children stood white and silent behind her, and Ambrose's mind recoiled at the thought of the shock they must suffer, seeing their invincible mother reduced to sobs and tears. But George was master of the situation.

He drew his tall and dignified wife towards him, and put his arms protectively about her. Her proud head rested gladly upon his shoulder. He stroked her hair gently.

Ambrose checked the ever-sensitive barometer of Norah's children, but they were staring at George and their mother with dawning relief.

Their expressions told Ambrose more about that marriage than any amount of words. Then Amy skipped and Eddy hopped away, released.

Ambrose made some excuse to depart, which nobody heard or cared about, and returned downstairs to his office.

Behind him, George was saying, 'That's right, my lass. Have a good greet. It's all over now, and I'm home for good. I'll take care o' thee, my lass. Tha's got nowt to worry about now *I'm* home.'

Part Five

Postscript 1851

A Great Excursion

chapter twenty nine

What marvellous event is this which draws people of all colour, creed, class and political conviction from the four corners of the earth, to lift their hands and eyes in astonishment?

What could possibly persuade Ambrose Longe to leave *The Northern Correspondent* for an entire week? For Hal Vivian to be awakened from his latest dream and bestir himself to see a greater vision? For Jamie Standish to let the Council alone and allow Wyndendale to be sick without him? For Dick Howarth of Kit's Hill, who had never travelled further than Millbridge in his seventy-six years, to set forth for the unknown like some agricultural Christopher Columbus? For the Longes, the Vivians and the Standishes to undertake the trouble and expense of transporting themselves *en famille* some two hundred miles, to find lodgings in the capital city?

What in the world could be so wonderful as to achieve all these professional and domestic miracles?

Ladies and Gentlemen, and Lesser Mortals, and Servants and Little Children too – it is nothing less than the First Great International Exhibition, being held in London, England, in 1851!

On the platform of Millbridge Central Station, in the summer of that year, a large group of some fifteen persons was chatting together animatedly, as they awaited the local train which was to take them as far as Preston, where they would join the London & North Western Railway.

Only two members of that group could be called children, and they were not going to keep each other company. For Jack

Longe, at eleven years old, refused to talk to a girl of seven, even if she was his much-loved sister. So he moved closer to Nat and Toby and Matthew Standish and stood as tall as he could, and knitted his brows knowledgeably as he listened to their discourse. Only the twin forks of a catapult, sticking out of his trouser pocket, betrayed his true interests.

Alice and Cicely, almost ready to come out into society as marriageable young ladies, chatted vivaciously together like the feminine stars of an occasion; watched by Philomena whose own star had never been bright. While Jessica, too young to envy any of them, and loving her father best, slipped her small gloved hand in his and held a whispered monologue with her doll. Naomi, Mary and Dorcas, as became family matrons, were poised, handsome and fashionable, discussing everyone else. The patriarchs stood slightly apart.

'Of course, though it is an age since I visited the place, I am a Londoner by birth!' Ambrose was saying.

His hair had silvered, but his silk top hat was still set at a killing angle, his figure as youthful, his attitude as jaunty as ever.

'I have never been there in all my life!' Jamie answered.

His red whiskers had turned a creamy-gold. The long struggle with typhus and cholera had left him lean and gaunt. In contrast, Hal Vivian in his late fifties had grown powerful in build and manner like his father the ironmaster. And like the ironmaster he worshipped his son, who was a slimmer, darker and more vivid edition of himself.

He was not alone in this. Mary tended to take Santo's arm in a proprietary manner when they were in public together, and look proudly on the handsome fellow who had survived a hectic childhood. And now and then, though apparently wrapped in conversation, pretty little Cicely Standish would glance at him to see if he was noticing her. Which he was, as best he could, though deep in talk of railways.

'For, of course, the success of this exhibition would not have been possible without a national and international network of fast transport!' Hal Vivian was saying to his son.

'Look how many people have come from abroad, simply because they can get here easily and quickly. Take our own railways! With all these cheap excursions, even factory workers can afford a day at the seaside, and a great number of ordinary folk can afford to visit the exhibition. Seven shillings return from Millbridge to London is not expensive.'

And he looked with tremendous pride at the rails glistening in the morning sun, leading them away to foreign parts.

Ambrose poked him gently in the back with his cane.

'You've proved to be a public benefactor by accident, Hal!' he observed, smiling. 'Devil a fig did you give for poor people's pleasures before!' Then fearing to mar the happiness of the day, even by so light a joke, he added, 'And what an improvement this station is on the original. I remember, Santo,' gracefully including the young man, 'when your father began the Wyndendale Railway with *Pioneer* back in 'twenty-eight, this place was no more than a platform and a hut for a booking office, with a board on which some unskilled workman had painted MILLBRIDGE!'

From those humble beginnings had risen a glass and iron palace with an imposing booking hall, two platforms connected by an iron bridge and flights of iron steps, a white-washed waiting room with wooden benches along its walls, a station-master's house of blackened brick, and a large and dignified sign announcing MILLBRIDGE CENTRAL.

Gratified, Hal Vivian said, 'We have not done badly. Twenty-three years to connect this valley to the outside world! Eh, Santo?'

'Very well indeed, sir!' Santo replied.

But to him, at twenty-one, that length of time seemed forever.

'By the by,' said Ambrose, looking round, 'I thought Uncle Dick Howarth was supposed to be travelling down with us by this train.'

'Aye! Did I not hear that your uncle had some piece of wood-carving accepted by the Exhibition?' asked Jamie Standish.

'Yes. His winter whittlings by the fireside have borne fruit!'

'It was Mamma's idea to send it up to the Exhibition,' said Santo, grinning. 'She went over to Kit's Hill to interview Aunt Hatty for her magazine series about "Old Farms of Wyndendale" – and found that my grandfather had carved an absolute replica of the hill farms on Garth Fell from a log of wood.'

'So Mamma *pounced* on him!' cried Alice, who had come up to be admired and to improve her brother's narrative. '*Twitched* the carving from his aged hands, *forced* some poor artist to copy it to illustrate her article, posted it off to London without *asking* him, and announced the result in *triumph*!'

'Mamma really is too awful!' said Santo proudly.

'And then, my dears,' Alice continued, 'she told grandfather that *of course*,' and here she imitated Mary to perfection, '*of course* he must go all the way to London to see it in the Exhibition! I'm surprised the poor old thing didn't drop dead of a heart attack!'

'That's enough impudence from you, Miss,' said Hal automatically.

Alice smiled radiantly on all of them, and twirled her parasol.

'The train's coming!' shouted Jack, who had moved to the very edge of the platform unobserved. 'The rails are throbbing!'

His ears were sharper than theirs. They had to stop talking in order to hear the approaching sounds of whistle and wheels.

'Jack would like to be an engine-driver,' Ambrose confided, 'and I have a treat in store for him today which he does not expect.'

'What treat, Papa?' Jack asked.

As his question remained unanswered, he asked another as a matter of principle.

'Which engine will it be, Uncle Hal?' *The Ironmaster* or *The Lancashire Messenger*?'

'Oh, *The Messenger*!' Hal replied. 'Or else your father couldn't give you such a splendid surprise!'

354

For his knowledge of the Pennine Railway Company extended even to its engine-drivers, and this train was being driven by a new one.

A whistle screamed for attention. In a rush, a roar, and a cloud of steam, *The Lancashire Messenger* was upon them, shining with brass and importance. And behind the engine trundled a line of carriages like a snake; ranging from the smart yellow coachwork and upholstered seats of the first-class, to plain, wooden second-class, to hard, open third-class, and ending with goods wagons and a guard's van.

The great iron wheels of the locomotive ground slowly to a halt, and most of the three family parties converged upon the carriages.

But Ambrose said, 'Jack!' and something in his tone fetched the lad hurrying to his side. 'Do you want to meet the engine-driver?'

Jack nodded, too excited to speak.

Jessica tugged his hand to remind him of her presence.

'I know,' said Ambrose, smiling. 'You can come too! But keep on the far side of me. We don't want smuts on you and Isabella or there'll be hell to pay with Mamma!'

Hal and Jamie were busy escorting the ladies into their carriage. A porter carried their luggage to the guard's van. Passengers in the first and second class had the advantage of the platform for boarding purposes, but the third-class carriages stood beyond it. So there was much hurrying down the line, and hoisting of women and children up the carriage steps, and many broad jokes about the size of the goods.

Hunks of glittering black fuel were piled high on the coal-wagon. Jack could feel the warmth of the engine and smell the oil as he walked quickly by his father's side, and when they reached the cab of the locomotive a black face, like that of a coal-miner, smiled on them and waved an oily rag. Jack swallowed with excitement. Even the prospect of London paled beside a real engine-driver. And between this little monarch of the railroad and his stoker, weathered and rosy with pride, stood a familiar figure.

'It's my Uncle Dick!' cried Jessica, and waved her doll's arm at him in tribute. 'You're the surprise, aren't you?'

'Eh, I've surprised myself, my lass!' said Dick heartily.

Then he nodded his head sideways at the driver and spoke to Ambrose in a highly confidential manner.

'I come down wi' him from t'railway shed in Garth Fowt! And I must say it's been a fair treat. I reckon I'll go on to Preston wi' him, and all!'

Jack never took his eyes off the driver, who was of middle height, and fair-skinned under the oil and coal-dust, with cheerful grey-green eyes and a wide smile as though he knew everybody well.

'Jack, my lad,' said Ambrose. 'This is your cousin, Herbert Howarth. Uncle Dick's – what number is it? The *sixth* son?'

Jack held out his hand and said, 'Honoured to meet you, sir!'

But Herbert would not shake it because of the coal-dust.

'Do you want to come up here a minute then, Jack, lad?' he asked in a friendly fashion. And to his father, 'Do you mind getting out for a bit, Dad? There's not a lot o' room in here!'

'Have we got time, Papa?' Jack asked, looking for permission.

'Well, they canna start th'engine without me!' said Herbert humorously, and raised a laugh.

It was early days on the Pennine Railway. No one minded if the train was held up for a few minutes. No one cared if it stopped at unofficial halts as well as the usual ones. And like the mail-coaches it had to stop at certain intervals for the convenience of passengers, though unlike them it could not choose hostelries but must find a nice wood or sheltered field.

So Jack came up on the foot-plate and was shown how the engine started, and he stored away every word and motion of the instructions, just in case a train broke down sometime and he was asked to take over. And just wait until I get back to Millbridge Grammar School next week, he thought, and I tell the chaps that I've been to the Great Exhibition and my cousin Herbert is an *engine-driver*!

With what reluctance did he jump down into Uncle Dick's arms, and watch him mount again in his stead. He was too well mannered to cry out that he would give his giant striped marble to travel to Preston on the foot-plate, but he ventured to open his heart to Naomi when they got back to the carriage, and woke memories in Mary Vivian.

'Oh, I know exactly how you feel!' she cried, suddenly young again. 'Oh, Hal, do you remember when *I* rode on the foot-plate with you and Mr Edgeworth in *Pioneer*?'

The Cornishman could not recollect it in detail, but saw that his wife could and that it meant much to her. So he picked up her hand and kissed it, and said of course he did.

'I lost my parasol in the coal-box!' Mary said.

'We touched on six-and-twenty miles an hour!' Hal remembered.

Naomi and Ambrose smiled at each other in mutual understanding. So did Jamie and Dorcas. But Alice and Cicely, ripe for love, and believing it to be the exclusive province of the young, put their Bibi bonnets together and giggled.

If Millbridge Central Station was grand, if *The Northern Correspondent* was a fine newspaper, if the cultural centres of Manchester and Liverpool were growing in number and splendour, and Lancashire welcomes were traditionally warm and hospitable, then London was all these things and more, rolled into one.

The great hall at Euston towered above the thousands who buzzed to and fro within its hive. The city had cleaned itself up for visitors, and was concerned that they should find their way to everywhere and see everything without getting lost. On W. H. Smith's bookstall inside the station Ambrose bought maps and guide books for his party, and saw that the orderly rows of London daily and evening newspapers had columns printed in different languages to welcome guests from abroad.

And no sooner had they arrived than London provided them with their first sight of the Ladies' Reform Dress, while the porter assembled their luggage.

'I don't believe it!' cried Mary.

'Is it a man or a woman?' Naomi asked ironically.

For a Bloomer was strolling past with an air of nonchalance. No one could have quarrelled with her straw hat, bound by wide scarlet ribbons, nor with her tight-fitting black jacket cut snugly to the waist. Even her spotted voile skirt was pretty, if only it had not stopped at the knees, and so displayed in all their vulgarity – a pair of bloomers. But, worse than that, far far worse, was the cigar gripped lightly between the lady's teeth. And as she passed them she took the fine brown cylinder from her lips, blew a perfect smoke ring, and deliberately and most impudently winked at them. Transfixed, the Wyndendale party watched her go by.

'She must be an American. Perhaps Mrs Bloomer herself!' whispered Mary, horribly impressed.

'I think,' said Naomi distinctly, 'that she is quite dreadful!'

'Oh, I don't know!' Mary murmured, watching the Turkish trousers sway away. 'The cigar is rather dashing!'

Then Hal Vivian woke up for perhaps the first and last time in all his married life, and read his wife's mind. He uttered one word in a distinct and final tone.

'*No!*' said the Cornishman.

Dick Howarth was apparently with them for moral support rather than company. He had chosen the same London excursion trip, one of many organised by a young man called Thomas Cook, but insisted on travelling third-class, though Ambrose offered to pay the difference so he could join them. Now, in spite of being among foreigners in foreign parts, he hung on the outskirts of the group purely as a temporary measure, to see where they were lodging.

Naomi, never at a loss for connections, had rented a house overlooking the common at Wimbledon for them all, including himself. But once he had their address written down on a piece of paper, Dick made up his mind to try the modest hospitality of Mr Thomas Harrison in Pimlico, who had created a vast establishment near the Pier, where one thousand members of the working-class at a time could enjoy a good bed, breakfast and dinner for two shillings and threepence, plus the added convenience of a newsroom, a smoking room, light music on the premises, the services of a surgeon and barber if required, and a penny omnibus from the very door.

'And if I canna get in,' said Dick, 'I'st find a clean place somewhere else, wi' a bed to spare!'

Admiring but concerned, the family gathered round him. Ambrose insisted on lending him three sovereigns, which Mary had to sew into the hem of his old jacket forthwith, sitting on a platform bench.

Jamie Standish thrust a map into his pocket, with strategic points marked in red ink, and directions to the Great Exhibition written in the margin.

Hal Vivian wrote the date and time of Dick's return train on another piece of paper, and gave him a Bradshaw's Railway Guide as an extra precaution.

The men synchronised their silver watches with Dick's old repeater, and shook hands with him. The women kissed him fervently.

'We'll meet you at ten o'clock tomorrow morning in the Exhibition Hall at the Crystal Fountain!' Ambrose shouted after him.

'T'day's half over by then!' Dick shouted back. 'I'st have walked London by ten o'clock.'

They watched him dodge his way resolutely between the evening omnibuses, carpet bag in hand.

359

'I never expect to see my father again!' cried Mary dramatically.

'Oh, I don't know,' said Ambrose. 'There's something immensely durable about Kit's Hill Howarths!'

Window on a Future World

chapter thirty

The Crystal Palace was all space and light and air. Fragile and iridescent it seemed, as if they were at the centre of a vast soap bubble and a puff of wind could blow it away.

So that the ladies all cried, 'Oh, what a work of *art!*'

Art? Two thousand workmen taking no more than nine months to construct a building one third of a mile long, on a foundation of concrete which covered eighteen acres of Hyde Park! Art? Thirty-four miles of iron pipes run through iron base-plates to carry hollow iron columns! Art? Four hundred tons of sheet glass set into its iron framework without the use of scaffolding!

'What a feat of *engineering!*' cried the gentlemen.

Sparkling in the sunlight, fluttering with the flags of all nations, its atmosphere was incredibly light-hearted: as light of heart and lively as the millions of people who streamed in and out of its portals.

From the practical point of view everything worked splendidly. There were three entrances and seventeen exits. Ten staircases gave access to a mile of galleries and courts, connected by bridges. And Chelsea Waterworks Company supplied three hundred thousand gallons a day to keep the fountains and other conveniences going. For in three parts of the building Public Comfort Stations had been installed for the visitors: an innovation which was highly appreciated. Light snacks and non-alcoholic drinks were supplied by Messrs Schweppe at moderate charges. Silvery medals, commemorating the event, could be bought from trayholders at the gates or along the roads.

This was the first shop window of the world, and countries all over the world from America to Russia hastened to advertise their wares. Products of every art and craft and industry were there: tons of sculpture, rooms full of modern machinery, gadgets and novelties of all descriptions, articles of use and ornament, something to suit the taste and capture the interest of everyone.

Nothing had been regarded as impossible. Even old and noble elms were incorporated rather than hewn down, and spread their branches with dignity beneath the glass dome. Excepting Fridays, when the admission price rose to half-a-crown, and Saturdays when it became five shillings, the cost of viewing this fairy-land was only one shilling a day. Fifty guardians of the law, top-hatted and truncheoned, made sure that peace prevailed. And the rules were few. You might not drink alcohol on the premises. You might not bring your dog. And the palace was closed on Sundays.

True to his word, Dick Howarth was there before ten o'clock the following morning, waiting under a potted palm tree near the fountain. He had been up at five o'clock, sailed the river by steam-boat from Pimlico to the city, and seen all manner of marvels. On arrival at the Crystal Fountain, he had drunk some of its filtered water, wetted his neckerchief and bathed his face, and was feeling the better for it. One hand gripped his carpet bag for safety. The other held a cold ham sandwich well laced with mustard, from which he had taken a couple of healthy bites. If a wanderer could ever be said to look at home, Dick Howarth was in his element.

'I had trouble at t'gate, I did,' said Dick cheerfully, when he had shaken hands all round. 'They'll not change a florin, tha knows. You have to give 'em t'shilling. I daresay they want to get folk in quick. Well, I hadna getten a shillin'. So I turned round and asked a chap behind me if he had change for a florin. Once we'd made us-selves understood he were very agreeable, but I tell thee summat, Ambrose – they don't half talk funny down here!'

'Ah! that's what comes of mixing with foreigners!' said his nephew gravely. 'Did you lodge with Mr Thomas Harrison?'

'Nay, he were full up, but I found a nice quiet widder woman in Ranelagh Street, and she had a sofa to spare in t'parlour. I'm going back there tonight, and all!'

'And what's our Hatty going to say about that, I should like to know?' Mary asked playfully, kissing him.

Then she caught sight of her husband wandering away towards the Machinery Rooms, and cried, 'Hal! Come back! We must all see Father's carving first!'

A crystal of many facets, the exhibition bade them reflect upon it, and as they peered into its shining depths they saw themselves reflected back, enhanced and magnified. They were to emerge something richer for the experience.

Dick Howarth discovered to his immense astonishment that he had two faces. One had grown old in all weathers and wore a dusty hat, and its mouth would dominate farming conversation ever after.

'Aye, that's all very well, Fred. But what you want, my lad, is one o' them McCormick's reapers for Sluther Field. It'd make a clean sweep in half an hour, and as for *threshing*! Well, I'd chuck that owd thresher into t'river if I was you, and find yourself one of them new improved machines like I saw in t'Great Exhibition!'

So would the oracle speak to his son-in-law, thumbs well down in his waistcoat pockets, chewing his pipe as he had seen a Yankee gentleman chewing his cigar. And how was Fred to know that these American marvels were designed to reap and thresh whole prairies of wheat, in the midst of which his crop of barley would be lost ten thousand times over? He did not. He could only thank Dick for his advice, and consider him to be the ultimate authority on such matters.

The other face Dick had taken for granted, and never

known for what it was: the face of a fine craftsman.

'Eh, by Gow!' cried Dick, looking round on his admiring family in wonder.

For between a cardboard model of St Paul's, and a set of carved fruit stones contributed by the Duke of Saxe-Coburg-Gotha, lay the whole of his humble world in miniature.

Garth Fell, Lancashire. By Richard Howarth, farmer. Carved in the evenings with a penknife, by candlelight.

'Eh! Eh, by Gow!' cried Dick, and could not see for tears.

Once they had viewed his work and praised him, the families split into separate groups, making arrangements to meet at specific times and places, and re-mingle to form different parties. But what a dreadful thing happened to Jack Longe!

His brothers and Matthew Standish were playing a new game, inspired by the wilder Novelties in the exhibition. It began with the words, 'My Favourite Novelty is . . .' and ended in peals of laughter.

'. . . is undoubtedly – *The Window Cleaner for the Protection of Female Servants from Fatal Accidents and Public Exposure*!' said Nathan in the beautiful dry tone inherited from his father.

The three youths slapped each other's shoulders and crowed with delight.

'No! No!' cried Toby, who always had to best his elder brother. 'What about *The Collapsible Piano for a Gentleman's Yacht*?'

Whereupon he collapsed with laughter, and the others followed.

'I say!' cried Matthew. 'What about *The Expanding Hearse*?'

They fell about. They imitated a row of corpses and the bulging vehicle. They made jokes about the cholera epidemic which showed how strong a nerve they had, or how black a sense of humour.

Jack laughed dutifully with them but was not really amused, so after a while he wandered away in search of his mother, who had given him an itinerary of her movements.

364

And there, directly in front of him, was an amazing little textile machine called 'The Tailor', being fed with pieces of cloth to demonstrate its powers. Jack was enthralled. He watched first one and then another pair of trousers cut out, stitched, and thrown down for inspection. He came closer. And closer.

At one stage – Jack could not remember when – he had offered to carry his mother's dust-cloak, which now hung over his arm. The Tailor finished its latest creation, tossed it aside, and looked for more. Intent on the textile machinery, Jack did not notice that one corner of the cloak had floated within its grasp.

Programmed to respond to the touch of cloth, the Tailor went into a ferment of agitation, whipped Naomi's mantle from him, gave a shrill scream, and began to ply a pair of mechanical scissors.

'Oh!' cried Jack. 'Oh, no, don't do it!'

Heedless of the boy's protests, or the sympathy and amusement of those around him, the tailor's needle flashed in and out of the snipped cloak with tremendous industry.

'Oh, please help me, somebody!' Jack cried, turning from one to another person. 'Please, sir, please ma'am, this machine has taken my Mamma's . . . my Mamma's . . .'

Contemptuously, the Tailor tossed him a pair of mangled trousers.

Hal Vivian had been a lost cause since he caught sight of the improved double turbine engine from France. But Santo's stomach, and his interest in a certain young lady, brought them back to reality.

'Excuse me, sir,' said Santo, addressing his father's back, 'but didn't Mamma say we were to meet everyone in the Central Area for luncheon at one o'clock?'

'I – believe – she – did,' Hal replied slowly, fascinated by James Nasmyth's steam-hammer, which was very tenderly cracking an egg to show them how wonderfully great power could be controlled.

'Well, it's half past two already, sir!'

There was a long pause, at the end of which the Cornishman realised he was supposed to say something.

'Is it, by Jove?' said Hal, trying to sound interested.

Still he did not look at the perturbed face of his son and heir.

'Half past two, by Jove!' he repeated.

This was an old trick, to show that he had heard and understood what was said to him.

Another egg was placed beneath the mammoth, and again cracked so lightly that the perfection of adjustment made Hal Vivian shake his head in silent admiration. As the hammer rose again, hissing, he became aware that he was expected to remark upon the time.

'It seems we shall be a little late,' said the Cornishman mildly.

To Cicely Standish the Exhibition was one enormous trousseau and furniture store laid out especially for her benefit. Even the fountain of Maria Farina Eau de Cologne provided its hint of romance. A young policeman, standing by, had kindly perfumed her handkerchief in the jet and returned it with a look of respectful admiration.

In her mind she trod an Aubusson carpet in a marble mansion. She was clad in silks, specially imported from Lyons, rich in handmade lace. She chose Dresden figurines for her parlour mantelpiece. The Carriage Court provided so much choice that she had difficulty in deciding on a closed carriage by Clapp of Boston, and thought she should need a light park phaeton as well. Her establishment was almost complete when Alice spotted the monumental console table and mirror.

'Isn't that the most *enormous* and glorious thing you have *ever* seen in *all* your days?' cried Alice, true daughter of Mary.

A dream of grandeur, garlanded with carved swags and vases and cherubs and roses. Cicely rustled forward to look, and found herself small and exquisite in its glossy depths. Prophetically, in the distance, stood Santo Vivian, and saw her from afar. They shared the same trance: the pretty girl in summer muslin, the handsome fellow watching her. Nothing had been said between them as yet. Nothing needed to be said. The looking glass spoke for them both.

Alice Vivian saw it happen, and the moment which created their fusion set her apart.

Cicely and Santo. Santo and Cicely, she thought. This is their beginning. But what will the middle and end be, and what will become of them? Imagine that this is the first and last time they see each other for many years. For some very good reason – his work perhaps – they will be separated. Would she be faithful? Yes! Would he? I'm not at all sure! She's ready for marriage. He wants freedom. Reflections in a looking glass. Why, I could write a novel about that!

She was a vivid girl, tall like her father, copper-haired like her mother, with those narrow, dark, amber eyes which seemed to be her own inheritance – for there were no others like them in the family. A girl quick to laugh, slow to cry, and simmering with vitality. As he swaggered by, a cavalry officer winked at her. Alice never saw him, lost in her imaginary world.

She thought, 'I must write it under another name, and not say a word to anyone until it is published. Not that Mamma wouldn't be wholly entranced by the idea, but she'd never give me a moment's peace to write it! Dearest Mamma, I shall do it without any help from you – and surprise you enormously. Now, what *nom de plume* should I choose?'

Santo had come up to them and was gazing at Cicely, who was gazing fixedly at the toe of her little slipper. They were enchanting. Children on the verge of an old adventure.

Yes, love's all very well, thought Alice, but I shan't have time for it just yet!

Jessica and Jack had found the patent freezing machine and were enjoying a sixpenny ice-cream apiece.

'I've had an ice-cream maker at home for over fifty years!' Dick Howarth said to the vendor.

'Ah! You're a bit of a caution, you are!' said the man, speaking in a familiar fashion, disbelieving him.

For what would a red-faced fellow in leather gaiters be doing with an ice-cream maker?

Immediately, Jack spoke to his great-uncle with extreme courtesy, intending to make the vendor cringe.

'Yours is an incredibly good ice-house, sir! Was it not made by your brother, the ironmaster?'

This subtlety was lost on Dick, the true democrat. Like his father before him, he could admire and pay homage to the great without feeling that he was lowly. It was young Jack, steeped in middle-class consciousness, who demanded the tokens of outward respect.

'Aye, our Will had it put up,' said Dick quite naturally. 'And it served to make ice-cream for his wedding, back in 'ninety-five.'

'Then you might be interested in this here machine, sir,' said the vendor, 'which is the latest model. Run entirely by steam, sir.'

'Nay, I can't abide the stuff!' said Dick honestly. 'I were only making a remark. Would you two young 'uns like another?'

They hesitated, wondering whether this would be greedy.

Then Jessica said, '*I* wouldn't, uncle, thank you. But *Isabella* quite fancies one, and she hasn't had any!'

Jack shook his head like a gentleman, wishing he were young enough to call upon the services of Little Voice.

'Here. Give us a couple o' shilling 'uns for the childer!' said Dick, understanding them both. And as he took the silver from his old leather purse, 'See that, young man? That were made from one of our sheeps' hides for me when I were one-and-twenty! And I tell thee, in those days my father paid me seven shilling a week in wages to be his carter. And what's that, nowadays? Seven big ice-creams, sithee!'

'Not a great deal on which to bring up a family, sir,' said Jack, well versed in *Correspondent* doctrine.

'No, but I'm still here to tell t'tale!' said Dick factually.

There would be yet another tale for him to tell, for him and for no other member of the party.

'I were on my own,' he would say, 'harming nobody and having a quiet gander round by mysen, when I heard – nay, I don't know how to describe it!'

A rustle, a murmur, a multitude of whispers. Then a man's voice just beside him said quietly and clearly, 'It's the Queen!'

'The Queen?' Dick cried. 'What? Our Queen?'

And he looked about him for trumpets and fanfares, for heralds and beefeaters and officers of the guard, and a thousand regal fancies connected with his notion of royalty.

'Where?' cried Dick, amazed.

'Why, here, man,' said the military gentleman beside him. 'The Queen comes here quite often, God bless her. No fuss. No ceremony. Just another visitor, moving among us all.'

'Without her sojers?' said Dick, horrified to think of royalty unprotected.

'Safe as houses with all of us, sir, and proud of it you may be sure. Such trust would be out of place abroad, of course. You never can depend on foreigners. But here in England, sir, we know how to behave to our monarch, and this is how she behaves with us!'

The crowd parted as quietly and efficiently as the river opened to allow Moses and his people to pass through to the Promised Land. And there, not an arm's length from him, walked a little lady in a rose-coloured silk bonnet and gown and a white lace shawl, entirely at her ease, followed a few paces behind by two other ladies.

'Just like it might be Mrs Bowker wi' a couple o' neighbours,' Dick was wont to say, and then wont to add, 'Well, not like Mrs Bowker exackerly, but you know what I mean!'

369

No, not in the least like Mrs Bowker, nor like anyone he had ever seen before or would ever see again. Not particularly young or striking or fashionable. Simply unique.

'I can't describe it,' said Dick, 'but as soon as I set eyes on her I knew. It were summat about her. She were our Queen Victoria.'

Something, whether myth or symbol or superstition, which caused him to sweep off his farmer's hat and bow as low as any courtier when she passed. Something which aroused more than ordinary respect or curiosity.

Was her smile and nod directed at him, or was she so adept by this time that she could convey a personal interest to every member of the crowd? She smiled. She nodded. It was enough to last him the rest of his life, and though he was an old man there were years yet.

For the second time that day he wiped the tears from his cheeks, and could not speak for a while.

Applegath and Cowper's latest printing-machine resembled two four-posters connected by a large wash-boiler. From where they stood, Ambrose and Nathan could see five men employed. The method of printing paper on a flat bed had been scrapped. Now the wash-boiler spun the sheets off in a rotary motion. They were printing *The Illustrated London News* while people watched.

At his father's request, Nathan moved close to the nearest worker and asked him how many copies an hour the machine could do.

'Five thousand, young sir!'

'So we enter the age of mass production,' Ambrose said.

And it would not be too long, he expected, before the government lifted all the duties from newspapers, and so allowed them to sell more cheaply and in greater numbers.

'Five thousand!' Ambrose repeated.

He doffed his hat to the machine, and gave an ironic little bow. Nathan watched him, smiling. Mamma had said to keep an eye on him, but not to let him know.

'Why, we shall see *The Northern Correspondent* printed every day in its tens of thousands and sold for twopence a copy, yet!' cried Ambrose to his eldest son, following a train of thought.

'And why not *The Evening Correspondent,* sir, coming out nightly, in an early and late edition?' Nathan remarked lightly.

Ambrose laughed, and capped this serious jest.

'I can even imagine a *Sunday Correspondent* at that!' he cried.

Then he stopped himself and put one hand inside his coat, for his heart was hopping in his breast like a mad thing.

'Are you all right, sir?' Nathan asked, concerned.

'Certainly!' said Ambrose.

For he saw how ridiculous it would be to die of a dream.

'Certainly, I am. And it's all possible, Nat. It's all possible. Perhaps not in my lifetime,' he added, 'but in yours, at any rate.'

Then this splendid son of his, who was a little taller and not quite so lean, but brown of skin and hair and eyes, undeniably flesh of his flesh, slipped an arm through his.

'In *both* our lifetimes, sir!' said Nathan firmly.

'How old are you, Nat?' Ambrose asked, for he never knew.

'Sixteen, sir.'

'Ah. A little way to go yet, then.'

Still, he should last five years. Get the boy on his feet. See him ensconced as future editor.

'We must keep her in the family, Nat!' he said, almost anxiously.

'Oh, we shall, sir. Never fear. *The Northern Correspondent* and the Longes are one and the same thing.'

'Nat!' said Ambrose. 'It is high time you and I had a talk over a glass of brandy one evening when the other lads are asleep.'

He clapped his top hat to one side of his head at a jauntier angle than ever before. And as they walked away he was whistling softly, and swinging his cane.

23 May, 1982 – 17 October, 1983